A SPY BY NATURE

CHARLES CUMMING

A SPY BY NATURE

ST. MARTIN'S PRESS   NEW YORK

This is a work of fiction. All of the characters, organizations, and events portrayed in this novel are either products of the author's imagination or are used fictitiously.

A SPY BY NATURE. Copyright © 2001 by Charles Cumming. All rights reserved. Printed in the United States of America. No part of this book may be used or reproduced in any manner whatsoever without written permission except in the case of brief quotations embodied in critical articles or reviews. For information, address St. Martin's Press, 175 Fifth Avenue, New York, N.Y. 10010.

www.stmartins.com

"Fake Plastic Trees." Words and music by Thom Yorke, Edward O'Brien, Colin Greenwood, Jonathan Greenwood, and Philip Selway. © 1994 Warner/Chappell Music Ltd. (PRS). All rights in the U.S. and Canada administered by WB Music Corp. (ASCAP). Used by permission of Alred Publishing Co., Inc. All rights reserved.

Library of Congress Cataloging-in-Publication Data

Cumming, Charles, 1971–
    A spy by nature / Charles Cumming.—1st ed.
        p. cm.
    ISBN-13: 978-0-312-36635-3
    ISBN-10: 0-312-36635-3
    1. Intelligence officers—Fiction. 2. Undercover operations—Fiction. I. Title.

PR6103.U484S69 2007
823'.92—dc22

2007011582

First published in the United Kingdom in 2001 by Michael Joseph, Ltd., a division of Penguin General Books

First St. Martin's Press Edition: July 2007

10 9 8 7 6 5 4 3 2 1

For my wife, Melissa

AUTHOR'S NOTE

Were the events of this story entirely true, they would inevitably breach clauses in The Official Secrets Act of the United Kingdom. Nevertheless, members of the intelligence community both in London and in the United States may find that they catch their reflection in the account which follows.

"The Foreign and Commonwealth Office"—or "Foreign Office"—is the rough equivalent of the United States Foreign Service. Its members refer to it simply as "The Office." The Secret Intelligence Service (SIS), commonly referred to as MI6, or "Six," is the United Kingdom's foreign intelligence agency. MI5, or "Five," handles domestic intelligence. GCHQ is a signals intelligence agency located near Cheltenham, England.

—C.C.

London, 2006

I remember, in fact, the Lebanese woman I knew at Berkshire College saying to me, after I told her how much I loved her: "I'll always tell you the truth, unless of course I'm lying to you."

—RICHARD FORD, *The Sportswriter*

PART ONE

1995

If we hope to live not just from moment to moment, but in true conscious-ness of our existence, then our greatest need and most difficult achievement is to find meaning in our lives.

—BRUNO BETTELHEIM, *The Uses of Enchantment*

1

AN EXPLORATORY CONVERSATION

The door leading into the building is plain and unadorned, save for one highly polished handle. No sign outside saying FOREIGN AND COMMON-WEALTH OFFICE, no hint of top brass. There is a small ivory bell on the right-hand side, and I push it. The door, thicker and heavier than it appears, is opened by a fit-looking man of retirement age, a uniformed policeman on his last assignment.

"Good afternoon, sir."

"Good afternoon. I have an interview with Mr. Lucas at two o'clock."

"The name, sir?"

"Alec Milius."

"Yes, sir."

This almost condescending. I have to sign my name in a book and then he hands me a security dog tag on a silver chain, which I slip into the hip pocket of my suit trousers.

"Just take a seat beyond the stairs. Someone will be down to see you in a moment."

The wide, high-ceilinged hall beyond the reception area exudes all the splendor of imperial England. A vast paneled mirror dominates the far side of the room, flanked by oil portraits of gray-eyed, long-dead diplomats. Its soot-flecked glass reflects the bottom of a broad staircase, which drops down in right angles from an unseen upper story, splitting left and right at ground level. Arranged around a varnished table beneath the mirror are two burgundy leather sofas, one of which is more or less completely occupied by an overweight, lonely-looking man in his late twenties. Carefully, he reads and rereads the same page of the same section of *The Times,* crossing and uncrossing his legs as his bowels swim in caffeine and nerves. I sit down on the sofa opposite his.

Five minutes pass.

On the table the fat man has laid down a strip of passport photographs, little color squares of himself in a suit, probably taken in a booth at Waterloo station sometime early this morning. A copy of *The Daily Telegraph* lies folded and unread beside the photographs. Bland non-stories govern its front page: IRA hints at new ceasefire; rail sell-off will go ahead; 56 percent of British policemen want to keep their traditional bobbies' helmets. I catch the fat man looking at me, a quick spot-check glance between rivals. Then he looks away, shamed. His skin is drained of ultraviolet, a gray flannel face raised on nerd books and *Panorama.* Black oily Oxbridge hair.

"Mr. Milius?"

A young woman has appeared on the staircase wearing a neat red suit. She is unflustered, professional, demure. As I stand up, Fat Man eyes me with wounded suspicion, like someone on his lunch break cut in line at the bank.

"If you'd like to come with me. Mr. Lucas will see you now."

This is where it begins. Following three steps behind her, garbling platitudes, adrenaline surging, her smooth calves lead me up out of the hall. More oil paintings line the ornate staircase.

Running a bit late today. Oh, that's okay. Did you find us all right? Yes.

"Mr. Lucas is just in here."

Prepare a face to meet the faces that you meet.

A firm handshake. Late thirties. I had expected someone older. Christ, his eyes are blue. I've never seen a blue like that. Lucas is dense boned and tanned, absurdly handsome in an old-fashioned way. He is in the process of growing a mustache, which undercuts the residual menace in his face. There are black tufts sprouting on his upper lip, cut-rate Errol Flynn.

He offers me a drink, an invitation seconded by the woman in red, who seems almost offended when I refuse.

"Are you sure?" she says, as if I have broken with sacred tradition. Never accept tea or coffee at an interview. They'll see your hand shaking when you drink it.

"Absolutely, yes."

She withdraws and Lucas and I go into a large, sparsely furnished room nearby. He has not yet stopped looking at me, not out of laziness or rudeness but purely because he is a man entirely at ease when it comes to staring at people. He's very good at it.

He says, "Thank you for coming today."

And I say, "It's a pleasure. Thank you for inviting me. It's a great privilege to be here."

There are two armchairs in the room, upholstered in the same burgundy leather as the sofas downstairs. A large bay window looks out over the tree-lined Mall, feeding weak, broken sunlight into the room. Lucas has a broad oak desk covered in neat piles of paper and a framed black-and-white photograph of a woman whom I take to be his wife.

"Have a seat."

I drop down low into the leather, my back to the window. There is a coffee table in front of me, an ashtray, and a closed red file. Lucas occupies the chair opposite mine. As he sits down, he reaches into the pocket of his jacket for a pen, retrieving a blue Mont Blanc. I watch him, freeing the trapped flaps of my jacket and bringing them back across my chest. The little physical tics that precede an interview.

"Milius. It's an unusual name."

"Yes."

"Your father, he was from the Eastern bloc?"

"His father. Not mine. Came over from Lithuania in 1940. My family have lived in Britain ever since."

Lucas writes something down on a brown clipboard braced between his thighs.

"I see. Why don't we begin by talking about your present job. The CEBDO. That's not something I've heard much about."

All job interviews are lies. They begin with the résumé, a sheet of word-processed fictions. About halfway down mine, just below the name and address, Philip Lucas has read the following sentence:

I have been employed as a Marketing Consultant at the Central European Business Development Organization (CEBDO) for the past eleven months.

Elsewhere, lower down, are myriad falsehoods: periods of work experience on national newspapers ("Could you do some photocopying please?"); a season as a waiter at a leading Genevan hotel; eight weeks at a London law firm; the inevitable charity work.

The truth is that CEBDO is run out of a small, cramped garage in a mews off Edgware Road. The kitchen doubles for a toilet; if somebody has a crap, no one can make a cup of tea for ten minutes. There are five of us: Nik (the boss), Henry, Russell, myself, and Anna. It's very simple. We sit on the phone all day talking to businessmen in central—and now eastern—Europe. I try to persuade them to part with large sums of money, in return for which we promise to place an advertisement for their operation in a publication known as the *Central European Business Review*. This, I tell my clients, is a quarterly magazine that enjoys a global circulation of four hundred thousand copies, "distributed free around the world." Working purely on commission I can make anything from two to three hundred pounds a week, sometimes more, peddling this story. Nik, I estimate, makes seven or eight times that amount. His only overheads, apart from telephone calls and electricity, are printing costs. These are paid to his brother-in-law who desktop publishes five hundred copies of the *Central European Business Review* four times a year. These he posts to a few selected embassies across Europe and to all the clients who have placed advertisements in the magazine. Any spares, he throws in the bin.

On paper, it's legal.

I look Lucas directly in the eye.

"The CEBDO is a fledgling organization that advises new businesses in central—and now eastern—Europe about the perils and pitfalls of the free market."

He taps his jaw with the bulbous fountain pen.

"And it's entirely funded by private individuals? There's no grant from the EC?"

"That's right."

"Who runs it?"

"Nikolas Jarolmek. A Pole. His family have lived in Britain since the war."

"And how did you get the job?"

"Through the *Guardian*. I responded to an advertisement."

"Against how many other candidates?"

"I couldn't say. I was told about a hundred and fifty."

"Could you describe an average day at the office?"

"Broadly speaking, I act in an advisory capacity, either by speaking to people on the telephone and answering any questions they may have about setting up in business in the UK or by writing letters in response to written queries. I'm also responsible for editing our quarterly magazine, the *Central European Business Review*. That lists a number of crucial contact organizations that might prove useful to small businesses that are just starting out. It also gives details of tax arrangements in this country, language schools, that kind of thing."

"I see. It would be helpful if you could send me a copy."

"Of course."

To explain why I am here.

The interview was set up on the recommendation of a man I barely know, a retired diplomat named Michael Hawkes. Six weeks ago I was staying at my mother's house in Somerset for the weekend, and he came to dinner. He was, she informed me, an old university friend of my father's.

Until that night I had never met Hawkes, had never heard my mother mention his name. She said that he had spent a lot of time with her and Dad when they were first married in the 1960s. But when the Foreign Office posted him to Moscow, the three of them had lost touch. All this was before I was born.

Hawkes retired from the Diplomatic Service earlier this year to take up a directorship at a British oil company called Abnex. I don't know how Mum tracked down his phone number, but he showed up for dinner alone, no wife, on the stroke of eight o'clock.

There were other guests there that night, bankers and insurance brokers in bulletproof tweeds, but Hawkes was a thing apart. He had a blue silk cravat slung around his neck like a noose and a pair of velvet loafers embroidered on the toe with an elaborate coat of arms. There was nothing ostentatiously debonair about any of this, nothing vain; it just looked as if he hadn't taken them off in twenty years. He was wearing a washed-out blue shirt with fraying collar and cuffs and stained silver cuff links that looked as though they had been in his family since the Opium Wars. In short, we got on. We sat next to each other at dinner and talked for close on three hours about everything from politics to infidelity. Three days after the party my mother told me that she had spotted Hawkes in her local supermarket, stocking up on Stolichnaya and tomato juice. Almost immediately, like a task, he asked her if I had ever thought of "going in for the Foreign Office." My mother said that she didn't know.

"Ask him to give me a ring if he's interested."

So on the telephone that night my mother did what mothers are supposed to do.

"You remember Michael, who came to dinner?"

"Yes," I said, stubbing out a cigarette.

"He likes you. Thinks you should try out for the Foreign Office."

"He does?"

"What an opportunity, Alec. To serve Queen and Country."

I nearly laughed at this, but checked it out of respect for her old-fashioned convictions.

"Mum," I said, "an ambassador is an honest man sent abroad to lie for the good of his country."

She sounded impressed.

"Who said that?"

"I don't know."

"Anyway, Michael says to give him a ring if you're interested. I've got the number. Fetch a pen."

I tried to stop her. I didn't like the idea of her putting shape on my life, but she was insistent.

"Not everyone gets a chance like this. You're twenty-four now. You've only got that small amount of money your father left you in his Paris account. It's time you started thinking about a career and stopped working for that crooked Pole."

I argued with her a little more, just enough to convince myself that if I went ahead it would be of my own volition and not because of some parental arrangement. Then, two days later, I rang Hawkes.

It was shortly after nine o'clock in the morning. He answered after one ring, the voice crisp and alert.

"Michael. It's Alec Milius."

"Hello."

"About the conversation you had with my mother."

"Yes."

"In the supermarket."

"You want to go ahead?"

"If that's possible. Yes."

His manner was strangely abrupt. No friendly chat, no excess fat.

"I'll talk to one of my colleagues. They'll be in touch."

"Good. Thanks."

Three days later a letter arrived in a plain white envelope marked PRIVATE AND CONFIDENTIAL.

Foreign and Commonwealth Office

No. 46A————Terrace

London SW1

PERSONAL AND CONFIDENTIAL

Dear Mr. Milius,

It has been suggested to me that you might be interested to have a discussion with us about fast-stream appointments in government service in the field of foreign affairs which occasionally arise in addition to those covered by the Open Competition to the Diplomatic Service. This office has a responsibility for recruitment to such appointments.

If you would like to take this possibility further, I should be grateful if you would please complete the enclosed form and return it to me. Provided that there is an appointment for which you appear potentially suitable, I shall then invite you to an exploratory conversation at this office. Your travel expenses will be refunded at the rate of a standard return rail fare plus tube fares.

I should stress that your acceptance of this invitation will not commit you in any way, nor will it affect your candidature for any government appointments for which you may apply or have applied. As this letter is personal to you, I should be grateful if you could respect its confidentiality.

Yours sincerely,
Philip Lucas
Recruitment Liaison Office

Enclosed was a standard-issue, four-page application form: name and address, education, brief employment history, and so on. I completed it within twenty-four hours—replete with lies—and sent it back to Lucas. He replied by return post, inviting me to the meeting.

I have spoken to Hawkes only once in the intervening period.

Yesterday afternoon I was becoming edgy about what the interview would entail. I wanted to find out what to expect, what to prepare, what to say. So I queued outside a Praed Street phone box for ten minutes, far enough away from the CEBDO office not to risk being seen by Nik. None of them know that I am here today.

Again Hawkes answered on the first ring. Again his manner was curt and to the point. Acting as if people were listening in on the line.

"I feel as if I'm going into this thing with my trousers down," I told him. "I know nothing about what's going on."

He sniffed what may have been a laugh and replied, "Don't worry about it. Everything will become clear when you get there."

"So there's nothing you can tell me? Nothing I need to prepare for?"

"Nothing at all, Alec. Just be yourself. It will all make sense later on."

How much of this Lucas knows, I do not know. I simply give him edited highlights from the dinner and a few sketchy impressions of Hawkes's character. Nothing permanent. Nothing of any significance.

In truth, we do not talk about him for long. The subject soon runs dry. Lucas moves on to my father and, after that, spends a quarter of an hour questioning me about my school years, dredging up the forgotten paraphernalia of my youth. He notes down all my answers, scratching away with the Mont Blanc, nodding imperceptibly at given points in the conversation.

Building a file on a man.

2

OFFICIAL SECRETS

The interview drifts on.

In response to a series of bland, straightforward questions about various aspects of my life—friendships, university, bogus summer jobs—I give a series of bland, straightforward answers designed to show myself in the correct light: as a stand-up guy, an unwavering patriot, a citizen of no stark political leanings. Just what the Foreign Office is looking for. Lucas's interviewing technique is strangely shapeless; at no point am I properly tested by anything he asks. And he never takes the conversation to a higher level. We do not, for example, discuss the role of the Foreign Office or British policy overseas. The talk is always general, always about me.

In due course I begin to worry that my chances of recruitment are slim. Lucas has about him the air of someone doing Hawkes a favor. He will keep me in here for a couple of hours, fulfill what is required of him, and the process will go no further. Things feel over before they have really begun.

However, at around three thirty I am again offered a cup of tea. This seems significant, but the thought of it deters me. I do not have enough conversation left to last out another hour. Yet it is clear that he would like me to accept.

"Yes, I would like one," I tell him. "Black. Nothing in it."

"Good," he says.

In this instant something visibly relaxes in Lucas, a crumpling of his suit. There is a sense of formalities passing. This impression is reinforced by his next remark, an odd, almost rhetorical question entirely out of keeping with the established rhythm of our conversation.

"Would you like to continue with your application after this initial discussion?"

Lucas phrases this so carefully that it is like a briefly glimpsed secret, a sight of the interview's true purpose. And yet the question does not seem to deserve an answer. What candidate, at this stage, would say no?

"Yes, I would."

"In that case, I am going to go out of the room for a few moments. I will send someone in with your cup of tea."

It is as if he has changed to a different script. Lucas looks relieved to be free of the edgy formality that has characterized the interview thus far. There is, at last, a sense of getting down to business.

From the clipboard on his lap he releases a small piece of paper, printed on both sides. This he places on the table in front of me.

"There's just one thing," he says, with well-rehearsed blandness. "Before I leave, I'd like you to sign the Official Secrets Act."

The first thing I think of, even before I am properly surprised, is that Lucas actually trusts me. I have said enough here today to earn the confidence of the state. That was all it took: sixty minutes of half-truths and evasions. I stare at the document and feel suddenly cata-pulted into something adult, as though from this moment onward things will be expected and demanded of me. Lucas is keen to assess my reaction. Prompted by this, I lift the document and hold it in my hand like a courtroom exhibit. I am surprised by its cursoriness. It is simply a little brown sheet of paper with space at the base for a signa-ture. I do not even bother to read the small print, because to do so might seem odd or improper. So I sign my name at the bottom of the page, scrawled and lasting. Alec Milius. The moment passes with what seems an absurd absence of seriousness, an absolute vacuum of drama. I give no thought to the consequence of it.

Almost immediately, before the ink can be properly dry, Lucas snatches the document away from me and stands to leave. Distant traffic noise on the Mall. A brief clatter in the secretarial enclave next door.

"Do you see the file on the table?"

It has been sitting there, untouched, for the duration of the inter-view.

"Yes."

"Please read it while I am gone. We will discuss the contents when I return."

I look at the file, register its hard red cover, and agree.

"Good," says Lucas, moving outside. "Good."

Alone now in the room, I lift the file from the table as though it were a magazine in a doctor's surgery. It is bound in cheap leather and well thumbed. I open it to the first page.

> Please read the following information carefully. You are being appraised for recruitment to the Secret Intelligence Service.

I look at this sentence again, and it is only on the third reading that it begins to make any sort of sense. I cannot, in my consternation, smother a belief that Lucas has the wrong man, that the intended candidate is still sitting downstairs flicking nervously through the pages of *The Times.* But then, gradually, things start to take shape. There was that final instruction in Lucas's letter: "As this letter is personal to you, I should be grateful if you could respect its confidentiality." A remark that struck me as odd at the time, though I made no more of it. And Hawkes was reluctant to tell me anything about the interview today: "Just be yourself, Alec. It'll all make sense when you get there." Jesus. How they have reeled me in. What did Hawkes see in me in just three hours at a dinner party to convince him that I would make a suitable employee of the Secret Intelligence Service? Of MI6?

A sudden consciousness of being alone in the room checks me out of bewilderment. I feel no fear, no great apprehension, only a sure sense that I am being watched through a small paneled mirror to the left of my chair. I swivel and examine the glass. There is something false about it, something not quite aged. The frame is solid, reasonably ornate, but the glass is clean, far more so than the larger mirror in the reception area downstairs. I look away. Why else would Lucas have left the room but to gauge my response from a position next door? He is watching me through the mirror. I am certain of it.

So I turn the page, attempting to look settled and businesslike.

The text makes no mention of MI6, only of SIS, which I assume to be the same organization. This is all the information I am capable of absorbing before other thoughts begin to intrude.

It has dawned on me, a slowly revealed thing, that Michael Hawkes was a Cold War spy. That's why he went to Moscow in the 1960s.

Did Dad know that about him?

I must look studious for Lucas. I must suggest the correct level of gravitas.

The first page is covered in information, two-line blocks of facts.

> The Secret Intelligence Service (hereafter SIS), working independently from Whitehall, has responsibility for gathering foreign intelligence . . .
>
> SIS officers work under diplomatic cover in British embassies overseas . . .

There are at least twenty pages like this one, detailing power structures within SIS, salary gradings, the need at all times for absolute secrecy. At one point, approximately halfway through the document, they have actually written: "Officers are certainly *not* licensed to kill."

On and on it goes, too much to take in. I tell myself to keep on reading, to try to assimilate as much of it as I can. Lucas will return soon with an entirely new set of questions, probing me, establishing whether I have the potential to do this.

It's time to move up a gear. *What an opportunity, Alec. To serve Queen and Country.*

The door opens, like air escaping through a seal.

"Here's your tea, sir."

Not Lucas. A sad-looking, perhaps unmarried woman in late middle-age has walked into the room carrying a plain white cup and saucer. I stand up to acknowledge her, knowing that Lucas will note this display of politeness from his position behind the mirror. She hands me the tea, I thank her, and she leaves without another word.

No serving SIS officer has been killed in action since World War Two.

I turn another page, skimming the prose.

The meanness of the starting salary surprises me: only seventeen thousand pounds in the first few years, with bonuses here and there to reward good work. If I do this, it will be for love. There's no money in spying.

Lucas walks in, no knock on the door, a soundless approach. He has a cup and saucer clutched in his hand and a renewed sense of purpose. His watchfulness has, if anything, intensified. Perhaps he hasn't been observing me at all. Perhaps this is his first sight of the young man whose life he has just changed.

He sits down, tea on the table, right leg folded over left. There is no ice-breaking remark. He dives straight in.

"What are your thoughts about what you've been reading?"

The weak bleat of an internal phone sounds on the other side of the door, stopping efficiently. Lucas waits for my response, but it does not come. My head is suddenly loud with noise and I am rendered incapable of speech. His gaze intensifies. He will not speak until I have done so. Say something, Alec. Don't blow it now. His mouth is melting into what I perceive as a disappointment close to pity. I struggle for something coherent, some sequence of words that will do justice to the very seriousness of what I am now embarked upon, but the words simply do not come. Lucas appears to be several feet closer now than he was before, and yet his chair has not moved an inch. How could this have happened? In an effort to regain control of myself, I try to remain absolutely still, to make our body language as much of a mirror as possible: arms relaxed, legs crossed, head upright and looking ahead. In time— what seem vast, vanished seconds—the beginning of a sentence forms in my mind, just the faintest of signals. And when Lucas makes to say something, as if to end my embarrassment, it acts as a spur.

I say, "Well . . . now that I know . . . I can understand why Mr. Hawkes didn't want to say exactly what I was coming here to do today."

"Yes."

The shortest, meanest, quietest *yes* I have ever heard.

"I found the pamphl—the file very interesting. It was a surprise."

"Why is that exactly? What surprised you about it?"

"I thought, obviously, that I was coming here today to be interviewed for the Diplomatic Service, not for SIS."

"Of course," he says, reaching for his tea.

And then, to my relief, he begins a long and practiced monologue about the work of the Secret Intelligence Service, an eloquent, spare résumé of its goals and character. This lasts as long as a quarter of an hour, allowing me the chance to get myself together, to think more clearly and focus on the task ahead. Still spinning from the embarrassment of having frozen openly in front of him, I find it difficult to concentrate on Lucas's voice. His description of the work of an SIS officer appears to be disappointingly void of macho derring-do. He paints a lusterless portrait of a man engaged in the simple act of gathering intelligence, doing so by the successful recruitment of foreigners sympathetic to the British cause who are prepared to pass on secrets for reasons of conscience or financial gain. That, in essence, is all that a spy does. As Lucas tells it, the more traditional aspects of espionage—burglary, phone tapping, honey traps, bugging—are a fiction. It's mostly desk work. Officers are certainly *not* licensed to kill.

"Clearly, one of the more unique aspects of SIS is the demand for absolute secrecy," he says, his voice falling away. "How would you feel about not being able to tell anybody what you do for a living?"

I guess that this is how it would be. Nobody, not even Kate, knowing any longer who I really was. A life of absolute anonymity.

"I wouldn't have any problem with that."

Lucas begins to take notes again. That was the answer he was looking for.

"And it doesn't concern you that you won't receive any public acclaim for the work you do?"

He says this in a tone that suggests that it bothers him a great deal.

"I'm not interested in acclaim."

A seriousness has enveloped me, nudging panic aside. An idea of the job is slowly composing itself in my imagination, something that is at once very straightforward but ultimately obscure. Something clandestine and yet moral and necessary.

Lucas ponders the clipboard in his lap.

"You must have some questions you want to ask me."

"Yes," I tell him. "Would members of my family be allowed to know that I am an SIS officer?"

Lucas appears to have a checklist of questions on his clipboard, all of which he expects me to ask. That was obviously one of them, because he again marks the page in front of him with his snub-nosed fountain pen.

"Obviously, the fewer people that know, the better. That usually means wives."

"Children?"

"No."

"But obviously not friends or other relatives?"

"Absolutely not. If you are successful after Sisby, and the panel decides to recommend you for employment, then we would have a conversation with your mother to let her know the situation."

"What is Sisby?"

"The Civil Service Selection Board. Sisby, as we call it. If you are successful at this first interview stage, you will go on to do Sisby in due course. This involves two intensive days of intelligence tests, interviews, and written papers at a location in Whitehall, allowing us to establish if you are of a high enough intellectual standard for recruitment to SIS."

The door opens without a knock and the same woman who brought in my tea, now cold and untouched on the table, walks in. She smiles apologetically in my direction, with a flushed, nervous glance at Lucas. He looks visibly annoyed.

"I do apologize, sir." She is frightened of him. "This just came through for you, and I felt you should see it right away."

She hands him a single sheet of fax paper. Lucas looks over at me quickly and proceeds to read it.

"Thank you." The woman leaves and he turns to me. "I have a suggestion. If you have no further questions, I think we should finish here. Will that be all right?"

"Of course."

There was something on the fax that necessitated this.

"You will obviously have to think things over. There are a lot of issues to consider when deciding to become an SIS officer. So let's end this discussion now. I will be in touch with you by post in the next few days. We will let you know at that stage if we want to proceed with your application."

"And if you do?"

"Then you will be invited back here for a second interview with one of my colleagues."

As he stands up to leave, Lucas folds the piece of paper in two and slips it into the inside pocket of his jacket. Leaving the recruitment file on the table, he gestures with an extended right arm toward the door, which has been left ajar by the secretary. I walk out ahead of him and immediately begin to feel all the stiffness of formality falling away from me. It is a relief to leave the room.

The girl in the neat red suit is standing outside waiting, somehow prettier than she was at two o'clock. She looks at me, gauges my mood, and then sends out a warm broad smile that is full of friendship and understanding. She knows what I've just been through. I feel like asking her out for dinner.

"Ruth, will you show Mr. Milius to the door? I have some business to attend to."

Lucas has barely emerged from his office: he is lingering in the doorway behind me, itching to get back inside.

"Of course," she says.

So our separation is abrupt. A last glance into each other's eyes, a grappled shake of the hand, a reiteration that he will be in touch. And then Philip Lucas vanishes back into his office, firmly closing the door.

3

TUESDAY, 4 JULY

At dawn, five days later, my first waking thought is of Kate, as though someone trips a switch behind my closed eyes and she blinks into the morning. It has been like this, on and off, for four months now. Sometimes, still caught in a half dream, I will reach for her as though she were actually beside me in bed. I try to smell her, try to gauge the pressure and softness of her kisses, the delicious sculpture of her spine. Then we lie together, whispering quietly, kissing. Just like old times.

Drawing the curtains, I see that the sky is white, a cloudy midsummer morning that will burn off at noon and break into a good blue day.

All that I have wanted is to tell Kate about SIS. At last something has gone right for me, something that she might be proud of. Someone has given me the chance to put my life together, to do something constructive with all these mind wanderings and ambition. Wasn't that what she always wanted? Wasn't she always complaining about how I wasted opportunities, how I was always waiting for something better to come along? Well, this is it.

But I know that it will not be possible. I have to let her go. Finding it so difficult to let her go.

I shower, dress, and take the tube to Edgware Road, but I am not the first at work. Coming down the narrow, sheltered mews, I see Anna up ahead, fighting vigorously with the lock on the garage door. A heavy bunch of keys drops from her right hand. She stands up to straighten her back and sees me in the distance, her expression one of unambiguous contempt. Not so much as a nod. I push a splay-fingered hand through my hair and say good morning.

"Hello," she says archly, twisting the key in the lock.

She's growing her hair. Long brown strands flecked with old high-lights and trapped light.

"Why the fuck doesn't Nik give me a key that fucking works?"

"Try mine."

I steer my key in toward the garage door, a movement that causes Anna to pull her hand out of the way like a flick knife. Her keys fall onto the gray step and she says fuck again. Simultaneously, her bicycle, which has been resting against the wall beside us, topples to the ground. She walks over to pick it up as I unlock the door and go inside.

The air is wooden and musty. Anna comes through the door behind me with a squeezed smile. She is wearing a summer dress of pastel blue cotton dotted with pale yellow flowers. A thin layer of sweat glows on the freckled skin above her breasts, soft as moons. With my index finger I flick the switches one by one. The strip lights in the small office strobe.

There are five desks inside, all hooked up to phones. I weave through them to the far side of the garage, turning right into the kitchen. The kettle is already full and I press it, lifting two mugs from the drying rack. The toilet perches in the corner of the narrow room, topped by rolls of pink paper. Someone has left a half-finished cigarette on the tank that has stained the ceramic. The kettle's scaly deposits crackle faintly as I open the door of the fridge.

Fresh milk? No.

When I come out of the kitchen Anna is already on the phone, talk-ing softly to someone in the voice that she uses for boys. Perhaps she left him slumbering in her wide, low bed this morning, the smell of her sex on the pillow. She has opened up the wooden doors of the garage so that daylight has filled the room. I hear the kettle click. Anna catches me looking at her and swivels her chair so that she is facing out onto the mews. I light a cigarette, my last one, and wonder who he is.

"So," she says to him, her voice a naughty grin, "what are you going to do today?" A pause. "Oh, Bill, you're so *lazy*. . . ."

She likes his being lazy, she approves of it.

"Okay, that sounds good. Mmmm. I'll be finished here at six, maybe earlier if Nik lets me go."

She turns and sees that I am still watching her.

"Just Alec. Yeah. Yeah. That's right."

Her voice drops as she says this. He knows all about what happened between us. She must have told him everything.

"Well, they'll be here in a minute. Okay. See you later. Bye."

She turns back into the room and hangs up the phone.

"New boyfriend?"

"Sorry?" Standing up, she passes me on her way into the kitchen. I hear her open the door of the fridge, the minute electric buzz of its bright white light, the soft plastic suck of its closing.

"Nothing," I say, raising my voice so that she can hear me. "I just said, is that your new boyfriend?"

"No, it was yours," she says, coming out again. "I'm going to buy some milk."

As she leaves, a telephone rings in the unhoovered office, but I let the answering machine pick it up. Anna's footsteps clip away along the cobbles and a car starts up in the mews. I step outside.

Des, the next-door neighbor, is buckled into his magnesium E-type Jag, revving the engine. Des always wears loose black suits and shirts with a sheen, his long silver hair tied back in a ponytail. None of us has ever been able to work out what Des does for a living. He could be an architect, a film producer, the owner of a chain of restaurants. It's impossible to tell just by looking into the windows of his house, which reveal expensive sofas, a wide-screen television, plenty of computer hardware, and, right at the back of the sleek white kitchen, an industrial-size espresso machine. On the rare occasions when Des speaks to anyone in the CEBDO office, it is to complain about excessive noise or car-parking violations. Otherwise, he is an unknown quantity.

Nik shuffles his shabby walk down the mews just as Des is sliding out of it in his low-slung, antique fuck machine. I go back inside and look busy. Nik comes through the open door and glances up at me, still moving forward. He is a small man.

"Morning, Alec. How are we today? Ready for a hard day's work?"

"Morning, Nik."

He swings his briefcase up onto his desk and wraps his old leather jacket around the back of the chair.

"Do you have a cup of coffee for me?"

Nik is a bully and, like all bullies, sees everything in terms of power. Who is threatening me; whom can I threaten? To suffocate the constant nag of his insecurity he must make others feel uncomfortable. I say,

"Funnily enough, I don't. The batteries are low on my ESP this morning, and I didn't know exactly when you'd be arriving."

"You being funny with me today, Alec? You feeling confident or something?"

He doesn't look at me while he says this. He just shuffles things on his desk.

"I'll get you a coffee, Nik."

"Thank you."

So I find myself back in the kitchen, reboiling the kettle. And it is only when I am crouched on the floor, peering into the fridge, that I remember Anna has gone out to buy milk. On the middle shelf, a hardened chunk of overly yellow butter wrapped in torn gold foil is slowly being scarfed by mold.

"We don't have any milk," I call out. "Anna's gone out to get some."

There's no answer, of course.

I put my head around the door of the kitchen and say to Nik, "I said there's no milk. Anna's gone—"

"I hear you. I hear you. Don't be panicking about it."

I ache to tell him about SIS, to see the look on his cheap, corrupted face. Hey, Nik, you're twice my age and this is all you've been able to come up with: a low-rent, dry-rot garage in Paddington, flogging lies and phony advertising space to your own countrymen. That's the extent of your life's work. A few phones, a fax machine, and three secondhand computers running on outdated software. That's what you have to show for yourself. That's all you are. I'm twenty-four, and I'm being recruited by the Secret Intelligence Service.

It is five o'clock in the afternoon in Brno, one hour ahead of London. I am talking to a Mr. Klemke, the managing director of a firm of building contractors with ambitions to move into western Europe.

"Particularly France," he says.

"Well, then I think our publication would be perfect for you, sir."

"Publicsation? I'm sorry. This word."

"Our publication, our magazine. The *Central European Business Review*. It's published every three months and has a circulation of four hundred thousand copies worldwide."

"Yes, yes. And this is new magazine, printed in London?"

Anna, back from a long lunch, sticks a Post-it note on the desk in front of me. Scrawled in girly swirls she has written, "Saul rang. Coming here later."

"That's correct," I tell Klemke. "Printed here in London and distributed worldwide. Four hundred thousand copies."

Nik is looking at me.

"And, Mr. Mills, who is the publisher of this magazine? Is it yourself?"

"No, sir. I am one of our advertising executives."

"I see."

I envision him as large and rotund, a benign Robert Maxwell. I envision them all as benign Robert Maxwells.

"And you want me to advertise, is that what you are asking?"

"I think it would be in your interest, particularly if you are looking to expand into western Europe."

"Yes, particularly France."

"France."

"And you have still not told me who is publishing this magazine in London. The name of person who is editor."

Nik has started reading the sports pages of *The Independent*.

"It's a Mr. Jarolmek."

He folds one side of the newspaper down with a sudden crisp rattle, alarmed.

Silence in Brno.

"Can you say this name again, please?"

"Jarolmek."

I look directly at Nik, eyebrows raised, and spell out J-a-r-o-l-m-e-k with great slowness and clarity down the phone. Klemke may yet bite.

"I know this man."

"Oh, you do?"

Trouble.

"Yes. My brother, of my wife, he is a businessman also. In the past he has published with this Mr. Jarolmek."

"In the *Central European Business Review*?"

"If this is what you are calling this now."

"It's always been called that."

Nik puts down the paper, pushes his chair out behind him, and stands up. He walks over to my desk and perches on it. Watching me. And there, on the other side of the mews, is Saul, leaning coolly against the wall smoking a cigarette like a private investigator. I have no idea how long he has been standing there. Something heavy falls over in Klemke's office.

"Well, it's a small world," I say, gesturing to Saul to come in. Anna is grinning as she dials a number on her telephone. Long brown slender arms.

"It is my belief that Jarolmek is a robber and a con man."

"I'm sorry, uh, I'm sorry, why . . . why do you feel that?"

A quizzical look from Nik, perched there. Saul now coming in through the door.

"My brother paid a large sum of money to your organization two separate times—"

Don't let him finish.

"—And he didn't receive a copy of the magazine? Or experience any feedback from his advertisement?"

"Mr. Mills, do not interrupt me. I have something I want to say to you and I do not wish to be interrupted."

"I'm sorry. Do go on."

"Yes, I will go on. I will go on. My brother then met with a British diplomat in Prague at a function dinner who had not heard of your publication."

"Really?"

"And when he goes to look it up, it is not listed in any of our documentation here in Czech Republic. How do you explain this?"

"There must be some misunderstanding."

Nik stands up and spits, "What the fuck is going on?" in an audible whisper. He presses the loudspeaker button on my telephone and Klemke's riled gravelly voice echoes out into the room.

"Misunderstanding? No, I don't believe it is. You are a fraud. My brother of my wife has made inquiries into your circulation and it appears that you do not sell as widely as you say. You are lying to people in Europe and making promises. My brother was going to report you. And now I will do the same."

Nik stabs the button again and pulls the receiver out of my hand.

"Hello. Yes. This is Nikolas Jarolmek. Can I help you with something?"

Saul looks at me quizzically, nodding his head at Nik, fishing lazily about in the debris on my desk. He has had his hair cut very short, almost shaved to the skull.

Suddenly Nik is shouting, a clatter of a language I do not understand. Cursing, sweating, chopping the air with his small stubby hands. He spits insults into the phone, parries Klemke's threats with raging animosities, hangs up with a bang.

"You stupid fucking arsehole!"

He turns on me, shouting, his arms spread like push-ups on the desk.

"What were you doing keeping that fucker on the phone? You could get me in jail. You stupid fucking . . . cunt!"

Cunt sounds like a word he has just learned in the playground.

"What, for fuck's sake? What the fuck was I supposed to do?"

"What were you . . . you stupid. Fucking hell, I should pay my dog to sit there. My fucking dog would do a better job than you."

I am too ashamed to look at Saul.

"Nik, I'm sorry, but—"

"Sorry? Oh, well then, that's all right. . . ."

"No, sorry, but—"

"I don't care if you're sorry."

"Look!"

This from Saul. He is on his feet. He's going to say something. Oh, Jesus.

"He's not saying he's sorry. If you'd just listen, he's not saying he's sorry. It's not his fault if some wanker in Warsaw catches on to what you're up to and starts giving him an earful! Why don't you calm down, for Christ's sake?"

"Who the fuck are you?" says Nik. He really likes this guy.

"I'm a friend of Alec's. Take it easy."

"And he can't take care of himself? You can't take care of yourself now, Alec, eh?"

"Of course he can take care of himself. . . ."

"Nik, I can take care of myself. Saul, it's all right. We'll go and get a coffee. I'll just get out of here for a while."

"For more than a while," says Nik. "Don't come back. I don't want to see you. You come back tomorrow. This is enough for one day."

"Jesus, what a cunt."

Now Saul is someone who really knows the time and place for effective use of the word *cunt*. I feel like asking him to say it again.

"I can't believe you work for that guy."

We are standing on either side of a table football game in a café on Edgware Road. I take a worn white ball from the trough below my waist and feed it through the hole onto the table. Saul traps the ball with the still black feet of his plastic man before gunning it down the table into my goal.

"The object of the game is to stop that kind of thing from happening."

"It's my goalkeeper."

"What's wrong with him?"

"He has personal problems."

Saul gives a wheezy laugh, lifts his cigarette from a Coca-Cola ashtray, and takes a drag.

"What language was it that Nik was speaking?"

"Czech. Slovak. One of the two."

"Play, play."

The ball thunders and slaps on the rocking table.

"Better than Nintendo, eh?"

"Yes, Grandpa," says Saul, scoring.

"Shit."

He slides another red counter along the abacus. Five–nil.

"Don't be afraid to compete, Alec. Carpe diem."

I attempt a deft sideways shunt of the ball in midfield, but it skewers away at an angle. Coming back down the table, Saul saying, "Now *that* is skill," it rolls loose in front of my center half. I grip the clammy handle with rigid fingers and whip it so that the neat row of figures rotates in a propeller blur. Saul's hand flies to the right and his goalkeeper saves the incoming ball.

"That's illegal," he says. The shorter haircut suits him.

"I'm competing."

"Oh, right."

Six–nil.

"How did *that* happen?"

"Because you're very bad at this game. Listen, I'm sorry if I interfered back there. . . ."

"No."

"What?"

"It's okay."

"No, I mean it. I'm sorry."

"I know you are."

"I probably shouldn't have stuck my foot in."

"No, you probably shouldn't have stuck your foot in. But that's how you are. I'd rather you spoke your mind and stood up for your friends than bit your tongue for the sake of decorum. I understand. You don't have to explain. I don't care about the job, so it's okay."

"Okay."

We tuck the subject away like a letter.

"So what are you doing up here?"

"I just thought I'd come up and see you. I've been busy with work, haven't seen you for a week or so. You free tonight?"

"Yeah."

"We can go back to mine and eat."

"Good."

Saul is the only person in whom I have considered confiding, but now that we are face-to-face it does not seem necessary to tell him about SIS. My reluctance has nothing to do with official secrecy: if I asked him to, Saul would keep his mouth shut for thirty years. Trust is not an element in the decision.

There has always been something quietly competitive about our friendship—a rivalry of intellects, a need to kiss the prettier girl. Adolescent stuff. Nowadays, with school just a vague memory, this competitiveness manifests in an unspoken system of checks and balances on each other's lives: who earns more money, who drives the faster car, who has laid the more promising path into the future. This rivalry, which is never articulated but constantly acknowledged by both of us, is what prevents me from talking to Saul about what is now the most important and significant aspect of my life. I cannot confide in him when the indignity of rejection by SIS is still possible. It is, perversely, more important to me to save face with him than to seek his advice and guidance.

I take out the last ball.

———

We eat stir-fry chicken side by side off a low table in the larger of the two sitting rooms in Saul's flat, hunched forward on the sofa, sweating under the chili.

"So is your boss always like that?"

It takes me a moment to realize that Saul is talking about the argument with Nik this afternoon.

"Forget about it. He was just taking advantage of the fact that you were there to ridicule me in front of the others. He's a bully. He gets a kick out of scoring points off people. I couldn't give a shit."

"Right."

Small black-and-white marble squares are sunk into the top of the table, forming a chessboard, which is chipped and stained after years of use.

"How long have you been there now?"

"With Nik? About a year."

"And you're going to stay on? I mean, where's it going?"

I don't like talking about this with Saul. His career, as a freelance assistant director, is going well, and there's something hidden in his questions, a glimpse of disappointment.

"What d'you mean, where's it going?"

"Just that. I didn't think you'd stay there as long as you have."

"You think I ought to have a more serious job? Something with a career graph, a ladder of promotion?"

"I didn't say that."

"You sound like a teacher."

We are silent for a while. Staring at walls.

"I'm applying to join the Foreign Office."

This just comes out. I didn't plan it.

"You're what?"

"Seriously." I turn to look at him. "I've filled in the application forms and done some preliminary IQ tests. I'm waiting to hear back from them."

The lie falls in me like a dropped stitch.

"Christ. When did you decide this?"

"About two months ago. I just had a bout of feeling unstretched, needed to take some action and sort my life out."

"What, so you want to be a diplomat?"

"Yeah."

It doesn't feel exactly wrong to be telling him this. At some point in the next eighteen months, a time will come when I may be sent overseas on a posting to a foreign embassy. Saul's knowing now of my intention to join the Diplomatic Service will help allay any suspicions he might have in the future.

"I'm surprised," he says, on the brink of being opinionated. "You sure you know what you're letting yourself in for?"

"Meaning?"

"Meaning, why would you want to join the Foreign Office?"

A little piece of spring onion flies out of his mouth.

"I've already told you. Because I'm sick of working for Nik. Because I need a change."

"You need a change."

"Yes."

"So why become a civil servant? That's not you. Why join the Foreign Office? Fifty-seven old farts pretending that Britain still has a role to play on the world stage. Why would you want to become a part of something that's so obviously in decline? All you'll do is stamp passports and attend business delegations. The most fun a diplomat ever has is bailing some British drug smuggler out of prison. You could end up in Albania, for fuck's sake."

We are locked into the absurdity of arguing about a problem that does not exist.

"Or Washington."

"In your dreams."

"Well, thanks for your support."

It is still light outside. Saul puts down his fork and twists around. A flicker of eye contact, and then he looks away, the top row of his teeth pressing down on a reddened bottom lip.

"Look. Whatever. You'd be good at it."

He doesn't believe that for a second.

"You don't believe that for a second."

"No, I do." He plays with his unfinished food, looking at me again. "Have you thought about what it would be like to live abroad? I mean, is that what you really want?"

For the first time it strikes me that I may have confused the notion of serving the state with a longstanding desire to run away from London, from Kate, and from CEBDO. This makes me feel foolish. I am suddenly drunk on weak American beer.

"Saul, all I want to do is put something back in. Living abroad or living here, it doesn't matter. And the Foreign Office is one way of doing that."

"Put something back into what?"

"The country."

"What is that? You don't owe anyone. Who do you owe? The queen? The empire? The Conservative Party?"

"Now you're just being glib."

"No, I'm not. I'm serious. The only people you owe are your friends and your family. That's it. Loyalty to the Crown, improving Britain's image abroad, whatever bullshit they try to feed you, that's an illusion. I don't want to be rude, but your idea of putting something back into society is just vanity. You've always wanted people to rate you."

Saul watches carefully for my reaction. What he has just said is actually fairly offensive. I say, "I don't think there's anything wrong with wanting people to have a good opinion of you. Why not strive to be the best you can? Just because you've always been a cynic doesn't mean that the rest of us can't go about trying to improve things."

"Improve things?" He looks astonished. Neither of us is in the least bit angry.

"Yes. Improve things."

"That's not you, Alec. You're not a charity worker."

"Don't you think we've been spoiled as a generation? Don't you think we've grown used to the idea of take, take, take?"

"Not really. I work hard for a living. I don't go around feeling guilty about that."

I want to get this theme going, not least because I don't in all honesty know exactly how I feel about it.

"Well, I really believe we have," I say, taking out a cigarette, offering one to Saul. "And that's not because of vanity or guilt or delusion."

"Believe what?"

"That because none of us have had to struggle or fight for things in our generation we've become incredibly indolent and selfish."

"Where's this coming from? I've never heard you talk like this in your life. What happened, did you see some documentary about the First World War and feel guilty that you didn't do more to suppress the Hun?"

"Saul . . ."

"Is that it? Do you think we should start a war with someone, prune the vine a bit, just to make you feel better about living in a free country?"

"Come on. You know I don't think that."

"So—what? Is it morality that makes you want to join the Foreign Office?"

"Look. I don't necessarily think that I'm going to be able to change anything in particular. I just want to do something that feels . . . significant."

"What do you mean 'significant'?"

Despite the fact that our conversation has been premised on a lie, there are nevertheless issues emerging here about which I feel strongly. I stand up and walk around, as if being upright will lend some shape to my words.

"You know—something worthwhile, something meaningful, something constructive. I'm sick of just surviving, of all the money I earn being plowed back into rent and bills and taxes. It's okay for you. You don't have to pay anything on this place. At least you've met your landlord."

"You've never met your landlord?"

"No." I am gesticulating like a TV preacher. "Every month I write a check for four hundred and eighty quid to a Mr. J. Sarkar—I don't even know his first name. He owns an entire block in Uxbridge Road: flats, shops, taxi ranks, you name it. It's not like he needs the money. Every penny I earn seems to go toward making sure that somebody else is more comfortable than I am."

Saul extinguishes his cigarette in a pile of cold noodles. He looks suddenly awkward. Money talk always brings that out in him. Rich guilt.

"I've got the answer," he says, trying to lift himself out of it. "You need to get yourself an ideology, Alec. You've got nothing to believe in."

"What do you suggest? Maybe I should become a born-again Christian, start playing guitar at Holy Trinity Brompton and holding prayer meetings."

"Why not? We could say grace whenever you come round for dinner. You'd get a tremendous kick out of feeling superior to everyone."

"At university I always wanted to be one of those guys selling *Living Marxist*. Imagine having that much *faith*."

"It's a little passé," Saul says. "And cold during the winter months."

I pour the last dregs of my beer into a glass and take a swig that is sour and dry. On the muted television screen the *Nine o'Clock News* is beginning. We both look up to see the headlines. Then Saul switches it off.

"Game of chess?"

"Sure."

We play the opening moves swiftly, the thunk of the pieces falling regularly on the strong wooden surface. I love that sound. There are no early captures, no immediate attacks. We exchange bishops, castle kingside, push pawns. Neither one of us is prepared to do anything risky. Saul keeps up an impression of easy joviality, making gags and farting away the stir-fry, but I know that, like me, he is concealing a deep desire to win.

After twenty-odd moves, the game is choking up. If Saul wants it, there's the possibility of a three-piece swap in the center of the board that will reap two pawns and a knight each, but it isn't clear who will be left with the advantage if the exchange takes place. Saul ponders things, staring intently at the board, occasionally taking a gulp of wine. To hurry him along I say, "Is it my go?" and he says, "No. Me. Sorry, taking a long time." Then he thinks for another three or four minutes. My guess is he'll shift his rook into the center of the back rank, freeing it to move down the middle.

"I'm going for a piss."

"Make your move first."

"I'll do it when I come back," he sighs, standing up and making his way down the hall.

What I do next is achieved almost without thinking. I listen for the sound of the bathroom door closing, then quickly advance the pawn on the f-file a single space. I retract my right hand and study the difference in the shape of the game. The pawn is protected there by a knight and another pawn, and it will, in three or four moves' time, provide a two-pronged defense when I slide in to attack Saul's king. It's a simple, minute adjustment to the game that should go unnoticed in the thick gathering of pieces fighting for control of the center.

When he returns from the bathroom, Saul's eyes seem to fix immediately on the cheating pawn. He may have spotted it. His forehead wrinkles and he chews the knuckle on his index finger, trying to establish what has changed. But he says nothing. Within a few moments he has made his move—the rook to the center of the back rank—and sat back deep into the sofa. Play continues nervously. I develop king-side, looking to use the advanced pawn as cover for an attack. Then Saul, as frustrated as I am, offers a queen swap after half an hour of play. I accept, and from there it's a formality. With the pawn in such an advanced position, my formation is marginally stronger; it's just a matter of wearing him down. Saul parries a couple of attacks, but the sheer weight of numbers begins to tell. He resigns at twenty to eleven.

"Nice going," he says, offering me a sweaty palm.

We always shake hands afterward.

At 1:00 A.M., drunk and tired, I sit slumped on the backseat of an unlicensed minicab, going home to Shepherd's Bush.

There is a plain white envelope on my doormat, second post, marked PRIVATE AND CONFIDENTIAL.

Foreign and Commonwealth Office
No. 46A———Terrace
London SW1
PERSONAL AND CONFIDENTIAL

Dear Mr. Milius,
Following your recent conversation with my colleague, Philip Lucas, I should like to invite you to attend a second interview on Tuesday, July 25th, at 10 o'clock.

Please let me know if this date will be convenient for you.

Yours sincerely,
Patrick Liddiard
Recruitment Liaison Office

4

POSITIVE VETTING

The second interview passes like a foregone conclusion.

This time around I am treated with deference and respect by the cop on the door, and Ruth greets me at the bottom of the staircase with the cheery familiarity of an old friend.

"Good to see you again, Mr. Milius. You can go straight up."

Throughout the morning there is a pervading sense of acceptance, a feeling of gradual admission to an exclusive club. My first encounter with Lucas was clearly a success. Everything about my performance that day has impressed them.

In the secretarial enclave, Ruth introduces me to Patrick Liddiard, who exudes the clean charm and military dignity of the typical Foreign Office man. This is the face that built the empire: slim, alert, colonizing. He is impeccably turned out in gleaming brogues and a wife-ironed shirt that is tailored and crisp. His suit, too, is evidently custom-made, a rich gray flannel cut lean against his slender frame. He looks tremendously pleased to see me, pumping my hand with vigor, cementing an immediate connection between us.

"Very nice to meet you," he says. "Very nice indeed."

His voice is gentle, refined, faintly plummy, exactly as his appearance suggested it would be. Not a wrong note. There is a warmth suddenly about all this, a clubbable ease entirely absent on my previous visit.

The interview itself does nothing to dispel this impression. Liddiard appears to treat it as a mere formality, something to be gone through before the rigors of Sisby. That, he tells me, will be a test of mettle, a tough two-day candidate analysis comprising IQ tests, essays, interviews, and group discussions. He makes it clear to me that he has every confidence in my ability to succeed at Sisby and to go on to become a successful SIS officer.

There is only one conversational exchange between us that I consider especially significant. It comes just as the first hour of the interview is drawing to a close.

We have finished discussing the European monetary union—issues of sovereignty and so on—when Liddiard makes a minute adjustment to his tie, glances down at the clipboard in his lap, and asks me, very straightforwardly, how I would feel about manipulating people for a living.

Initially I am surprised that such a question could emerge from the apparently decent, old-fashioned gent sitting opposite me. Liddiard has been so courteous, so civilized up to this point, that to hear talk of deception from him is jarring. As a result, our conversation turns suddenly watchful, and I have to check myself out of complacency. We have arrived at what feels like the nub of the thing, the rich center of the clandestine life.

I repeat the question, buying myself some time.

"How would I feel about manipulating people?"

"Yes," he says, with more care in his voice than he has allowed so far.

I must, in my answer, strike a delicate balance between the appearance of moral rectitude and the implied suggestion that I am capable of pernicious deceits. It is no good telling him outright of my preparedness to lie, although that is the business he is in. On the contrary, Liddiard will want to know that my will to do so is born of a deeper dedication, a profound belief in the ethical legitimacy of SIS. He is clearly a man possessed of values and moral probity: like Lucas, he sees the work of the Secret Intelligence Service as a force for good. Any suggestion that the intelligence services are involved in something fundamentally corrupt would appall him.

So I pick my words with care.

"If you are searching for someone who is genetically manipulative, then you've got the wrong man. Deceit does not come easily to me. But if you are looking for somebody who would be prepared to lie when and if the circumstances demanded it, then that would be something I would be capable of doing."

Liddiard allows an unquiet silence to linger in the room. And then he suddenly smiles, warmly, so that his teeth catch a splash of light. I have said the right thing.

"Good," he says, nodding. "Good. And what about being unable to tell your friends about what you do? Have you had any concerns about that? We obviously prefer it that you keep the number of people who know about your activities to an absolute minimum. Some candidates have a problem with that."

"Not me. Mr. Lucas told me in my previous interview that officers are allowed to tell their parents."

"Yes."

"But as far as friends are concerned . . ."

"Of course not."

"That's what I'd come to understand."

Both of us nod simultaneously. Suddenly, however, for no better reason than that I want to appear solid and reliable, I do something quite unexpected. It is unplanned and dumb. A needless lie to Liddiard that could prove costly.

"It's just that I have a girlfriend."

"I see. And have you told her about us?"

"No. She knows that I'm here today, but she thinks I'm applying for the Diplomatic Service."

"Is this a serious relationship?"

"Yes. We've been together for almost five years. It's very probable that we'll get married. So she should know about this, to see if she's comfortable with it."

Liddiard touches his tie again.

"Of course," he says. "What is the girl's name?"

"Kate. Kate Allardyce."

Liddiard writes down Kate's name in his notes. Why am I doing this? They won't care that I am about to get married. They won't think any more of me for being able to sustain a long-term relationship. If anything, they would prefer me to be alone.

He asks when she was born.

"December twenty-eighth, 1971."

"Where?"

"Argentina."

A tiny crease saunters across his forehead.

"And what is her current address?"

I had no idea that he would ask so much about her. I give the address where we used to live together.

"Will you want to interview her? Is that why you want all this information?"

"No, no," he says quickly. "It's purely for vetting purposes. There shouldn't be a problem. But I must ask you to refrain from discussing your candidature with her until after the Sisby examinations."

"Of course."

Then, as a savored afterthought, he adds, "Sometimes wives can make a substantial contribution to the work of an SIS officer."

5

DAY ONE/MORNING

It's 6:00 A.M. on Wednesday, August 9. There are two and a half hours until Sisby.

I have laid out a gray flannel suit on my bed and checked it for stains. Inside the jacket there's a powder-blue shirt at which I throw ties, hoping for a match. Yellow with faint white dots. Pistachio green shot through with blue. A busy paisley, a sober navy one-tone. Christ, I have awful ties. Outside, the weather is overcast and bloodless. A good day to be indoors.

After a bath and a stinging shave I settle down in the sitting room with a cup of coffee and some back issues of *The Economist,* absorbing its opinions, making them mine. According to the Sisby literature given to me by Liddiard at the end of our interview in July, "all SIS candidates will be expected to demonstrate an interest in current affairs and a level of expertise in at least three or four specialist subjects." That's all I can prepare for.

I am halfway through a profile of Gerry Adams when the faint moans of my neighbors' early-morning lovemaking start to seep through the floor. In time there is a faint groan, what sounds like a cough, then the thud of wood on wall. I have never been able to decide whether she is faking it. Saul was over here once when they started up and I asked his opinion. He listened for a while, ear close to the floor, and made the solid point that you can only hear her and not him, an imbalance that suggests female overcompensation. "I think she wants to enjoy it," he said, thoughtfully, "but something is preventing that."

I put the dishwasher on to smother the noise, but even above the throb and rumble I can still hear her tight, sobbing emissions of lust. Gradually, too rhythmically, she builds to a moan-filled climax. Then I am left in the silence with my mounting anxiety.

Time is passing. It frustrates me that I can do so little to prepare for the next two days. The Sisby program is a test of wits, of quick thinking and mental panache. You can't prepare for it, like an exam. It's survival of the fittest.

Grab your jacket and go.

The Sisby examination center is at the north end of Whitehall. This is the part of town they put in movies as an establishing shot to let audiences in South Dakota know that the action has moved to London: a wide-angle view of Nelson's Column, with a couple of double-decker buses and taxis queuing up outside the broad, serious flank of the National Gallery. Then cut to Harrison Ford in his suite at The Grosvenor.

The building is a great slab of nineteenth-century brown brick. People are already starting to go inside. There is a balding man in a gray uniform behind a reception desk enjoying a brief flirtation with power. He looks shopworn, overweight, and inexplicably pleased with himself. One by one, Sisby candidates shuffle past him, their names ticked off on a list. He looks nobody in the eye.

"Yes?" he says to me impatiently, as if I were trying to gate-crash a party.

"I'm here for the Selection Board."

"Name?"

"Alec Milius."

He consults the list, ticks me off, gives me a flat plastic security tag.

"Third floor."

Ahead of me, loitering in front of a lift, are five other candidates. Very few of them will be SIS. These are the prospective future employees of the Ministry of Agriculture, Social Security, Trade and Industry, Health. The men and women who will be responsible for policy decisions in the governments of the new millennium. They all look impossibly young.

To their left a staircase twists away in a steep spiral and I begin climbing it, unwilling to wait for the lift. The stairwell, like the rest of the building, is drab and unremarkable, with a provincial university aesthetic that would have been considered modern in the mid-1960s. The third-floor landing is covered in brown linoleum. Nicotine-yellow paint clings to the walls. My name, and those of four others, have been typed on a sheet of paper that is stuck up on a pockmarked notice board.

COMMON ROOM B3: CSSB (SPECIAL)

ANN BUTLER
MATTHEW FREARS
ELAINE HAYES
ALEC MILIUS
SAM OGILVY

A woman—a girl—who can't be much older than twenty is standing in front of the notice board, taking in what it has to say. She appears to be reading an advertisement requesting blood donors. She doesn't turn to look at me; she just keeps on reading. She has pretty hair, thick black curls tied halfway down with a dark blue velvet band. Strands of it have broken free and are holding on to the fabric of her tartan jacket. She is tall with thin spindly legs under a knee-length skirt. Wearing tights. A pair of thick National Health glasses obliterates the shape and character of her face.

A middle-aged man comes around the corner and passes her at the top of the stairs. She turns to him and says, "Hello. By any chance you wouldn't know where Common Room B3 is, would you?"

She has a Northern Ireland accent, full of light and cunning. That was brave of them to take her on. Imagine the vetting.

The man, probably a Sisby examiner, is more helpful than I expect him to be. He says yes of course and points to a room no more than ten feet away on the far side of the landing with B3 clearly written on the door. The girl looks embarrassed not to have noticed this but he makes nothing of it and heads off down the stairs.

"Good start, Ann," she says under her breath, but the remark is directed at me. "Hello."

"Hi. I'm Alec."

"This Alec?" She is tapping ALEC MILIUS on the notice board.

"The same."

Her skin is very pale and lightly freckled. She has a slightly witchy way about her, a creepy innocence.

"I'm so nervous," she says. "Are you? Did you find it okay?"

"Yes, I did. Where are you from?"

"Northern Ireland."

We are walking into B3. Cheap brown sofas, dirty windowpanes, a low MFI table covered in newspapers.

"Oh. Which town?"

"Do you know Enniskillen?"

"I've heard of it, yes."

Old men with medals pinned to their chests, severed in two by the IRA. Maybe an uncle of hers, a grandpa.

"And you?"

"I'm English."

"Aye. I could tell by your accent."

"I live here. In London."

The small talk here is meaningless, just words in a room, but the beats and gaps in the conversation are significant. I note Ann's sly glances at my suit and shoes, the quick suspicion in her wide brown eyes.

"Which part of London?"

"Shepherd's Bush."

"I don't know that."

No talk for a moment while we survey the room, our home for the next forty-eight hours. The carpet is a deep, worn brown.

"Do you want a drink?" she asks, but her smile is too full of effort. There is a machine in the corner surrounded by polystyrene cups, threatening appalling coffee.

"I'm all right, thanks."

A gnomic man appears now in the doorway of the common room, carrying a brown leather satchel. He looks tired and bewildered, encumbered by the social ineptitude of the fabulously intelligent.

"Is this B3?" he asks. His hair is unbrushed.

"Yes," Ann says, keenly.

He nods, clearly heavy with nerves. A hobbit of a man. He shuffles into the room and sits across from me in an armchair that has sponge pouring out of its upholstery. Ann seems to have decided against coffee, moving back toward the window at the back of the room.

"So you're either Sam or Matthew," she asks him. "Which one?"

"Matt."

"I'm Alec," I tell him. We are near each other and I shake his hand. The palm is damp with lukewarm sweat.

"Nice to meet you."

Ann has swooped in, bending over to introduce herself. The Hobbit is nervous around women. When she shakes his hand, his eyes duck to the carpet. She fakes out a smile and retreats below a white clock with big black hands that says half past eight.

Not long now.

I pick up a copy of *The Times* from the low table and begin reading it, trying to remember interesting things to say about Gerry Adams. Matt takes a cereal bar out of his jacket pocket and begins tucking into it, oblivious of us, dropping little brown crumbs and shards of raisin on his Marks & Spencer blazer. It has occurred to me that in the eyes of Liddiard and Lucas, Matt and I have something in common, some shared quality or flaw that is the common denominator among spies. What could that possibly be?

Ann looks at him.

"So what do you do, Matt?"

He almost drops the cereal bar in his lap.

"I'm studying for a master's degree at Warwick."

"What in?"

"Computer science and European affairs."

He says this quietly, as though he is ashamed. His skin is fighting a constant, losing battle with acne.

"So you just came down from Warwick last night? You're staying in a hotel?"

She's nosy, this one. Wants to know what she's up against.

"Yeah," he says. "Not far from here."

I like it that he does not ask the same question of her.

A young man appears in the doorway. This must be Sam Ogilvy, the third male candidate. He has an immediate, palpable influence on the room that is controlling. He makes it his. Ogilvy has a healthy, vitamin-rich complexion, vacuous turquoise eyes, and a dark, strong jawline. He'll be good at games, for sure, probably plays golf off eight or nine; bats solidly in the middle order and pounds fast, flat serves at you that kick up off the court. So he's handsome, undoubtedly, a big hit with the ladies, but a drink with the lads will come first. His face, in final analysis, lacks character, is easily forgettable. I would put money on the fact that he attended a minor public school. My guess is that he works in oil, textiles, or finance, reads Grisham on holiday, and is chummy with all the secretaries at work, most of whom harbor secret dreams of marrying him. That's about all there is to go on.

"Good morning," he says, as if we have all been waiting for him and can now get started. He has broad athletic shoulders that manage to make his off-the-peg suit look stylish. "Sam Ogilvy."

And, one by one, he makes his way around the room, shaking hands, moving with the easy confidence of an £80,000 per annum salesman used to getting what he wants—a closed deal, a wage increase, a classy broad.

Ann goes first. She is reserved but warm. It's a certainty that she'll find him attractive. Their handshake is pleasant and formal; it says we can do business together.

The Hobbit is next, standing up from the armchair to his full height, which still leaves him a good five or six inches short. Ogilvy looks to get the measure of him pretty quickly: a bright shining nerd, a number cruncher. The Hobbit looks suitably deferential.

And now it's my turn. Ogilvy's eyes swivel left and scope my face. He knew as soon as he came in that I'd be the one he's up against, the biggest threat to his candidacy. I knew it, too. Ann and Matt won't cut it.

"How do you do? Sam."

He has a strong, captain-of-the-school grip on him.

"Alec."

"Have you been here long?" he asks, touching the tip of his tanned nose.

"About ten minutes," Ann replies behind him.

"Feeling nervous?"

This goes out to anyone who feels like answering. Not me. Matt murmurs "mmmm," which I find oddly touching.

"Yeah, me too," says Sam, just so we know he's like the rest of us, even if he does look like Pierce Brosnan. "You ever done anything like this before?"

"No," says Matt, sitting down with a deep, involuntary sigh. "Just interviews for university."

Matt picks up a Sisby booklet from the table and starts flicking through it like a man shuffling cards. For a moment, Ann is stranded in the middle of the room, as if she was on the point of saying something but decided at the last minute to remain silent on the grounds that it would have been of no consequence. Sam smiles a friendly smile at me. He wants me to like him but to let him lead. I stand up, a sudden attack of nerves.

"Where are you off to?" Ann asks, quick and awkward. "If you're looking for the toilet it's down the hall to the right. Just keep on going and you'll come to it."

She stretches out a pale arm and indicates the direction to me by swatting it from left to right. A ring on her middle finger bounces a spot of reflected sunlight around the common room.

The loo is a clean, white-painted cuboid room with smoked-glass windows, three urinals, a row of push-tap basins, and two cubicles. Half-a-dozen other candidates are crowded inside. I squeeze past them and go into one of the cubicles. It is 8:40 A.M. Outside, one of the candidates says, "Good luck," to which another replies, "Yeah." Then the door leading out into the corridor swishes open and clunks shut. Somebody at the sink nearest my cubicle splashes cold water onto his face and emits a shocked, cleansing gasp.

I remain seated and motionless, feeling only apprehension. I just want to focus, to be alone with my thoughts, and this is the only place in which to do so. The atmosphere in the building is so at odds with the princely splendor of Lucas's and Liddiard's offices as to be almost comic. I put my head between my knees and close my eyes, breathing slowly and deliberately. Just pace yourself. You want this. Go out and get it. I can feel something inside my jacket weighing against the top of my thigh. A banana. I sit up, take it out, peel away the skin, and eat it in five gulped bites. Slow-burn carbohydrates. Then I lean back against the tank and feel the flush handle dig hard into my back.

The water has stopped running out of the taps on the other side of the cubicle door. I check my watch. The time has drifted on to 8:50 A.M. without my keeping track of it. I slam back the lock on the door and bolt out of the cubicle. The room is empty. The corridors, too. Just get there, move it, don't run. My black shoes clap on the linoleum floors, funneling down the corridor back to B3. I reenter, trying to look nonchalant.

"Right, he's here," says a man I haven't seen before who obviously works in the building. He has a strangulated Thames Valley accent. "Everything all right, Mr. Milius?"

"Fine, sorry, yes."

Leaning against the window in the far corner of the common room is the fifth and last candidate, Elaine Hayes. I don't have time to have a proper look at her.

"Good. We can make a start then."

I find a seat between Ogilvy and Matt on one of the sofas, dropping down low into its springless upholstery. One of them is wearing industrial-strength aftershave with a curiously androgynous fragrance. Must be Ogilvy. The man hands me a piece of paper with my timetable on it for the next two days.

"As I was saying, my name is Keith Heywood."

Keith's sparse hair is grease combed and badger gray. He has skin the color of chalk and puffy hairless arms. He looks sixty-five but is probably twenty years younger. Most of his working life has been spent in this building. He wears a light blue short-sleeved shirt and black flannel trousers with meandering creases. His shoes, also black, are at least five years old: no amount of polishing could save them now. He looks, to all intents and purposes, like a janitor.

"I'm your intake manager," he says. "If you have any questions about anything at all over the course of the next two days, you come to me."

Everyone nods.

"I'll also be monitoring the cognitive tests. You won't, of course, be permitted to talk to me during those."

This is obviously Keith's big opening-speech gag. Ogilvy is polite enough to laugh at it. As he smiles and sniggers, he looks across and catches my eye. Rivalry.

"Now," Keith says, clapping his hands. "Do you have any questions about your timetables?"

I look down at the sheet of paper. It is headed AFS NON-QT CANDIDATES, a phrase that I do not understand. I am known only as Candidate 4.

"No. No questions," says Ann, answering for us all.

"Right," says Keith. "Let's get started."

Keith lumbers down the corridor to a small classroom filled with desks in rows and orange plastic chairs. We follow close behind him like children in a museum. Once inside, he stands patiently at one end of the room beside a large wooden examiner's table while each of us chooses a desk.

Ann sits immediately in front of Keith. Matt settles in behind her. He places a red pencil case on the desk in front of him, which he unzips, retrieving a chewed blue Bic and a fresh pencil. Ogilvy heads for the back of the room, separating himself from the rest of us. Elaine, who is older than me, sits underneath a single-pane window overlooking the trees of St. James's Park. She looks bored. I position myself at the desk nearest the door.

"I have in my hand a piece of paper," says Keith, surprisingly. "It's a questionnaire that I am obliged to ask you to complete."

He begins dishing them out. Ann, helpfully, takes two from his pile, swiveling to hand one back to Matt. She moves stiffly, from the waist and hips, as if her neck were clamped in an invisible brace.

"It's just for our own records," says Keith, moving between the desks. "None of your answers will have any bearing on the results of the Selection Board."

The first page of the questionnaire is straightforward: name, address, date of birth. It then becomes more complicated.

1. What do you think are your best qualities?
2. And weaknesses?
3. What recent achievement are you most proud of?

These are big subjects for nine o'clock in the morning. I ponder evasive answers, wild fictions, blatant untruths, struggling to get my brain up to speed.

"Of course," says Keith, as we begin filling out the forms, "you're not obliged to answer all of the questions. You may leave any section blank."

This suits me. I complete the first page and ignore all three questions, sitting quietly until the time elapses. The others, with the exception of Elaine, begin scribbling furiously. Within ten minutes, Ann is on her third page, unraveling herself with a frightening candor. Matt treats the exercise with a similar seriousness, letting it all out, telling them how he really feels. I turn to look at Ogilvy, but he catches my glance and half smiles at me. I turn away. I can't see how much, if anything, he has written. Surely he'd be smart enough not to give anything away unless he had to?

It's over after twenty minutes. Keith collects the questionnaires and returns to his desk. I turn around to see Ogilvy leaning back in his chair, staring at the ceiling like a matinee idol.

Keith coughs.

"In just over ten minutes you'll begin the group exercise," he says, leaning to pick up a small pile of papers from the top right corner of his desk. "This involves a thirty-minute discussion among the five of you on a specific problem described in detail in this document."

He flaps one of the sheets of paper beside his ear and then begins distributing them, one to each of us.

"You have ten minutes to read the document. Try to absorb as much of it as possible. The board will explain how the assessment works once you have gone into the second examination area. Any questions?"

Nobody says a word.

"Right, then. Can I suggest that you begin?"

This is what it says:

A nuclear reprocessing plant on the Normandy coast, built jointly in 1978 by Britain, Holland, and France, is allegedly leaking minute amounts of radiation into a stretch of the English Channel used by both French and British fishermen. American importers of shellfish from the region have run tests revealing the presence of significant levels of radiation in their consignments of oysters, mussels, and prawns. The Americans have therefore announced their intention to stop importing fish and shellfish from all European waters, effective immediately.

The document—which has been written from the British perspective by a fictional civil servant in the Ministry of Agriculture, Fisheries and Food—suggests that the American claims are nebulous. Their own tests, carried out in conjunction with the French authorities, have shown only trace levels of radiation in that section of the English Channel, and nothing in the shellfish from the area that might be construed as dangerous. The civil servant suspects an ulterior motive on the part of the Americans, who have objected in the past to what they perceive as unfair fishing quotas in European waters. They have asked for improved access to European fishing grounds, and for the French plant to be shut down until a full safety check has been carried out.

The document suggests that the British and French ministries should present a united, pan-European resistance to face off the American demands. But there are problems. An American car company is one step away from signing a contract with the German government to build a factory near Berlin that would bring over three thousand jobs to an economically deprived area. The Germans are unlikely to do anything at this stage to upset this agreement. Ditto the Danes, who have an ongoing row with the French over a recent trade agreement. The Spanish, who would suffer more than anyone under any prolonged American export ban, will side firmly with the British and French, though their position is weakened by the fact that the peseta is being propped up by the U.S. dollar.

It's a fanciful scenario, but this is what we are required to talk about.

Keith has given each of us a sheet of blank paper on which to scribble notes, but I write as little as possible. Eye contact will be important in front of the examiners: I must appear confident and sure of my brief. To be constantly buried in pages of notes will look inefficient.

Ten minutes pass quickly. Keith asks us to gather up our things and accompany him to another section of the building. It takes about four minutes to get there.

Two men and an elderly lady are lined up behind a long rectangular desk, like judges in a bad production of *The Crucible*. They have files, notepads, full glasses of water, and a large chrome stopwatch in front of them. The classroom is small and cheaply furnished, with just the one window. Somehow I expected a grander setup: varnished floors, an antique table, old men in suits peering at us over half-moon spectacles. A stranger might walk in here and be offered no hint that the three people inside are part of the most secret government department of them all. And that, of course, is as it should be. The last thing we are supposed to do is draw attention to ourselves.

"Good morning," says the older of the two men. "If you'd all like to take a seat, we'll make a start."

From his accent, he is unmistakably English, yet his suntan is so pronounced that he might almost be Indian. He looks well into his fifties.

There is a table with five chairs positioned around it no more than two feet away from the examiners. We move toward it and are suddenly very polite to one another. *Shall I go here? Is that all right? After you.* Ann, I think, overdoes it, actually holding Elaine's chair for her. I find myself in the seat farthest from the door, flushed with shirt sweat, trying to remember everything I have read while at the same time appearing relaxed and self-assured. An age passes until we are all comfortably seated. Then the man speaks again.

"First off, allow us to introduce ourselves. My name is Gerald Pyman. I am a recently retired SIS officer. I'll be chairing the Selection Board for the next two days."

Pyman's eyes are like black holes, as if they have seen so much that is abject and contemptible in human nature that they have simply withdrawn into their sockets. He wears a tie, a smart one, but no jacket in the heat.

"To my left is Dr. Hilary Stevenson."

"Good morning," she says, taking up his cue. "I'm the appointed psychologist to the board. I'm here to evaluate your contributions to the group exercises and—as you will all have seen from your timetables—I will also be conducting an interview with each of you over the course of the next two days."

She has a kind, refined way of speaking, the trusting softness of a grandmother. The room is absolutely still as she speaks. Each of us has adopted a relaxed but businesslike body language: arms on laps or resting on the table in front of us. Ogilvy is the exception. His arms are folded tight against his chest. He seems to realize this and lets them drop to his sides. It is the turn of the man on Pyman's right to speak. He is a generation younger, overweight by about forty pounds, with a pale, rotund face that is tired and paunchy.

"And I'm Martin Rouse, a serving SIS officer working out of our embassy in Washington."

Washington? Why do we need intelligence operations in Washington?

"Can I just emphasize that you are not in competition. There's nothing at all to be gained from scoring points off one another."

Rouse has a faint Manchester accent, diluted by a life lived overseas.

"Now," he says, "we'll just go around the table and allow you to introduce yourselves to us and to each other. Beginning with Mr. Milius."

I experience the sensation of breathing in both directions at once, inhalation and exhalation canceling each other out. Every face in the room shifts minutely and settles on mine.

I look up and for some reason fix Elaine in the eye as I say, "My name is Alec Milius. I am a marketing consultant."

Then I slide my gaze away to the right, taking in Stevenson, Rouse, and Pyman, a sentence for each of them.

"I work in London for the Central European Business Development Organization. I'm a graduate of the London School of Economics. I'm twenty-four."

"Thank you," says Rouse. "Miss Butler."

Ann dives right in, no trace of nerves, and introduces herself, quickly followed by the Hobbit. Then it's Ogilvy's turn. He visibly shifts himself up a gear and, in a clear, steady voice, announces himself as the sure-fire candidate.

"Good morning."

Eye contact to us, not to the examiners. Nice touch. He stares me right down without a flinch and then turns to face Elaine. She remains unmoved.

"I'm Sam Ogilvy. I work for Rothmans Tobacco in Saudi Arabia."

This information knocks me sideways. Ogilvy can't be much older than I am, yet he's already working for a major multinational corporation in the Middle East. He must be earning thirty or forty grand a year with a full expense account and company car. I'm on less than fifteen thousand and live in Shepherd's Bush.

"I graduated from Cambridge in 1992 with a first in economics and history."

Bastard.

"Thank you, Mr. Ogilvy," says Rouse, planting a full stop on his pad as he looks up at Elaine and smiles for the first time. He doesn't need to say anything to her. He merely nods, and she begins.

"Good morning. I'm Elaine Hayes. I'm already employed by the Foreign Office, working out of London. I'm thirty-two, and I can't remember when I graduated from university it was such a long time ago."

Both Pyman and Rouse laugh at this and we follow their cue, mustering strained chuckles. The room briefly sounds like a theater in which only half the audience has properly understood a joke. It intrigues me that Elaine is already employed by the Foreign Office. If she was looking to join SIS, surely they would promote her internally without the bother of going through Sisby?

"We'd like to proceed now with the group exercise," Pyman says, interrupting this thought. "The discussion is unchaired, that is to say you are free to make a contribution whenever you choose to do so. It is scheduled to conclude after thirty minutes, at which time you must all have agreed upon a course of action. If you find yourselves in agreement before the thirty minutes are up, we shall call a stop then. I must emphasize the importance of making your views known. There is no point in holding back. We cannot assess your minds if you will not show them to us. So do participate. There's a stopwatch here. Miss Hayes, if you'd like to start it up and set it on the desk where everyone can see it."

Elaine is closest to Rouse, who takes the stopwatch from Pyman and hands it to her with his right arm outstretched. She takes it from him and sets it down on the table, positioning the face in such a way that we can all see it. Then, with her thumb, she pushes the bulbous steel knob at the top of the stopwatch, starting us off.

It has a tick like chattering teeth.

"Can I just say to begin with that I think it's very important that we maintain a tight alliance with the French, though the problem is of their making. Initially, at least."

Ann, God bless her, has had the balls to kick things off, although her opening statement has a forced self-confidence about it that betrays an underlying insecurity. Like a pacesetter in a middle-distance track event, she'll lead for a while but soon tire and fall away.

"Do you agree?" she says, to no one in particular, and her question has a terrible artificiality about it. Ann's words hang there unanswered for a short time, until the Hobbit chips in with a remark that is entirely unrelated to what she has said.

"We have to consider how economically important fish exports are to the Americans," he says, touching his right cheekbone with a chubby index finger. "Do they amount to much?"

"I agree."

I say that, and immediately regret it, because everyone turns in my direction and expects some sort of follow-up. And yet it doesn't come. What happens now, for a period of perhaps five or six seconds, is appalling. I become incapable of functioning within the group, of thinking clearly in this unfamiliar room with its strange, artificial rules. This happened with Lucas and it is happening again. My mind is just terrible blank white noise. I see only faces, looking at me. Ogilvy, Elaine, Ann, Matt. Enjoying, I suspect, the spectacle of my silence. Think. Think. What did he say? I agree with what? What did he say?

"I happen to know that annual exports of fish and shellfish to the United States amount to little more than twenty or thirty million pounds."

The Hobbit, tired of waiting, has kept on going, has dug me out of a hole. Immediately attention shifts back to him, allowing me the chance to blank out what has just happened. I have to think positively. I may not have betrayed my anxiety to the others, or to Pyman, Rouse, or Stevenson. It may, after all, have been just a momentary gap in real time, no more than a couple of beats. It just felt like a crisis; it didn't look like one.

Stay with them. Listen. Concentrate.

I look over at Elaine, who has taken a sip from a glass of water in front of her. She appears to be on the point of saying something in response to the Hobbit. She has a perplexed look on her face. You *happen* to know that, Hobbit? How can someone *happen* to know something like that?

Ann speaks.

"We can't just abandon exports of fish and shellfish to America on the grounds that they only bring in a small amount of revenue. That's still twenty million pounds' worth of business to the fishing community."

This is the humanitarian angle, the socialist's view, and I wonder if it will impress Rouse and Pyman, or convince them that Ann is intellectually unevolved. I suspect the latter. Elaine shapes as if to put her straight, moving forward in her chair, elbows propped on the table. A woman in her twenties who is not a socialist has no heart; a woman in her thirties who is still a socialist has no brain. Instead, she ignores what Ann has said and takes the conversation off on a different tack. We are all of us rushing around this, just trying to be heard. Everything is moving too fast.

"Can I suggest trying to persuade the Americans to accept imports of fish from European waters that are not affected by the alleged nuclear spillage? We can accept a temporary export ban on shellfish, but to put a stop to all fish exports to the U.S. seems a bit draconian."

Elaine has a lovely, husky voice, a been-there, done-that, low-bullshit drawl with a grin behind it. All the time the examiners are busy scribbling. I have to operate at a level of acute self-consciousness: every mannerism, every gesture, every smile is being minutely examined. The effort is all-consuming.

A pause opens up in the discussion. My brain fog has cleared completely, and a sequence of ideas has formed in my mind. I must say something to erase the memory of my first interruption, to make it look as though I can bounce back from a bad situation. Now is my chance.

"On the other—"

Ogilvy, fuck him, started speaking at the same time as me.

"Sorry, Alec," he says. "Go ahead."

"Thank you, Sam. I was just going to say that I think it's going to be difficult to make a distinction between fish and shellfish in this instance. Nuclear contamination is nuclear contamination. The Americans have a very parochial view of Europe. They see us as a small country. Our waters, whether they be the English Channel or the Mediterranean, are connected geographically in the minds of the Americans. If one is polluted, particularly by nuclear waste, then they all are."

"I think that's quite a patronizing view of America."

This comes from Elaine. I had made the mistake of perceiving her as an ally. In my peripheral vision I see Rouse and Pyman duck into their pads.

"Okay, perhaps it is, but consider this."

This had better be good or I'm finished.

"Any lasting export ban of radioactive shellfish to America will quickly become an international ban. No one wants to eat contaminated food. If we don't put a stop to it soon, other countries, even in Europe, will refuse to buy shellfish and fish from British and French waters. It's a domino effect."

This goes down well. Both Ann and the Hobbit nod respectfully. But Ogilvy has decided he has been silent too long. He leans forward, like a chess grand master on the point of making a telling move in the endgame. He's going to make me look ineffectual.

"The question is an interesting one," he says, drawing us into his web of good-naturedness. A bird sounds territorially outside. "Is this a direct face-off between the United States of America and a United States of Europe? Do we as British citizens want to see ourselves that way, as part of a federal Europe? Or do we value our sovereignty too much, our prerogative to dictate terms to other European states and to the world at large?"

This is inch-perfect, not a fluffed line. He goes on.

"I suggest that we see this problem in those terms. There are too many conflicting European interests to mount an effective British campaign. We must do it with the assistance of our European partners and present a united front to the Americans. We hold many of the cards. Our major problem is Germany, and that is what we have to address. Once they're on board, the rest will follow."

This is the smart move. He has set the foundations for the conversation, given it a clear starting point from which it can develop and assume some shape. Ogilvy has essentially proposed to chair the discussion, and this aptitude for leadership will not go unnoticed.

Ann takes up the argument.

"I don't see why we have to present pan-European resistance to America as the civil servant in this document suggests."

As she says this, she taps the printed sheet quite vigorously with the point of her middle finger. She is not as good at this as Ogilvy is, and she knows it. Every contour of her body language betrays this to the rest of us, but some dark stubbornness in her, some Ulster obstinacy, will not allow her to back down. So she will wade in, deeper and deeper, pretending to know about things she barely understands, feigning a self-confidence she does not possess.

"To put it bluntly, this is France's problem," she says, and her voice is now overexcited. "It's a French nuclear reprocessing"—her tongue trips on this last word several times—"plant that is leaking. I suggest that, perhaps with EU funding, you know, we conduct some definitive checks on the plant with American observers on site. On the site. If it proves to be clean, then there's no reason why the Americans shouldn't begin rebuying European fish. If it's leaking, we demand that the French get it fixed. We then try to persuade the Americans to buy fish and shellfish from non-French, uncontaminated waters."

"So you're suggesting we just abandon the French?" I ask, just so that my voice is heard, just to make it look like I'm still taking part.

"Yes," she says impatiently, hardly taking the time to look at me.

"There's a problem with that solution."

Ogilvy says this with the calm bedside manner of a family GP.

"What?" says Ann, visibly unsettled.

"The plant was built in 1978 with joint British, French, and Dutch cooperation."

This trips everyone up. Nobody had recalled it from the printed sheet except Ogilvy, who is happy to let this fact make its way across the room to the impressed examiners.

"Yes, I'd forgotten that," Ann admits, to her credit, but she must know that her chance has passed.

"I still think Ann has a point," says a gallant Hobbit. He is surely too kind to be caught up in this. "The French facility needs to have a thorough checkup with American observers. If it's leaking, we all have to put it right collectively and be completely open about that. But I suspect it's fine, and that these American claims are disingenuous."

In the tight lightless classroom, this last word sounds labored and pretentious. Ann's face has flushed red and the hand in which she is holding her pen is shaking. Ogilvy inches forward.

"Let's look at it this way," he says. "We don't know all the facts. What we do know is that the Americans are playing games. And in my view, the best way to deal with a bully is to bully them back."

"What are you suggesting?"

"I'm suggesting, Alec, that if the Americans are proposing to squeeze us, then we in turn should squeeze them."

They'll like this. We're supposed to play hardball. We're supposed to be capable of a trick or two. Ogilvy glances across at Rouse, then back at the Hobbit.

"Matthew, you seem to know about the levels of import and export of fish and shellfish going to and fro between Britain and America."

The Hobbit, flattered, says, "Yes."

"Well, I suspect that the Americans export significantly higher numbers of fish and shellfish to Europe than we export to them. Is that right?"

"Off the top of my head, yes, as much as three times the amount," says the Hobbit.

It's just between the two of them for now, and it's an impressive thing to watch. Ogilvy is giving us all a lesson in man management, in how to make the little guy feel good about himself. A trace of sweat has formed above the Hobbit's upper lip, a little vapor of nerves, but he is otherwise entirely without self-consciousness. Just getting the words out, happy to talk in facts. Maybe even enjoying himself. Ogilvy has rested his elbows on the table, fingers interlocked and raised to his dark face.

"So a ban on American fish and shellfish imports would hit them even harder?"

"In theory," says Elaine, a dismissiveness in her voice.

"Of course," says Ogilvy, cutting her off before she has a chance to tell him how unworkable a trade embargo with the United States would be, "I actually don't think that we'll have to go as far as reciprocating their ban with one of our own."

He wants to show Rouse and Pyman that he's seen all the angles.

"The key to this, as I've said, is the Germans. If we can get them on our side, and as long as any problem with the reprocessing plant can be addressed, I can't foresee the Americans continuing with their demands. It's important that we be seen to stand up to them."

It's time to steal some ideas from Ogilvy, before he runs away with it.

"The sticking point is the automobile manufacturer. We have to make sure that that contract is secured and goes ahead. At the same time, we might offer the Germans a sweetener."

"What kind of a sweetener?" Elaine asks. She lingers on *sweetener* as if it is the most absurd word she has ever heard.

"Sell them something. At a bargain price. Or we could buy more of their exports."

This sounds meek and ill-informed. It is clear that I have not thought it through. But Ogilvy bails me out, saying yes with a degree of enthusiasm that I had not anticipated. Ironically, this leads to a bad mistake. He says, "We could offer to buy up deutsch marks, to push up their value briefly against the pound."

This is ludicrous, and Elaine tells him so.

"You try it. You'd have to be owed some pretty big favors at the Exchequer to get something like that done."

She delivers this in a tone of weary experience and for a moment Ogilvy is stumped. His square jaw tremors with humiliation, and it gives me a small buzz of pleasure to watch him ride it out. It's important that I don't let this opportunity slip. Shut him down.

"I have to agree with Elaine, Sam. We mustn't pass the buck to another department. It's difficult, without knowing more about our other negotiations with the Germans, to determine how exactly we might go about persuading them to side with us. It may not even be necessary, for two reasons. The first has already been made clear. The French plant may in fact be safe and the Americans may be acting illegally. If that's the case, we're in the clear. But if it does prove necessary to get the Germans onside, we could try another tactic."

"Yes, I—" Ann tries to grab the floor, but I'm not about to be interrupted.

"If I could just finish. Thank you. If we succeed in convincing a majority of other European states to form a united front against the Americans, the Germans will not relish being isolated. While they may not want to be seen to be taking issue with the United States, at the same time they won't want to be seen by their European partners to be forming an unholy alliance with America. We can, in effect, shut them up."

"We shouldn't underestimate the Germans or their influence," the Hobbit mumbles. "Nobody here wants to acknowledge the truth of this situation, which is that the Germans are the dominant economic force in European politics. They are, in effect, our masters."

This annoys me.

"Well, if that's what they're teaching you on your European affairs course at Warwick, I'm not signing up."

Elaine, Pyman, and Rouse emit snorty laughs. I'm winning this, I'm coming through. The Hobbit's cheeks rouge nicely. He can't think of a comeback, so I carry on.

"This notion of the Germans as the European master race is contrived. Their economy will slow in the next few years, unemployment is chronic since unification, and Kohl's days are numbered."

I read this in *The Economist*.

"Let's not get off the point." Ogilvy wants back in. "Let's talk about how to get the Spaniards and the Danes onboard."

Suddenly Ann sneezes, a great lashing *a-choo* that she only half covers with her hand. In stereo, Ogilvy and I say, "Bless you," to which he adds, "Are you okay?" Ann, not one to be patronized, lets her guard drop and says, "Yeah," with sullen indifference. Her voice, with its sour accent, sounds impatient and spoiled. In this brief moment, we can all see her for what she really is: a tough nut of steely ambition, looking for a one-way ticket to London and a better life. In the wake of it, Ogilvy glides away, talking with great efficiency about how to get the Spaniards and Danes "on board." As time ticks away, the stopwatch edging toward our thirty-minute limit, he is left more or less on his own, with occasional interjections from the Hobbit, whose knowledge of European Union bylaws is as extensive as it is tedious. He must be the star pupil at Warwick. Ann, for the most part, turns in on herself and merely disagrees for the sake of disagreeing. Elaine barely speaks. From my point of view, I feel that I have done enough to please the examiners, both by what I have said and by my personal conduct, which has been forthright but respectful of the other candidates. I also feel that Ogilvy and the Hobbit are flogging a dead horse. Most of the points that were there to be made have been made saliently some time ago. Nevertheless, it will look good if I try to wrap things up.

"If I could just interrupt you there, Sam, because we're running out of time, and I think we should try to reach some sort of conclusion."

"Absolutely."

He gives me the floor. Don't fuck it up.

"I think we've covered most of the angles on this problem. Judging from the last ten minutes or so, we're mostly agreed on a course of action."

"Which is?" says Ann, coldly.

"That we need to—as you pointed out right at the start—present a united front to the Americans. We must conduct conclusive tests on the French plant. If needs be, we should bargain with the Germans to get them on our side."

"We never said how we were going to do that." The manner in which Elaine says this, with just under a minute to go, implies that this is largely my responsibility.

"No, we didn't. But that's not something that should worry us. I think the Germans would be unlikely to do anything that would undermine the EU."

"And what do we do about the American export ban?" the Hobbit asks, looking in my direction as he tips forward on his chair. It was a mistake to take this on.

"Well, there's very little we can do. . . ."

"I don't agree," says Ann, cutting me off short so that my incomplete sentence sounds weak and defeatist.

"Me too," says Ogilvy, but he too is interrupted.

"I'm afraid that your thirty minutes is up."

Rouse has tapped his pen twice—*tap tap*—on the hard surface of the examiners' table. We all turn to face him.

"Thank you all very much. If you'd like to gather up your things and make your way back to the common room, where Mr. Heywood is waiting for you."

I think we all share a sense of disappointment at not managing to conclude the discussion within the allocated time. It will reflect badly on the five of us, although I may score points for trying to tidy things up toward the end. Ogilvy is first up and out of the room, followed by the rest of us in a tight group, waddling out like tired ducks. Elaine is the last to leave, closing the door behind her. She does this with too much force, and it slams shut with a loud clap.

Keith is waiting for us in the common room, idling near the coffee machine. As soon as we are all inside, he instructs us to follow him back down the corridor to begin the first of the written examinations. There is no time to relax, no time to ruminate or grab a drink. They won't let the pressure off until five o'clock this evening, and then it starts all over again tomorrow.

On the way to the classroom, Elaine and Ann peel away from the group to go to the loo. This flusters Keith. While Ogilvy, the Hobbit, and I are taking our seats in the classroom, he lurks nervously in the corridor, waiting for their return.

The Hobbit, who has taken a seat by the window, grabs this opportunity to tuck into yet another cereal bar. Ogilvy returns to his previous spot at the back of the room. To annoy him I move to the desk nearest his, close in and to the left. For a moment it looks as though he may move, but politeness checks him. He looks across at me and smiles very slowly.

With no sign of Elaine and Ann, Keith trundles back in, head bowed, and starts handing out thick pink booklets, which he leaves facedown on every candidate's desk. The Hobbit thanks him through the crumbly munch of his midmorning snack, and Ogilvy begins twirling a pencil in his right hand, rotating it quickly through his fingers like a helicopter blade. It's a poser's party trick and it doesn't come off: the pencil spins out of his hand and clatters onto the lino between our two desks. I make no attempt to retrieve it, so Ogilvy has to bend down uncomfortably to pick it up. As he is doing so, Elaine and Ann bustle in, sharing the cozy mutual smiles and solidarity of women returning from a shared trip to the loo.

"This section of the Sisby program is known as the Policy Exercise," Keith says, beginning his introductory talk before they have had a chance to sit down. He's on a strict timetable, and he's sticking to it. "It is a two-hour written paper in which you will be asked to analyze a large quantity of complex written material, to identify the main points and issues, and to write a thorough and cogently argued case for one of three possible options."

I stare at the pink booklet and pray for something other than shellfish.

"You may start when you are ready. I will let you know when one hour of the examination has passed, and again when there are ten minutes of the exercise remaining."

A crackle of paper, an intake of breath, the incidental noises of beginning.

Here we go again.

6

DAY ONE/AFTERNOON

After lunch—a ham and cheese sandwich at the National Gallery—we sit in the stifling classroom faced by a phalanx of numerical facility tests divided into three separate sections: Relevant Information, Quantitative Relations, and Numerical Inferences. Each batch of twenty questions lasts exactly twenty-two minutes, after which Keith allows a brief interlude before starting us on the next paper. Each problem, whether number- or word-based, must be solved in a matter of seconds, with no time available for checking the accuracy of the answer. Calculators are forbidden. It is by far the most testing part of Sisby so far, and the mind-thud of intellectual fatigue is overwhelming. I crave water.

We are all of us squeezed by time, clustered in the classroom like caged hens as the heat intensifies. Everything—even the most testing arithmetic calculation—has to be answered more or less on instinct. At one point I have to estimate 43 percent of 2,345 in under seven seconds. Often my brain will work ahead of itself or lag behind, concentrating on anything but the problem at hand. The tests blur into a soup of numbers, traps of contradictory data, false assumptions, and trick questions. Any apparent simplicity is quickly revealed as an illusion: every word must be examined for what it conceals, every number treated as an elaborate code. My ability to process information gradually wanes. I don't complete any of the three batches of tests to my satisfaction.

Shortly before four o'clock, Keith asks us with nasal exactitude to stop writing. Ogilvy immediately glances across to gauge how things have gone. He tilts his head to one side, creases his brow, and puffs out his cheeks at me, as if to say, *I fucked that up, and I hope you did, too.* For a moment I am tempted into intimacy, a powerful urge to reveal to him the extent of my exhaustion, but I cannot allow any display of weakness. Instead, I respond with a self-possessed, almost complacent shrug to suggest that things have gone particularly well. This makes him look away.

A few minutes later, we emerge narrow-eyed into the bright white light of the corridor. Better air out here, cool and clean. The Hobbit and Ann immediately walk away in the direction of the toilets, but Ogilvy lingers outside, looking bloodshot and leathery.

"Christ," he says, pulling on his jacket with an exaggerated swagger. "That was tough."

"You found it difficult?" Elaine asks. My impression has been that she does not like him.

"God, yeah. I couldn't seem to concentrate. I kept looking at you guys scribbling away. How did it go for you, Alec?"

He smiles at me, like we're long-term buddies.

"I don't go in for postmortems much." To Elaine: "You got a cigarette?"

She takes out a pack of high-tar Camels.

"I only have one left. We can share."

She lights up, crushing the empty pack in her hand. Ogilvy mutters something about giving up smoking, but looks excluded and weary.

"I need to get some fresh air," he says, moving away from us down the hall. "I'll see you later on."

Elaine exhales through her nostrils, two steady streams of smoke, watching him leave with a critical stare.

"Have you got anything else today?" she asks me. "An interview or anything?"

I don't feel like talking. My mind is looped around the penultimate question in the last batch of tests. The answer was closer to 54 than 62, and I circled the wrong box. Damn.

"I have to meet Rouse. The SIS officer."

She glances quickly left and right.

"Careless talk costs lives, Alec," she whispers, half smiling. "Be careful what you say. The five of us are the only SIS people here today."

"How do you know?"

"It's obvious," she says, offering the cigarette to me. The tip of the filter is damp with her saliva and I worry that when I hand it back she will think the wetness is mine. "They only process five candidates a month."

"According to who?"

She hesitates.

"It's well known. A lot more reach the initial interview stage, but only five get through to Sisby. We're the lucky ones."

"So you work in the Foreign Office already. That's how you know?"

She nods, glancing again down the corridor. My head has started to throb.

"Pen pushing," she says. "I want to step up. Now, no more shoptalk. What time are you scheduled to finish?"

"Around five."

Her hair needs washing and she has a tiny spot forming on the right side of her forehead.

"That's late," she says, sympathetically. "I'm done for the day. Back tomorrow at half past eight."

The cigarette is nearly finished. I had been worried that it would set off a fire alarm.

"I guess I'll see you then."

"Guess so."

She is turning to leave when I say, "You don't have anything for a headache, do you? Dehydration."

"Sure. Just a moment."

She reaches into the pocket of her jacket, rustles around for something, and then uncurls her right hand in front of me. There in the palm of her hand is a short strip of plastic containing four aspirin.

"That's really kind of you. Thanks."

She answers with a wide, conspiratorial smile, dwelling on the single word, "Pleasure."

In the bathroom, I turn on the cold tap and allow it to run out for a while. Flattery is implicit in Elaine's flirtations. She has ignored the others—particularly Ogilvy—but made a conscious effort to befriend me. I puncture the foil on the plastic strip of pills and extract two aspirin, feeling them dry and hard in my fingertips. Drinking water from a cupped hand, I tip back my head and let the pills bump down my throat. My reflection in the mirror is dazed and washed out. Have to get myself together for Rouse.

Behind me, the door on one of the cubicles unbolts. I hadn't realized there was someone else in the room. I watch in the mirror as Pyman comes out of the cubicle nearest the wall. He looks up and catches my eye, then glances down, registering the strip of pills lying used on the counter. What looks like mild shock passes quickly over his face. I say hello in the calmest, it's-only-aspirin voice I can muster, but my larynx cracks and the words come out subfalsetto. He says nothing, walking out without a word.

I spit a hoarse "fuck" into the room, yet something body-tired and denying immediately erases what has just occurred. Pyman has seen nothing untoward, nothing that might adversely affect my candidacy. He was simply surprised to see me in here, and in no mood to strike up a conversation. I cannot be the first person at Sisby to get a headache late in the afternoon on the first day. He will have forgotten all about it by the time he goes home.

This conclusion allows me to concentrate on the imminent interview with Rouse, whose office—B14—I begin searching for along the corridors of the third floor. The room is situated in the northwestern corner of the building, with a makeshift nameplate taped crudely to the door: MARTIN ROUSE: AFS NON-QT/CSSB SPECIAL.

I knock confidently. There is a loud, "Come in."

His office smells of bad breath. Rouse is pacing by the window like a troubled general, the tail of a crumpled white shirt creeping out the back of his trousers.

"Sit down, Mr. Milius," he says. There is no shaking of hands.

I settle into a hard-backed chair opposite his desk, which has just a few files and a lamp on it, nothing more. A temporary home. The window looks out over St. James's Park.

"Everything going okay so far?"

"Fine, thank you. Yes."

He has yet to sit down, yet to look at me, still gazing out the window.

"Candidates always complain about the Numerical Facility tests. You find those difficult?"

It isn't clear from his tone whether he is being playful or serious.

"It's been a long time since I had to do maths without a calculator. Good exercise for the brain."

"Yes," he says, murmuring.

It is as if his thoughts are elsewhere. It was not possible during the group exercise to get a look at the shape of the man, the actual physical presence, but I can now do so. His chalky face is entirely without distinguishing characteristics, neither handsome nor ugly, though the cheekbones are swollen with fat. He has the build of a rugby player, but any muscle on his broad shoulders has turned fleshy, pushing out his shirt in unsightly lumps. Why do we persist with the notion of the glamorous spy? Rouse would not look out of place behind the counter of a butcher's shop. He sits down.

"I imagine you've come well prepared."

"In what sense?"

"You were asked to revise some specialist subjects."

"Yes."

His manner is almost dismissive. He is fiddling with a fountain pen on his desk. Too many thoughts in his head at any one time.

"And what have you read up on?"

I am starting to feel awkward.

"The Irish peace process . . ."

He interrupts before I have a chance to finish.

"Ah! And what were your conclusions?"

"About what?"

"About the Irish peace process," he says impatiently. The speed of his voice has quickened considerably.

"Which aspect of it?"

He plucks a word out of the air.

"Unionism."

"I think there's a danger that John Major's government will jeopardize the situation in Ulster by pandering to the Unionist vote in the House of Commons."

"You do?"

"Yes."

"And what would you do instead? I don't see that the prime minister has any alternative. He requires legislation to be passed, motions of no confidence to be quashed. What would you do in his place?"

This quick, abrasive style is what I had expected from Lucas and Liddiard. More of a contest, an absence of civility.

"It's a question of priorities."

"What do you mean?"

He is coming at me quickly, rapid jabs under pressure, allowing me no time to design my answers.

"I mean does he value the lives of innocent civilians more than he values the safety of his own job?"

"That's a very cynical way of looking at a very complex situation. The prime minister has a responsibility to his party, to his MPs. Why should he allow terrorists to dictate how he does his job?"

"I don't accept the premise behind your question. He's not allowing terrorists to do that. Sinn Fein/IRA have made it clear that they are prepared to come to the negotiating table and yet Major is going to make decommissioning an explicit requirement of that, something he knows will never happen. He's not interested in peace. He's simply out to save his own skin."

"You don't think the IRA should hand over its weapons?"

"Of course I do. In an ideal world. But they never will."

"So you would just give in to that? You would be prepared to negotiate with armed terrorist organizations?"

"If there was a guarantee that those arms would not be used during that negotiating process, yes."

"And if they were?"

"At least then the fault would lie with Sinn Fein. At least then the peace process would have been given a chance."

Rouse leans back. The skin of his stomach is visible as pink through the thin cotton of his shirt. Here sits a man whose job it is to persuade Americans to betray their country.

"I take your point."

This is something of a breakthrough. There is a first smile.

"What else, then?"

"I'm sorry, I don't understand."

"What else have you prepared?"

"Oh." I had not known what he meant. "I've done some research on the Brent Spar oil platform and some work on the Middle East."

Rouse's face remains expressionless. I feel a droplet of sweat fall inside my shirt, tracing its way down to my waist. It appears that neither of these subjects interests him. He picks up a clipboard from the desk, turning over three pages until his eyes settle on what he is looking for. All these guys have clipboards.

"Do you believe what you said about America?"

"When?"

He looks at his notes, reading off the shorthand, quoting me, " 'The Americans have a very parochial view of Europe. They see us as a small country.' "

He looks up, eyebrows raised. Again it is not clear whether this is something Rouse agrees with, or whether his experience in Washington has proved otherwise. Almost certainly, he will listen to what I have to say and then take up a deliberately contrary position.

"I believe that there is an insularity to the American mind. They are an inward-looking people."

"Based on what evidence?"

His manner has already become more curt.

"Based on the fact that when you go there, they think that Margaret Thatcher is the queen, that Scotland is just this county in a bigger place called England. That kind of ignorance is unsettling when you consider that American capitalism is currently the dominant global culture. To anyone living in Texas, global news is what happens in Alabama. The average American couldn't care less about the European Union."

"Surely you can appreciate that in our line of work we don't deal with 'the average American'?"

I feel pinned by this.

"I can see that. Yes."

Rouse looks dissatisfied that I have capitulated so early. I press on.

"But my point is still valid. Now that America is the sole super-power, there's a kind of arrogance, a tunnel vision, creeping into their foreign policy. They don't make allowances for the character and outlook of individual states. Unless countries fall into line with the American way of thinking, they risk making an enemy of the most economically pow-erful nation on earth. This is the position that Britain finds itself in all the time."

"In what respect?"

"In order to keep the special relationship alive, successive governments have had to ignore their better judgment and do some pretty unsavory things when called upon to do so by the United States. They would defend that by saying it's in the nature of politics."

"You don't think the special relationship is worth preserving?"

"I didn't say that. I think it's worth preserving at any cost. Maintaining close ties with America will make the UK a pivotal force within the European Union."

Rouse nods. He knows this is true.

"But you remain cynical about the government in Washington?"

Now I take a risk.

"Well, with respect, so do you."

That may have been a mistake. Rouse appears to withdraw slightly from the improving familiarity of our conversation, stopping to write something in longhand on the clipboard.

"I'm not sure I follow you," he says, bringing the pen to his mouth.

"You're a serving SIS officer in Washington. It's your job to be cynical."

He goes cold on me.

"I'm afraid I can't discuss that."

"Of course. I'm sorry I brought it up."

I have gone too far.

"Not a problem," he says, as suddenly relaxed as he was distant just seconds before. I am relieved by this, yet the swing in his mood was eerie. He can be all things to all people. "At Sisby we are perfectly free to discuss the work of an SIS officer in general terms. That, after all, is one of the reasons why you are here."

"Yes."

"So is there anything in particular you would like to ask?"

That he is permitting me to question him on matters of national secrecy is in itself astonishing, yet the blank slate provided somehow makes the process of thinking up a question more difficult. Rouse glances coolly at his watch. I have to say something.

"It would interest me to know what sort of work SIS is involved in now that the Cold War is over. Is industrial espionage the main focus?"

Rouse knits his fingers.

"For obvious reasons, I can't talk about the specifics of my own operation. But, yes, industrial espionage, competitive intelligence—whatever you want to call it—poses a very grave threat to British interests. Purely in economic terms, allowing British secrets to pass into the hands of rival organizations and companies is catastrophic. There is an argument, in fact, that industrial spies are more damaging to British interests in the long term even than Cold War traitors. That's not to say that we aren't still concerned with traditional counterespionage measures."

"What about organized crime?"

Rouse stalls. I may have hit upon his area of expertise.

"You're talking about Russia, I assume?"

"Yes."

"A local problem, though one that will spread to the West if allowed to go unchecked. Likewise, the danger posed by religious fundamentalism. These are the kinds of issues we also take an interest in."

Rouse has folded his arms across his belly, where they rest defensively. He will say no more on this subject.

"Can I ask a more specific question about your lifestyle?"

"Of course," he says, apparently surprised by the frankness of my request. He moves forward in his chair, all of that weight now bulked on the desk in front of him.

"Have you lost contact with the friends you had before you joined the intelligence service?"

Rouse runs a finger down the left side of his cheek.

"Have I lost contact with my friends?" A wistful silence lingers. "You're perhaps talking to the wrong man. I've never been one for cultivating friendships." A grin appears at the side of his mouth, a little memory tickling him. "In fact, when I was applying for the job, I was asked for a number of written references and had trouble finding enough people who knew me well enough to give an account of my character."

I smile. It seems the right thing to do. Rouse sees this.

"Is that something that has been worrying you? Losing touch with your friends?"

I reply quickly, "Not at all. No."

"Good. It shouldn't necessarily. During my initial two-year training period in London, I worked alongside an officer who had a very busy social life. Seemed to enjoy himself a great deal. There's no absolute standard."

"But you have friends in Washington? Professional associates? People that you are able to see on a private basis away from work?"

Rouse emits a stout snort. And what he says now crystallizes everything.

"Let me tell you this," he says, his eyes fixed on mine. "An SIS officer is asked to blend his private and professional selves into a seamless whole. We make no distinction between the two. An officer has, in a sense, no private life, because it is through his private life that much of his professional work is done. He uses his friendships, brokers trusts outside of the professional world, in order to gather information. That is how the system operates."

"I see."

He glances at his watch, a digital.

"It appears that our time is up." It isn't, but he knows where this conversation is going. They cannot risk telling me too much. "Why don't I leave you with that thought?"

He stands up out of his chair, the white shirt more disheveled now. A man with no friends.

"Thank you for coming in," he says, as if it had been a matter of choice.

"It's been interesting talking to you."

I start backing away toward the door.

"I'm glad I could be of some assistance," he says. "We will see you in the morning, I trust."

"Yes."

And with that I close the door. No handshake, no contact. I walk briskly in the direction of the common room with a light, flushed sense of success. The building is strangely quiet. The doors to the various classrooms and offices leading off the corridor have been closed. In the distance I hear a Hoover being dragged up and down on a worn floor.

The common room, too, is empty. Everyone has gone home. There are plastic cups strewn across the low table in the center of the room, one of which has tipped over and soaked a portion of the pink business insert of the *Evening Standard*. Chewed broadsheet pages lie stiffly against the back of the sofa, fanned out like a tramp's bed. I just look in and turn away.

Elaine is in the downstairs foyer, slouched against the wall. She is inspecting her nails. They are clear-varnished, neatly manicured.

"Fancy a postmortem drink?" she asks.

"Oh, no. No, thanks. I'm just going to go home. Watch some TV."

"Just like the others."

"Just like the others. They've all gone home, have they?"

"Mmmm."

"How come you're still here?" I ask. "I thought you finished an hour ago."

"Met an old friend. Went for a coffee and forgot my bag."

A lie.

"Tomorrow, then," I tell her unconvincingly. "Tomorrow we'll all go out."

"Yeah," she says. "Tomorrow."

7

DAY TWO

The morning of the second day is taken up with more written papers, beginning at nine o'clock.

The In-Tray Exercise is a short, sharp, sixty-minute test of nerve, a lengthy document assessing both the candidate's ability to identify practical problems arising within the Civil Service and his capacity for taking rapid and decisive action to resolve them. The focus is on leadership, management skills, and the means to devolve responsibility and "prioritize" decisions. SIS is big on teamwork.

Most of us seem to cope okay: Ogilvy, Elaine, and Ann finish the test within the allocated time. But the Hobbit looks to have messed up. At his desk, his shoulders heave and slump with sighing frustration, and he writes only occasionally, little halfhearted scribbles. He has not responded well to having his mind channeled like this: concision and structure are contrary to his nature. When Keith collects his answer sheet at the end of the exercise, it looks sparse and blotched with ink, the script of a crosswired mind.

The Letter Writing Exercise, which takes us up to lunch, is more straightforward. A member of the public has sent a four-page letter to a Home Office minister complaining about a particular aspect of the legislation outlined in the In-Tray Exercise. We are asked to write a balanced, tactful reply, conscious of the government's legal position, but firm in its intent not to cave in to outside pressure. The Hobbit seems to find this significantly easier: sitting there in his blue-black blazer with its cheap gold buttons, he is no longer a sweating, panting blob of panic. The letter allows for a degree of self-expression, for leaps of the imagination, and with these he is more comfortable. There is a general sense that we have all returned here today locked into a surer knowledge of how to proceed.

I have lunch for the second time at the National Gallery and again buy a ham and cheese sandwich, finding something comforting in the routine of this. Then the greater part of the final afternoon is taken up with more cognitive tests: Logical Reasoning, Verbal Organization, two Numerical Facility papers. Again there is not enough time, and again the tests are rigorous and probing. Yet, much of the nervousness and uncertainty of yesterday has disappeared. I know what's required now. I can pace myself. It's just a question of applying the mind.

At three thirty, I find Elaine in the common room, alone and drinking coffee. She is sitting on a radiator below one of the windows, her right leg lifted and resting on the arm of the sofa. Her skirt has ridden up to the midsection of her thighs, but she makes no attempt to cover herself, or to lower her leg when I come in.

"Nearly over," she says.

I must look exhausted. I settle into one of the armchairs and sigh heavily.

"My brain is numb. Numb."

Elaine nods in agreement. Bare-skinned thighs, no tights.

"You finished?"

"No," she says. "One more."

Our conversation is slow monosyllables. It feels as if we are talking like old friends.

"What is it?"

"Interview with the departmental assessor."

"Rouse? He's a straight-talker. You'll like him."

"What about you? What do you have?"

"Just the shrink. Four thirty."

"Nice way to finish off. Get to talk about yourself for half an hour."

"You've had her?"

"Yesterday. Very cozy. Like one of those fireside chats on *Songs of Praise*." Elaine stands up, smoothing down her skirt. "We're all going to the pub later. Sam's idea."

"He's a leader of men, isn't he? Takes control."

Elaine smiles at this. She agrees with me.

"So meet you back here around five fifteen?"

I don't feel like drinking with them. I'd rather just go home and be alone. So I ignore the question and say, "Sounds all right. Good luck with your interview."

"You too," she replies.

But in Dr. Stevenson's office I fall into a trap.

There are two soft armchairs in the corner of the hushed warm room. We face each other and it is as if I am looking into the eyes of a kindly grandmother. Stevenson's face has such grace and warmth that there is nothing I can do but trust it. She calls me Alec—the first time that one of the examiners has referred to me by my first name—and speaks with such refinement that I am immediately lulled into a false sense of security. The lights are dim, the blinds drawn. There is a sensation of absolute privacy. We are in a place where confidences may be shared.

Everything starts out okay. Her early questions are unobtrusive, shallow even, and I give nothing away. We discuss the format of Sisby, what improvements, if any, I would make to it. There is a brief reference to school—an inquiry about my choice of A levels—and an even shorter discussion about CEBDO. That these topics go largely unexplored is not due to any reticence on my part. Stevenson seems happy simply to skirt around the edges of a subject, never probing too deeply, never overstepping the mark. In doing so she brokers a trust that softens me up. And by the time the conversation has moved into a more sensitive area, my guard is down.

"I would like to talk about Kate Allardyce, if that would be all right?"

My first instinct here should have been defensive. Nobody ever asks Alec about Kate; it's a taboo subject. And yet I quickly find that I want to talk about her.

"Could you tell me a little bit about the two of you?"

"We broke up over six months ago."

"I don't understand," she says, and then, with sudden horror, I remember the lie to Liddiard. "I was led to believe that she was your girlfriend."

She looks down at her file, staring at it in plain disbelief. Mistakes of this kind do not happen. She moves awkwardly in her seat and mutters something inaudible.

It was a throwaway deceit. I only did it to make myself appear more solid and dependable, a rounded man in a long-term relationship. He asked for her full name, for a date and place of birth, so that SIS could run a check on her. And now that the vetting process is over they want to square their deep background with mine. They want to know whether Kate will make a decent diplomatic wife, a spy's accomplice. They want to hear me talk about her.

My left hand is suddenly up around my mouth, squeezing the ridge of skin under my nose. It is almost funny to have been caught out by something so crass, so needless, but this feeling quickly evaporates. The humiliation is soon total.

Out of it, I knit together a shoddy retraction.

"I'm sorry. No, no, it's my fault. I'm sorry. We just . . . we just got back together again, about three months ago. Secretly. We don't want anybody to know. We prefer things to be private. I'm just so used to telling people that we're not back together that it's become like a reflex."

"So you are together?"

"Very much so, yes."

"But no one else knows?"

"That's correct. Yes. Except for a friend of mine. Saul. Otherwise, nobody."

"I see."

There is disappointment in the tone of this last remark, as if I have let her down. I feel ten again, a scolded child in the head-teacher's study.

"Perhaps we should talk about something else," she says, turning a page in my file.

I have to rescue this situation or the game is up.

"No, no. I'm happy to talk about it. I should explain. Sorry. It's just that after we broke up I never spoke about it to anyone. No one would have understood. They might have tried to, but they would never have understood. They would have put things in boxes and I didn't want that. It would have trivialized it. And now that we are back together, both of us have made a decision to keep things between ourselves. So we're used to lying about it. Nobody else knows." An uneasy pause. "This must sound childish to you."

"Not at all." I may have got away with it. "But can I ask why you broke up in the first place?"

This is expressed in such a way that it would be easy for me not to answer the question. But my embarrassment at having been caught out by Stevenson is substantial, and I do not want to refuse her request.

"Largely on account of my selfishness. I think Kate grew tired of the fact that I was always withholding things from her. I had this insistence on privacy, a reluctance to let her in. She called it my separateness."

There is suddenly a look of deep satisfaction in the lined wise eyes of Hilary Stevenson. *Separateness.* Yes. A good word for it.

"But you don't have a problem with that anymore?"

"With privacy? No. Not with Kate at least. I'm still an intensely private person, but I've become far more open with her since we got back together."

This emphasis on privacy could even work in my favor. It is surely in the nature of intelligence work.

"And why did you want to give the relationship a second chance? Do stop me if you think I'm being unduly intrusive."

"No, no. There's no reason why you shouldn't know. I wanted to try again because I started thinking about the future. It was that simple. I looked around and thought about where I wanted to be in ten years' time. The sort of life I wanted to lead. And I realized I'd thrown away the best chance I had of a kind of happiness."

Stevenson nods encouragingly, as if this makes absolute sense to her. So I continue.

"It's one of the clichés of breaking up, but you simply don't know how much you love something until it's taken away from you. I'm sure you come across this all the time in your profession."

"All the time."

"That's the dangerous thing about being in a serious relationship with someone. In a very worrying sense, love guarantees you."

"And then all that was taken away from you?"

"Yes."

A first gathering of pain here. Don't show it to her. Tell her what you know she wants to hear.

"So I set myself a task. I tried to get it back. And luckily we hadn't killed too much of it off."

"I'm glad," Stevenson says, and I believe that she is. Everything I have told her is the truth about me, save for the plain fact that Kate has refused to come back. I *had* killed off too much of it, and she has now moved on.

Stevenson writes something in my file, at least three lines of notes, and for some time the room is quiet save for the whisper of her pen. I wonder if the others were as open with her as I have been.

"I was interested by what you said about not knowing how much you love somebody until they are taken away from you. Is that how you felt about your father?"

This comes out of the silence, spoken into her lap, and it takes me by surprise. I don't recall mentioning my father's death either to Liddiard or to Lucas. Hawkes must have told them.

"In a way, yes, though it's more complicated than that."

"Could you say why?"

"Well, I was only seventeen at the time. There's a toughness in you then. An unwillingness to feel. What do Americans call it—'denial'?"

A lovely amused laugh. Making out that she is charmed by me.

"But more recently?"

"Yes. Recently his death has affected me more."

"Could you say why?"

"On a basic level because I saw the relationships my male friends were having with their fathers in that transitional period from their late teens into early twenties. That was obviously a key period for some of them, and I missed out on that."

"So the two of you weren't particularly close when you were a child? You felt that your father kept you at a distance?"

"I wouldn't say that. He was away from home a lot."

Oddly, to speak about Dad in this way feels more deceptive than what I have told Stevenson about Kate. It is not a true account of him, nor of the way we were together, and I want to explain some of this to her.

"This is difficult for me," I tell her. "I am rationalizing complex emotions even as I am talking to you."

"I can understand that. These matters are never simple."

"I can hear myself say certain things to you about my father and then something else inside me will contradict that. Does that make sense? It's a very confusing situation. What I'm trying to say is that there are no set answers."

Stevenson makes to say something, but I speak over her.

"For example, I would like my father to be around now so that we could talk about Sisby and SIS. Mum says that he was like me in a lot of ways. He didn't keep a lot of friends, he didn't need a lot of people in his life. So we shared this need, this instinct for privacy. And maybe because of that we might have become good friends. Who knows? We could have confided in one another. But I don't actively miss him because he's not here to fulfill that role. Things are no more difficult because he's not available to offer me guidance and advice. It's more a feeling that I'll never see his face again. Sometimes it's that simple."

Stevenson's tender eyes are sunk in rolls of skin.

"How do you think he would have felt about you becoming an SIS officer?"

"I think he would have been very proud. Perhaps even a little envious."

"What do you mean?"

"It's every young man's dream, isn't it, to join MI6, to serve his country. Dad wouldn't have thought ideas like that were out-of-date, and neither do I. And I think he would have been good at the job. He was smart, concealed, he could keep a secret. In fact, sometimes I feel like I'm doing this for him, in his memory. That's why it's so important to me. I want to show him that I can be a success. I want to make him proud of me."

Stevenson looks perplexed and I feel that I may have gone too far.

"Yes," she says, writing something down. "And Kate? How does she feel?"

This may be a test: they will want to know if I have broken the Official Secrets Act.

"I haven't told her yet. I didn't see that there was any point. Until I actually became one."

Stevenson smiles.

"Don't you think you ought to tell her?"

"I don't think it's necessary at this stage. And I was advised against it by Mr. Liddiard. If I advance to the next level, then it would become increasingly difficult to keep things from her."

"Yes," she says, giving nothing away. Stevenson looks at her watch and her eyebrows hop. "Good Lord, look at the time."

"Are we finished?"

"I'm afraid so. I hadn't realized how late it is."

"I thought the interview would last longer."

"It can do," she replies, uncrossing her legs and allowing her right foot to drop gently to the floor. "It depends on the candidate."

Abruptly I am concerned. The implication of this last remark is troubling. I should have been less candid, made her work harder for information. Stevenson looks too satisfied with what I have given her. She closes my file with knuckles that are swollen with arthritis.

"So you're happy with what I've told you? Everything's okay?"

That was a dumb thing to ask. I am letting my concern show.

"Oh, yes," she says, very calmly. "Do you have anything else you might want to ask?"

"No," I say immediately. "Not that I can think of."

"Good."

She moves forward, beginning to stand. Things have shut down too quickly. She sets my file on a small table beside her chair.

"I should have thought you were keen to be off. You must be tired after all your exertions."

"It's been hard work. But I've enjoyed it."

Stevenson is on her feet, barely taller than the back of the chair. I stand up.

"I've enjoyed talking to you," she says, moving toward the door. There is a distance about her now, a sudden coldness. "Good luck."

What does she mean by that? Good luck with what? With SIS? With CEBDO?

She is holding the door open, a pale tweed suit.

What did she mean?

Brightness in the corridor. I look back into the office to check that I have left nothing behind. But there is only low light and Stevenson's papers in a neat pile beside her chair. I want to go back in and start again. Without shaking her hand, I move out into the corridor.

"Good-bye, Mr. Milius."

I turn around.

"Yes. Good-bye."

I walk back down the corridor feeling light and stunned. Ogilvy, Elaine, the Hobbit, and Ann are waiting for me in the common room. They stand up and approach me as I come in, a surge of kinship and relief, smiling broadly. This is the thrill of finishing, but I feel little of it. We have all done what we came here to do, but I experience no sense of solidarity.

"What happened to you, Alec?" Ann asks, touching my arm.

"I had a tough one with the shrink. Grilled me."

"You look exhausted. Did it go badly?"

"Difficult to say. Sorry to keep you waiting."

"You didn't," Ogilvy says warmly. "Matt only finished ten minutes ago."

I look across at the Hobbit, whose nod confirms this.

"Pub, then?" Ogilvy asks.

"You know what? I may just go home," I tell them, hoping they'll just let me leave. "I have to have dinner with a friend later on. I'd like to have a shower, get my head together."

Elaine appears offended.

"Don't be stupid," she says. "Just have a couple of drinks with us."

"I'd love to. Really. But I have so much I have to do before—"

"What? Like having a shower? Like getting your head together?"

Her mimicry irritates me, and only hardens my resolve.

"No. You guys go ahead. I'm done for. I'll see you all in the autumn."

I smile here, and it works. The joke relaxes them.

"Well, if you're sure," Ogilvy says. He's probably relieved. Center stage will be his.

"I'm sure."

"Either way," says Ann, and this seals it, "we should go now, 'cos I've got a flight to Belfast at half past nine."

So we say our good-byes, and Sisby is over.

8

PURSUIT OF HAPPINESS

In the early hours of the following Sunday morning, I wake with a specific dream image of Kate being fucked by another man.

She is in a strange, lightless room, almost suffocating with the pleasure of it. Her body is arched in a seizure of lust, but the lovemaking is so intense that she makes no sound. To desire and to be desired this much is inspiring in her a kind of awe. She has discovered a sexual pleasure far greater than the one that we shared in our innocence. She is relishing it because it has nothing to do with compromise or responsibility, nothing to do with the stagey romance of first love. She feared that she would never again experience the passion and tenderness that she knew in those first years with me. But now I look into her face and see that all of that has been consigned to the past.

My room is in absolute darkness as these thoughts peck away at my heart. The shock of them has quickened my breathing to something approaching the panic of an asthma attack, and I have to sit up in bed and then walk slowly around the room, gathering myself together.

I open the curtains and look outside. The color of the sky is caught between the city's reflected glow and the first light of dawn. She is out there with him somewhere, lying against pale sheets.

I take out Kate's T-shirt from the bottom of my chest of drawers and bury my face in its soft cotton folds. Her perfume has disappeared from it entirely. From a bottle of scent that I keep in the bathroom, I replenish the smell, tipping droplets of Chanel No. 19 onto the material before scrunching it up in a tight ball. It is the fourth time that I have had to do this since we separated. Time is passing by.

I cannot get back to sleep, so I sit in the kitchen drinking coffee, my mind shuttling between memories of Kate and apprehension over the results of Sisby.

Whatever happens now, win or lose, I can't go back to CEBDO. Not after all this. I couldn't shrink myself. So tomorrow, first thing, there's something I must do.

"Look, Nik, here's the thing. I want to move on."

This has been coming for months. It feels good to tell him.

"You want to move on."

This isn't said as a question. More as a statement. Nik swallowing the news whole.

"I feel I've achieved everything that I can working for you. And things have got very bad between me and Anna. We can't work together anymore. It's better that one of us should go."

I have brought him to a small greasy spoon café on Edgware Road. It is ten A.M. Traffic and people clapping by outside. There's a red plastic bottle containing ketchup—probably not Heinz—sitting on the table between us. Nik stares at it.

"Okay," he says.

I had expected more of a reaction, a trace of hurt.

"I've been offered a chance to do something . . . larger. Something more meaningful. You know?"

Nik shakes his head, still looking at the ketchup.

"No, I don't know. You tell me what that is, Alec. I'm not a mind reader."

"I'm sorry. I've hurt your feelings. You've invested a lot of time in me and I've let you down."

Now he lifts his head and looks me straight in the eye. There may be pity in his leering, condescending grin.

"Oh, Alec. That's what I always hated about you. You always think you're the most important person in the room. Let me tell you something. The world is bigger than you. You understand? You don't hurt my feelings. You think something like you handing in your notice could hurt my feelings? You think I can't go out onto that street right now and find someone to replace you? You think I can't do that?"

This is more like it. This is what I was expecting.

"I'm sure you can, Nik. I'm sure you can. You're amazing like that."

"Don't make fun of me, all right? I gave you a job of work. You come into my offices and all you're interested in doing is fucking my staff, fucking Anna. And now you say you cannot speak with her. This is your problem. I gave you a job of work. That is a precious thing. . . ."

"Oh, *please*."

I really draw out the *please* here, and it deflects him. I often wonder when he is angry like this how much gets lost in translation, how much of what he wants to say is denied to him by his mediocre English.

"This operation I have," he says, gesturing freely with his right hand. He's about to embark on one of his delusional monologues. "You're just a tiny fragment of something much larger. Something that you can't even comprehend. I plan expansion, more offices, more people and workers. And do you know why you can't comprehend that?"

"Is it just too complicated for me, Nik? Is it just too global and secret and amazing?"

"I tell you why. It's not because I don't allow you to comprehend it. No. It's because you won't allow *yourself* to see it. You see only what's in front of your nose. You never see the bigger picture, the possibilities your work can offer. You and me, we could go places, make some money. The world is bigger than you, Alec. The world is bigger than you."

"What does that fucking mean, Nik? What exact brand of shit are you talking?"

"You're a clever boy. I thought this when I first met you. I still think it. But you need to take your head out of your arse. You're soft."

It's time to draw things to a close.

"Nik, I'm not about to take life lessons from you. These plans, these ambitions you talk about. I can't tell you how little I care about them. You're not running Ogilvy and Mather. You're a crook, a petty thief."

"You want to be careful what you—"

I interrupt him.

"I don't have much stuff at the office. Someone will come and get it next week."

"Fine."

And with that he stands up, pivots away from the table, and walks out of the café, leaving me with the bill.

———

Now it's just a question of waiting for SIS to call.

I don't go outside for twenty-four hours in case the telephone rings, but by three o'clock on Tuesday I am growing impatient. The only person to have rung since lunchtime on Monday is Saul, who is just back from Spain. Perhaps SIS wants us to call them?

I dial Liddiard's office and a woman answers.

"Seven-two-zero-four."

They never say anything other than the number of the extension. It might just as well be a launderette.

"Patrick Liddiard, please."

"May I say who's speaking?"

"Alec Milius."

"Yes. Just one moment."

Five seconds of dead noise. Ten. Then a click and Liddiard picks up.

"Alec."

"Good afternoon. How are you?"

"Very well, thank you."

I can't tell anything by the tone of his voice. He's cheery and polite, but that is his manner.

"I was ringing about the results of Sisby."

"Yes. Of course."

Well, say something, then. Tell me. Good or bad.

"I wondered if you knew anything."

"Yes, we do."

And there's a terrible beat now, a gathering of courage before bad news.

"I'm afraid that the board felt you were not up to the very high standards required. I'm sorry, Alec, but we won't be able to take your application any further."

My first instinct is that he has mistaken me for somebody else: the Hobbit, perhaps even Ogilvy. But there has been no confusion. Soon every glimpse of promise I have ever shown is ebbing from me like a wound. Liddiard is talking, but I cannot pick up the words. I feel debilitated, bone weak, crushed. In the circumstances I should try to say something dignified, accept defeat graciously, and withdraw. But I am too shocked to react. I stand in the hall holding the phone against my ear, ingesting failure. And because I am not saying anything, Liddiard tries to placate me.

"Would you like me to indicate to you where we felt the weakness was in your application?"

"Okay."

"It was the group exercise primarily. The board felt you did not display sufficient depth of knowledge about the subjects under discussion."

"Did anybody else make it through? Sam? Matthew?"

This is all I want to know. Just tell me that I came the closest out of all of them.

"For obvious reasons I can't reveal that."

I think I detect contempt in the way he says this, as if my asking such a stupid question has only verified their decision not to hire me.

"No, of course you can't."

"But thank you for your enthusiastic participation in the recruitment procedure. We all very much enjoyed meeting you."

Oh, fuck off.

"It's nice of you to say so. Thank you."

"Good-bye."

9

THIS IS YOUR LIFE

My first instinct, and this shames me, is to ring Mum. No sooner have I put the phone down on Liddiard than I am picking it up again and dialing her number in Somerset. She never goes out in the afternoon. She'll tell me everything's all right.

The number rings out shrill and clean. I can tell her everything, I can get it all off my chest. And I can do so in the full assurance that she will actually express relief at my failure. She might even be horrified to learn that I had even considered employment in such a murky organization. That her only child, her son, could have gone into such a thing without telling his mother . . .

I hang up. She'll never know. It's as simple as that.

Receiving bad news is always like this: there's too much information to process, too much at stake that has been irretrievably lost. Something similar happened when Mum told me that my father had died. My mind went absolutely numb, and there was nothing I could do to put his loss into perspective.

The telephone rings, a volt of shock in my chest. I don't even think about screening the call on my answering machine. I know it's Hawkes.

"Alec?"

"Yes. Hello, Michael."

"I've just heard the news. I'm very sorry. I really thought you'd go the whole way."

"You weren't the only one."

"They telephoned me about an hour ago."

"Why? Why did they call you? I thought you'd retired?"

He stalls here, as if making something up.

"Well, given that it was me who initiated your candidacy, they wanted to keep me informed."

"But I thought you'd left? I thought you were in the oil business now."

"You never really leave, Alec. It's an ongoing thing."

"So you're not doing that anymore?"

"Don't be concerned about me. Let's talk about your situation."

"Okay."

His voice has thinned out, flustered, concealing something.

"They suggested to me that your cognitive tests were fractionally below par. That's all they said."

"They told me it was the group exercise, not the cognitive tests."

Another awkward pause.

"Oh?"

"Yes. Said I wasn't fully in control of my brief or something. Hadn't covered all the angles."

"Well, yes, there was that, too."

He has obviously squared what to tell me with Liddiard, but one of them has fucked up. It must have been the interview with Stevenson. They know I lied about Kate.

"Did they give you any other reason why I failed?"

"Don't see it as a failure, Alec."

"That's what it is, isn't it?"

Why can't he just be honest about it? I've let him down. He recommended me and I've embarrassed him. I was so sure it was going to be all right.

"The vast majority of candidates don't even make it through to Sisby. To have progressed beyond the initial interviews is an achievement in itself."

"Well, it's good of you to say so," I say, suddenly wanting to be rid of him. "Thanks for recommending me in the first place."

"Oh, not at all. What will you do now? Go back to your old job?"

"Probably."

He pauses briefly before saying, "We haven't exhausted every avenue, of course. There are alternatives."

For now this is of no interest to me. I simply want the conversation to end.

"You've done enough. Don't worry. Thank you for everything."

"You're sure?" He sounds disappointed. "Think about it, Alec. And in the meantime, if there's anything I can do, just let me know."

"That's kind. Thank you."

"I'll be in touch."

A lie. Why would he bother contacting me again? My usefulness to him has passed.

"I'll look forward to it," I tell him.

"Don't be too down, Alec. As I say, there are other options."

At around six I go over to Saul's, for company and for some way of shaking off the gloom. It takes about three-quarters of an hour to get there, driving through the rush-hour traffic and then finding somewhere to park. He has put up a notice on the door of his flat: JUST AS MUCH JUNK MAIL AS YOU CAN SPARE, PLEASE. When I see it, I smile for the first time in hours.

He pours two vodkas—mine without ice—and we sit in front of the television in the sitting room. A balding actor on *This Is Your Life* has just been surprised by the host, Michael Aspel, sporting his big red book. Saul says something about minor celebrities in Britain being "really minor" and retrieves a cigarette he had going from an ashtray.

"Who's that?" he asks as a middle-aged woman in pink emerges onto the stage, mugging to the camera.

"No idea."

She starts telling a story. Saul leans back.

"Christ. Is there anything more tedious than listening to people telling anecdotes on *This Is Your Life*?"

I do not respond. There is a constant, nagging disquiet inside me that I cannot shake off.

"What've you been up to?" he asks. "Day off as well?"

"Yeah. I've had a lot happening."

"Right."

He twists toward me on the sofa.

"Everything all right?"

"Yeah."

"You look worn out."

"I am."

There shouldn't be any need to, but I try to convey a greater sense of melancholy than may be visible, just in case Saul hasn't detected it.

"Alec, what is it?"

He switches the television off with the remote control. The image sucks into itself until it forms a tiny white blob, which then snuffs out.

"Bad news."

"What? Tell me."

"I've done a stupid thing. I handed in my notice to Nik."

"That isn't stupid. It's about time."

This irritates me. He always thought I was wasting away at CEBDO. Fiddling while Rome burns.

"I did it for the wrong reason. I did it because I was sure I was set at the Foreign Office."

"That job you were applying for?"

"Yes."

"And you didn't get it?"

"No. I found out today."

"I'm sorry."

"You didn't tell anyone else I was applying for it, did you?"

"No. Course not. You told me not to."

I believe him.

"Thanks."

"So what happened? Did you fuck up the exams?"

"Yeah. Toughest thing I've ever done."

"You shouldn't be disappointed. I've heard they're like that. Hardly anyone gets through."

"It's more shame than disappointment. It's as if my worst fears about myself have been confirmed. I thought I was clever enough to make a career out of it. It really seemed to make sense. I spent so long thinking I was good enough to do top-level work, but now it turns out I was just deluding myself."

I don't like admitting failure to Saul. It doesn't feel right. But there's an opportunity here to talk through a few things, in confidence, which I want to take advantage of.

"Well, I never knew why you wanted to join in the first place," he says.

I drain the vodka.

"Because I was flattered to be asked."

"To be asked? You never said anything about being asked. You didn't say anything about anyone approaching you."

Careful.

"Didn't I? No. Well, I met someone at a dinner party at Mum's. He'd just retired from the Diplomatic Service. Put me onto it. Gave me a phone number."

"Oh."

Saul offers me a cigarette, lights one of his own.

"What was his name?"

"George Parker."

"And why did you want to join?"

"Because it was exciting. Because I wanted to do it for Dad. Because it beat ripping Czechs off for a living. I don't know. This meant so much to me. I'll never get a chance like that again. To be on the top table."

The conversation dies now for a second or two. I don't think Saul is really in the mood for it: I've come around uninvited on his day off.

"Listen," he says. "I think you're lucky not to have got in."

This is exactly the wrong thing to say to me.

"Why? Why am I in any way lucky? This was my big chance to get ahead, to start a career."

"I'm sorry, I didn't think—"

"It's been every day for four months."

"I had no idea—"

"You're not the only one who's ambitious, you know. I have ambitions."

"I didn't say you didn't."

He is being defensive now, a little patronizing. My anger has unnerved him.

"I wanted to work abroad, to have some excitement. I wanted to stop pissing away my youth."

"So what's stopping you? Go out and get a different job. The Foreign Office isn't the only organization that offers positions overseas."

"What's the point? What's the point in a corporate job when you can get downsized or sacked whenever the next recession comes along?"

"Don't exaggerate. Don't just repeat what you've heard on TV."

"Anyway, it's too late. I should have done it straight out of LSE.

That's the time to spend two or three years working away from home. Not now. I'm supposed to be establishing myself in a career."

"That's bullshit."

"Look around, Saul. Everybody we knew at university did the job fair circuit, did their finals, and then went straight into a sensible career where they'll be earning thirty or forty grand in a couple of years' time. These were people who were constantly stoned, who never went to lectures, who could barely string a sentence together. And now they're driving company cars and paying fifty quid a month into pension plans and 'health insurance.' That's what I should be doing instead of sitting around waiting for things to happen to me. It doesn't work that way. You have to make your own luck. How did they know what to do with their lives when they were only twenty-one?"

"People grow up."

"Evidently. I should've gone into the City. Read law. Taken a risk. What was the point in spending four years reading Russian and business studies if I wasn't going to use them?"

"Jesus, Alec. You're twenty-four, for Christ's sake. You can still do whatever you like. It just requires a bit of imagination."

There's a glimmer here of something hopeful, a zip of optimism, but the stubbornness in me won't grasp it.

"If you could have just met some of the people I did the entrance exams with. To think that they could have got the job and not me. There was this one Cambridge guy. Sam Ogilvy. Smooth, rich, vacuous. I bet they took him."

"What does it matter if they did? You jealous or something?"

"No. No, I'm not. He was . . . he was . . ." How to describe Ogilvy to Saul? In an uncomfortable way, they reminded me of each other. "What did that man on TV call Tony Blair? 'A walking Autocue in a sensible suit.' That's exactly what this guy was like. In order to get anywhere these days we have to be like Sam Ogilvy. An ideas-free zone. A platitude in patent leather shoes. That's what employers are looking for. Coachloads of Tony Blairs."

There is a message from Hawkes on my answering machine when I get home at eight fifteen. Were it not for the fact that I have had four vodkas, I might be more surprised to hear from him.

"Alec. It's Michael. I'm coming to London tomorrow and I suggest we get together for lunch. Have a chat about things. Give me a ring in the country."

His voice sounds stern. He leaves a contact number and I say, "Yeah, whatever," to the machine, but out of inquisitiveness scribble it down on a pad.

For dinner I microwave some pasta and watch television for an hour, unable to concentrate on much beyond the shock of SIS. The rejection begins to act like heartbreak. Just when I think I've found some respite, after six hours of soul-searching and self-pity, something triggers the pain again—a memory of Stevenson, of Rouse standing firm in the window. So many ideas and plans, so many secret aspirations that will now remain untested. I was absolutely prepared to live my life as a shadow of who I really am. Surely they saw that? Surely there was something I could have done for them? I cannot understand why I have been discarded with such speed and ruthlessness. It makes no sense. To be left with this shaming feeling, the grim realization that there is nothing that marks me out from the crowd.

At around nine, after finishing a half-empty bottle of wine in the fridge, I go out to the corner shop and buy a four-pack of Stella. By the time I have finished the first can, I have written this in longhand:

Alec Milius
111E Uxbridge Road
London W12 8NL
15 August 1995
Patrick Liddiard
Foreign and Commonwealth Office
No. 46A————Terrace
London SW1

Dear Mr. Liddiard:
Further to our conversation on the telephone this morning, there are one or two points I would like to raise in relation to my failed application to join the Secret Intelligence Service.

It concerns me that your department is in possession of a file that contains detailed information about me, ranging across my background and education, with further confidential material about my professional and personal life.

Could you please confirm by return of post that this file has been destroyed?

Yours sincerely,
Alec Milius

I read it back a couple of times and extract "by return of post," which doesn't sound right. Then, with the letter stamped, addressed, and in my pocket, I lock up the flat and head for a bar in Goldhawk Road.

10

MEANING

I am woken at nine forty-five by the noise of the telephone, the sound of it moving toward me out of a deep sleep, growing louder, more substantial, incessant. At first I turn over in bed, determined to let it ring out, but the answering machine is switched off and the caller won't relent. I throw back the duvet and stand up.

It is as if one part of my brain lurches from the right side of my head to the left. I almost fall to the floor with the pain of it. And the phone keeps on ringing. Naked, stumbling across the hall, I reach the receiver.

"Hello?"

"Alec?"

It's Hawkes. With the sound of his voice I immediately reexperience the stab of my failure at SIS, the numb regret and the shame.

"Michael. Yes."

"Did I wake you?"

"No. I was just listening to the radio. Didn't hear it ring."

"My apologies."

"It's fine."

"Can you meet me for lunch?"

The thought of gathering myself together sufficiently to spend two or three hours with Hawkes feels impossible with such a hangover. But there is a temptation here, a sense of unfinished business. I spot his telephone number scribbled on the pad beside the phone.

We haven't exhausted every avenue. There are alternatives.

"Sure. Where would you like to meet?"

He gives me an address in Kensington and hangs up.

There had better be something in this. I don't want to waste my time listening to Hawkes tell me where I went wrong, saying over and over again how sorry he is. I'd rather he just left me alone.

He cooks lunch for the two of us in the kitchen of a small flat on Kensington Court Place, beef Stroganoff and rice that is still crunchy, with a few tired beans on the side. Never been married, and he still can't cook. There is an open bottle of Chianti, but I stick to mineral water as the last of my hangover fades.

We barely discuss either SIS or Sisby. His exact words are, "Let's put that behind us. Think of it as history," and instead the subjects are wide-ranging and unconnected, with Hawkes doing most of the talking. I have to remind myself continually that this is only the second occasion on which we have met. It is strange once again to encounter the man who has shaped the course of my life these last few months. There is something capricious about his face. I had forgotten how thin it is, drawn out like an addict's. He is still wearing a frayed shirt and a haphazard cravat, still the same pair of velvet loafers embroidered on the toe with a coat of arms. How odd that a person who has given his life to secrecy and concealment should be so willing to stand out from the crowd.

Afterward, scraping creamy leftovers of rice into a garbage bin, he says, "I often like to go for a walk after lunch. Do you have time?"

And largely because there has not yet been any talk of improving my situation, I agree to go.

Hyde Park is buzzing with rollerbladers and a warm wind is blowing north to south across the grass. I have a desire for good, strong coffee, a double espresso to give me a lift after lunch. My energy feels sapped by the exercise.

We have been talking about Mum when Hawkes says, "You remind me very much of your father. Not just in the way you look—he always seemed about twenty-one, never appeared to age—but in manner. In approach."

"You'd lost touch? You said when we met . . ."

"Yes. Work took me away. It's what happens in the Office, I'm afraid."

I don't feel like asking a lot of questions about Dad. I'd rather Hawkes brought up another subject. As we are passing the Albert Memorial he says, "I admired his tenacity tremendously. He was entrepreneurial almost before the word had been invented. Always working on a plan, a scheme for making money. Not a fast buck. Not to cheat anyone. But he loved working, he was ambitious. He wanted to make the best of himself."

And this intrigues me. I remember Dad more as an absence, always away on business, and never wanting to talk about work when he came home. Mum has certainly never spoken about him in such a way.

"How do you mean?"

"Let me give you an example," he says. "I imagine that you have friends from school or university who spend a lot of their time just sitting around or wasting away in dead-end jobs."

I sure do. I'm one of them.

"I don't have that many friends," I tell him. "But yes, there are a lot of people who come out of higher education and feel that their choices are limited. People with good degrees with nowhere to go."

Hawkes coughs, as if he hasn't been listening. "And this job you're doing at the moment. I suspect it's a waste of your time, yes?"

The remark catches me off guard, but I have to admire his nerve.

"Fair enough." I smile. "But it's not a waste of time anymore. I quit over the weekend."

"Did you now?" His reply does not disguise a degree of surprise, perhaps even of pleasure. Is it possible that Hawkes really does have some plan for me, some opportunity? Or am I simply clinging to the impossible hope that Liddiard and his colleagues have made an embarrassing mistake?

"So what are you going to do?" he asks.

"Well, right now it looks as though I'm going to become one of those people who spend a lot of their time just sitting around."

He laughs at this, breaking into a rare smile that stretches his face like a clown. Then he looks me in the eye, that old paternal thing, and says, "Why don't you come and work for me?"

The offer does not surprise me. Somehow I had expected it. A halfway house between CEBDO and the coveted world of espionage. A compromise. A job in the oil business.

"At your company? At Abnex?"

"Yes."

"I'm very flattered."

"You have Russian, don't you? And a grounding in business?"

"Yes," I reply confidently.

"Well then, I would urge you to think about it."

We have stopped walking. I look down at the ground, drawing my right foot up and down on the grass. Perhaps I should say more about how grateful I am.

"This is extraordinary," I tell him. "I'm amazed by how—"

"There is something I would need to ask in return," he says, before I become too gushy.

I look at him, trying to gauge what he means, but his face is unreadable. I simply nod as he says, "If you decided that you wanted to take up a position . . ." Then he stalls. "What are your feelings, instinctively? Is oil something you'd like to become involved in?"

In my confused state, it is almost impossible to decide, but I am intrigued by Hawkes's caveat. What would he ask for in return?

"I would need to get my head together a little bit, to think things through," I tell him, but no sooner have the words come out than I am thinking back to what he said about my father. His ambition. His need to improve himself, and I add quickly, "But I can't think of any reason why I would want to throw away an opportunity like that."

"Good. Good," he says.

"Why? What would you need me to do?"

The question sets us moving again, walking slowly down a path toward Park Lane.

"It's nothing that would be beyond you."

He smiles at this, but the implication is clandestine. There is something unlawful here that Hawkes is concealing.

"Sorry, Michael. I'm not understanding."

He turns and looks behind us, almost as if he feels we are being followed. A reflex ingrained into his behavior. But it's just a group of four or five schoolchildren kicking a football fifty meters away.

"Abnex has a rival," he says, turning back to face me. "An American oil company by the name of Andromeda. We would need you to befriend two of their employees."

"Befriend?"

He nods.

"Who is 'we'?" I ask.

"Let's just say a number of interested parties, both from the government side and private industry. All I can tell you firmly at this stage is that you would need to maintain absolute secrecy, in exactly the same way as was described to you during your selection procedure for SIS."

"So this has something to do with them?"

He does not respond.

"Or MI5? Are they the 'alternative' you were talking about on the phone yesterday?"

Hawkes breathes deeply and looks to the sky, but a satisfied expression on his face seems to confirm the truth of this. Then he continues walking. "Five might be interested in using you as a support agent," he says. "On a trial basis."

I am astonished by this. "Already?"

"It's something that just popped up in the last couple of weeks. A rather discreet operation, in actual fact. Off the books." A dog runs across our path and vanishes into some long grass. "My contact there, John Lithiby, can't use his regular employees and needs some fresh fruit off the tree. So I suggested your name. . . ."

"I can't believe this."

"There'd be a job for you at the other end," he says, "if the operation is a success."

I feel flattered, stunned. "You're talking about a job with MI5?" I am shaking my head, almost laughing. "Just for befriending some Americans?"

Hawkes turns and looks back down the path, as if searching for the dog, then faces me and smiles. He appears oddly proud, as if he has fulfilled a longstanding pledge to my father. "Questions, questions," he mutters. Then he puts his arm across my back, the right hand squeezing my shoulder, and says, "Later, Alec. Later."

PART TWO

1996

Making millions on sheer gall. American Dream.

—JOHN UPDIKE, *Rabbit Redux*

11

CASPIAN

The offices of Abnex Oil occupy five central stories in an eyesore Broadgate high-rise about six minutes' walk from Liverpool Street station.

The company was founded in 1989 by a City financier named Clive Hargreaves, who was just thirty-five years old at the time. Hargreaves had no A levels and no formal higher education, just a keen business sense and an instinctive, immediate grasp of the market opportunities presented by the gradual collapse of communism in the Eastern bloc and, later, the former Soviet Union. With private investment attached to a chunk of money he'd made in the City during the Thatcher–Lawson boom, Hargreaves expanded Abnex from a small outfit employing fewer than one hundred people into what is now the third largest oil-exploration company in the UK. At the start of the decade, Abnex had minor contracts in Brazil, the North Sea, Sakhalin, and the Gulf, but Hargreaves's masterstroke was to realize the potential of the Caspian Sea before many of his competitors had done so. Between 1992 and early 1994, he negotiated well-workover agreements with the nascent governments of Kazakhstan, Turkmenistan, and Azerbaijan, and sent down teams of geologists, contractors, and lawyers to Baku with a view to identifying the most promising well sites in the region. The Caspian is now awash with international oil companies, many of them acting as joint ventures and all competing for their chunk of what are proven oil reserves. Abnex is better placed than many of them to reap the benefits when the region goes online.

On New Year's Day 1995, Hargreaves was killed riding pillion on a motorcycle in northern Thailand. The driver, his best friend, wasn't drunk or high; he was just going too fast and missed a bend in the road. Hargreaves, who was single, left the bulk of his estate to his sister, who immediately sold her controlling stake in Abnex to a former cabinet minister in the Thatcher government. This is where Hawkes came in. A new chairman, David Caccia, had been appointed by the board of directors. Caccia was also ex–Foreign Office, though not SIS. The two men had been posted to the British embassy in Moscow in the 1970s and become close friends. Caccia, knowing that Hawkes was approaching retirement, offered him a job.

I work undercover for MI5 as a business development analyst in a seven-man team specializing in emerging markets, specifically the Caspian Sea. On my first day, just four or five hours in, the personnel manager asked me to sign this agreement:

CODE OF CONDUCT

To be complied with at all times by employees and associates of Abnex Oil.

- The Company expects all of its business to be conducted in a spirit of honesty, free from fraudulence and deception. Employees—and those acting on behalf of Abnex Oil—shall use their best endeavors to promote and develop the business of the Company and its standing both in the UK and abroad.
- All business relationships—with government representatives, clients, and suppliers—must be conducted ethically and within the bounds of the law. On no account should inducements or other extracontractual payments be made or accepted by employees or associates of Abnex Oil. Gifts of any nature must be registered with the Company at the first opportunity.
- Employees and associates are forbidden to publish or otherwise disclose to any unauthorized person trading details of Abnex Oil or its clients, including—but not limited to—confidential or secret information relating to the business, finances, computer programs, data, client listings, inventions, know-how, or any other matter whatsoever connected with the business of Abnex Oil, whether such information may be in the form of records, files,

correspondence, drawings, notes, computer media of any
description, or in any other form including copies of or excerpts
from the same.

- Any breach of the above regulations will be construed by the
Company as circumstances amounting to gross misconduct, which
may result in summary dismissal and legal prosecution.

August 1995

All the guys on my team are university graduates in their mid-to-late
twenties who came here within six months of leaving university. With
one exception, they are earning upward of thirty-five thousand pounds
a year. The exception, owing to the circumstances in which I took the
job, is myself. I am over halfway through the trial period imposed by the
senior management. If, at the end of it, I am considered to have per-
formed well, my salary will be bumped up from its present level—
which is below twelve thousand after tax—to something nearer thirty,
and I will be offered a long-term contract, health coverage, and a company car. If Alan Murray, my immediate boss, feels that I have not con-
tributed effectively to the team, I'm out the door.

This probationary period, which ends on 1 December, was a condition of my accepting the job imposed by Murray. Hawkes and Caccia
knew that they had brought me in over the heads of several more highly
qualified candidates—one of whom had been shadowing the team, unpaid, for more than three months—and they were happy to oblige.
From my point of view it's a small price to pay. Like most employers
nowadays, Abnex knows that they can get away with asking young
people to work excessively long hours, six or seven days a week, without
any form of contractual security or equivalent remuneration. At any one
time there might be fifteen or twenty graduates in the building doing
unpaid work experience, all of them holding out for a position that in
all likelihood does not exist.

So, no complaints. Things have swung around for me since last year
and I have Hawkes to thank for that. The downside is that I now work
harder, and for longer hours, than I have ever worked in my life. I am up
every morning at six, sometimes quarter past, and take a cramped tube to
Liverpool Street just after seven. There's no time for a slow, contemplative

breakfast, those gradual awakenings of my early twenties. The team is expected to be at our desks by eight o'clock. There is a small, aggressively managed coffee bar near the Abnex building where I sometimes buy an espresso and a sandwich at around nine A.M. But often there is so much work to do that there isn't time to leave the office.

The pressure comes mainly from the senior management, beginning with Murray and working its way steadily up to Caccia. They make constant demands on the team for reliable and accurate information about geological surveys, environmental research, pipeline and refining deals, currency fluctuations, and—perhaps most important of all—any anticipated political developments in the region that may have long- or short-term consequences for Abnex. A change of government personnel, for example, can dramatically affect existing and apparently legally binding exploration agreements signed with the previous incumbent. Corruption is at an epidemic level in the Caspian region, and the danger of being outmaneuvered, either by a competitor or by venal officials, is constant.

A typical day will be taken up speaking on the telephone to clients, administrators, and other officials in London, Moscow, Kiev, and Baku, often in Russian or, worse, with someone who has too much belief in his ability to speak English. In that respect, little has changed since CEBDO. In every other way, my life has taken on a dimension of intellectual effort that was entirely absent when I was working for Nik. I look back on my first six months at Abnex as a blur of learning: files, textbooks, seminars, and exams on every conceivable aspect of the oil business, coupled with extensive MI5/SIS weekend and night classes, usually overseen by Hawkes.

In late September, he and I flew out to the Caspian with Murray and Raymond Mackenzie, a senior employee at the firm. In under eight days we took in Almaty, Tashkent, Ashgabat, Baku, and Tbilisi. It was the first time that Hawkes or I had visited the region. We were introduced to Abnex employees, to representatives from Exxon, Royal Dutch Shell, and BP, and to high-ranking government officials in each of the major states. Most of these had had ties with the former Soviet administration; three, Hawkes knew for certain, were former KGB.

It is not that I have minded the intensity of the work or the long hours. In fact, I draw a certain amount of satisfaction from possessing what is now a high level of expertise in a specialist field. But my social life has been obliterated. I have not visited Mum since Christmas, and I can't remember the last time I had the chance to savor a decent meal, or to do something as mundane as going to the cinema. My friendship with Saul is now something that has to be timetabled and squeezed in, like sex in a bad marriage. Tonight—he is coming to an oil industry party at the In and Out Club on Piccadilly—will be only the third time that I have had the opportunity to see him since New Year's. He resents this, I think. In days gone by, it was Saul who called the shots. He had the glamorous job and the jet-set lifestyle. At the last minute, he might be called off to a shoot in France or Spain, and any arrangements we might have made to go to a movie or meet for a drink would have to be canceled.

Now the tables have turned. Freelancing has not been as easy as Saul anticipated. The work hasn't been coming in, and he is struggling to finish a screenplay that he had hoped to have financed by the end of last year. It may even be that he is jealous of my new position. There has been something distrustful in his attitude toward me since I joined Abnex, almost as if he blames me for getting my life in order.

It's a Thursday evening in mid–May, just past five o'clock. People are starting to leave the office, drifting in slow pairs toward the lifts. Some are heading for the pub, where they will drink a pint or two before the party; others, like me, are going straight home to change. If everything goes according to plan, tonight should mark a significant development in my relationship with Andromeda, and I want to feel absolutely prepared.

Back at the flat, I put on a fresh scrape of deodorant and a new shirt. At around seven o'clock I order a taxi to take me to Piccadilly. This early part of the evening is not as awkward as I had anticipated. I am clearheaded and looking forward finally to making progress with the Americans.

There are flames leaping from tall Roman candles in a crescent forecourt visible from the cab as it shunts down a bottlenecked Hyde Park toward the In and Out Club. I pay the driver, check my reflection in the window of a parked car, and then make my way inside.

An immaculate silver-haired geriatric, wearing a gold-buttoned red blazer and sharp white tie, is greeting guests at the door. He checks my invitation.

"Mr. Milius. From Abnex. Yes, sir. Just go straight through."

Other guests in front of me have been ushered into a high-ceilinged entrance hall. Most of them are, at a guess, over thirty-five, though a hand-in-hand, good-looking couple of about my age are gliding around in a circular room immediately beyond this one. The boyfriend is guiding an elaborate blonde counterclockwise around a large oak table, pretending to admire some cornice work on the oval ceiling. He points at it intelligently, and the girlfriend nods, openmouthed.

I walk past them and turn right down a darkened corridor leading into a spacious, paved garden where the party is taking place. The noise of it grows sharper with every pace, the rising clamor of a gathered crowd. I walk out onto a terraced balcony overlooking the garden from the club side and take a glass of champagne from a teenage waiter who breezes past me, tray held at head height. The party is in full swing. Polite laughter lifts up from the multitudes in their suits and cocktail dresses, oil people in dappled light amid the ooze of small talk.

Piers, Ben, and J.T., three members of my team, are standing in the far right corner of the garden, thirty or forty feet away, sucking back champagne. As usual, Ben is doing most of the talking, making the others laugh. Harry Cohen, at twenty-eight the oldest and most senior member of the team after Murray, is just behind them, schmoozing some mutton-dressed-as-lamb in a little black dress. No sign of Saul, though. He must have been held up.

Just below me, to my left, I see the Hobbit talking to his new girlfriend. It is still extraordinary to witness the change that has come over him. Gone are the spots and greasy skin, and his once-raggedy hair has now been cropped short and combed forward to shield a gathering baldness. There are things that he still gets wrong. On his lapel he is wearing a bright orange badge imprinted with the name MATTHEW FREARS above the logo of his company, Andromeda. And his glance up at me is nervous, almost intimidated. Yet he is reliable, and honest to the point of candor. We make eye contact, nothing more. He'll be as fired up as me.

I walk down a short flight of stone steps and make my way through the crowd to the Abnex team. J.T. is the first to spot me.

"Alec. You're late."

"Not networking?" I say to them.

"Pointless at parties," Piers replies.

"Why's that?"

"Everyone's up to the same game. You're never going to make an impression. Might as well neck the free booze and fuck off home."

"It's your optimism I admire," says Ben. "Life-affirmin'."

"Murray arrived?"

"Coming later," he says, as if it were inside knowledge.

"Why'd you go home?" Piers asks me.

"Change of shirt."

"Sweaty boy," says Ben. "Sweaty boy."

"You haven't met someone called Saul, have you?"

He is a vital component in tonight's plan, and I need him to get here. Ben says, "What kind of a name is Saul?"

"He's a friend of mine. I'm supposed to be meeting him here. He's late."

"Haven't seen him," he says, taking a sip from his drink.

Cohen separates himself from the middle-aged woman with the facelift and turns toward us. His coming into our small group has the effect of tightening it up.

"Hello, Alec."

"Harry."

The woman gives him a final smile before disappearing into the crowd.

"Mum come with you?" Ben says to him, trying on a joke. Cohen does not react.

"Who was she?" J.T. asks.

"A friend of mine who works for Petrobras."

"Sleeping with the enemy, eh?" Ben mutters under his breath, but Cohen ignores him.

"She's involved with exploration on the Marlin field," he says, turning to me. "Where's that, Alec?"

"You giving me a test, Harry? At a fucking party?"

"Don't you know? Don't you know where the Marlin field is?"

"It's in Brazil. Marlin is in Brazil. Offshore."

"Very good," he says with raw condescension.

J.T. looks at me and rolls his eyes. An ally of mine.

"Glad I could be of some assistance," I tell him.

"Now, now, boys. Let's all try to enjoy ourselves," Ben says, grinning. He must have been drinking for some time. His round face has taken on a rosy, alcoholic flush. "Plenty of skirt here."

J.T. nods.

"You still seeing that journalist, Harry?" Ben asks.

Cohen looks at him, irked by the intrusion into his private life.

"We're engaged. Didn't you know?"

"Matter of fact, I think I did know that," he says. "Set a date?"

"Not as such."

None of us will be invited.

"Who's that young bloke next to Henderson, the one with the dark hair?"

Cohen is half pointing at a lean, jaded-looking man in a crushed linen suit standing to the right of our group.

"Hack from the *FT*," says Piers, taking a satay stick from one of the waiters. "Joined from the *Telegraph* about three months ago. Going places."

"Thought I recognized him. What's his name?"

"Peppiatt," Piers tells him. "Mike Peppiatt."

This is registered by Cohen, the name stored away. Before the evening is out, he will have spoken to the journalist, made contact, chatted him up. *Here's my card. Call me anytime you have a query.* Cohen has the patience to forge contacts with the financial press, to feed them their little tidbits and scoops. It gives him a sense of power. And Peppiatt, of course, will return the favor, putting another useful name in his little black book. This is how the world goes round.

I spot Saul now, sloping into the party on the far side of the garden, and feel relieved. There is a look of wariness on his face, as if he is here to meet a stranger. He looks up, sees me immediately through the dense, shifting crowd, and half smiles.

"There he is."

"Your mate?" says Ben.

"That's right. Saul."

"Saul," Ben repeats under his breath, getting used to the name.

The five of us turn to greet him, standing in an uneven semicircle. Saul, nodding shyly, shakes my hand.

"All right, man?" he says.

"Yeah. How was your shoot?"

"Shampoo ad. Canary Wharf. Usual thing."

Both of us, simultaneously, take out a cigarette.

"These are the people I work with. Some of them, anyway."

I introduce Saul to the team. This is J.T., this is Piers, this is Ben. Harry, meet an old friend of mine, Saul Ricken. There are handshakes and eye contacts, Saul's memory lodging names while his manner does an imitation of cool.

"So how are things?" I ask, pivoting away from them, taking us out of range.

"Not bad. Sorry I was late getting here. Had to go home and change."

"Don't worry. It was good of you to come."

"I don't get much of a chance to see you these days."

"No. Need a drink?"

"Whenever someone comes round," he says, flatly.

Both of us scan the garden for a waiter. I light Saul's cigarette, my hand shaking.

"Nervous about something?" he asks.

"No. Should I be?"

No reply.

"So what sort of shampoo was it?"

"You really care?" he says, exhaling.

"Not really, no."

This is how things will start out. Like our last meeting, in March, the first few minutes will be full of strange, awkward silences and empty remarks that go nowhere. The broken rhythm of strangers. I can only hope that after two or three drinks Saul will start to loosen up.

"So it's good to finally meet the guys you work with," he says. "They seem okay."

"Yeah. Harry's a bit of a cunt, but the rest are all right."

Saul puffs out his lips and stares at the ground. There is a waitress about ten feet away moving gradually toward us, slim and nineteen. I try to catch her eye. A student, most probably, making her rent. She sees me, nods, and comes over.

"Glass of champagne, gentlemen?"

We each take a glass. Clear marble skin and a neat black bob, breasts visible as no more than faint shapes beneath the thin white silk of her shirt. She has that air of undergraduate self-confidence that gradually ebbs away with age.

"Thanks," says Saul, the side of his mouth curling up into a flirty smile. It is the most animated gesture he has made since he arrived. The girl moves off.

We have been talking for only ten or fifteen minutes when Cohen sidles up behind Saul with a look of intent in his eye. I take a long draw on my champagne and feel the chill and fizz in my throat.

"So you're Saul," he says, squeezing in beside him. "Alec's often spoken about you."

Not so.

"He has?"

"Yes."

Cohen reaches across and touches my shoulder, acting like we're best buddies.

"It's Harry, isn't it?" Saul asks.

"That's right. Sorry to interrupt but I wanted to introduce Alec to a journalist from the *Financial Times.* Won't you come with us?"

"Fine," I say, and we have no choice other than to go.

Peppiatt is tall, almost spindly, with psoriatic flakes of chalky skin grouped around his nose.

"Mike Peppiatt," he says, extending an arm, but his grip goes dead in my hand. "I understand you're the new kid on the block."

"Makes him sound like he's in a fucking boy band," Saul says, coming immediately to my defense. I don't need him to do that. Not tonight.

"That's right. I joined Abnex about nine months ago."

"Mike's interested in writing a piece about the Caspian," Cohen tells me.

"What's the angle?"

"I thought you might have some ideas." Peppiatt's voice is plummy, precise.

"Harry run out of them, has he?"

Cohen clears his throat.

"Not at all. He's been very helpful. I'd just welcome a second opinion."

"Well, what interests you about the region?" I ask, turning the question back on him. Something about his self-assuredness is irritating. "What do your readers want to know? Is it going to be an article on a specific aspect of oil and gas exploration or a more general introduction to the area?"

Saul folds his arms.

"Let me tell you what interests me," Peppiatt says, lighting a cigarette. He doesn't offer the pack around. Journalists never do. "I want to write an article comparing what's going on in the Caspian with the Chicago of the 1920s."

No one responds to this. We just let him keep talking.

"It's a question of endless possibilities," he says, launching a slim wrist into the air. "Here you have a region that's rich in natural resources, twenty-eight billion barrels of oil, two hundred and fifty trillion cubic feet of gas. Now there's a possibility that an awful lot of people are going to become very rich in a very short space of time because of that."

"So how is that like Chicago in the twenties?" Saul asks, just before I do.

"Because of corruption," Peppiatt replies, tilting his head to one side. "Because of man's lust for power. Because of the egomania of elected politicians. Because somebody somewhere, an Al Capone if you like, will want to control it all."

"The oligarchs?" I suggest.

"Maybe. Maybe a Russian, yes. But what fascinates me is that no country at the present time has a clear advantage over another. No one knows who owns all that oil. That hasn't been decided yet. Not even how to divide it up. It's the same with the gas. Who does it belong to? With that in mind, we're talking about a place of extraordinary potential. Potential for wealth, potential for corruption, potential for terrible conflict. And all of that concentrated into what is a comparatively small geographical area. Chicago, if you like."

"Okay—"

I had tried interrupting, but Peppiatt has still not finished.

"—But that's just one angle on it. The former Soviet states—Azerbaijan, Armenia, Kazakhstan—are just pawns in a much bigger geographical game. Look at a map of the region and you see the collision of all the great powers. China on the eastern flank of the Caspian Sea, Russia on its doorstep, the EU just a few hundred miles away to the west of Turkey. Then you have Afghanistan in the southeast and a fundamentalist Islamic republic right next door to that."

"Which one?" Saul asks.

"Iran," Cohen says, without looking at him.

"So you can see why the Yanks are in there," Peppiatt says, as if none of us was aware of an American presence in the Caspian. "They're over-reliant on Middle East oil and they're trying to get a piece of the action. And their best way of doing that is to toady up to the Turks. And why not? We Europeans treat the government in Ankara as though they were a bunch of good-for-nothing towel heads."

Saul snorts out a laugh here and I look around, just in case anyone has heard. But Peppiatt is on a roll. This guy loves the sound of his own voice.

"In my view it's an outrage that Turkey hasn't been offered membership in the EU. That will come back to haunt us. Turkey will be Europe's gateway to the Caspian, and we're allowing the Americans to get in there first."

"That's a little melodramatic," I tell him, but Cohen immediately looks displeased. He doesn't want me offending anyone from the *FT*.

"How so?" Peppiatt asks.

"Well, if you include Turkey in the EU, your taxes will go up and there'll be a flood of immigrants all over western Europe."

"Not my concern," he says, unconvincingly. "All I know is that the Americans are being very clever. They'll have a foot in the door when the Caspian comes online. There's going to be a marked shift in global economic power and America is going to be there when it happens."

"That's true," I say, my head doing an easy bob back and forth. Saul smiles.

"Only to an extent," Cohen says, quick to contradict me. "A lot of British and European oil companies are in joint ventures with the Americans to minimize risk. Take Abnex, for example." Here comes the PR line. "We got in at about the same time as Chevron in 1993."

"Did you?" says Peppiatt. "I didn't realize that."

Cohen nods proudly.

"Well, you see, that in itself will be interesting for my readers. I mean, are all these joint ventures between the multinational oil conglomerates going to make millions for their shareholders in five or ten years' time, or are they all on a hiding to nothing?"

"Let's hope not," says Cohen, giving Peppiatt a chummy smile. It's sickening how much he wants to impress him.

"You know what I think you should write about?" I say to him.

"What's that?" he replies briskly.

"Leadership. The absence of decent men."

"In what respect?"

"In respect of the increasing gap between rich and poor. If there aren't the right kind of politicians operating down there, men who care more about the future of their country than they do about their own comfort and prestige, nothing will happen. Look what happened to Venezuela, Ecuador, Nigeria."

"And what happened to them?" Peppiatt asks, his brow furrowing. I've found another gap in his knowledge.

"Their economies were crippled by oil booms in the 1970s. Agriculture, manufacturing, and investments were all unbalanced by the vast amounts of money being generated by oil revenues in a single sector of the economy. Other industries couldn't keep up. There was no one in power who foresaw that. The governments in the Caspian are going to have to watch out. Otherwise, for every oil tycoon fucking a call girl in the back of his chauffeur-driven Mercedes, there'll be a hundred Armenian farmers struggling to make enough money to buy a loaf of bread. And that's how wars start."

"I think that's a bit melodramatic, Alec," Cohen says, again smiling at Peppiatt, again trying to put a positive spin on things. "There's not going to be a war in the Caspian. There's going to be an oil boom for sure, but no one is going to get killed in the process."

"Can I quote you on that?" Peppiatt asks.

Cohen's eyes withdraw into calculation. That is what he wants most of all. His name in the papers, a little mention in the financial press.

"Of course," he says. "Of course you can quote me. But let me tell you a little bit about what our company is doing down there."

Saul catches my eye. I can't tell whether he's bored.

"Fine," says Peppiatt.

Cohen takes a step back.

"Tell you what," he says, suddenly looking at me. "Why don't you tell him, Alec? You could explain things just as effectively as me."

"All right," I reply, slightly off balance. "But it's quite straightforward. Abnex is currently conducting two-dimensional seismic surveys in several of Kazakhstan's one hundred and fifty unexplored offshore blocks. It's one of our biggest projects. Some of this is being done in conjunction with our so-called competitors as a joint venture, and some of it is being done independently without any external assistance. I can have details faxed to you tomorrow morning, if you like. What we want to do is start drilling exploration wells in two to three years' time if evidence of oil is found. We have sole exploration rights to six fields, thanks to the well-workover agreements negotiated by Clive Hargreaves, and we're very hopeful of finding something down there."

"I see." This may be too technical for Peppiatt. "That's a long and expensive business, I take it?"

"Sure. Particularly when you don't know what you're going to find at the end of the rainbow."

"That's just it, isn't it?" says Peppiatt, with something approaching glee. "The truth is you boys don't know *what* you've got down there. Nobody does."

And Saul says, "Print that."

12

MY FELLOW AMERICANS

This is when I see her for the first time, standing just a few yards away through a narrow break in the crowd. A sudden glimpse of the future.

She is wearing a backless cotton dress. For now, all that is visible is the delicate heave of her pale shoulder blades and the faultless valley of skin that lies between them. It is not yet possible to see her face. Her husband, twenty years older, is standing opposite her, bored as a museum guard. His back is stooped and his thick graying hair has been blown about by the wind that is whipping around the garden. You can tell right away that he is an American. It's in the confident breadth of his face, the particular blue of his shirt. He seems somehow larger than the people around him.

There is an older man standing with them, thinned out by age, his cheeks like little sacks. This is Doug Bishop, former CEO of Androm-eda, moved upstairs in 1994 but with one hand still on the tiller. The fourth member of the group is a monstrous suburban matron wearing pearls and Laura Ashley, her hair piled up in a beehive like an astronaut's wife. The pitch and yaw of her voice whinnies across the garden. These words are actually coming out of her mouth:

"And this is why I told my friend Lauren that feng shui is an ab-solute scandal. And Douglas agrees with me. Don't you, Doug?"

"Yes, dear," says Bishop, in a voice of great fatigue.

"And yet not only ordinary members of the public but actual cor-porations are prepared to pay hundreds of thousands of dollars to these Oriental tricksters just so's they can rearrange the alignment of their plant pots."

Listening to this, Katharine takes a sip of her drink and smiles weakly. Then she turns and her face is more clearly visible. Male heads in the immediate vicinity spring to catch a glimpse of her, alert as dogs.

"When were you thinking of writing the piece?" Cohen is asking Peppiatt. "In the near future or is this an ongoing project?"

"The latter, most definitely," Peppiatt replies, accepting a champagne refill from a passing waiter. "I want to talk to the tobacco industry, to car manufacturers, to all of these huge corporations who are making big moves into Central Asia."

The Hobbit comes up behind me.

"Can I have a word, Alec?"

I nod at the others and say, "Excuse me a moment. Back in a second."

"Sure," says Cohen.

When both of us are a few paces away, moving toward a corner of the garden, the Hobbit turns and says, "That's them. That's Katharine and Fortner."

"I know," I tell him, smiling, and he grins sheepishly, realizing that he has stated the obvious. He wouldn't have wanted to let on how nervous he is.

"We should do it now," he says "While Bishop is with them. I know him and I can introduce you."

"Good. Yes." I feel a slight lift in my stomach. "She's beautiful, isn't she?"

"Yeah," the Hobbit says wearily. "The whole fucking office fancies her."

And in that instant, Katharine seems to sense that we are talking about her. She turns her head and looks directly at me through the crowd, smiling in a single movement. It is as if the shape of her glance, the timing of it, has been minutely planned. My face freezes, and I cannot summon a smile. I merely stare back and then almost immediately look away. The Hobbit acts smartly, quick on his feet. He has smiled back at her, a colleague's acknowledgment, using the eye contact to legitimize our approach.

"Here we go," he says, moving toward her. "Bring Saul."

So, as we pass Cohen and Peppiatt, I extract him from their conversation.

"Come with me, will you, mate?" I say to him. "You remember Matt, don't you?" They met at my flat a few months ago, to ease this evening's events. "He wants to introduce us to some people he works with."

"Sure," Saul replies, acknowledging the Hobbit with a nod. "You don't mind, do you, guys?"

"No," they say in unison.

And we are on our way, the three of us moving through the crowd toward the Americans. My sense of nervousness is suddenly over-whelming.

"Mr. Bishop," the Hobbit says as we arrive, playing the ingratiating underling to great effect. "Could I just introduce you to an old friend of mine? Alec Milius. And Saul . . ."

"Ricken," says Saul.

"Of course."

Bishop transfers a glass of champagne to his left hand so that he can effect the handshakes.

"Good to make your acquaintance," he says. "How do you know Matthew here?"

"Long story," I tell him. "We met traveling in 1990 and just bumped into each other at a social occasion a few months ago."

This is also the story I told Saul.

"I see. Well, allow me to introduce my wife, Audrey."

"Pleased to meet you." She scans the two of us up and down.

"And this is Katharine Lanchester and her husband, Fortner Grice."

Katharine looks at me. There is now no flirtatiousness in her man-ner, not with Fortner so close.

"How do you do?"

"Very well, thank you," she says. Her hand is cool and soft.

Now it's Fortner's turn. He pumps my arm, doing a little side jerk with his head. His forehead is dark and creased by frown lines, as if he has spent a lifetime squinting up at a bright sun.

"Good to meet you guys," he says, very unruffled, very cool. "You in oil, like everybody else here?"

"With Abnex, yes. Caspian development."

"Oh right. Kathy and I work as consultants for Andromeda. Explo-ration. Geological surveying and so on."

"You spend much of your time down there?"

Fortner hesitates, clearing his throat with a stagey cough.

"Not for a while. They like to keep us in London. Yourself?"

"Ditto."

There is a gap in the conversation, to the point of becoming awkward. Doug takes a half step forward.

"We were just talking about politics back home," he says, taking a mouthful of champagne.

"We were," Beehive adds animatedly. "And I was asking why that grotesque man from Little Rock is living in the White House."

Bishop rolls his eyes as Fortner cuts in. He must weigh 200 or 220 pounds, and not much of it is fat.

"Now hold on there, Audrey. Clinton's been doin' a lot of good. We've all just been away from home too long."

"You think so, honey?" Katharine asks, disappointed that he should hold such an opinion. She's from Republican stock, New England money.

"Damn right I do," he replies forcefully, and the Hobbit laughs politely. Things are awkward again.

"Is anybody else hot?" Bishop asks.

"I'm okay, actually," Saul tells him.

"Me too," says Fortner. "Maybe you should be wearing a cocktail dress, Doug. You'd feel more comfortable."

I smile at this and Saul lights another cigarette.

"Can we go back to Clinton, for a moment?" Audrey is saying. Somebody on the far side of the garden drops a glass and there is a momentary hush. "What I mean to say is . . ." She loses herself, struggling to find the words. "Is it your interpretation that Clinton will be re-elected this year?"

"What do you guys think? You reckon our president will be re-elected in November?"

Katharine looked at Saul rather than me as she asked this, but it is the Hobbit who answers, "I think he'll be reelected, if only because Dole is too old."

"Mind what you're saying there, son," Douglas says to him, his voice low and sly. "Old Dole's only got a few years on me."

"So do the Brits like him, then?"

This comes from Audrey. She must have used up a can of hairspray tonight. Her beehive hasn't budged an inch in the wind.

"I think he has the most impressive grasp of insincerity that I've ever seen," I tell her, though that isn't the first time that I've used that phrase. It just sounds good coming out now. "I think the British people like him. We tend to admire your politicians more than our own, but it's a hypocritical approval. We wouldn't want any of them running our country."

"Why in hell not?" Fortner asks, and for a moment I am concerned that I may have annoyed him. Saul drops his half-finished cigarette on the ground and steps on the butt.

"Your political system is seen as being more corrupt than ours," I reply. "Unfairly, I think."

"Too right unfairly," he says. "What about Matrix Churchill? What about Westland? What about arms to Iraq?"

"The Scott Inquiry will clear everyone," Saul announces solemnly. "The old-boy network will see to that."

"Oh, yes," says Douglas wistfully. "The old-boy network."

"You wish you were a part of that, Doug?" Fortner says, nudging him. "An old Etonian? An Oxford man?"

"Princeton'll do me fine."

"So how long have you been with Abnex?"

Katharine wants to change the subject.

"About nine months."

"You enjoying it?"

"Yes and no. I've had to learn a lot in a short space of time. It's been a real eye-opener."

"An eye-opener," she says, as if she enjoys this expression. "So your background was in . . . ?"

"Russian and business studies."

"You just out of college?"

"No. I worked in marketing for a bit."

"Right."

Now Saul joins in. "How long have you and your husband been living here?"

"Long time now. About four years."

The Hobbit has cleverly started up a separate conversation with Bishop and Audrey, one that I cannot hear.

"And you enjoy it?"

"Oh, yeah." The heavy, interjectory way that Fortner comes forward, answering the question on Katharine's behalf, seems to reveal something about the dynamic of their relationship. "We love it here. Spending time with the allies. What do you do for a living, Saul?"

"I'm in advertising. Commercials. I'm an assistant director."

"And, what? That will lead into television, into movies?"

"Something like that," he replies. "I'm working on a script at the moment, trying to get some development money."

"What's it about?" Katharine asks.

"It's a kind of spoof thriller. A comedy about a serial killer."

"No shit," Fortner says, laughing. "A comedy about a serial killer?" He clearly thinks the idea is ludicrous. "I gotta say I prefer different kinds of movies myself. Old Bogarts and Cagneys. Westerns mainly."

"Really?" Saul replies enthusiastically. He is, albeit unwittingly, playing his role to perfection. "You like Westerns? Because the National Film Theatre is doing a John Wayne season at the moment."

"Is that right?" Fortner looks genuinely interested. "I didn't know that. I'd love to catch one or two. *The Searchers, Liberty Valance* . . ."

"Me too." I sensed immediately that I could use this as a way of establishing a bond between us. "I love Westerns. I think John Wayne is great."

"You do?" Saul has screwed up his face in surprise. I have to be careful that he doesn't undermine me.

"Yeah. It's a little fetish of mine. I used to watch them with Dad when I was growing up. Henry Fonda. Jimmy Stewart. But especially John Wayne."

Katharine clears her throat.

"So you like him too, Saul?" she asks, as if it is a test of character.

"Not as much as Clint," he replies. "But Wayne's great. One of the best."

"The best," says Fortner with emphasis. "Eastwood's just a pretty boy."

"Maybe it's a generational thing, honey," Katharine suggests. "Sorry, guys. My husband has a weakness for draft dodgers."

I don't know what she's referring to, and Fortner says, "What's that supposed to mean?"

"John Wayne didn't fight in World War Two," Saul informs him. "He did everything he could to avoid conscription."

"Right," says Katharine triumphantly.

"So what?" Fortner replies. Although his tone is aggressive, he may be enjoying the argument. "Wayne did more for the war effort as an actor than he ever coulda done getting shot at on Omaha Beach. He was a patriot, an anti-Communist—"

"—Who hated riding horses, hated wearing his cowboy outfits, and actively encouraged American participation in the Vietnam War," Katharine interrupts him in full flow. She has a brazen, mischievous intelligence, a self-confidence not dissimilar to Kate's.

"But he made some great films," Saul says, perhaps as a way of defusing what he thinks is tension.

And then the idea comes to me. As simple as it is shrewd. A way of guaranteeing a second encounter.

"Well, I have an idea," I suggest. "We should solve this by going to see one of these films at the NFT. I was going anyway. Why don't you join me?"

And without any hesitation, Fortner says, "Great," shrugging his shoulders. "You wanna go too, Saul?"

"Sure," he replies.

Katharine looks less enthused, a reaction that may be more instinctive than premeditated.

"Count me out," she says. "I can't stand Westerns. You fellas go right ahead. I'll stay home with Tom Hanks."

The Hobbit, Bishop, and Audrey have by now been pulled away into a larger group of six or seven people, two of whom are employees of Abnex. And, across the garden, David Caccia is coming down a short flight of stone steps, joining the party late. He catches my eye, but when he sees that I am with the Americans a mild look of concern passes across his face. In his right hand he is balancing a little pastry parcel oozing feta cheese.

"Is that David Caccia?" Fortner asks. "That guy looking at ya?"

"That's right."

"He and I had a couple of meetings back in the New Year. Tough negotiator. We were discussing the joint venture. You know about that?"

"A little. Fell through, I hear."

"That's right. Not a smart move if you ask me."

"I have to say—off the record—I agree with you."

My voice is quiet here, collaborative.

"You do?" Katharine seems surprised by my candor. This may be a good time to leave.

"Look, I have to have a word with him about something. Will you excuse us?"

Saul takes an instinctive step backward and Fortner says, "Sure, no problem. It sure was nice to meet you fellas."

He takes my hand and the shake is firmer than it was before. But I am worried that the plan to visit the NFT will be forgotten as a casual passing remark. I cannot mention it again at the risk of appearing pushy. The invitation will have to come from them.

Fortner now turns to Saul, and Katharine takes me to one side.

"Do you have a card?" she asks, holding a slim piece of embossed white plastic in her hand. "So Fort can get in touch about the movie."

Luck is on my side.

"Of course."

We exchange cards. Katharine studies mine carefully.

"Milius, huh? Like the name."

"Me too," says Fortner, breaking in from behind and slapping me hard on the back. "So we're set for John Wayne? Leave the womenfolk at home?"

Katharine adopts an expression of good-humored exasperation.

"Looking forward to it," I tell him. "I'll give you a call."

An hour later the Hobbit weaves toward me carrying a glass of sparkling mineral water. Saul is inside the club, talking to the waitress.

"Hi, Matt."

He looks slightly sheepish.

"How did you get on?"

"Very well. I think we're going to see each other again. I just bumped into them as they were leaving and we chatted for another ten minutes."

"Good," he says, picking a piece of lemon out of his drink and dropping it to the ground.

"Manners, Matthew."

"Nobody saw," he says, looking quickly left and right. "Nobody saw."

13

THE SEARCHERS

"So how did it go?"

Hawkes is leaning back in a molded plastic chair on the second floor of the Abnex building. The blinds are drawn in the small gray conference room, the door closed. His feet are up on the table, hands clasped behind his neck.

"Fine. Really well."

He arches his eyebrows, pressing me.

"And? Anything else? What happened?"

I lean forward, putting my arms on the table.

"I met Saul at seven for a drink in the bar. You know, where they have all those bookstalls under Waterloo Bridge."

Hawkes nods. The soles of his shoes are scuffed to the color of slate.

"Fortner was on time. Seven fifteen. We had another round of drinks, bought our tickets, and went in."

"Who paid?"

"For the drinks or the tickets?"

"Both."

"Everybody went dutch. Don't worry. There was no largesse."

Somebody walks past outside at a fast clip.

"Go on," he says.

As it always is when we are talking business, Hawkes's manner is abrupt to the point of being rude. Increasingly he has become a withdrawn figure, an enigma at the back of the room.

"Saul sat between us. There was no planning to it. It just worked out that way. We saw *The Searchers,* and afterward I told him we had to go to a party. Which we did."

"Did you invite him along?"

"I thought that would be pushing things."

"Yes," he says after a moment's contemplation. "But in your view Grice wasn't offended by that?"

I light a cigarette.

"Not at all. Look, I've obviously been thinking about what I was going to tell you this afternoon. And it's a measure of how well things went that I feel as if I have nothing of any significance to reveal. It was all very straightforward, very normal. It went exceptionally well. Fortner has a youthful side to his personality, like someone much younger. Just as you said he did. He fitted in, and if I'd invited him to the party, he would have fitted in there, too. He was making an effort, of course, but he's one of those middle-aged men who are hanging on to something youthful in their nature."

Hawkes folds his arms.

"So it wasn't at all awkward," I tell him. "When we were having the drink beforehand, we talked like we were old friends. It was a boys' night out."

"And how do you want to play it now?"

"My instinct is that they'll call."

"Why do you think that?"

"Because he likes me. Isn't that what you wanted?"

No reaction. Hawkes is assessing whether I have read the situation correctly.

I continue, "He left saying that Katharine wanted to have dinner sometime. He also wants to introduce Saul to a friend of his in advertising who used to be an actor. He's interested, believe me."

"But in Saul or in you?"

"What do you think?"

"That's what I'm asking," he says, not impatiently.

"Look. Saul has a lot of friends. Far more than I do. He likes Fortner, they laugh at each other's jokes, but there's no connection between them. Saul will fall by the wayside and resume his day-to-day life without even realizing he has brought the Americans to me. And then it'll just be the three of us."

14

THE CALL

Exactly two weeks later, at around three o'clock in the afternoon, J.T. walks over to my desk and presses a single sheet of Abnex-headed paper into my hand.

"You seen this?" he says.

"What is it?"

I save the file on my computer and turn to him.

"New staff memo. Unbelievable."

I begin to read.

While Abnex Oil fully respects the privacy of employees' personal affairs, it expects them to discharge fully their obligations of service to the company. It also requires them to be law-abiding, both inside and outside working hours. Remember that any indiscreet and/or antisocial behavior could not only affect an employee's performance and position, but also reflect badly on Abnex Oil.

"Jesus," I mutter.

"Too right. Fucking nanny state."

"Next they'll be telling us what to eat."

Cohen's desk faces mine. We work staring into each other's eyes. He looks up from his computer terminal and says, "What is that?"

"New memo. Just came up from personnel." J.T. looks at him. "Call it up on your e-mail. They've labeled it urgent. Some big-brother piece of shit instructing employees on how to conduct their private lives. Fucking disgrace."

"Did you manage to get those figures I asked you for at lunch?" Cohen asks him, ignoring the complaint entirely. He will not tolerate any hint of dissent on the team.

"No. I can't seem to get hold of the guy in Ankara."

"Well, will you keep trying, please? They'll be closing up and going home now."

"Sure."

J.T., suitably rebuked and sheepish, slopes back to his desk and picks up the phone. He leaves the memo beside my computer and I slide it into a drawer.

All seven members of the team, including Murray and Cohen, share a secretary. Tanya is an anglophone Canadian from Montreal with strong views on Quebec separatism and a boyfriend called Dan. She is big boned, thickset, and straightforward, and has been with the company since it started. Tanya wears a lot of makeup and piles her hair up high in a thick ebony bunch, which she never lets down.

"Only Dan gets to see my hair," she says.

No one has ever met Dan.

At half past three the telephone rings on my desk.

"Who is it, Tanya?"

"Someone from Andromeda."

I think that it may be the Hobbit, but then she says, "Katharine Lanchester. You want me to take a message?"

Cohen looks up, just a half glance, registering the name.

"No. I'll take it."

I was a day away, no more, from calling them myself.

From his desk nearby, Ben mutters, "Play hard to get, Alec. Birds love that."

"I'm putting her through."

"Okay."

Adrenaline now, my hand in my hair, pushing it out of my face.

"Alec Milius."

"Alec? It's Katharine Lanchester at Andromeda. Fortner's wife."

"Oh, hello. What can I do for you?"

"How are you?"

"Fine, thanks. It's good to hear from you."

"Well, Fort so enjoyed going to the movies with you. Said he had a great time."

Her voice is quick and enthused.

"Yes. You missed a good film."

"Oh, I can't stand Westerns. Guys in leather standing in the middle of the street twirling six-shooters, seeing who blinks first. I prefer something more contemporary."

"Sure."

"Still, I had a nice dinner with Fortner afterward and he told me all about it. Matter of fact, that's why I was calling. I was wondering if you and maybe Saul would like to have dinner sometime?"

"Sure, I—"

"I mean I don't know if you're free, but . . ."

"No, no, not at all, I'd like that very much. I'll ask him and I'm sure he'd like to."

"Good. Shall we set a date?"

"Okay."

"When are you not taken up?"

"Uh, anytime next week except—just let me check my diary."

I know that I'm free every night. I just don't want it to appear that way.

"How about Wednesday?"

"Terrific. Wednesday it is. So long as Saul can make it."

"I'm sure he'll be able to."

Cohen's eyes are fixed on the far wall. He is listening in.

"How's Fortner?" I ask.

"Oh, he's good. He's in Washington right now. I'm just hoping that he'll be back in time. He's got a lot of work to get through out there."

"So where shall we meet?"

"Why don't we just say the In and Out again? Just at the gate there, eight o'clock?"

She had that planned.

"Fine."

"See you there, then."

"I'll look forward to it."

I hang up and there is a rush of blood in my head.

"What was all that?" Cohen asks, chewing the end of a pencil.

"Personal call."

15

TIRAMISU

The only spy who can provide a decent case for ideology is George Blake. Young, idealistic, impressionable, he was posted by SIS to Korea and kidnapped by the Communists shortly after the 1950 invasion. Given *Das Kapital* to read in his prison cell, Blake became a disciple of Marxism, and the KGB turned him after he offered to betray SIS. "I'd come to the conclusion that I was no longer fighting on the right side," he later explained.

Upon his release in 1953, Blake returned to England a hero. He had suffered terribly in captivity and was seen to have survived the worst that communism could throw at him. There is television footage of Blake at Heathrow Airport, modest before the world's press, a bearded man hiding a terrible secret. For the next eight years, working as an agent of the KGB, he betrayed every secret that passed across his desk, including Anglo-American cooperation on the construction of the Berlin Tunnel. His treachery is considered to have been more damaging even than Philby's.

Blake was caught more by a process of elimination than by distinguished detective work. SIS summoned him to Broadway Buildings, knowing that they had to extract a confession from him or he would walk free. After three days of fruitless interrogation, in which Blake denied any involvement with the Soviets, the SIS officer in charge of the case played what he knew was his final card.

"Look," he said, "we know you're working for the Russians, and we understand why. You were a prisoner of the Communists, they tortured you. They blackmailed you into betraying SIS. You had no choice."

This was too much for George.

"No!" he shouted, rising from his chair. "Nobody tortured me! Nobody blackmailed me! I acted out of a belief in communism."

There was no financial incentive, he told them, no pressure to approach the KGB.

"It was quite mechanical," he said. "It was as if I had ceased to exist."

The platforms and escalators of Green Park underground station are thick with trapped summer heat. The humidity follows me as I clunk through the ticket barriers and take a flight of stairs up to street level. The tightly packed crowds gradually thin out as I move downhill toward the In and Out Club.

I am casually dressed, in the American style: camel-colored chinos, a blue button-down shirt, old suede loafers. Some thought has gone into this, some notion of what Katharine would like me to be. I want to give an impression of straightforwardness. I want to remind her of home.

I see Fortner first, about fifty yards farther down the street. He is dressed in an old, baggy linen suit, wearing a white shirt, blue deck shoes, and no tie. At first I am disappointed to see him. There was a possibility that he would still be in Washington, and I had hoped that Katharine would be waiting for me alone. But it was inevitable that Fortner would make it: there's simply too much at stake for him to stay away.

Katharine is beside him, more tanned than I remember, making gentle bobbing turns on her toes and heels, her hands gently clasped behind her back. She is wearing a plain white T-shirt with loose charcoal trousers and light canvas shoes. The pair of them look as if they have just stepped off a ketch in St. Lucia. They see me now, and Katharine waves enthusiastically, starting to walk in my direction. Fortner lumbers just behind her, his creased pale suit stirring in the breeze.

"Sorry. Am I late?"

"Not at all," she says. "We only just got here ourselves."

She kisses me. Moisturizer.

"Good to see ya, Milius," says Fortner, giving me a butch, pumping handshake and a wry old smile. But he looks tired underneath the joviality, far off and jet-lagged. Perhaps he came here directly from Heathrow.

"I like your suit," I tell him, though I don't.

"Had it for years. Made in Hong Kong by a guy named Fat."

We start walking toward The Ritz.

"So it was great that you could make it tonight."

"I was glad you rang."

"Saul not with you?"

"He couldn't come in the end. Sends his apologies. Had to go off at the last minute to shoot an advert."

I never asked Saul to come along. I don't know where he is or what he's up to.

"That's too bad. Maybe next time." Katharine moves some loose hairs out of her face. "Hope you won't be bored."

"Not at all. I'm happy it being just the three of us."

"You gotta girlfriend, Milius?"

I don't mind it too much that Fortner has decided to call me that. It suggests a kind of intimacy.

"Not at the moment. Too busy. I used to have one but we broke up."

This is quietly registered by both of them, another fact about me. We continue along the street, the silence lengthening.

"So where are we heading?" I ask, trying to break it, trying to stop any sense that we might have nothing to say to one another. I must keep talking to them. I must earn their trust.

"Good question," says Fortner, loudly clapping his hands. It is as if I have woken him up from a nap. "Kathy and I have been going to this place for years. We thought we'd show it to you. It's a small Italian restaurant that's been owned by the same Florentine family for decades. Maître d' goes by the name of Tucci."

"Sounds great."

Katharine's attention has been distracted. There are hampers, golf bags, and elegant skirts on display in the windows of Fortnum & Mason and she has stopped to look at them. I am watching her when Fortner puts his hand on my shoulder and says, "I like this part of town." He's decided to play the avuncular card right away. "It's so . . . *anachronistic,* so Merchant Ivory, you know? Round here, an English gentleman can still get his toast done on one side, have an ivory handle attached to his favorite shooting stick, get a barber to file his nails down and rub his neck with cologne. You got your bespoke shirts, your customized suits. Look at all this stuff."

"You like that, honey?" Katharine asks, pointing at a smart two-piece ladies' outfit in a window.

"Not a whole lot," Fortner replies, his mood abruptly fractious. "Why, you wanna get it?"

"No. Just askin'."

"Well, I'm hungry," he says. "Let's go eat."

The restaurant has an outside staircase flaked with dried moss leading down to a basement. Fortner, walking ahead of us, clumps down the steps and through the heavy entrance door. He doesn't bother holding it open for Katharine. He just wants to get inside and start eating. Katharine and I are left on the threshold and I hold the door open for her, letting her glide past me with a whisper of thanks that is almost conspiratorial.

The restaurant is only half full. There's a small clearing immediately inside the entrance, where we are met by a paunchy, hair-oiled Italian in late middle-age. Fortner already has his arm wrapped around him, with a big, fulfilled smile all over his face.

"Here they come now," he is saying as we come through the door, his voice hearty and full of good cheer. "Tucci, let me introduce you to a young friend of ours, Mr. Alec Milius. Very smart guy in the oil business."

"Nice to meet you, sir," says Tucci, shaking my hand, but he hasn't even looked at me. His eyes have been fixed on Katharine since she walked in.

"And your beautiful wife, Mrs. Grice," he says. "How are you, my dear?"

Katharine bends to meet Tucci's puckered kiss, offering him a smooth, pale cheek. She doesn't bother explaining that Grice isn't her surname.

"You look as beautiful as ever, madam."

"Oh, you're incorrigible, Tucci. So charming."

The slimy old bastard leads us downstairs into a dark basement where we are shown to a small table covered in a faded red cloth and cutlery. The decor is very seventies, but it isn't consciously retro. Cheap wood carvings line the walls and there are candles in old wicker flasks on shelves. Hardened wax clings to their sides like jewelery.

Fortner shuffles onto a sofa attached to the wall and Tucci pins the table up against his legs. I take the chair to Fortner's right and Katharine sits opposite me. Three of us in a booth. Rather than have one of his dumb-looking Sicilian studs do it, Tucci then goes back upstairs and brings down three menus and a wine list, thereby giving himself as much time as possible with Katharine. All of his premeal small talk is addressed to her. *That's a lovely dress, Mrs. Grice. Have you been on holiday? You look so well.* By contrast, Fortner and I are treated with something approaching contempt. Eventually, Fortner loses his cool and tells Tucci to bring us some drinks.

"Right away, Mr. Fortner. Right away. I have a nice bottle of Chianti you try. And some Pellegrino, perhaps?"

"Whatever. That'd be great."

Fortner takes off his jacket to eat, tossing it in a crumpled heap onto the sofa beside him. Then he undoes the top three buttons of his shirt and inserts a napkin, mafia-style, below his neck. His chest hair is clearly visible, tight black curls like cigarette burns.

In the early part of the meal we do not talk about any aspect of the oil business. I am not tapped for information, for tips and gossip, nor do Katharine and Fortner discuss ongoing projects at Andromeda. I have ordered veal, but it is tough and bland. Both Americans are having the same thing—plump breasts of chicken in what appears to be a mushroom cream sauce; it looks a lot better than mine. We share out french beans and potato croquettes and get through the first bottle of red wine within half an hour.

We get along fine, better even than I had expected. Everything is easy and enjoyable. The generation gap between us, as was proved by the trip to the NFT, is no hindrance at all. Although Fortner's age is in some ways accentuated by the vigor of his younger bride, he has that certain playfulness about him that largely offsets his age.

Still, I cannot work out why Katharine would ever have chosen to marry him. Fortner is handsome, yes, with a certain gruff charm and a full head of hair, but close up, sitting near her in the dim light of the restaurant, the virility dissipates: he suffers by comparison, looking blotchy and liquor-sick, just another man on the wrong side of fifty. With a few drinks inside him, Fortner has a nice, sly sarcastic manner that he can get away with on account of his age—in a younger man, it would look like arrogance—yet there is a quality of solipsism about him that overshadows any occasional glints of mischief. As I felt when I first met him, though Fortner looks to have experienced a great deal, he appears to have learned very little from those experiences. There is even an element of stupidity in him. He can at times appear almost a fool.

Yet his attitude toward Katharine is not one of deference and admiration. He is often short with her, critical and dismissive. At one point, just as I am finishing off my veal, she embarks on a story about her college days at Amherst. Before she has really begun, Fortner is interrupting her, telling her not to bore Alec with stories from her youth. Then he simply takes the conversation off on a separate tangent with which he is more at ease. This is done consciously, as a premeditated recrimination, but Katharine barely seems to mind. It is as if she has accepted the subjugatory role of pupil, like a student who has moved in with her tutor and finds herself living in his shadow. This is not how things should be. Katharine is smarter, quicker-witted, and more subtle, in her views and manner, than Fortner. He is gauche by comparison.

Just once or twice her face registers impatience when Fortner goes too far, though I sense that this may be largely for my benefit, another tactic she employs in flirtation. Nevertheless, it is all the more pointed for being concealed from him. By the time the pudding menus arrive I am convinced that she is starved of simple affections and would cherish a little attention.

Tucci recommends the tiramisu and flatters Katharine by telling her that she is the last person on earth who should worry about putting on weight. She will not be persuaded and orders fruit instead. Fortner asks if the restaurant still serves ice cream, and Tucci gives him a slightly withering look before saying yes. Fortner then orders a large bowl of mint choc chip. I ask for the tiramisu, and Tucci disappears upstairs with our order.

This is when they finally ask me a question about Abnex.

"How long have you been there?" Katharine inquires, rearranging her napkin so that it forms a neat square on her lap.

"About nine months."

"You like it?"

She has asked me this before. At the party.

"Yes. I find the work interesting. I'm underpaid and the hours are antisocial, but I have prospects."

"Boy, you really know how to sell it," Fortner mutters.

"You've just got me on a bad day. I had an argument with my boss earlier. He comes down hard when things don't go his way."

"What did you do wrong?" Katharine asks.

"That's just it. I didn't."

"Okay then," she says patiently. "What does he think you did wrong?"

I get all the components of the story straight in my mind, then kick off.

"He told me to set up a meeting with an associate of his, who I think is unreliable. Name of Warner. This guy is an old friend of Alan's, so he feels a residual loyalty toward him. In other words, he's prepared to overlook the fact that Warner's a loser. Alan knows I think this, and it's almost as if he enjoys giving me as much contact with him as possible."

Fortner's head drops slightly, his eyes moving slowly across the table.

"Anyway, Warner didn't return any of my calls for a week. I must have been ringing him five times a day. I needed some figures. Eventually I gave up and just got them from someone else. Alan went spastic, said I'd gone over his head and questioned his authority. And I'm at Abnex on a trial basis, so it doesn't bode well."

"A trial basis?" says Fortner, looking up immediately. He hadn't stopped listening to me. "You mean you're not a full-time employee?"

"I'm halfway through a trial period. I have to attain a consistently high standard of work or they'll kick me out."

"Jesus," says Katharine, swallowing a mouthful of Chianti. "That's a lot of pressure to work under."

"Yeah," adds Fortner. "You're a human being, not a Cadillac."

I laugh at this, making a snorting noise loud enough to cause someone at a neighboring table to look up and stare at me. I bring my napkin to my face and dab away an imaginary speck. Keep going.

"The trouble is that they don't give me any indication of how well I'm doing. There's very little in the way of compliments or praise."

"I think people need that, the encouragement," Katharine says.

"That's right," says Fortner, his voice going deep and meaningful. "So is that usual for young guys like yourself to get hired by a company and then, you know, just see how it pans out?"

"I guess so. I have friends in a similar kind of position. And there's not a hell of a lot we can do about it. It's work, you know?"

The pair of them nod sympathetically, and, sensing that this is the best opportunity, I decide to tell them now about my interviews with SIS last year. It is a great risk, but Hawkes and I have decided that to tell the Americans about SIS may actually draw me further into their confidence. To conceal the information might arouse suspicion.

"It's funny," I say, taking a sip of wine. "I nearly became a spy."

Katharine looks up first, vaguely startled.

"What?" she says.

"I probably shouldn't be telling you, Official Secrets Act and all that, but I got approached by MI6 a few months before I got the job at Abnex."

Not missing a beat, Katharine says, "What is MI6? Like your version of the CIA?"

"Yes."

"Jesus. That's so . . . so James Bond. So . . . are you . . . I mean, are . . . ?"

"Of course he's not, honey. He's not gonna be sitting here telling us all about it if he's in MI6."

"I'm not a spy, Katharine. I didn't pass the exams."

"Oh," she says. "I'm sorry."

"Why? Why are you sorry?"

"Well, weren't you disappointed?"

"Not at all. If they didn't think I was good enough for the job, then fuck 'em."

"That's a great attitude," Fortner exclaims. "A great attitude."

"How else am I supposed to react? I went through three months of vetting and interviewing and IQ tests and examinations, and at the end of it all, after they'd more or less told me I was certain to get in, they turned around and shut me out. With a *phone* call. Not a letter or a meeting. A phone call. No explanation, no reason why."

My sense of disappointment should be clear to them.

"You must have been devastated."

But I don't want to overplay the anger.

"At the time, I was. Now I'm not so sure. I had a pretty idealistic view of the Foreign Office, but from what I can gather it's not like that at all. I had images of exotic travel, of dead drops and seven-course dinners in the Russian embassy. Nowadays it's all pen pushing and equal opportunities. Right across the board, the Civil Service is being filled up with bureaucrats and suits, people who have no problem toeing the party line. Anybody with a wild streak, anyone with a flash of the unpredictable, is ruled out. There are no rough edges anymore. The oil business has more room for adventure, don't you think?"

They both nod. It looks as though the gamble has paid off.

"Sorry. I don't mean to rant."

"No, no, not at all," says Katharine, laying her hand on my sleeve. A good sign. "It's good to hear you talk about it. And I have two things I wanna say." She refills my glass, draining the bottle in the process. "One, I can't believe that a guy as smart and together as you didn't make it. And two, if your government doesn't have sense enough to know a good thing when it sees one, well then, that's their loss."

And with that she raises her glass and we do a three-way clink over the table.

"Here's to you, Alec," says Fortner. "And screw MI6."

While we are eating pudding something odd happens between Fortner and Katharine, something I had not expected to see.

I have been given a large bowl of tiramisu and Katharine is insisting on tasting it. Fortner tells her to leave me alone, but she ignores him, sliding her spoon into the ooze on my plate and retrieving it with her hand held underneath, catching stray droplets of cream.

"It's good," she says, swallowing, and turns to Fortner.

"Can I try yours, sweetie?"

He rears back, shielding his bowl with his hand.

"No way," he says indignantly. "I don't want your germs."

There is a startled pause before she says, "I'm your wife, for Chrissakes."

"Makes no difference to me. I don't want any foreign saliva on my mint choc chip."

Katharine is embarrassed, as am I, and she stands up just a few seconds later to go to the ladies'.

"Sorry, Milius," Fortner grunts, now shamed into regret. "I get real touchy about that kinda thing."

"I understand," I tell him. "Don't worry."

To smooth things over, he starts telling me a story about how the two of them met, but the ease has gone out of the evening. Fortner knows that he has slipped up, that he has shown me a side of himself he had intended to remain concealed.

"You want coffee, honey?" he asks timidly when Katharine comes back. I can tell straight away that she has forgiven him, gathered herself together in the ladies' and taken a deep breath. There is no hint of admonishment or frustration on her face.

"Yeah. That'll be nice," she says, grinning. She has put on a new coat of lipstick. "You boys having one?"

"We are."

"Good. Then I'll have an espresso."

And the incident passes.

Half an hour later we emerge into the darkness of W1. Fortner, who has picked up the bill, puts his arm around Katharine and walks east, looking around for a cab. The weight of his arm seems to be pulling her down on one side.

"We gotta do this again sometime," she says. "Right, honey?"

"Oh, yeah."

High up to the left, Katharine gazes at the postcard lights of Piccadilly Circus and says how she never grows tired of looking at them. We walk down the hill toward Waterloo Place and pass the statue commemorating the Crimea.

There are no cabs in sight, but an old red Audi curb-crawls us on the corner of Pall Mall. An unlicensed taxi. Fortner looks over nervously as the driver lowers the window on the passenger side and mutters, "Cab?" under his breath. I lean down and tell him no thanks. He pulls away.

"Did you want to go with him?" I ask.

"No, we'll get a black," Fortner replies firmly.

And no sooner has he said this than one shows up.

"You sure you don't want it?" Katharine says, kissing me on both cheeks.

"No," I tell her. "I'm going to catch a train from Charing Cross."

"Well, it was lovely seeing you."

"Give me a ring," I say as she climbs in behind Fortner. I can see the slim outline of her arse and a long slender thigh taut against the cloth of her charcoal trousers.

"We will," he shouts out.

It went well.

16

HAWKES

Hawkes leaves the country for the next four and a half months, ostensibly on Abnex business, although I am increasingly of the view that he is involved in other projects with at least one other company. In his absence my encrypted reports are sent to John Lithiby, who has not contacted me directly since the beginning of the year. I have taken this as a sign of his approbation.

There is a rumor in the office—no more than that—that Hawkes has a girlfriend in Venice. When we meet in the gray conference room on the second floor for our first debriefing of the summer, he has just returned from a ten-day break "in northern Italy."

"Nice this time of year?" I ask him.

"Crowded," he says.

Lithiby will have informed Hawkes of the progress of my relationship with Katharine and Fortner: the Sunday lunch I cooked for them at my flat in May, with the Hobbit, his girlfriend, and Saul in attendance; the night we watched England lose on penalties to Germany in a pub on Westbourne Grove; the Saturday afternoon when Fortner got sick, and Katharine and I ended up going to the cinema together. It is the record of a gradually improving acquaintance, all of it planned and analyzed to the last detail.

"John said something about a drive you took with Fortner the week before last. Could you tell me more about that?"

I have been fiddling with my mobile phone, which I now place on the table in front of me.

"He wanted to see Brighton, said he'd never been there."

"Where was Katharine?"

"Visiting a pregnant friend."

"What did you talk about?"

"It's in the report, Michael."

"I want to hear it from you."

I have difficulty casting my mind back to that afternoon. There is an important call coming through from an Abnex client in Russia this evening, and I am eager to get back to my desk to prepare for it.

"It was normal. I told him about my problems at Abnex."

"What kind of problems?"

"Made-up stuff. Not getting enough money, that kind of thing."

"Don't overplay that," he says, one of the few times that Hawkes has hinted at any concern over the way I am handling things.

"I won't," I tell him, lighting a cigarette. "Fort likes to give me advice about the business, tells me how to handle Alan and Harry. He gets a kick out of it."

"Playing the father figure?"

I hesitate here, uncomfortable with the analogy.

"If you want to call it that, yes. He likes to think of himself as someone who helps out the younger generation. He tried to set Saul up with a contact he had in advertising."

"Did anything come of that?"

"Don't think so. Anyway, we chatted, drove around, had some coffee. I managed to bring up that conversation you suggested."

"Which one?"

"You wanted me to complain to them about our government doing anything the Americans tell it to."

"I do recall that, yes."

"As a matter of fact, I think I used your phrase: 'We've been hanging on to the shirttails of every presidential administration since Franklin Roosevelt.'"

"And how did Fortner respond?"

"Coolly, I would say. That's the word I used in my report. I told him I felt Britain had become the fifty-first American state. Ask nicely, and we'll bomb Baghdad. Just say the word and you can use our runways. You know the kind of argument. Cut us a deal and you can borrow our aircraft carriers, our military installations. Even our soldiers, for Christ's sake."

"You're not trying to defect, Alec," he says suddenly, cackling at his own joke. "I trust you didn't go too far?"

"Relax," I tell him. "Fortner agreed with everything I said."

"And Katharine. How is she?"

"Very flirtatious. That's still the predominant tactic. Little arguments every now and again with Fortner, then a little glance at me for sympathy. She's very touchy-feely. But that may be just a Yank thing."

Hawkes straightens up in his chair.

"Keep using the sexual element," he says, with the detachment of a doctor discussing a prescription. "Don't go too far, but don't shut her out."

"I won't."

"When are you next seeing them?"

"This weekend. Fortner's gone to Kiev for the pipeline conference. Katharine called me almost as soon as he left for the airport."

"She did?"

"Yeah. Asked if I wanted to spend Saturday with her. Go for a walk in Battersea Park."

"Let me know how it goes," he says.

Feeling oddly confident, I decide to press him on something.

"Any news on the job? Has Lithiby said anything about taking me on full-time?"

Hawkes withdraws slightly, as if offended by the question. As far as he is concerned, this matter has already been dealt with.

"Things remain as they were," he says. "If the operation is a success, the Security Service will consolidate its relationship with you. Your position will become permanent."

"That was always the precondition," I say, speaking for him. And in a tired echo, Hawkes says, "Yes. That was always the precondition."

17

THE SPECIAL RELATIONSHIP

Standing easy against the fridge in the kitchen at Colville Gardens, Katharine sweeps hair out of her face and says, "Alec, I'm gonna take a shower, is that all right? I'm kinda hot after our walk. If the phone rings, the machine'll pick it up. You be okay for a bit; watch TV or something?"

"Sure."

Her cheeks have rouged to a healthy flush after being outside in the fresh air of Battersea Park.

"Why don't you fix us a drink while I'm gone?"

I know what she likes: a fifty-fifty vodka tonic in a tall glass with a lot of ice and lemon.

"You want a vodka and tonic?"

She smiles, pleased by this. "That'd be great. I've got olives in the refrigerator."

"Not for me."

"Okay. Leave 'em. They're really for Fort. He eats them like candy."

The kitchen is open plan, chrome, gadget filled. Their entire apartment is expensively decked out, but clearly rented, with no evidence of personal taste. Just a few photographs, some CDs, and an old clock on the wall.

"You like a lot of lemon, don't you?" I ask as Katharine crosses to a cupboard above the sink. She takes down two highball glasses and a bottle of Smirnoff Blue and sets them on the counter. She is tall enough to reach up without standing on tiptoe.

"Yeah. A lot of lemon. Squeeze it in."

I move toward the fridge and open the freezer door.

"That'll be the best ice you ever had," she says from behind me.

"The best *ice*? How come?"

"Fort's started putting Volvic in the tray. Says he read somewhere it's the only way to avoid getting too much lead or something."

I half laugh and retrieve the tray. By the time I turn round, Katharine has left the room. I break out two cubes and throw them gently into a glass. Then I pour myself a double vodka and sink it in a single gulp.

Gladiators is on ITV.

I look around the other three channels, but there's nothing on, so I mute the sound and flick through a copy of *Time Out*. There's a swamp of plays and films on in London that I will never get to see because of work. All that entertainment, all those ideas and stories just passing me by.

After about ten minutes, I hear a rustle at the sitting-room door and look up to see Katharine coming in. She is wearing a dark blue dressing gown over white silk pajamas, her hair still wet from the shower, combed back in long, straight even strands. She looks up at me and smiles with softened wide eyes.

"Good shower?" I ask, just to disguise my surprise.

"Great, thanks. Oh, are you watchin' *Gladiators*?" She sounds excited, picking up the remote control and putting the sound back on. The thin silk of her dressing gown flutters as she sits beside me, releasing an exquisite mist of warm lathered soap. "The British version of this show is much better than ours."

"You actually watch this?"

"I find it intriguingly barbaric. She's pretty, huh, the blond one?"

The dour Scots referee says, "Monica, you will go on my first whistle. Clare, you will go on my second whistle," and before long two tracksuited PE teachers are chasing each other around the Birmingham NEC.

"So, you hungry?" Katharine asks, turning away from the screen to face me. "I'm gonna make us some supper."

"That'd be great."

I am still getting over the pajamas.

"You wanna stay here or help me out?"

"I'll come with you."

In the kitchen, Katharine goes to the fridge and takes out a tray of freshly made ravioli, which I make all the right noises about. *Did you make them yourself? That's amazing. So much better than the packaged stuff.* The delicate shells are coated in a thin dusting of flour, and she sets them down beside the fridge. I help by putting a large pan of salted water on the stove, placing a lid on top, and turning the gas up high. The speed of the ignition makes me jerk my head back and Katharine asks if I'm okay. Oh, yes, I say, as the blue flames glow and roar. Then I sit on a tall wooden stool on the far side of the kitchen counter and watch as she prepares a salad.

"I'll teach you a trick," she says, crunching down on a stick of celery, like a toothpaste ad. "If you've got yourself a tired lettuce like this one, just stick it in a bowl of cold water for a while and it'll freshen right up."

"Handy."

I can think of nothing worthwhile to say.

"You never had your drink," I tell her, looking over at the sink, where the ice in her vodka tonic has melted into a tiny ball.

"Oh that's *right*," she exclaims. "I knew there was something missing. Will you fix me a fresh one?"

"Of course."

The bottle of Smirnoff is still sitting out and I mix two fresh vodka and tonics as she washes a colander at the sink. This will be my third drink of the evening.

"There you go," I say, handing it to her. Our fingers do not touch. She takes a sip and lets out a deep sigh.

"God, you make these so good. How'd you know how to do that?"

"My father taught me."

She sets the glass on the counter and starts slicing up some tomatoes, a cucumber, and the sticks of celery on a wooden chopping board, throwing them gently into a large teak bowl. Steam has started to rise in thick clouds from the pan on the stove, rattling the lid, but rather than do anything about it, I say, "Water's boiling, Kathy."

"You wanna get it, honey? I'm kinda busy."

"Sure."

I remove the lid, twist the dial to low, and watch the water subside into little ripples.

Honey. She called me honey.

Katharine stops chopping and comes to stand beside me. She has a wooden spoon in her hand and says, "Let's put the pasta on, shall we?"

And now very carefully, one by one, she lowers the ravioli pillows into the water on the wooden spoon, intoning, "This is the tricky bit, this is the tricky bit," in a low voice that is almost a whisper. I am beside her, watching, doing nothing, my shoulder inches from hers. When she is done I walk away from the stove and sit back down on the stool. Katharine brings out a large white plate, a flagon of olive oil, some balsamic vinegar, and a basket of sliced ciabatta. These she places on the counter in front of me. Still clutching the basket, she turns around to face the stove and the silk of her dressing gown rides up to the elbow. Her bared arm is slender and brown, the long fingers of her flushed pink hands crowned by filed white nails.

"The trick is not to let the water boil too fast," she says, talking to the opposite wall. "That way the ravioli doesn't break up."

She turns back to face me and the sleeve of her gown slips back down her arm. Even with all the flavors and steam around us, the smell of her is lifting from her hair and shower-warmed skin.

"You'll love this," she says, looking down at the counter. She picks up the flagon of oil and pours it onto the plate in a thin, controlled line that creates a perfect olive circle. Then she allows tiny droplets of balsamic vinegar to fall into the green center of the plate, forming neat black orbs that float loose in the viscous liquid.

"Dip the bread in," she says, showing me how with a crusty slice of her own. "It tastes so good."

I take a smaller chunk of bread from the basket and run it through the oil.

"Try to get a little more of the oil than the vinegar," she says.

I swirl the bread around and leave cloudy crumbs amid the black and green spirals.

"Sorry. Messy."

"Don't worry," she says, licking her lips. I take my first mouthful, sweet and rich. "Tastes good, huh?"

We eat the ravioli sitting at the kitchen table, and consume the better part of a bottle of Chablis by quarter past nine. As Katharine is taking the plates to the sink, the telephone rings and she goes next door to answer it, padding there softly in bare feet. From the tone of the conversation, I presume that it's Fortner. There's no forced politeness in Katharine's voice, just the easy familiarity of long-term couples. At no point does she mention that I am in the next room, though there's a section of the conversation that I can't hear owing to a car alarm triggering in Colville Gardens. When it is finally shut off, I overhear Katharine say, "You could say that, yes," and, "Absolutely," with a guardedness that leads me to assume they are talking about me. It will be past midnight in Kiev.

"That was Fort," she says, breezing back into the kitchen a few moments later. "He says hi. Jesus, those fucking vehicle alarms."

She wouldn't ordinarily say "fucking" unless she'd had a few drinks.

"I know, I heard it."

"What's the point of them, anyway? Nobody pays any attention when they go off. They don't prevent car crime. Everybody just ignores them. You wanna coffee or something? I'm making myself one."

"Instant?"

" 'Fraid so."

"No, thanks."

"You're such a snob about coffee, Alec."

"Nescafé is just an interestingly flavored milk drink. You shouldn't tolerate it. I'm going for a pee, okay?"

"You do what you have to, sweetie."

The bathroom is at the far end of the apartment, through the sitting room and down a long corridor that passes the entrance to the flat. The bathroom door is made of light wood with an unoiled hinge that squeaks like a laughing clown when I open it. I walk in and slide the lock. There is a mirror hung above the sink and I check my reflection, seeing tiny pimples dotted along my forehead, which can't look good in the stark white light of the kitchen. The rest of my face is blanched and I push out my lips and cheeks to bring some color back into them. Once a little red flush has appeared, I go back outside.

Walking toward the sitting room, I steal a look through the door of their bedroom, which Katharine has left open after her shower. This is the most basic sort of invasion, but it is something I have to do. There are clothes, shoes, and several issues of *The New Yorker* strewn on the floor. I walk farther inside, my eyes shuttling around the room, taking in every detail. There is a fine charcoal sketch of a naked dancer on the wall above the bed, and a discarded bottle of mineral water by the window.

I go back out into the corridor and hear the distant running of water at the kitchen sink. Katharine is washing up. There is another bedroom farther down on the right side of the passage, again with its door open. Again I look through it as I am passing, prying behind her back. An unmade bed is clearly visible on the far side, with one of Fortner's trademark blue shirts lying crumpled on the sheets. An American paperback edition of *Presumed Innocent* has been balanced on the windowsill, and there are bottles of cologne on a dresser near the door. Is it possible that they no longer share a room? There are too many of Fortner's possessions in here for him simply to have taken an afternoon nap.

I walk quietly back to the first bedroom. This time I notice that the bed has been slept in only on one side. Katharine's creams and lotions are all here, with skirts and suits on hangers by the door. But there are no male belongings, no ties or shoes. A photograph in a gilt frame by the window shows a middle-aged man on a beach with a face like an old sweater. But there are no pictures of Fortner, no snaps of him arm in arm with his wife. Not even a picture from their wedding.

No noise in the corridor. On a side table I spot a heavy, leatherbound address book and pick it up. The alphabetized guides are curled and darkened with use, each letter covered in a thin film of dirt. I check the *A*s, scanning the names quickly.

AT&T
Atwater, Donald G.
Allison, Peter and Charlotte
Ashwood, Christopher
AM Management
Acorn Alarms

No Allardyce. That's a good sign.

To *B,* on to the *C*s, then a flick through to *R*. Sure enough, at the bottom of the third page:

Bar Reggio
Royal Mail
Ricken, Saul

His full address and telephone number are there as well. I have to get back to the kitchen. But there is just time for *M*.

M&T Communications
Macpherson, Bob and Amy
Maria's Hair Salon
Milius, Alec

Suddenly I hear footsteps nearby, growing louder. I shut the book and place it back on the table. I am turning to leave when Katharine comes in behind me. We almost collide, and her face sparks into rage.

"What are you doin' in here, Alec?"

"I was just . . ."

"What? What are you doing?"

I can think of nothing to say and wait for the wave of anger in her eyes to break over me. In the space of a few seconds, the evening has been ruined.

But something happens now, something entirely artificial and against the apparent nature of Katharine's mood. It is as if she applies brakes to herself. Had I been anyone else, there would have been an argument, a venting of spleen, but the fury in her quickly subsides.

"You get lost?" she asks, though she knows that this is unrealistic. I have been to the bathroom in their flat countless times.

"No. I was snooping. I'm sorry. It was an intrusion."

"It's all right," she replies, moving past me. "I just came to get something to wear. I'm kinda cold."

I leave immediately, saying nothing, and return to the sitting room. When Katharine comes back—some time later—she is wearing thick Highland socks and a blue Gap sweatshirt beneath her dressing gown, as if to suppress anything that I may earlier have construed as erotic. She sits on the sofa opposite me, her back to the darkening sky, and fills the silence by reaching for the CD player. Her index finger prods through the first few songs on *Innervisions,* and Stevie comes on, the volume set low.

"Oh, that's right," she says, as if "Jesus Children of America" had prompted her. "I was going to fix us some coffee."

"I'm not having any," I tell her as she leaves the room, and even that sounds rude. She does not reply.

I should deal with this, do it now. I follow her into the kitchen.

"Listen, Kathy, I'm sorry. I had no right to be in your bedroom. If I caught you looking around my things, I'd go crazy."

"Forget about it. I told you it was okay. I have no secrets."

She tries to smile now, but there is no hiding her annoyance. She is clearly upset; not, perhaps, by the fact that I was in her room, but because I have discovered something intimate and concealed about her relationship with Fortner that may shame her. I do not think she saw me with the address book. Leaning heavily on the counter, she spoons a single mound of Nescafé into a blue mug and fills it with hot water from the kettle. She has not looked directly at me since it happened.

"I need you to know that it doesn't matter to me, what I saw."

"What?"

Katharine stares at me, her head at an angle, tetchy.

"I think every married couple goes through a stage where they don't share a room."

"What the hell makes you think you can talk to me about this?" she says, straightening up from the counter with a look of real disappointment in her eyes.

"Forget it. I'm sorry."

"No, Alec, I can't forget it. How is that any of your business?"

"It's not. I just didn't want to leave without saying something. I don't want you thinking that I know something about you and Fort and that I'm jumping to conclusions about it."

"Why would I think that? Jesus, Alec, I can't believe you're being like this."

We have never before raised our voices at each other, never had a cross word.

"I shouldn't have said anything."

"No, you're right. You shouldn't have. If I asked you personal stuff about Kate, you wouldn't like it too much, would you?"

"That was a long time ago."

"Was it? Does it feel that way? No. No it doesn't. These things are our most private . . . ."

I put my hands in the air defensively, moving them up and down in a gesture of contrition.

"I know, I know."

"Jesus," she says, a rasp in her voice. "I don't wanna argue with you like this."

"Neither do I. I'm sorry."

Silence now, and the edge suddenly goes out of our rush of talk. We are left facing each other, quiet and spent.

"Let's just sit next door, she says, turning to pick up her coffee. "Let's just forget all about it."

We go into the sitting room, the breath of the fight still around us. Stevie is singing—ridiculously—"Don't You Worry 'Bout a Thing." Katharine flops down into one of the sofas and clutches her mug in both palms. She has the most beautiful hands. Eventually she says, "I hate fighting with you," as if we have done it many times before.

"Me too."

I sit on the sofa opposite hers.

"*Can* we talk about it?"

She emphasizes the word *can* here as if it were a test of character. I do not know how to respond except with the obvious: "About what?"

"About Fortner."

His name balloons out of her as if he were sick.

"Of course we can. If you want to."

Her voice is very quiet and steady. It is almost as if she has prepared something to say.

"We—Fortner and I—haven't shared a bed for more than a year. For longer than you've known us."

My pulse skips.

"I'm sorry. I had no idea."

I immediately regret saying this.

"We'll work it out," she says hopefully. "I just can't be beside him in a bed right now. It's not anyone's fault."

"No."

"We're just kind of going through this thing where we're not attracted to each other."

"Or where you're not attracted to him?"

She looks up at me, acknowledging with a softened expression that this is closer to the truth.

"Have you talked about it? Does he know how you feel?"

"No. He thinks he's moved into the spare room because I can't stand his snoring. He has no idea it's because I don't want to sleep with him."

A brief quiet falls on the room, the lull after a sudden revelation.

Katharine drinks her coffee and plays with a loose thread on her dressing gown.

"There's some history to it," she says softly, still staring into her lap. "When I met Fort, I was very vulnerable. I'd just come out of a long-term relationship with a guy I'd met in college. It ended badly, and Fort offered me the kind of support that I needed."

"Was he a rebound?"

Katharine doesn't want to admit this either to herself or to me, but she says, "I guess so. Yes."

She looks up at me, and I can only hope that my face looks receptive to what she wants to say.

"Before I'd even really thought about it, we were married. Fort had been hitched before—kids, divorce, the usual pattern—and he really wanted to make it work this time. He hasn't had access to his children for more than ten years. I was still kind of hung up on this guy, and Fortner knew that. He's always known it."

She takes a deep, possibly stagey breath.

"I wanted to have kids, to make a family, but he was reluctant to start again. Fort's daughters are your age, you know, and he doesn't think it's fair to children to become a parent when you're close to fifty. But I didn't agree with him. I thought he didn't want to have kids because he didn't really love me. That was the state my mind was in. And after my father died, I thought there was something almost reverent about being a parent, like if you had the chance to be one you shouldn't throw that away. Maybe you felt that too after your dad passed away. But I was . . . I was . . ."

She is suddenly tripping over her thoughts, too scared to hear them come out.

"Tell me."

"Alec, you can't ever tell him that I told you this. Okay? There's only a handful of people in the world who know about it."

"You can trust me."

"It's just I wanted children so badly. So I did a terrible thing. I tricked Fort into getting us pregnant. I stopped using birth control, and then when I got pregnant, I told him."

"How did he react?"

"He went crazy. We were living in New York. But Fort, you know, he's totally against termination, so he agreed that I could keep her."

There's only one possible outcome to this story, the worst outcome of all.

"But I lost her. Three months in, there was a miscarriage and . . ."

"I'm so sorry."

Katharine's face is an awful picture of despair. In an attempt to appear resilient, she is struggling to bury tears.

"Well, what can you do, huh?" she says, with a shrug. "It was just one of those things. I was paying the penalty for deceiving him."

"Is that how you see it?"

"It gives me a sort of comfort to see it that way. Maybe it isn't true. I don't know. Anyway, pretty soon after that, work brought us here to London, but it's never been the same between us. Never. We just have the friendship."

"He's Misstra Know-It-All" comes on the stereo system, a song I like, and it distracts me. What I should properly be feeling now is a sense of honor at being made privy to the secrets of their marriage, but even as Katharine is relating the most intimate history of her relationship with Fortner, my mind is caught between the loyalty demanded of friendship and a growing desire to take advantage of her vulnerability. When she is speaking, I have tried to look solely at her eyes, at the bridge of her nose, but every time she has looked away I have stolen glimpses of her calves, her wrists, the nape of her neck.

"You've repaired that?"

"It's a slow process. I was very honest with Fortner about how I'd gotten pregnant. I told him that it had been a deliberate act on my part. That was a mistake. It would have been better to lie, to blame the Pill or something. But somehow I wanted him to know, like an act of defiance."

"Sure, I can see that."

"It's so good having someone who understands," she says. "I mean, you've had your heart broken, you've been through some tough times. You know how all this feels."

"Perhaps," I say, nodding. "But not to the extent that you've been through it."

"It's not so bad," she says. She is attempting to come out of her contemplative mood into something more positive. "In a lot of ways, I'm lucky. Fort's great, you know? He's so smart and funny and laid-back and wise."

"Oh yeah, he's great."

"Hey," she says.

"What?"

"Thanks for listening. Thanks for being here for me when I needed you."

"That's all right. Don't mention it."

In a single fluid movement, she stands and crosses the room to where I am sitting, crouching down low in her thick Highland socks. Before I have had time to say anything, she has wrapped her arms around my neck, whispering, "Thank you, you're sweet," into my hair. The weight of her is so perfect. I put my hand lightly on her back.

She stops hugging first and withdraws. Now we are looking at each other. Still on her haunches, Katharine smiles and, very softly, touches the side of my face with her hand, drawing her fingers down to the line of my jaw. She lets them linger there and then slowly takes her hand away, bringing it to rest in her lap. There is a look in her eyes that promises the impossible, but something prevents me from acting on it. This is the moment, this is the time to do it, but after all the thought-dreams and the longings and the signals coding back and forth between us, I do not respond. Before I have even properly thought about it, I am saying, "I should get a cab."

It was pure instinct, something defensive, an exact intimation of the correct thing to do. I could not spend the night with her without jeopardizing everything.

"What, *now*?" She leans backward and her relaxed smile disguises well any disappointment she may be feeling. "It's not even eleven o'clock."

"But it's late. You'll want to—"

"No, it's not."

I don't want to offend her, so I say, "You want me to stick around?"

"Sure. Relax. I'll fix us a whiskey."

She gives my knee a squeeze and I simply can't believe that I have just let that happen. Just kiss her. Just give in to what is inevitable.

"Okay, then, maybe just a quick one."

She stands slowly, as if expecting me at any moment to pull her down onto the sofa. Just the action of her moving releases that exquisite scent as she turns and walks into the kitchen. I hear Fortner's frozen Volvic falling into glass tumblers, then the slow glug-glug of whiskey being poured onto ice. The noise of her moving quietly around on the polished wooden floor fills me with regret.

"You take water in it, don't you?" she asks, coming back in with the drinks.

"Yes."

She hands me a glass and sits beside me on the sofa.

"Can I ask you something?" she says, taking a sip of her whiskey straightaway. It is as if she has plucked up the courage for a big subject while she was in the kitchen.

"Of course."

Tucking a loose strand of hair behind her ear, she tries to make the question sound as easygoing as possible.

"Are you happy, Alec? I mean really happy?"

The question takes me by surprise. I have to be very careful what I say here.

"Yes and no. Why?"

"I just worry about you sometimes. You seem a little unsettled."

"It's just nerves."

"What d'you mean nerves? What about?"

It was a mistake to say that, to speak of nervousness. I'll have to shift the subject, work from memory.

"I was joking. Not nervousness exactly. I'm just in a constantly fraught state because of Abnex."

"Why?"

"Because of the pressure to do the best job that I can. Because of the feeling of being watched and listened in on all the time. Because of the demands Alan and Harry put on me. All that stuff. I'm so tired. It's so easy to get locked into a particular lifestyle in London, a particular way of thinking. And right now all I seem to worry about is work. There's nothing else."

Katharine has tilted her head to one side, eyes welled up with concern.

"You'll get the job, won't you?"

"Probably, yes. They wouldn't spend all that money training someone just to chuck them out after a year. But it still hangs over me." I take a sip from the whiskey tumbler and a slipped ice cube chills my top lip. "The truth is I have this deep-seated fear of failure. I seem to have lived with it all my life. Not a fear of personal failure, exactly. I've always been very sure and certain of my own abilities. But a fear of others' thinking that I'm a failure. Maybe they're the same thing."

Katharine smiles crookedly, as if she is finding it difficult to concentrate.

"It's like this, Kathy. I want to be recognized as someone who stands apart. But even at school I was always following on the heels of other students—just one or two, that's all—who were more able than I was. Smarter in the classroom, quicker witted in the playground, faster on the football pitch. They had a sort of effortlessness about them which I have never had. And I always coveted that. I feel as though I have lived my life suspended between brilliance and mediocrity, you know? Neither ordinary nor exceptional. Do you ever feel like that?"

"I think we all do, all the time," she replies, lightly shrugging. "We try to kid ourselves that we're in some way distinct from everyone else. More valuable, more interesting. We create this illusion of personal superiority. Actually, I think men in particular do that. A whole lot more than women, as a matter of fact."

"I think you're right."

I have a longing for a cigarette.

"Still," she says, "I gotta say that you don't seem that way to us."

"Who's us?"

"Fort and I."

"Don't seem vain?"

"No."

It's good that they think that.

"But are you disappointed to hear me say these things?"

She jumps at this: "No! Hell no. Talk, Alec, it's fine. We're friends. This is how it's supposed to be."

"I'm just telling you what I feel."

"Yes."

"Like for a long time now I've thought that things are down to luck. Success has nothing to do with talent, don't you think? It's just good fortune. Some people are lucky, some aren't. It's that simple."

Katharine tucks her feet under her thighs, curling up tight on the sofa, and she breathes out through a narrow channel formed between pursed lips. I can feel the wine now, the dissembling brew of vodka and whiskey.

"For example, I was predicted straight-A grades for university, but I got sick and took a string of Bs and Cs, so I didn't get my chance to go to Oxbridge. That would have changed everything. Oxford and Cambridge are the only truly optimistic places in England. Graduates come out feeling that they can do anything, that they can be anybody, because that's the environment they've been educated in. And what's to stop them? It's almost American in that sense. But I meet Oxbridge graduates, and there's not one of them who has something I don't, some quality I don't possess. And yet somehow they've found themselves in positions of influence or of great wealth, they've got ahead. Now what is that about if it isn't just luck? I mean, what do they have that I haven't? Am I lazy? I don't think so. I didn't sit on my arse at university screwing girls and smoking grass and raving it up. I just didn't get a break. And I'm not the sort of person who gets depressed. If I start feeling low, I tell myself it's just irrational, a chemical imbalance, and I pull myself out of it. I feel as if I have had such bad luck, you know?"

Katharine brings her eyes down from the ceiling and exclaims, "But you're doing such good work now, such important work. The Caspian is potentially one of the most vibrant economic and political areas in the world. You're playing a part in that. I had no idea you harbored these frustrations, Alec."

I shouldn't go too far with this.

"They're not constant. I don't feel like that all the time. And you're right—the Caspian is exciting. But look at how I'm treated, Kathy. Twelve and a half thousand pounds a year and no future to bank on. There's so little respect for low-level employees at Abnex, it's staggering. I can't believe what a shitty company it is."

"How are they shitty?" This has caught her interest. "Tell me," she says.

"Well . . ."

"Yes?"

"I've only just started admitting this to myself, but after what happened with MI6, Abnex was a bit of a rebound."

"MI6?" she says, as if she's never heard of it. "Oh yes, of course. Your interviews. How do you mean a rebound?"

"Well, that was my dream job. To do that."

"Yes," she says slowly. "I recall you saying."

I watch her face for a trace of deceit, but there is nothing.

"Not for Queen and Country—that's all shit—but to be involved in something where success or failure depended entirely on me and me alone. Working in oil is okay, but it doesn't compare to what I would have experienced if I'd been involved in intelligence work. And I'm not sure that I'm cut out for the corporate life."

"Why's that?"

"Let me put it like this. Sometimes I wake up and I think: is this it? Is this what I really want to do with my life? Is this the sum total of my efforts so far? I so much wanted to be a success at something. To be significant. And I still resent the Foreign Office for denying me that. It's childish, but that's how I feel."

"But you *are* a success, Alec," she says, and it sounds as if she really means it.

"No, I mean a successful individual. I wanted to make my own mark on the world. MI6 would have given me that. Is that too idealistic?"

"No," she says quietly, nodding her head in slow agreement. "It's not too idealistic. You know, it's funny. I look at you, and I think you have everything a guy your age could possibly want."

"It's not enough."

"Why not?"

"I want acclaim. I want to be *acknowledged*."

"That's understandable. A lot of young, ambitious guys are just like you. But do you mind if I give you a piece of advice?"

"Go ahead."

After a brief pause, she says, "I think you should relax a little bit, try to enjoy being young. What do you say?"

Katharine edges toward me, lending a bending emphasis to the question. For the first time since she returned from the kitchen, we find ourselves looking each other directly in the eye. We hold the contact, drawing out a candid silence, and I tell myself: this is happening again. She is giving it another try. She is guiding us gradually toward the bliss of an infidelity. And I think of Fortner, asleep in Kiev, and feel no loyalty to him whatsoever.

"Relax a little bit?" I repeat, moving toward her.

"Yes."

"And how do you suggest I do that?"

"I dunno," she says, leaning back. "Get out a bit more. Try not to care so much about what other people think about you."

In this split instant, I fear that I have read the situation wrongly. Her manner becomes suddenly curt, even distant, as if by flirting with her I have broken the spell between us, made it explicit.

"Easier said than done."

"Why?" she asks. "Why is that easier said than done?"

"I find it so hard, Kathy. To relax."

"Oh, come on," she says, tossing her face up to the ceiling. She finds my cautiousness disappointing.

"You're right. . . ."

"You know I am. I know what's best for you. What about Saul? Why don't you go out with him more?"

"With Saul? He's always busy. Always got a new girlfriend on the go."

"Yes," she says quietly, standing and picking up the two empty glasses from the table.

"Let me give you a hand with those."

"No no, that's okay." As she moves toward the kitchen she is shaking her head. "You're so serious, Alec. So serious. Always have been."

I don't reply. It is as if she is angry with me.

"You want another drink?" she calls out.

"No, thanks. I've had one too many."

"Me too," she says, coming back in. "I have to go to the bathroom."

"Fine."

"Be here when I get back?"

"I'm not going anywhere."

I had expected it. When she returns from the bathroom, Katharine is yawning, the elegant sinew and muscle on her neck stretched out in fine strands. She slumps down on the sofa and says, "Excuse me. Oh, I'm sorry. Must be tired."

I take the cue. The hint is broad enough.

"I should be going, Kathy. It's late."

"No, don't," she says, jerking up out of her seat with a suddenness that gives me new hope. "It's so nice having you here. I'm just a little sleepy, that's all."

She rests her hand lightly on my leg. Why is she blowing so hot and cold?

"That's why I should be going. If you're sleepy."

"Why don't you stay the night? It's Sunday tomorrow."

"No. You'll want to be on your own."

"Not at all. I hate being alone. Strange noises. It would be nice if you slept over."

"You sure?"

"Sure, I'm sure."

"Because that would be great if I could. I'd save the money on a taxi."

"Well there you go, then. It's settled." She beams, lots of teeth. "It'll be just me and you. You can look out for me. Be my protector."

"Well, if I'm going to do that, I should sleep on the sofa. See the burglars coming in."

"You won't be all that comfortable."

"Well, where do you suggest I sleep?"

I put as much ambiguity into this as is comfortable to risk, but Katharine doesn't pick it up.

"Well, there's always Fortner's room," she says. "I can change the sheets."

Not what I wanted her to say.

"That's a chore. You don't want to be doing that at this time of night."

"No really. It's no problem."

I scratch my temple.

"Look, maybe I should just get a taxi. Maybe you'd prefer it if I went."

"No. Stay. I'll fetch you a blanket."

"You have one spare?"

"Yeah. I got plenty."

She twists up from the sofa, her left sock hanging loose off the toes, and walks back down the corridor.

"There you go," she says, returning with a green checkered rug draped over her arm. She lays it on the sofa beside me. "Need a pillow?"

She yawns again.

"No, the cushions will be fine."

"Okay, then. Well, I'm gonna get some sleep. Shout if you need anything."

"I will."

And she leaves the room.

I am not sure that there was anything else I could have done. For a moment, sex was hovering in the background like a secret promise, but it was too much of a risk to make a move. I could not have been certain of her response. But now I am alone, still clothed, still wide awake, feeling cramped and uncomfortable on a Habitat sofa. I regret talking her into letting me stay the night. I only did it in the hope of being asked to join her in bed. I'd like to be on my way home, working back through the night's conversations, thinking them through and noting them down. Now I am stuck here for what will be at least six or seven hours.

At around two o'clock, perhaps a little later, I hear the noise of footsteps in the corridor. A quiet tiptoe in the dark. I turn on the sofa to face out into the darkened room, eyes squinting as a light comes on in the passage.

I make out Katharine's silhouette in the doorway. She pauses there, and the room is so quiet that I can hear her breathing. She is coming toward me, edging forward.

"Kathy?"

"Sorry." She is whispering, as if someone might hear. "Did I wake you?"

"No. I can't sleep."

"I was just gonna get a glass of water," she says. "Sorry to wake you. You want one?"

"No, thanks."

If I'd said yes, it would have brought her over here. That was stupid.

"Actually, maybe I will have one."

"Okay."

She turns on a side light in the kitchen and the low hum of the fridge compressor cuts out as she opens the door. A narrow path of bright light floods the floor. She pours two glasses of water, closes the fridge, and comes back into the sitting room.

"There you go," she says. I sit up, trying to catch her eye as she comes toward me. Her legs look tanned in the darkness.

"Thanks, Kathy."

"Sorry to disturb you."

She is not stopping. She turns, saying nothing more, moving back in the direction of her room.

"Can't you sleep?" I ask, desperate now to keep her here. My voice is loud in the room, foolish.

"No," she whispers. "I'll be fine after this. Move into Fortner's bed if you want. I'll see you in the morning."

18

SHARP PRACTICE

"So how was Kiev?"

"Kiev?" says Fortner, as if he has never heard of the place.

"Yeah. Kiev."

We walk another two or three paces down Ladbroke Grove before he replies, "Oh, yeah. Christ. Kiev. Not bad. Not bad."

I know he didn't go to Ukraine. The Hobbit told me yesterday on the phone.

"Were you working the whole time?"

"Flat out. Twenty-four/seven. A lotta talk."

"Nice weather?" I ask, with a grin that he doesn't see.

"Oh, yeah. Real nice. They sure don't know how to dress for it, though. Girls wearing nylon tights in the sunshine, and all the guys with these thick mustaches. What is that, a macho thing?"

"What, wearing nylon tights?"

"You're sharp tonight, Milius," he says, putting his arm across my shoulders. He does that quite frequently nowadays. "I like it when you're quick on your feet. Keeps us old guys on our toes."

Fortner and I are going for a drink together. It's something we've done three times before, just the two of us. Katharine cooks dinner, makes herself scarce, and leaves us to it. *You go enjoy yourself, honey,* she says, helping him on with his jacket. *Bring him back in one piece, y'hear?* And we walk the few blocks from their flat in Colville Gardens down to Ladbroke Grove, ready to drink through to last orders.

The setting is a spacious, brown, old-style pub that will be a themed bar and restaurant within twelve months, guaranteed. I hold the door

open for him and we go inside, finding a pair of stools at the bar. Fortner hangs his elbow-patched tweed jacket on a nearby hook, retrieving
his wallet from the inside pocket. Then he sits beside me and rests his
forearms on the wooden bar, breathing out heavily in anticipation of the
long night ahead. To his left there's a vast, *Sun*-reading builder, all biceps
and sinew, muscles packed tight into a lumberjack shirt. His neck has
been shaved to stubble and dropping from a scarred right earlobe is a
single silver stud that seems to contain his entire personality. The man
does not look up as we sit down. He just keeps on reading his paper.

"I'll get the first round," I say and reach into my hip pocket for a
handful of change. "You want a pint or something, Fortner?"

"A pint," he says slowly, as if, after four years in London, he is still
coming to terms with this strange Limey word. "Yes. That is a good
idea, young man. A pint."

"Guinness? I'm having one."

The barman hears this and brings down two tall glasses, starting to
pour the Guinness before I have even asked for them. He allows the
pints to settle for a while, using the time to take my money and cash it
in at the till.

"Nuts? Do you want any nuts?"

"Not for me," Fortner says. "Been tryin' to get back to my ideal
weight. Two hundred fifty pounds."

"There you go, guys," says the barman, setting the glasses down in
front of us. He has the slightly sweeter, higher semitone voice that dis-
tinguishes Kiwis from Australians.

"How was your flight?"

"From Ukraine? Lousy."

Imperceptibly, Fortner gathers together the lies.

"There's no chance of jet lag on account of the time difference, but
they do their best to exhaust you anyway. Airplane sat on the tarmac for
three straight hours. Fuckin' stewards gave us one complimentary drink
and then played cards until takeoff. Then the flight was diverted through
Munich and I had to spend the night in a goddamn Holiday Inn. Took
a day to get home."

This is utterly convincing. Perhaps the Hobbit got it wrong. Fortner
does look older tonight, aged by long-haul flights and the trickeries of
Kiev. Here is a man propping up a bar, a man in shirtsleeves and slacks,
with ovals of sweat under his arms and stubble cast across his face like a

rash. There will be questions he means to ask me, but his eyes look drained of will. He has no energy.

"You look tired," I tell him.

"Oh, I'm all right. This'll start me up."

He takes a long creamy swig of his Guinness and sets it back down on the bar with a thud.

"So what'd you and Kathy get up to while I was away?" he asks, licking his upper lip. We've already been over this at dinner, but it makes me do the talking.

"Like she told you at supper. We went walking in Battersea Park. Had dinner at your place afterward."

"Oh, yeah. She mentioned that."

"Why d'you ask, then?"

"I just wanted details. Kinda missed her while I was away. I like hearing stories about her, things she did and said."

The truth here would prove interesting. *Well, frankly, Fort, there's a lot of sexual tension between your wife and me and we nearly had sex on Saturday night.*

"She talked about you a lot," I tell him.

"Is that right?"

"Then I talked about me a lot."

"No change there, then."

"And finally we went to bed. I slept on the sofa."

"You stayed the night on the couch? Kathy never said."

Interesting.

"Didn't she?"

"No."

An awkward pause hovers over us. The builder turns the page of his newspaper and it crackles in the silence.

"Why do we always drink here?" I ask Fortner, turning back to face him and lighting a cigarette from my pack on the counter. "Why do you like it?"

"Don't you?"

"No, it's great. It's just that we haven't varied the venue."

"Consistency is a much undervalued asset in modern times, my friend. Best to get to know a place. And besides, there's good-lookin' women later on."

The builder vibrates slightly on his stool. Something about this unnerves him.

Fortner takes another long draw of Guinness. "So how are things?" he asks. "Everything okay at Abnex?"

"Good, actually. Alan's on holiday this week so we can get things done without him breathing down our necks."

"That's always good, when the big chief takes off. You gotta hope they never come back."

"But I'm broke. I got hit for a parking ticket and a tax bill first thing on Monday morning. That really pissed me off."

"You forget to feed the meter?"

"No. Parked it on a double yellow near Hammersmith. Got towed."

"Shit. They swoop those guys, like a fucking SWAT team. You gotta be careful."

"The tax is worse. I live in a shithole but I'm paying a fortune to the local council."

"You let it pile up?"

"Yeah, it's been building for the last year. I couldn't afford to pay so I just let it drift."

"Foolish, my friend. Foolish. You should have come to me. I'd have helped you out."

Fortner gives me a paternal pat on the back and I thank him, saying in the nicest possible way that I have no intention of borrowing money off him. Then he drains his pint with a long, satisfied gulp and says it's his round. Mine is still only half empty. It takes him some time to get the attention of the barmaid, a local girl who has served us before.

"How are you, gents?" she asks. She has a crisp East End accent. "Same again, is it?"

"That's right," says Fortner, taking a twenty-pound note from his wallet and snapping it between his fingers. He's started to pick up in the last few minutes. One more drink and things will be rolling.

"You mind if I make a slight criticism of you, Milius?" he says, still looking at the girl. "Would that be okay?"

It is as if the fact that he is buying me a drink has suddenly given him the confidence to ask a serious question.

"Sure."

"It's something I've been meaning to talk to you about for a while now and I thought tonight would give us a good opportunity."

"Go ahead."

"It's just that in the time that we've known each other—what is it, about six or seven months—you've shown a lot of hostility to the way things work over here. Does that sound unfair? I mean, stop me if I'm outta line."

He wants to sound me out.

"No, that's okay."

"So you know what I'm talkin' about?"

"Yes. Of course."

Encouraged by this, Fortner expands on his theme.

"There's just certain things you say, certain observations you make. For a guy your age you have a very jaded perspective on things. Maybe it's normal for your generation. I hope you don't mind me sayin' this."

I don't mind at all. The barmaid puts two more pints down in front of us and gives Fortner his change.

"Example. Do you really think that the concept of Queen and Country is just a lot of shit?"

"Why did you use that phrase? Queen and Country?"

"Because you did. With Kathy on Saturday night. She told me you'd said you didn't want to go into the Foreign Service for patriotic reasons because you thought that kind of stuff was a waste of time. Why d'you feel that way?"

"Maybe it's difficult for an American to understand," I say, trying to find a way of balancing expediency with opinions that I genuinely hold. "Although your country is divided in a lot of ways—down racial lines, in the gap between the very rich and the very poor—you're still bound together by flag-waving patriotism. It's drummed into you from child-hood. God bless America and put a star-spangled banner outside every home. You're taught to love your country. We don't have that here. We don't do things the same way. Loving the country is something blue-rinse Tories do at the party conference in Blackpool. It's seen as naïve, lacking the requisite degree of cynicism. We're a divided nation, like yours, but we seem to relish that divisiveness. We have no reason histor-ically to love our country."

"That's a crock. Look at the camaraderie you generated during World War Two."

"Right. And we've been living off that for fifty years. Let me tell you something. Four in ten people in England celebrate St. Patrick's Day every year. How many do you think do something to celebrate St. George's Day?"

"No idea."

"Four in every hundred. English pubs can get a special late license to serve on St. Patrick's Day. They can't if they want to do that on St. George's."

"That's pretty sad."

"Too right it's pretty sad. It's pretty fucking embarrassing, too. But that isn't the reason why I'm jaded, necessarily."

"Why, then?"

The builder suddenly scrapes back his stool, bundles up his copy of *The Sun,* and leaves. He's heard enough of this.

"I think we're living in an age of social disintegration," I tell Fortner, trying not to sound too apocalyptic.

"You do?" He looks nonplussed, as if everyone he has had a conversation with in the last few days has said exactly the same thing.

"Absolutely. Health and education in this country, the two bedrocks of any civilized society, are a disgrace."

I almost used the word time bomb there, but I can hear Hawkes's voice in my head: You're not trying to *defect,* Alec. Then his brisk, cackled laugh.

I continue, "For nearly twenty years the government has been more interested in installing pen-pushing bureaucrats into hospitals than it has been in making sure there are enough beds to tend for the sick. And why? Because in these days of enlightened capitalism and free markets, a hospital, just like everything else, has to turn a profit."

"Come on, Milius. You believe in free markets just as much as the next guy."

True. But I don't admit this.

"Just a second. So in order to make their money, they've created a culture of fear overseen by big-brother management consultants—no offense to you and Kathy—whose only concern is to get their annual bonus. The last thing it has anything to do with is curing people."

Fortner makes to interrupt me again, but I keep on going.

"Education is worse. Nobody wants to become a teacher anymore, because in the mind of the public, being a teacher is just a notch above cleaning toilets for a living. Just like doctors, they've been treated with utter contempt, subjected to endless form-filling, changes in the curriculum, low salaries, you name it. And all because the Tories don't have the guts to say that the real problem isn't the teachers, it's bad parenting. And you know why they don't say that? Because parents vote."

"You think that'll change if Labour wins?"

I give a spluttering laugh, more contemptuous than I had intended.

"No. No way. Maybe they'll try and make the difference in schools, but until the accumulation of knowledge stops being unfashionable, until kids are encouraged to stay at school past sixteen, and until they find parents who actually take responsibility for their kids when they go home in the evening, nothing will change. Nothing."

"It's no different in the States," Fortner says, curling his mouth downward and shaking his head. "In some cities we have kids checking in assault rifles before assembly. You go to a high school in Watts, it's like passing through security at Tel Aviv airport."

"Sure. But your system isn't a toss-up between private and public education. Only a very few people actually pay to go to high school in the States, right?"

"Right."

"That's not the case in this country. Here, you can buy your way out of the mess. And the worst of it is that the more state education goes into decline, the more parents are going to send their children to fee-paying schools, and the more teachers are going to want jobs outside the state sector because they don't need the grief of working in an inner-city comprehensive. So the gap between rich and poor will widen. It's exactly the same pattern with medical care. The only way not to have to wait three years for an operation is to pay for it. But you want to know what really sickens me?"

"I feel sure you're gonna tell me."

"Our fee-paying schools. They have unbelievable facilities, superb teaching resources, and they cost a fortune. But they're wasted on the people who can afford to go there."

"Why d'you say that?"

"Look at what the students do after ten years of being privately educated. Most of them go and work in the City with the sole objective of making money. Nobody ever puts anything back in. Nobody is taught to feel a responsibility toward their society. It's women and children first with those guys, but only if Tarquin isn't worried about losing the twelve percent bonus on his offshore-investment portfolio. That's the extent of his imagination."

"But these are bright guys, Milius. And maybe after working in the City they go into the law or politics, or they start their own small business and create jobs for other people."

"Bullshit. Excuse me, Fort, but that's bullshit. They'll just make sure they have enough money to send their son to Winchester, and then the whole cycle will begin all over again. Another generation of inbred fuckwits who are spoon-fed just enough of the right information by gifted teachers that they can scrape through their A levels, go to university, and waste some more of the taxpayer's money. You know what? We should have to pay to go to university like you do in the States. At least then we'd appreciate it more."

Fortner smirks and mutters, "Yeah," under his breath. A vapor of sweat has appeared on his forehead and he has a thin line of Guinness threaded across his upper lip.

I try a different tack: "Reminds me of a story my father told once."

"Your late father?"

"Yes."

Why did he need to stress that? *Late* father. Does it make him feel somehow closer to me?

"He said that whenever a Cadillac goes by in America, the man on the street will say, 'When I make my fortune, I'm gonna buy one of those.' But when a Rolls-Royce drives past in England, people look at it and say, 'Check out the wanker driving the Rolls. How come *he's* got one and I haven't?' "

This is actually a story Hawkes told me, which I thought would go down well with Fortner.

"That's what we're faced with here," I tell him. "A profound suspicion of anything that smacks of success. It's got so bad now in public life that I wouldn't be surprised if no one in my generation wants to go into politics. Who needs the grief?"

"There'll always be folks lookin' for power, Milius, whatever the cost to their personal lives. Those guys know how high the stakes are: that's why they get involved in the first place. Anyway, a minute ago you were attacking politicians. Now you feel sorry for them?"

I have to be careful not to build in too many contradictions, not to sound too rash. The trick, Hawkes told me, is not to play your hand too early. Sound them out, try to discover what it is that they want to hear, and then deliver it. You must become practiced at the art of the second guess. I cannot afford to overemphasize like this. Rest assured, he said, that everything you tell them will be infinitely examined for flaws.

Fortner leans toward me.

"I'll tell you, I think some of the worst offenders in this are CNN. That station has done more to decimate the art of television news than any other organization on the planet. For a start, it's just a mouthpiece for whoever happens to be in the White House. It's an instrument of American imperialism. And secondly, because of the pressure to do reports on the hour, every hour, the reporters never actually *go* anywhere. They sit in their hotels in Sarajevo or Mogadishu doing their hair and makeup, waiting for a live satellite linkup with the Atlanta studio based on information they gleaned from the guy who brought them room service."

It's surprising to hear these kinds of arguments from Fortner. They are the first anti-American sentiments he has ever revealed.

"Yes," I tell him. "But at least you *have* CNN. At least you had the vision and the balls to set the thing up. Why couldn't the BBC do that? They have the resources, the staff, the years of experience. And they would have done it a lot better than Ted Turner. Why did it take an American company to create a global news network? I'll tell you. Because you have the vision and we don't. It's just too daunting for us."

"You got a point," he says, tapping his glass. "You got a point."

My round again.

It's past nine thirty and this is as crowded as the pub usually gets. Every so often, Fortner and I are jostled by customers hollering orders from behind our stools. Standing between us, a twig-thin trust-fund hippy waits for the barman to finish pouring the last of the half-dozen pints he paid for with a Coutts & Co. check. His jacket smells, and he has no qualms about pushing his thigh up tight against mine. I move to the right to make more room, but he just keeps coming at me, getting closer to the bar, squeezing me up.

"This is intolerable," Fortner says. "Let's get outta here."

A small group of people are vacating one of the small tables up a short flight of steps to our right.

"I'll grab that table," I tell him. "Bring your stuff."

I step down off the stool and make my way over, loitering nearby as the students drain their drinks and make for the exit. When enough of them have gone, and before any of the other customers has had time to react, I slide onto one of the vacant chairs, its wood still warm. One girl remains, an expensive-looking brunette with sharp features and high-lights in her hair. She is checking her makeup in the mirror of a powder compact. Her black-lined eyes flick up at me momentarily, a fan of lash registering distaste.

Fortner comes up behind me as the girl moves off.

"I never bought that round," I tell him.

"What?"

"Of drinks."

"Oh sure, yeah," he says, looking down at the table. "Get me a bloody Mary this time, will ya, Milius? I can feel my insides turnin' black with all this Guinness."

I stand up to go back to the bar as one of the members of the staff comes past me with a tall column of pint glasses stacked high in his arms. He collects the empties from our table and goes on his way, leaving the ashtray full of butts and gum.

"Pint of lager and a bloody Mary," I tell the Kiwi barman. The boy-to-girl ratio around me is Alaskan: for every reasonably attractive woman, there are now six or seven men crowding up the pub.

"Tabasco, Worcester sauce in the bloody Mary?"

"Yeah."

The Kiwi pours the pint and sets it down on a cloth mat in front of me, turning to fill a tumbler with ice. He places that alongside the lager and lifts a half-empty bottle of Smirnoff from a rack below his waist. Rather than simply pour the vodka into the glass, he gives the bottle a 360-degree spin in the flat of his hand and upends it so that a good splash of liquid bounces out of the glass and onto the mat. Then, when he has finished pouring a contemptible measure of spirits, he whips the neck of the bottle out of the glass in a fast twist, and the same thing happens again: large drops of vodka land on the mat outside the tumbler, leaving no more than an inch in the glass itself.

"I would have preferred that in the drink," I tell him.

"Sorry, mate," he says, a fake smile frozen on his face like a game-show host's. He drop-slides the bottle back into its rack, fills the glass with bloody Mary mix, and says, "Four twenny."

I don't make a scene. How can you argue with a guy who, ten years after *Cocktail,* still thinks it's cool to act like Tom Cruise? He gives me my change and I head back to the table.

"So I've been thinking about what you were sayin' earlier," Fortner announces, as if I hadn't been away. I am still squeezing into my seat when he says, "About the difference between here and back home. You may have a point."

"I definitely have a point. And I haven't even started yet. You know the thing that frustrates me?" The music is turned up on a speaker above our heads, so I lean in a little closer. "It goes back to what we were say-ing about CNN. How come the world is crawling with mediocre American hamburger and ice cream outlets? Why does no one here get a piece of that?"

"Same reason you were sayin'. You guys just don't have the vision. You don't think globally. You tellin' me the ice cream in Penzance isn't better than Ben 'n' fuckin' Jerry's? No way. But those guys were smart for two hippies. They saw the opportunity and they weren't afraid to hang their balls out a little bit. But your man in Cornwall with his two scoops and his chocolate flake, he doesn't think like that. That's why he doesn't have any outlets in Wisconsin and Ben and Jerry have a store on every street corner in western Europe. And Häagen-Dazs, for that matter."

Fortner leans back in his chair. His eyes sweep briefly, suspiciously, around the room, and his mouth stretches out.

"You know Häagen-Dazs is a made-up name?"

"No kidding?" he says.

"I'm telling you. The guy wanted something that sounded aristo-cratic, something classy, so he played around with a few Scandinavian-sounding words and came up with that. Then he had his family change their surname by deed poll to Häagen-Dazs and now they have their picture taken for *Hello!* magazine."

"Shit," says Fortner. "I always thought they were descended from the Hapsburgs."

"No. They're descended from a thesaurus."

Fortner is an intriguing drunk. In the early stages, say after two or three beers or a half bottle of wine, all the better elements of his personality—the quick, sly humor, the anecdotes, the cynicism—fuse together and he operates with a sharpness that I have seen captivate Katharine. But this doesn't last. If he keeps knocking back the drinks, his questions become more blunt, his answers long-winded and tinged with a regret that can morph into self-pity. Right now, we are in the limbo between these two points. It could go either way.

Largely as a way of tapping me for industry rumor before his condition gets out of hand, Fortner starts talking shop for the next fifteen minutes. He tells me what he and Katharine have been up to and about Andromeda's plans for the short-term future. In return, Fortner expects information, much of which he knows I should not tell him. What is Abnex planning to do about X? What's the company line on Y? Is there any truth in the rumors about a merger with Z? My answers are carefully evasive.

"That was damn good," he says, tipping his head back and letting the last half mouthful of his bloody Mary seep through a mess of ice and lemon. "I like 'em spicy. You like 'em like that, Milius?"

"Kate did."

This just comes out. I hadn't planned to say it.

"You never talk about her much," he says, after a brief silence in which sincerity has suddenly swamped his mood.

"No. I don't."

"You feel like talkin' about her now?"

And the curious thing is that I do. To talk about Kate to this weathered Yank in a pub swirling with noise and bluster.

"How long has it been now since you broke up?"

"Over a year. More."

"D'you think you're over her?"

"There's always this pilot light of grief."

"Nice way of putting it," Fortner says. He is doing a good job of suppressing any instinct for flippancy.

"You were together what, six or seven years?"

"From school, yes."

"Long time. You ever see her?"

"Now and again," I tell him, just to see what happens. "You know how it is with couples who've been together a long time. They can't ever really break up. So we meet once in a while and spend these incredible nights together. But we can never seem to get it going again."

I like the idea of Fortner's thinking she still can't get over me.

"How often?"

"Every five or six weeks. I still confide in her. She's still the best friend I have."

"Really?" Fortner looks suitably intrigued, admiring, even. "She got another boyfriend?"

"Don't know. She's never said anything to me."

"So how come you broke up? What happened?"

"Same thing that happens to a lot of couples after university. Suddenly they find they have to go out and work for a living, and things aren't as much fun anymore. Priorities change, you have more responsibilities. You have to grow up so fast, and unless you can find a way of doing that together, the cracks are bound to show."

"And that's what happened with you and Kate?"

"That's what happened with me and Kate. We were living together, but for some reason that made things worse. We were trying to be our parents before our time."

This last remark doesn't appear to have made any sense to Fortner. He says, "What d'you mean?"

"Playing host and hostess to our friends. Dinner parties. Going to the Prado during the Easter holidays, renting villas in Tuscany. All of a sudden we were dressing smarter, choosing furniture, buying cookbooks. And we were barely twenty-one, twenty-two. We took everything so seriously."

"That's not like you," he says, arching his eyebrows and grinning.

"Funny," I reply.

"And Kate was getting a lot of work? She was finding success as an actress?"

"Partly. I was fucked up after college. I didn't want to commit myself to any one thing in case something better came along. I was afraid of hard work, afraid that my youth was prematurely over. And I was jealous of her success, yes. It was pretty pathetic."

"And she didn't help?"

"No, Christ, she was wonderful. She was sympathetic and understanding, but I pushed her away. She got tired of me. Simple as that."

"You think she was in love with you?"

I feel as though everyone sitting around us in the pub is listening in to our conversation, waiting for my response to this question. I falter, looking down at the worn brown carpet, then say, "I'll tell you a story."

"Okay," he says. "But first let me buy us a drink."

When Fortner returns he is clutching two whiskeys, mine a scotch and dry, his a double on the rocks. The bell sounds for last orders.

"Lucky I got there on time," he says. "Now, you were gonna tell me somethin'."

"You asked if Kate was ever in love with me."

"Yes, I did."

"This is what I know. During one of the summer breaks from college I went on holiday with Mum to Costa Rica. Without Kate."

"How come?"

"I didn't invite her."

"Why?"

"Because I saw it as a good opportunity to have some time away from her. We lived in each other's pockets and round about then Kate was very unsettled. And Mum wanted it to be just the two of us. She never really got on with Kate."

Fortner just nods, takes a sip of his drink.

"My mother and I had rooms quite far apart in the hotel, so that if I came back late at night I wouldn't disturb her. One night I went clubbing with some people who were also staying in the hotel. We drank a lot, danced, the usual stuff. There was a girl with us that I liked a lot. A Canadian. Don't remember her name. She'd been hanging around the pool and we'd talked every now and again. She was beautiful, really sexy, and I fancied my chances, y'know? But I'd been with Kate so long that I'd forgotten how to seduce someone."

"Sure," says Fortner, listening hard. My glass of whiskey has a taste of aniseed on its rim. I want to take it back and complain.

"So I bought her a few drinks, tried to make her laugh, tried to act cool, tried to dance without making a fool of myself. But nothing seemed to work. All night she seemed to be getting further and further away from me and I had no idea why. Anyway, after the club closed we found ourselves in the hotel lift together, going back to our rooms, and I tried to kiss her. I lunged in and waited for a response, even though deep down I knew it wasn't coming. I knew she didn't like me, and sure enough she veered away. Then the doors of the lift opened onto her floor and she said good night—I couldn't tell if she was giggling or offended—got out of the lift and went off down the corridor to her room."

"What happened then?" says Fortner.

"I went back to my room. Shame, guilt, embarrassment, you name it."

"You only tried kissin' her, for Christ's sake."

"You don't know Kate."

Fortner frowns.

"It was five in the morning and I was drunk and melancholy. The time difference with London was four or five hours so I decided to ring Kate, to hear her voice, just to make myself feel better so that I could get some sleep. So I picked up the phone and dialed her number. She answered almost straightaway."

"What'd she say?"

"She was crying."

"Crying?"

"Yeah. I said, 'What's wrong?' and without a second's hesitation she said, 'I just miss you. I woke up and you weren't beside me and I was all alone and I miss you.' That's how much she loved me."

Fortner absorbs the story, but his blank expression indicates that it's nothing he hasn't heard before. Once you've seen one broken heart, you've seen them all. He waits for a few seconds, just out of politeness, and then asks, "Was Kate always emotional? Cryin' all the time?"

It irritates me that he'll think of her now as meek and timid, a little lamb of insecurity unable to sustain herself without me. She wasn't like that at all.

"No. She's very strong. She's one of those people who are old before their time, who know exactly what they want and don't waste any time getting it. Kate's very low-bullshit. She has no ego."

"Bet you're wrong about that," he says, swallowing a mouthful of whiskey. "Everyone has an ego, Milius. Some are just better at hidin' it than others."

"You think Katharine has an ego?"

"Hell, yeah. Why, you don't think she does?"

I don't want to give Fortner the impression that I've given too much time to thinking about his wife.

"I dunno. But it's interesting. Kate seemed so perfect to me that by the end I just worshiped her. That had a lot to do with the fact that she was so kind. It didn't seem proper, or possible, that someone could be as good and as pure as she was. I was in awe of her beauty. It got to such a point that I felt I could no longer touch her. She actually made me feel unworthy of her. Perverted, even. She was too good for me."

"But you still see her?" he asks quickly, aware of an emerging contradiction. I'd forgotten that I'd lied about that.

"Yeah. But it's just sex now. Sex and the occasional chat. Nostalgia."

"If you could take her back, would you?" he asks. "Go back to having a full relationship, living together and all that?"

"Straightaway."

"Why?"

It feels so good to be telling him even a semblance of truth. I wouldn't be surprised if he suddenly took out a notebook and began taking shorthand.

"This is what I truly believe," I tell him, and this will be my last word on the subject. "I believe that people spend years looking for the right person to be with. They try on different personalities, different bodies, different neuroses, until they find one that fits. I just happened to find the right girl when I was nineteen years old."

"That the only time you cheated on her, in Costa Rica?"

"Yes."

No one knows about Anna. Only Kate and Saul, and the people at CEBDO.

"Truth?"

"Course it's the truth. Why? Do you ever contemplate screwing around on Katharine?"

"Do I ever *contemplate* it?" Fortner appears to examine the word for its various meanings, like a lawyer checking small print. Then he says, "No," with tremendous firmness.

"But you think about it?"

"Oh, sure, I think about it. Does Rose Kennedy have a black dress? Sure, I *think* about it. I'd been messin' around for years before I met Kathy, and it's been hard givin' all that up. But you know what I finally realized?"

"No. What?"

"I realized that there's a lot of attractive women out there, but you can't fuck 'em all. It just ain't possible. The problem with screwing around is you get yourself a taste for it. You fuck one woman, you start developing this lucky feelin', start thinking you can fuck the next one that comes along, and the next one after that. What you have to learn is how to prefer looking at women instead of touching them. You see what I'm saying? It's like giving up cigarettes. You might love to have a smoke, the smell of the tobacco on the air, but you know it'll kill you if you do. You can never let that filter touch your lips again. Same with women. You gotta let 'em go."

He takes another slug of scotch, as if anticipating applause, and lets the alcohol sloosh and sting around his mouth.

"It's like gettin' older." Fortner's hand ducks down below the table and he gives his balls a good, ill-disguised scratching. "When you're a young kid, you think you can change the world, right? You see a problem and you can articulate it to your college friends and suddenly the world's a much better fuckin' place to live. But then you start gettin' older, and you get yourself a whole new bunch of experiences. You're aware of a lot more points of view. So now it's not so easy sounding convinced about what you're thinkin' about, 'cos you know too many of the angles. You followin' me?"

I have been distracted by the gradual exodus of people in the pub, the clatter and wipe of closing. But I know I can drift out of the conversation and still come back in to follow Fortner's train of thought.

"Oh, yeah," I tell him. "That makes a lot of sense."

"Jeez, I'm hammered," he says suddenly, wiping his brow with his forearm. He had noticed that my attention was wandering. "We oughta be going, I guess. Hope my jacket's still here."

"It should be," I tell him.

Both of us finish our drinks and stand up. I take my pack of cigarettes off the table and check that the lighter is still in my trousers. As we head for the exit, Fortner pulls his jacket off the hook by the bar—it's the last one there—and flips it over his shoulder. He barks a friendly farewell to the Kiwi, who is busy emptying ashtrays into a blue plastic bucket. The barman looks up at us and says, "Night, guys, see y'again," and then goes back to work.

Out on the street, a few paces up the road, Fortner turns to me.

"Well, young man," he says, slapping me on the back. "It's been a pleasure as always. Stay in touch. I'm gonna go home, wake up Kathy, take a fistful of aspirin, and try to get some sleep. You gonna be okay gettin' back to your apartment? You wanna come up for a beer, a coffee or somethin'?"

"No. I'd better be off. Got work tomorrow."

"Sure. Okay, I'll see ya. Gimme a call in the next few days."

"Will do."

And he ambles up the street, a lost, faintly disheveled figure gradually moving out of focus. I have this sense that the evening has ended oddly, too quickly, but it's a barely registered concern.

I head up the hill as far as Holland Park Avenue, but there isn't a taxi in sight. Passing the underground station, my mobile phone goes off and I take it out of my jacket.

"Alec?"

"Yes."

It's Cohen.

"Harry. Hi. How are you?"

"I'm at the office."

I look at my watch.

"But it's past eleven."

"Do you think I'm not aware of that?"

"No, I simply—"

He interrupts me, his voice bullish and proud.

"Look. When did you speak to Raymond Mackenzie?"

"Off the top of my head I can't remember. Can't this wait until tomorrow?"

"Given that he's leaving for Turkmenistan in seven hours, no it can't."

"I think I spoke to him yesterday. In the afternoon. I had everything he needs faxed over to him. He's not going there with his trousers down."

The connection falters here, dead noise and then broken words.

"Harry, I can't hear you."

Cohen is raising his voice, but it's impossible to make out what he is saying.

"I can't hear you. Harry? My battery's dead. Listen, I'll call you from a landline—"

He is cut off.

There is a phone booth nearby, decorated with a patchwork quilt of whore cards. A man is standing inside, a worn-out husband wearing a raincoat and training shoes. I look straight at him and our eyes briefly meet, but with no regard for this he just rocks back on his heels and has a good look at what's on offer. He pans left and right, studying the cards, taking his time. Traffic sweeps by and suddenly I feel cold.

After a minute or so he makes up his mind, scribbling a number on a pad that rests on the thin metal shelf to the right of the phone. Then he drops a ten-pence piece into the slot.

I don't want to be doing this. I don't want to be waiting to make a phone call to Cohen at half past eleven at night. I tap on the glass, fast with the hard edge of my knuckle, but the man just ignores me, turning his back.

A cab drives past and I flag it down, riding back to Uxbridge Road. But when I try Cohen's number from home, there is no reply. Just the smug disdain of his voice mail and a low-pitched beep.

I hang up.

19

SEIZE THE DAY

The keypad on my telephone at home has four preprogrammed numbers: 1 is Mum; 2 is Saul; 3 is Katharine and Fortner; 0 is Abnex. The rest are blank.

I push Memory 3 and listen to the tone-dial symphony of their number ringing.

She answers. "Hello. Katharine Lanchester."

Here we go.

"I don't fucking believe it."

"Alec. Is that you?"

"I don't fucking *believe* it."

"Alec, what is it?"

"Abnex told me they're not satisfied with what I'm doing. With my work. They're not convinced I'm doing the best I can."

"Slow down, honey. Slow down."

"I can't get my head around it."

"What did they say?"

"That if I don't start pulling my weight they won't give me a contract when my trial period is over."

"When did they say this?"

She whispers, "It's Alec," to Fortner. He's there in the room with her.

"Today. Murray called me into his office and we both went upstairs and I was given a dressing down by David Caccia, the fucking guy who hired me in the first place. Obviously Murray's been on him about me. It was totally humiliating."

"Just you? Was anyone else criticized?"

I have to think about this before answering. It's all lies.

"Only Piers. But his job is safe, he's on contract. He's not in the same position as I am."

"It's possible they're just giving everybody a scare. Management likes to do that from time to time."

"Well then, fuck them for doing that, Kathy. I've worked my arse off for that company, learning my trade, doing overtime, making up for the fact that I came in through the back door. There isn't anything I wouldn't do to . . ."

"To what?"

"I just can't believe I'm being treated like this. And they have the nerve to pay me twelve thousand a year and still talk to me like that."

"It is kind of odd. I mean you're there every night until eight or nine, right? Later sometimes."

She's finding it difficult to know what to say. My voice is shaking. I have taken her by surprise.

"Wait a minute, Alec." There is a muffled noise on the line, like a piece of cloth being dragged across the receiver. "Fort's trying to say something. What, honey? . . . Yeah, that's a good idea. Why don't you come over here, for dinner, huh? We can talk about it. We haven't eaten yet, and besides, we haven't seen you in almost two weeks."

I wasn't expecting this. It could all happen quicker than I anticipated.

"Now? Are you sure it's not too late? Because that would be great."

"Sure it's not too late. Come on over. I got a chicken here needs roasting. There's easily gonna be enough for three. Get a cab and you'll be here in a half hour."

They both come to the door. Katharine's face is a haven of sympathy. Her hair is brushed out and she's wearing a long black dress with red roses printed on the cotton. Fortner looks unsettled, nervous, even. He is wearing flannel trousers and a white shirt with an old, canary-yellow tie knotted tight against his larynx.

"Come on in," says Katharine, putting her arm across my shoulders. They've obviously decided that she'll play the mother figure. "You've had a shitty day."

"I'm really sorry to bother you like this."

"No. God, no. We're your friends. We're here for you. Right, Fort?"

Fortner nods and says, "Of course," like he has something else on his mind.

"You wanna fix Alec a drink, honey? What do you feel like?"

"Do you have any vodka?"

"I think we have some left over from the last time you went at it," Fortner says, going into the kitchen ahead of me. "You have it straight, Alec, or with tonic?"

"Tonic and ice," Katharine calls after him, smiling at me broadly.

I am invited to come in and sit down, which I do, on the large window-facing sofa with the coffee table in front of it. All the lamps are on to make the room feel warm and cozy; there's even jazz drifting out of the CD player. It's John Coltrane or Miles Davis, one or the other. I light a cigarette and look over at Katharine, who has sat down on the sofa facing mine. I allow myself a courageous little smile, a gesture to suggest that things aren't as bad as I might have made out on the phone. I want to appear gutsy, while at the same time eliciting their sympathies.

Fortner emerges with my drink in a large tumbler. As far as I can make out they aren't having anything themselves. There's an ice-melted glass on the mantelpiece above the fire, but it's a leftover from early evening.

As Fortner hands me my drink, I smell shaving foam or aftershave on him, and indeed his face does look unduly smooth for this time of night. Is it possible that he has preened himself for me, as if I were the vicar coming for tea? He walks around the coffee table and falls heavily into his favorite armchair, the collapse of a man whose evening rhythm has been disturbed. There's a smile on his face that his eyes aren't backing up. My visit has thrown him: he'd like to have gone to bed with a Ludlum and seen the day off. Now he has to reengage his mind and give this situation his full attention.

"So come on. Spit it out," he says, not unkindly. "What'd they say to you?"

"Just what I said on the phone." He's made the vodka strong, at least a double, and I am wary of this. Have to keep my wits about me.

"Go through it again for Fort, sweetie. He didn't hear our conversation."

For the old man's benefit, I retread the shape of the threat from Abnex.

"You know, at least I've always told you, that I don't really get on with the two senior guys on my team."

"What are their names?" he asks. "Cohen, is that it, and Alan Murray?"

"Harry Cohen, yes. They're very tight, very good friends."

"And you feel that they . . . ?"

Katharine says, "Let him finish, honey."

"From day one they've treated me disrespectfully. I get given more work to do than any other member of the team. I have to work longer hours, I have to take more shit. If there's a letter that needs writing, a phone call that has to be made, if a client needs to talk with one of us or if Abnex needs somebody to stay in the office over the weekend, it's always me that has to do it. Alan swans up and says, 'Alec, do this, Alec do that,' or if he's not around, Harry does the same thing. Never a please or a thank-you. Just this expectation that I will fall into line. Don't get me wrong. I know I'm the junior partner. In a sense, I deserve to get given the menial tasks. But I am not *appreciated*. I am not afforded any respect. If I do a good job, it goes unnoticed. Either that or Harry will take the credit. But if I fuck something up, it sure as shit isn't forgotten."

Fortner's mouth has dropped into a deep scowl, like a horseshoe spilling its luck.

"And I've never been sure whether they treat me like this because they genuinely dislike me, or because of jealousy. . . ."

"The latter, most likely," he mutters.

"Or it could be because they feel threatened by me. I really can't believe that they think I'm no good at my job. That's just impossible. If you could just see the fuck-ups J.T. makes. Lost business, bad planning, *basic* fucking mistakes. But today it's me they chose to round on."

"What did they say?" Katharine asks.

"They say I screwed up with this guy called Raymond Mackenzie. He went to the Caspian for us, he's one of our top oil traders. I was supposed to do background for him, get logistical information about pipelines out there, how their refineries are set up, that kind of stuff."

"Yes," says Fortner slowly.

"I got hold of maps, spoke to a bunch of geologists, it was a normal job. And I did it well, you know?"

"Sure," he says.

"There are so many things that I could have slipped up on but didn't. I got the size of the export jetties—that took three days to discover—I got watertight information about pipelines that he was able to work with. But Mackenzie gets out there and he's ready to finalize a deal with the Turkmenbashi refinery when it turns out that the oil is going to be too sulfurous for them to handle. So it's looking like we're going to have to recommend spending a hundred and fifty million dollars on a brand-new distillate hydro treating unit to strip out the sulfur at the refinery."

"Surely that's not your responsibility," says Katharine. "Surely they would have found something like that out long ago?"

"Well, they didn't," I snap, though she does not look offended. "I was supposed to check it out, but it never crossed my mind. And now we have all this oil, an expectant market, and no way to fucking refine it and get it out to them."

"There's gotta be another refinery."

"That's what I've been working on. I'm trying the one in Baku. But the shit still hit the fan. Murray went fucking crazy."

"Guy's a chump," says Fortner. "Class-A dickhead."

Katharine looks upset.

"I can't believe this," she says. "After all you've done for them. I think it's despicable the way you're being treated."

To which Fortner adds, "You must be mad as hell," getting up from his chair to put some classical music on. The volume is louder than it needs to be. "Alan Murray is lucky to have a guy like you on board. Period."

"Well, I must be doing something wrong."

"No," Katharine says sharply. "I don't think so at all. In fact, quite the contrary. This is about personalities, it's not about the job. Obviously there are people within your organization who feel threatened by you."

Obviously.

"I've seen it a thousand times," says Fortner, now moving to the window and closing the curtains. "A thousand times."

"What do you think I should do?"

For once, the immediacy of their answers stalls. Fortner glances over at his wife and, only when a few seconds have passed, says, "We'll come to that."

"What do you mean?"

"We've been thinking, and we have a few ideas as to how we might help you."

"I don't understand."

My pulse starts to thump. It's coming.

"Before we get to that, there's something I'd like to say."

"Sure. What is it?"

Fortner moves away from the window, pacing to the kitchen door and then back to the drawn curtains. At times he is talking behind me. The anxiety he was showing when I first arrived has receded completely.

"There's a pattern of behavior here, Alec. Do you see it?"

Katharine is nodding confidently, as if she already knows what he's going to say.

"What pattern? Does this have something to do with what you were saying about ideas to help me?"

Don't rush them.

"You remember that conversation we had a while back about your interviews with MI6? Do you remember that?"

He's behind me now. Only Katharine can see the distinct characteristics of his face.

"Of course, yes."

"Well, it was my view then, and it still is, that if the British government could afford to throw away someone of your potential, then it's either in much better shape than anyone thinks, or it's just plain dumb. Now . . ."

He moves back to the bay window, turning to face me.

"Abnex appears to be doing the same thing. I get a sense that both of these organizations are overawed by you. You may think of that as an overstatement, but let me explain." He touches his tie, loosening it. "It seems to us that Abnex doesn't really know how to get the best out of you. It's almost as if they can't deal with an employee who shows a little flair or versatility. Now, I'm not blind, Alec. We both know that you can step out of line occasionally. But only—and this is crucial—only ever in the interests of the company."

"I'm just sick of being underestimated," I tell him, skirting the compliment. "I'm sick of being ignored and treated as a second-class citizen. I'm sick of knockbacks and failure."

"You haven't failed," says Katharine, interjecting. "Not at all. You're just in a very unfortunate situation."

As she says this, Fortner walks back behind his armchair with the deliberation of an actor hitting a mark.

Katharine says, "Alec, this isn't the first time that you've been upset, is it?"

"About Abnex? No."

"And your financial situation hasn't improved since you started there?"

I glance over at Fortner and there is a look of rocklike concentration on his face. His eyes are fixed on mine. The rest of the room has become invisible to me. It's just the three of us, closing in on something unimaginable.

"No. Why?"

Katharine does not answer. There is no knowing why she asked that question, other than to remind me that I am being badly paid. A little subconscious hook.

"You want another drink?"

I almost jump when Fortner says this, and he smiles warmly, taking my glass from the table. From my position low down on the sofa, he looks suddenly vast and strong.

"Sure, that would be great. You having something?"

"Yeah, I'm gonna open a bottle of wine."

"That'd be nice, honey," says Katharine, very mellow. It's as if they have both gone into a trance.

With Fortner out of the room, Katharine asks, "Do you still believe that Abnex is unprincipled in some of its activities?"

"When did I say I believed that?"

"So you don't?"

There's no noise at all coming from the kitchen. Fortner is listening.

"No, as a matter of fact I still do. Yes."

"How do you feel about that? About unprincipled behavior?"

"What, generally?"

"Yes."

"Kathy, it completely depends . . ."

"Of course . . ."

A cork pops in the kitchen.

"On the circumstances."

"Right."

"But I do think that a lot of the stuff that we're getting involved in now will be detrimental to the company, not necessarily in the short term, but in ten to fifteen years' time. That's why I have a problem with it. It's not the dishonesty that annoys me, so much as the stupidity of it."

"What are they paying you, exactly?" Fortner asks, coming back into the sitting room with a bottle of good red wine and three upside-down glasses threaded through the fingers of his right hand.

"Twelve."

"What's that, around eighteen thousand dollars a year?" he says, setting the glasses on the surface of the coffee table. "In America, for the job you're doing, that salary would be unsatisfactory. And we have lower taxes, medical plans built in, all that."

It's time to get it out of them.

"What are you saying?"

"What we're saying, Alec, is that we'd like to give you the opportunity to do something about your situation."

"I don't understand."

"You won't, immediately," he says, his eyes fixed on the table.

I shift uncomfortably in my seat as he says this and look over at Katharine for some indication of what is going on. Her face is entirely inscrutable. There is an atmosphere of very carefully chosen words. I hear the first swallowing glugs of wine as Fortner starts to fill the glasses. He twists the bottle to catch any drips, his hand as steady as a flat sea. There's just the rustle of clothing and distant traffic sounds as Fortner sits down. Each of us takes a glass from the table, sipping, registering the taste.

Fortner breathes in the bouquet and says, "We have something, we both have something we want to discuss with you."

I do not answer. The rush of expectation in me is so great that I don't want to risk anything on a few ill-chosen remarks. Better to react precisely to what he has to say, to let them do all the talking.

"How would you feel about coming over to our side?"

There's no liveliness in Fortner's face as he asks this, no widening of the eyes. He merely lets the question drift out of him with an uninflected stillness.

"What, you mean work for Andromeda?"

"Not exactly, no."

I don't have to look over at Katharine to know that she is watching me.

"How, then?"

"We want you to help us."

His words are phrased with care to ensure an ambiguity.

"To help you?"

"Yes."

I hold the pause longer than is necessary. What Fortner is asking is very plain to anyone who works in our business, but he has couched it in such a way that if I object, neither of them will be culpable. As if to confirm this, Fortner takes a very relaxed draw on his wine as he waits for my response, pausing to look at me only briefly. He's been here before.

I look across at Katharine, more out of nervousness than anything else, and I am surprised to see that she looks almost ashamed at what Fortner has suggested. She is blinking constantly and massaging the back of her neck.

"I don't understand," is all I can think to say. There's been a delay in the room like the disappearing echo of a long-distance phone call.

"It's quite simple. Would you like to help us?"

"You mean hand over information about what Abnex is doing? For money?"

He has made me say it, just as they said he would. I was the one who put it in concrete terms.

"That is correct."

"Kathy, do you know about this?"

"Of course. It occurred to us that you would be amenable."

At this, Fortner looks over at her quickly. It wasn't the right thing to say. She changes tack.

"That it would *suit* you. And us."

I take a sip of wine. My hand is shaking so violently that I can barely hold the glass.

"You'll obviously need some time to think it over," Fortner says, like a doctor who has just diagnosed a cancer. He is funneling any anxiety into the red plastic top of the wine bottle, turning it this way and that in his thick fingers. He has gradually molded the plastic cone into the shape of a toadstool, twirling the stem between the thumb and index finger of his left hand.

I know that at first I must appear to be offended.

"So our whole friendship has been based on the possibility that this might happen?"

"Alec, don't . . ." says Katharine, but I interrupt her.

"You've pretended to be something that you're not."

"You're bound to be a little shocked at first," Fortner says very flatly. He's absolutely certain that I'll come over. It's just a matter of time.

"How long have you been planning to ask me?"

"For some time now," Katharine replies, running her hands down her thighs so that the material of her dress stretches out.

"How long?"

"Four or five months," she says.

"Four or five months! That's practically when we met."

"Come on, Alec. We were first introduced before that."

"Yes. And you cultivated the friendship because you knew that this might happen."

"Now hold on there," says Fortner. "We just want a little help, that's all, and we're prepared to pay you handsomely for that."

This is smart: bring it back to the money. It's fascinating to see how Fortner operates. He wants to take my mind away from ethical considerations and just let me visualize the cash.

"How much?"

"We'll come to that in good time. There's a lot we need to discuss first."

"I'm not even sure about this. I'll need time to think it over."

"Of course."

And now it's my turn to pace. I am up on my feet, walking in random circles around the room, running my hand through my hair, lighting a cigarette.

"I need some air."

"What?"

Katharine looks up at me, a dying fall of panic in her voice.

"He says he needs some air. Alec, you mustn't talk to anyone about this. That could get us all in a lot of trouble. Now you understand that, don't you?"

"I'm not stupid, Fort. I just need to walk around, clear my head."

"So you'll be back?" she asks.

"Maybe," I reply, backing away to the front door. "Maybe."

20

CREATING JUSTIFY

An hour later, I climb the stairs to their apartment, not two at a time but singly, contemplatively, slowly making my way to the third-floor landing. Fortner is standing in the half-open door, his tie gone, a glass of whiskey in his hand. Our eyes meet for a good long time as I go toward him, my shoulders hung deliberately heavy, hair disheveled by the wind.

"Where d'you get to?" he says quietly, ushering me back inside.

"To Portobello Road. Around."

Katharine is sitting on the sofa, upright and very still. She looks to have been scolded. Her eyes are heavy, perhaps even with tears. It is as if a mask has been wrenched from her face, and all that is left is a frightened revelation of self. She looks up at me and gives a weak smile. Everything feels drained now.

"You wanna drink?"

"No, thanks, Fortner. I want to be very clear."

He sits beside his wife and I settle opposite them on the second sofa, our positions exactly reversed from before.

"We didn't think you'd come back," says Katharine. "We're really very sorry about what happened."

"I was walking. Thinking things through."

"Of course," she says.

"I . . ."

Fortner interrupts me as I make to say something.

"Alec, it was a bad idea asking you. We could get you in a lot of trouble if—"

"I'll do it."

Katharine's head jerks up and her bruised eyes flare open.

"You will?"

"Yes."

"Well, that's good news." Fortner seems less enthused than I had expected. He's known that I would bite all along. I tell them that we need to clarify a lot of things, and he says, "Indeed."

"And I'm sorry I got upset with you," I say, lighting another cigarette. "I was just very surprised."

"Of course you were." Fortner says this with no feeling in his voice. Katharine stirs, looking at me fondly. Relief has energized her.

"Alec, I really just wanna make one thing absolutely clear, okay?"

"Sure."

"I just wanna say that our friendship wasn't predicated on this happening. It was interdependent . . . uh . . . more of a product of our becoming friends."

Fortner seconds this, saying, "Absolutely, it's very important to make that clear," but it's a lie, because his eyes sink to the floor as he says it. He and Katharine are strangely out of sync, as if every development is new to them, untested.

"So what is it exactly that you want me to do?"

Katharine suddenly laughs with nervous relief.

"Golly," she says breathlessly. "Where do we start?"

Golly isn't a word that I've heard her use before. This is all getting to her in a way that Fortner cannot have anticipated.

"We're not gonna get anything resolved this evening in any detail," he says, with a steadiness suggesting that from now on he will take charge. "The most important thing to stress to you is that what we're about to embark on must be undertaken with a view to total secrecy. You can tell no one, Alec. Not a girlfriend, not your mother, not Saul, not some stranger you meet in a bar you're never gonna see again. No one."

"Of course."

"Believe me, that will be the most difficult part. But you'll quickly come to understand the kinds of sacrifices involved, and I don't foresee that for someone of your integrity it would be a problem."

How deft are his little flatteries.

"Integrity? This doesn't feel all that principled."

"You'll be substantially remunerated for any and all information that you can give us."

"I want that to start tonight," I tell him, exhaling smoke in a tight cylinder, which may look self-conscious. "I want some sort of initial down payment this evening."

There's a fractional skip as Fortner weighs this before saying, "Of course." As he should, he thinks I'm greedy, but it's more important to him to keep me sweet.

"We'll deposit ten thousand dollars in a U.S. bank account right away. You start getting irregular activity on your High Street bank account, and those guys are obliged to tell their money-laundering people, who'll go straight to the cops."

This is intended to worry me, but I say nothing in response. I'm waiting for Fortner to do what's right.

"What we can do for you is give you a small amount of cash as an initial gesture of good faith. Say a thousand sterling. That suit ya?"

"Pocket money. But it'll be okay to be getting on with."

"Don't worry about it, Alec, all right? We'll see to it that the financial side of things is very satisfactory for you. You're not gonna have any complaints. We're also in a position to offer you employment at Andromeda if Abnex doesn't pick up your option at the end of the year. And if they do, and if you're still happy with our arrangement, we can keep things just as they are. But that's all in the future."

"I'll need this in writing."

"No," he says firmly, his voice raised for the first time. "That's imperative. Write nothing down. You let us do all the paperwork."

"Why? Isn't it better to cloak everything in some sort of code? Isn't that how this is done? I don't want it coming back to me."

Fortner slowly shakes his head, trying his best to be patient with my apparent lack of expertise.

"It won't come back to you. Not if there's nothing to come back in the first place. And there won't be if you don't write any of it down. That's the first rule you gotta learn."

This is what it's all about for Fortner: the lure, the approach, the sting. He's relishing this situation for all the demands it is going to make on his tradecraft. He has lifted right out of himself, and all the old tingles are coming back. This is the way things used to be in the old days. This is the way he likes it.

"You have any other questions?"

"What about getting the information to you? How do I do that?"

Katharine leans forward in her chair. She's prepared to field this one.

"We have an entire setup that will assist you with that."

"What do you mean, an entire setup? At Andromeda?"

She looks across at Fortner, who is slowly lolling his neck from side to side, loosening tightened muscles. He stands and slides his hands into his pockets, beginning to pace the room once again.

"You explain, honey," Katharine says to him, in a quiet, almost respectful voice. Fortner steadies himself, turns around, and smiles at me. A man preparing to reveal his hand.

"Alec," he says, "let me put it to you this way." He takes another couple of paces and briefly glances at the mantelpiece. "The end of the Cold War has meant an increasingly blurred line between state-sponsored intelligence gathering and private-sector espionage. Do you follow me?"

"I think so. Yes."

"I made the crossover."

He coughs, a throat clearer.

"You mean you used to work for the CIA?"

Asking him this feels very ordinary, very straightforward, like inquiring after his star sign.

"Yes," he says.

I look at Katharine, whose head is very slightly bowed.

"And you?"

She looks up at her husband, waiting for him to give her clearance.

"Katharine is still with the Agency," he says. "She has a formal relationship with Andromeda, but the federal government pays her salary."

"Jesus."

"I can understand your sense of shock."

"It's not . . . No . . ." I begin to mumble incoherently. "I always thought . . . Jesus."

"Please, if I could just say at this stage that anything you might have heard or read or understood about the Agency—put that immediately to one side. The CIA is not a sinister operation—"

"I didn't say it was."

"It's just the American equivalent of your Secret Intelligence Service. With a bigger budget."

"Well, everything's bigger in America."

This is clever. It breaks the ice and both of them laugh. Katharine looks up and gives me a broad, flirty smile.

"Would you like to know something about what we do?" she says. "Would that make it easier for you? Get it down to a more realistic level?"

"Sure," I say. "But I'm sitting here wondering why you need me. Why don't you just bug the Abnex phones and get the information you need from a satellite somewhere?"

That was always going to be a naïve question, but Fortner gives it a patient, considered response.

"Only about ten percent of our intelligence is scooped by birds. We still need guys like you on the ground. The Agency has a budget of twenty-eight billion dollars a year. Only six of that goes for satellites. Agents like Katharine and myself still provide the backbone of the intelligence operation, and guys like you are our lifeblood."

"So this is what you do all the time? Jesus, it's overwhelming."

Fortner smiles, like he's glad to have everything out in the open.

"This is it."

They are looking at each other, an undisguised relief shuttling between them.

"So what kind of stuff do you get up to? I can't believe this, it's so . . ."

"Primarily nowadays the Agency is involved in reducing the influence of Russian organized crime," Katharine says, with the confidence of someone moving into an area of expertise. "Last June, for example, we arrested three guys who were trying to sell nuclear-grade zirconium to some of our federal agents posing as Iraqis in New York. That's just an example."

"FBI agents. Not the CIA?"

"That's right," she replies. I am amazed at her candor.

"More and more since Ames we've been working with the FBI," says Fortner.

I should ask who Ames is.

"Who's Ames?"

"You know. The trait—" Katharine stops herself short and adjusts swiftly. "The CIA agent who was spying for the KGB. He was our head of counterintelligence in Washington."

"Oh yeah. I think I read about him."

Fortner sits on the sofa beside Katharine and juts his chin toward the floor. Bad memories.

"How long have you guys been doing this?"

He looks up.

"Let's not talk too much about it now, okay? We can fill you in on everything you need to know some other time."

"Sure. Fine. Whatever."

Almost to himself, he says, "Shit, it's not like you'll be doing anything in the same sphere as Rick Ames. What we're asking you to do isn't anything like that. What you'll be doing for Andromeda isn't gonna get people killed."

"I understand that. I wouldn't do it if it did."

"Good," he says, looking at Katharine. "That's good to know. I think it's important to have standards, and I respect you for that, Alec, I really do. Matter of fact, I wouldn't even compare the two. So let's not get sidetracked. What remains to be said right now—the most important thing as far as you're concerned—is that there's a common misconception about how all this works."

Katharine, who has been listening quietly, stands and offers us coffee. We both accept.

"All you gotta do is bring us as much information as you can without arousing suspicion with any of your colleagues or with Abnex security. Those offices are under twenty-four-hour camera surveillance, ditto the Xerox room."

"So you want me to photocopy stuff?"

"We'll go over it. I'm just giving you some basic ground rules. Everything you do on your computer terminal will be logged." He starts to chop the air with his hand, marking out each point. "Presume that your telephone is tapped. Never communicate with us using e-mail or cell phone. These are just basic precautions."

"I see."

I hear Katharine in the kitchen taking down mugs from a cupboard.

"There's also a problem that's unique to your situation. We share a lot of intelligence with your government, and a lot of the codes and ciphers we use are identical to those employed by Five and SIS. We start using them, and they'd be on to us right away. So we can't encrypt text or scramble conversations. I wouldn't wanna scare you. You just have to be smart. We can go over all this in much finer detail when we're a lot less pumped up. For now, all I would emphasize to you is to keep it simple. Go home with that thought. Don't ever try to do too much, especially at first. Just make everything look as natural as possible."

"That's it?"

Fortner laughs.

"That's it. If you don't make a big deal about it, no one else will. Years gone by, we might have asked you to take a couple of weeks' vacation so we could get you off to a safe house back home and give you some basic training in equipment and communications. In your case, none of that will be necessary. This is just a small operation. Like I said, we're just gonna keep things real simple. That's the mistake a lot of people make. They make things too complicated for themselves, start feeling like the whole world is watching them when in fact the whole world doesn't have a goddamn clue what's going on. You're just plain old Alec Milius to Abnex, and it'll stay that way as long as you don't do anything that's gonna arouse anyone's suspicion. Don't go looking for extra information that wouldn't ordinarily cross your desk. Keep it real simple. We'll get into isolated dead-drops, surveillance exercises, and audio penetrations only when it's absolutely necessary. Otherwise, it doesn't need to get complicated."

"What sort of information do you want? Memos, financial reports, business plans . . . ?"

"That kinda thing, yes," he says, though his expression hints at greater prizes. "Get us everything you safely can. Even information about your operation that you might consider to be of no interest to us. Don't make any judgment on the validity of documentation on our behalf. Are we clear?"

"Sure."

Katharine comes back in with the tray of coffee. She distributes the mugs quietly, settles back down on the sofa, and says, "Did you say anything about Caspian exploration, Fort? Did you mention 5F371?"

Fortner does very well here. She has made a bad mistake, but he betrays no sign of it.

"How do you know about that?" I ask. "How do you know about 5F371?"

And he says, very coolly, "It's common knowledge, right? Look, we'll get to that some other time. Later. No need to talk about specifics at the moment."

"All we need for you now is a code name," Katharine says, also recovering well.

"Yes," says Fortner, sipping his coffee, then putting the mug on the table. "Kathy came up with JUSTIFY. How do you feel about that?"

I like it.

"Sounds fine to me. Why do I need one?"

"In the unlikely event that there's any kind of an emergency, that's the name you would use to contact us. We call it a cryptonym. It's also how you'll be known to our case officer at the Agency."

"I see."

"So are we clear?" he asks, rubbing his hands together with a broad smile. "Is this thing under way?"

"Oh yes," I reply. "I'm clear. Absolutely."

This thing is definitely under way.

21

BEING RICK

When Aldrich Ames made the decision to become an agent for the KGB, he did it swiftly and without moral compunction. His treachery was motivated solely by greed. He walked into the Soviet embassy in Washington on a sunlit mideighties afternoon, presented himself to the nearest intelligence operative, and offered up his services in exchange for large sums of money. The Russians couldn't believe their luck.

Treason is rarely explained by ideology. Nobody really knows why Blunt crossed over. He only got into Marxism as a way of understanding paintings. The others—Burgess, Maclean, Philby—were twisted in on themselves, corrupt from the soul up. Marxism was only theoretically attractive to them; their attachment to it was not deeply felt. What mattered more was the secret thrill of betrayal, the proper fulfillment of their vast egotism. All the traitor ever craves is respect.

Take Ames. He needed to live with the constant, incontrovertible knowledge that his actions were cherished at a higher level, that what he was doing was world shifting, deeply consequential. To be merely run-of-the-mill was intolerable to him. Up to a point, Ames was disenchanted with the CIA, sick of going out in the name of American imperialism and risking his life to obtain intelligence that was then overlooked by the Agency's masters on Capitol Hill for reasons of political expediency. But the satisfaction of his vanity was crucial, and money provided that. Ames later explained that he wanted money for "what it could guarantee": a sports car, an apartment in Europe, a fur coat for his foxy Colombian wife. The trappings of wealth also provided him with the material proof of his importance to the other side.

It was the money that was to prove his undoing. Conspicuous and inexplicably vast reserves of cash and possessions led the molehunt, after months of blind alleys and false leads, directly to Ames's door. He was arrested at his home in Virginia and bundled into the back of an FBI Pontiac by a huddle of G-men wearing flak jackets and mirrored shades.

"Think," he was heard repeating to himself, over and over again. "Think."

A few days after the meeting in Colville Gardens, Fortner and Katharine call me at Abnex to arrange a rendezvous at the swimming pool in Dolphin Square, a vast, brown-brick residential cube on the north bank of the Thames.

The reception area, off Chichester Street in Pimlico, is a hotel lobby. Fortner and Katharine are sitting on a small two-seater sofa just inside the main doors, both looking out of place and friendless. They seem quite unable to shed that unassimilated quality that marks them out as Americans. Katharine is wearing a white tennis dress and clean plimsolls over pale yellow socks. Fortner has on a blue tracksuit with expensive Reebok pumps and two sweatbands secured tightly around his wrists. They seem too healthy, too big boned, to be British, like tourists off the red-eye whom I have been asked to show around.

As we greet one another, it is immediately plain that a shift in the emphasis of our relationship has already taken place. When I kiss Katharine's cheek, it seems colder, and my handshake with Fortner is rigid with meaning. He holds the eye contact a beat too long. We are bound up in one another now, each of us capable of ruining the other. That knowledge acts as a background to our exchange of pleasantries. During the short walk from the lobby to the pool, there's something forced about the level of civility between us.

Fortner is carrying a heavy sports bag bulging with towels and clothing. We walk downstairs to the sports complex and he places it on the ground at the ticket desk, paying for the three of us to swim.

"That's kind of you, Fort," I tell him as he puts his wallet in a side pocket of the holdall.

"Least I can do, Milius."

"So I'll see you guys in there?" Katharine calls out as she walks off in the direction of the ladies' changing rooms. "Got your ten pence for the lockers?"

"Don't you worry 'bout that, honey," Fortner shouts after her—too loudly, I think, for such a small public space. "We got plenny."

The changing room is hot with steam. Men are drifting in and out of showers and there is a stench of mingled deodorants. Walking in, I am confronted by the tuberous cock and balls of a man of Fortner's generation, vigorously drawing a towel across his back like someone waving a scarf at a football match. I look away and find a small area of bench at which to undress. Fortner slots in beside me, cramping up the space.

"All right if I slide in here, buddy?" he says.

I don't want to do the nude thing with him. Not at all.

"Sure," I reply.

Gradually he unpacks his affairs: a too-small pair of Speedo trunks, a set of sky-blue goggles, and, to my surprise, a large black bathing cap. Quite quickly he is undressed, Adam-naked for the world to see. Fortner's skin is white and, with the exception of the upper part of his chest, comparatively hairless. But the shoulders are broad and strong, and his rib cage juts out proudly, as though packed with voluminous lungs. He looks tougher with his clothes off. I glance away as he puts on the Speedos.

"You not gettin' changed there, Alec?"

This is said brazenly, and two men sitting nearest us on the bench glance over suspiciously. We must look like a couple of queers: rent boy and papa.

"I was just wondering if I had a ten pee."

"I got one," he says, reaching into his trouser pocket on the clothes hook, withdrawing a fistful of loose change and handing me a shiny ten-pence piece. "That do ya?"

I thank him and clasp the coin in my hand. Then I wrap a towel around my waist before sliding on my Bermudas. In the meantime, Fortner shoulders his bag and walks to the locker rooms. He has thick stubby legs dotted with freckles, and a faded pink scar running down the back of his right thigh. I hear the metal clatter of a locker opening, then the slide of his bag being stowed within.

"Flashy shorts," he says as he comes back in, and the two men again look over at me. I drop my head, gathering my clothing into a tight round ball, which I place in a locker in the next room. There's nothing worth stealing, but it would be irritating to be robbed: I have a wallet with a picture of Kate inside and a decent pair of shoes that cost me seventy quid.

By the time I have returned to the changing room, Fortner has already showered off and entered the pool. There are two men dressed in suits, preparing to leave, hair wet and faces flushed with exercise. I switch on the taps in an open shower cubicle and soap away the sweat and surface grime of an average London day, trying to clear my head for what is about to follow. I must remain alert to everything they say or imply. We have not spoken about JUSTIFY for seventy-two hours and there will be details that they will want to clarify.

My dive into the pool goes badly wrong. I haven't been swimming in a long time, and I land too flat on the surface of the water with a loud, clapping belly flop. The hard slap against my stomach is painful and stinging. I swim briefly underwater, long enough for any embarrassment to subside, and surface in the center of the pool. Fortner and Katharine are standing in the shallow end, talking to each other, but they stop when they see me coming toward them.

Being tall, Katharine is only up to her waist in the water. She is wearing a blue bikini and her stomach looks flat and supple to the touch. I dare not look directly at her breasts in case Fortner notices. He looks absurd in the black bathing cap. It is wrapped so tightly around his head that all the blood has vanished from the upper part of his face, leaving his forehead looking white and ill. The goggles, too, are sucking down hard on his eyeballs, bulging out the surrounding skin.

"Nice temperature, don'tcha think?" he says.

"Ideal."

"You been here before, Milius?"

"Never. You picked a good spot for the meeting."

"That's right," he tells me. "Everything we say gets lost in the clamor."

"Is that the idea?"

It's a well-known technique.

"That's the idea."

Fortner splashes water onto his face and says, "You wanna go about halfway down and talk there?"

I nod and he pushes off, leading the way with a gentle crawl. Katharine follows in the slipstream and I swim with her, still adjusting to the sting and warmth of the pool. We swim directly beside each other, both of us breaststroking, and at one point our hands touch very briefly near the surface of the water. Katharine laughs instinctively as they slip apart, looking across at me with a smile. Her wet hair has glossed to jet black, thick as seaweed.

An elderly man passes us, swimming in the opposite direction. He moves with a painful slowness, as though he is here under duress. Thin gray hairs are glued across his forehead, and his face is strained from effort. His thin legs barely kick at all. Ahead of us, Fortner reaches the edge of the pool, touches down, and waits for us to join him.

"So how you doin'?" he says to me when we get there. "Everything feel okay?"

He removes the goggles, and his eyes are bloodshot and sore.

"Fine," I reply, with no inflection. "Better than I thought it would."

"No nerves? Second thoughts?"

"None."

"Good. We couldn't explain on the phone, but Kathy and I felt we should meet here today to give you the opportunity to ask any questions you may have."

A child's high-pitched shriek bounces off the water, piercing the space around us. I turn and see a mother coming out of the ladies' changing room, holding a wriggling toddler by the hand.

"There is one thing," I say, trying to keep things light and easy.

"What's that?" Katharine asks.

"How did you know I'd do it?"

Fortner's face retracts very slightly. This is not the question he was expecting.

"Do what?" he asks.

"How did you know I would agree?"

Fortner considers his answer for some time. Katharine, who is holding on to the ceramic edge of the pool, watches his face for clues. Finally she makes to speak, but Fortner interrupts her.

"I felt—we both felt—that you fit a certain personality type. You're a very sensitive person, Alec. You enjoy your solitude. You expressed to us on a number of occasions a certain understandable dissatisfaction with your job. . . ."

"And I'm short of money."

This prompts a smile in both of them, and Fortner says, "Yes. That's true. Things like that are not irrelevant."

The old man passes us again, slow weightless kicks toward the deep end.

"So there is such a thing as a psychological profile?" I ask. "There's a certain type of person who is more willing to commit an act of betrayal than another?"

"I don't put all that much faith in them myself," Katharine says. "I tend to go on instinct. And we always had a great feeling about you, Alec. Like you would want to do the right thing."

"Yes," I reply quietly.

A fit-looking man in his midthirties, wearing navy trunks and dark goggles, dives neatly into the pool and starts doing fast lengths. The blue water, which is covering me up to my shoulders, is suddenly warmer than the surrounding air. The mother and child are in the shallow end. She is teaching him how to swim.

"You have anything else you wanna ask?" Fortner says.

I must stress to them my ignorance of the intelligence world, ask something naïve about espionage.

"Yes. You said something about your organization sharing a lot of codes and stuff with MI5 and MI6. How much intelligence do we share with the Americans?"

"It's a good question," Katharine says, holding on to the side with outstretched arms and beginning to kick very gently underwater. "And, like Fort said, it's relevant to your situation. Usually, we share a great deal. The Agency sits in on weekly meetings of the Joint Intelligence Committee, for example. Some time ago, the British government paid our National Security Agency about eight hundred million dollars to share satellite-signals intelligence. But there's a problem right now with MI5. They feel that sensitive information about terrorist activities in Northern Ireland is finding its way back to the IRA via the Clinton White House. They're blaming Kennedy Smith, our ambassador in Dublin, who they think is soft on republicanism on account of her Irish roots. It's all bullshit of course, but the Security Service is understandably upset. They're being a little more economical with what they hand over."

This is certainly true. I recall Lithiby talking about it in one of our first meetings. It was just the latest in a long line of disputes with the Americans. He was also incensed that they had eavesdropped on British troops in Bosnia. At the time, I recall thinking that Lithiby's antagonism toward the CIA may have justified the entire Abnex/Andromeda project in his eyes.

I stare down at the clear blue pool and try to think of something else to say, something that will further convey my lack of expertise and a sense of my enthusiasm about JUSTIFY. But my mind is a blank. Katharine lifts a small handful of water and lets it fall.

"You're lookin' a little raggedy there," Fortner says. "You okay?"

Our lack of movement in the water has stilled my muscles. I am starting to shiver with cold.

"Sure. I'm fine. I'm just going to swim for a bit," I tell them. "Let's have another talk in a while."

Ten minutes later, resting in the shallow end after six brisk lengths, my eyes are stinging with chlorine and my head aches with the effort of concentration. The pool is almost deserted. The child and her mother have gone, as has the old man. Only the man in navy trunks remains, plowing up and down the lanes with his vigorous front crawl.

Fortner's black-capped head is bobbing up and down in the water, the goggles coming slowly toward me like lizard's eyes. Katharine is about seven feet to his left, arms describing elegant arcs of backstroke. They touch the shallow-end wall simultaneously and move across to talk to me. Fortner rubs his eyes and makes a low noise that is only halfway to civility. He wants to get down to business.

"We need to talk about your first drop," he says. "You wanna do that now?"

"Sure."

"What do you think you can get us?" Katharine asks.

My answer comes out swift and easy. This is what I had planned to say today.

"Abnex has just done some commercial price sets, which include our assumptions about how the global economy is going to pan out over the next few years. They'd give Andromeda some idea of our short-term plans, where we think the price of oil is going, that kind of thing."

"Sounds good," she says, flatly. They expected more.

"It's available in e-mail format, but I suppose that'll be traceable if I send it to you."

"That's the right way to be thinking," Fortner says, keeping his voice low. "Safety first. You could direct your messages via a remailing service that will strip them of their identifying features, but that's probably too risky as a first venture. We can't simply encrypt them. We'll have to think of another method. Maybe on floppy or a straight printout."

"That wouldn't be a problem," I tell him, trying to appear amenable and cooperative.

Katharine comes in with a suggestion: "If you just ran it off the printer at the Abnex office under the pretext that you wanted to do some work at home, would that be okay? I'm sure everyone does that as a means of staying on top of his workload."

Fortner nods in agreement, as though there were nothing more to be said on the subject, but something about this worries me. Just standing here watching the two of them discuss these vital first stages with such apparent calm makes me feel edgy and rushed. Katharine drops her hair back into the pool and a thin film of water on her neck glistens in the light. When she brings her head back up, she looks directly at me in anticipation of some sort of response.

"Yes," I tell her. "We do it all the time. It won't be a problem."

But it might be. How can I get the information onto the printer and out of the office without running the risk of somebody at Abnex noticing? There is constant movement in the office, constant observation. I cannot be certain that someone won't start asking questions. In an attempt to avoid looking nervous, I try to convince myself that it is best to let the Americans dictate things at this early stage. All of us are keen for the first handover to be completed and out of the way. Their experience here is greater than mine, but I do not like letting others make decisions on my behalf. There is already the danger that my best interests could be undermined by forces beyond my control. With this development, it feels almost as if the Americans are laying traps for me, and yet I know that this can surely not be the case.

"The actual process of handing over any information should be simple and straightforward," says Fortner, who halts momentarily as the swimmer approaches us, does a brisk turn, and moves away. He continues, "There's an absence of risk if you just keep to the basics. Let me give you a few examples of how we can work all this to our mutual advantage."

Hot chemical air is rising off the water and continuing to sting my eyes, but I manage a nod that I hope looks alert and concentrated.

"To start out, you can make duplicates of disks on the laptop at your apartment and photocopy any sensitive documentation at a convenience store in your neighborhood without arousing undue suspicion. Who's in those places, after all? Old ladies buying scratchcards and teenage kids sifting through porno magazines. Nobody's gonna notice. Better to do it there than under the cameras at Abnex, right?"

"What about getting the documents to you?" I ask.

"Just get a cab or subway over to our apartment like you would any other time. Or you can meet me in a restroom, a movie theater, any public area where an exchange will go unnoticed. Or we can do it at your apartment in Shepherd's Bush. The key is variety, to avoid anything that may look like a routine to a possible tail."

I bob my head without responding. This is the first time they have mentioned anything about my being followed.

Katharine says, "The only thing I would add . . ."

The man is already back again, swimming fast and hard to burn himself out. The three of us stare wanly out at the pool as he touches down, somersaults, and swims away. When he is safely out of earshot, Katharine continues.

"The only thing I would add is that it's better to say as little as possible about JUSTIFY when you're visiting Colville Gardens, or if we're meeting at your apartment. Just in case there's any audio surveillance. We'll put some background music on whenever you show up, and you should do the same when we come to Shepherd's Bush. And don't just do it when it's us that's visiting. Make a habit of putting on a CD whenever somebody comes round. That way it won't stand out as unusual if anyone happens to be listening in. Now, is there anywhere in particular that you would like to use as a location for the first drop?"

Her voice is full of patience. Without thinking, I reply, "What about Saul's flat on Saturday night? We're all going for dinner anyway, so it might just as well be there."

Fortner's response is tentative: "You cannot be seen handing any information to us. That's critical, Alec."

"Yeah. Maybe it's not such a good idea."

He narrows his eyes, working things through in his mind.

"Not necessarily," he says, as two young girls come out of the changing room and make their way gingerly down the steps into the pool. "There is a way we could work it."

"How?"

He waits for the girls to swim away.

"What's the combination on your briefcase, the one you take to work?"

"One sixty-two."

"On both sides?"

I nod.

"All right, then." He shifts his legs under the water, moving his left hand in the shallows. "Just bring the information to Saul's apartment at, say, seven thirty, and at some point during the evening either Kathy or myself will get to the case, open it up, and take out whatever's there."

"That's not making things too complicated?"

"Piece a cake," he replies confidently. "Once that's done, and we've had a chance to examine the price sets, we'll arrange for ten thousand dollars to be deposited in the account that our operation is setting up for you in Philadelphia."

"Pounds."

"What?"

"I said pounds. I want it in pounds."

"That wasn't a part of our initial agreement."

Katharine nervously passes her hand over her hair, flattening it down.

"I'm making it one now," I tell him, my voice still light and friendly. "I understood that payment would be in sterling."

"Alec, this is highly irregular."

"I don't think so. And don't tell me the Agency can't afford it."

"That's not the point. There's a principle involved."

I say nothing. Fortner's hands are tied, and he will have to consent.

"We'll see what we can do," he says quietly.

Katharine looks away.

"Thank you."

I feel bad now, like I've gone too far.

"What if there's no opportunity to get to the case during dinner?"

"Most probably there will be, Alec, if you put it somewhere smart." There's now a hint of irritation in Fortner's voice. "If we can't do it safely, we won't do it at all. And if that happens, just take the case home and bring it to us some other time. But just remember one thing. . . ."

He brings his hand out of the water to make his point firmly and with great care. "Nobody is expecting you to do what you're doing. That's the beauty of it. Nobody's watching us anymore. That should help to calm any nerves you might have."

I do not answer this, merely nod my head.

"That's settled then," he says, crouching down until the water is up to his neck. Katharine does the same. "Just leave the case in the hall of Saul's apartment. We'll take care of the rest. It's gonna be real easy. Now let's do some laps."

It has started to rain as we make our way through the lobby doors and out on to Chichester Street. A strong wind is blowing along the face of the building. Katharine comments on how quickly the summer has passed. Fortner tells us to stay indoors while he fetches the car, so we head back inside and sit down.

Katharine immediately leans forward and adopts the manner of a concerned friend. She wants to get back that closeness we had, that shared understanding by which I was first ensnared.

"Alec, it's difficult for you, I know," she says. "You wanna do everything right by Fortner, you don't want to let him down. But all this must be quite a shock for you. You sure you don't have any concerns?"

"Of course," I tell her with a confident smile. "I'm completely okay about it."

"You sure? Because back there in the pool you seemed a little spaced out, a little tense."

It's bad that she thought this.

"Not at all, no. I was just a bit apprehensive about using Saul's flat. You know, the friend thing."

"We can change that if you want."

"It's fine. It makes sense. I've thought about it now. Don't worry."

"You sure? Because you know you can always come to me if there's a problem."

And with this she reaches across to touch my sleeve, her fingers pressing against my wrist.

"I'm sure," I tell her, looking away.

Clearly, this is how they will proceed from now on. The pattern has been set. Fortner will handle the business end of things while Katharine takes care of the emotional side, coddling me whenever I am beset by doubt. It's pointless, of course, to confide in her, for my every word will be reported back to him for careful analysis. All my conversations, no matter who they are with, have this quality of evasion about them. They are significant not for what is said in the everyday to and fro of mutual trickery, but rather for what is left unspoken. It's all about hidden meanings, reading between the lines, teasing out the subtext. This is where the skill resides.

The first handover, for example, is not about the leaking of sensitive information. Its true purpose is more subtle than that. Katharine and Fortner set it up with such ease in the pool because they know that a duplicate of our commercial price sets is of no more use to them than a copy of *The Economist*. The true value of the exchange at Saul's flat lies in giving JUSTIFY a dummy run. Katharine and Fortner want to see how effectively I can operate within our new arrangement; whether, in the heat of the action, I become sloppy, forgetful, thrown by nerves. More crucially, it is essential from their point of view that I commit an act of industrial espionage—however slight—as soon as possible. That will bind me into the treachery and give them leverage with which to threaten me should I develop cold feet at a later date.

Fortner pulls up in the car outside. Katharine moves to the door. Just as I am standing up to leave, Cohen's girlfriend walks into the lobby. I recognize her from the Christmas party. She is tall and self-confident, with an older face that she will grow into. We catch each other's eye and stare lingeringly without words. In different circumstances, the moment might even be construed as flirtatious. We both consider the prospect of a brief, embarrassed greeting in which neither of us knows the other's name, but she soon looks the other way and walks off toward the reception desk.

There is no doubt in my mind that she recognized me, at least as an Abnex employee or, more exactly, as a member of Murray's team. She will tell Cohen of this encounter when she sees him tonight, perhaps giving him a description in the hope of discovering my name. He will piece it together from there.

Was he with anyone?

Yes, she will reply.

Really? Cohen will say. *A woman in her thirties, tall, good-looking? An older man, too?*

Yes, she'll say. *As a matter of fact he was.*

22

PLAUSIBLE DENIABILITY

To: Alec Milius
Address: Alec—Milius@abnex.co.uk
Subject: Dinner Sat

Alec
Hi. Hope you get this and your system doesn't fuck it up like last time. What's happening about tomorrow night? Let me know what time you're picking up Fortner & Katharine. I've invited a guy who was working on the Spain film to come to dinner with his girlfriend—haven't met her before.

I'm trapped in a vortex of daytime television. Looking forward to Saturday. I don't see enough of you these days, my friend—it'll be good to catch up.

Saul

Q: What's the difference between an egg and a wank?
A: You can beat an egg.

Tanya walks past and floats a single sheet of paper into my in-tray. It's a circular about restricting noncommercial use of the Internet within the office. There is a tangerine on my desk and I tear open its skin. The smell of Christmas billows up out of the fruit.

I hit Reply.

To: Saul Ricken
Address: sricken5471@compuserve.com
Subject: Re: Dinner Sat

Meeting F+K at your place—seven thirty okay with you? I have to work, so coming direct from here.

Can't believe you've never heard the egg joke before.

See you tomorrow night.
Alec

I have a long meeting on Saturday morning between nine o'clock and twelve thirty with Murray and Cohen in one of the small conference rooms on the sixth floor. With the exception of George on security duty downstairs, the office is deserted. Even the canteen is closed.

I am the last to arrive and the only one of us not wearing a suit. Cohen remarks on this immediately, and Murray reminds me about "company policy" as we sit at the start of the meeting. Another black mark against my name. Cohen, of course, looks trim and showered, elegantly attired in a bespoke navy herringbone. You could take him anywhere, the little fucker.

His attitude toward me throughout the meeting is spiteful and manipulative. At one point, he presses me for details about a research project he knows I have yet to begin working on. When I can't give a full answer, a shadow of irritation falls across Murray's face and he coughs lightly, writing something down. They are both sitting opposite me at the conference table so that the relationship between us takes on the characteristics of an interrogation. My mind is slipped and weak. I woke up late and missed breakfast, and I have a gathering nervousness about the handover tonight. Cohen, by contrast, is sharp and alert. He listens with faked overattentiveness to Murray's every word, nodding vigorously in agreement and taking detailed minutes on his laptop with neat little punches on the keyboard. If Murray cracks a joke, Cohen laughs. If Murray wants a cup of coffee, Cohen fetches it for him. The whole affair is sickening. By lunchtime, my gut feels hollow, and my mood is one of blank anger.

I eat alone in a pub on Hewett Street, haddock and chips with plastic sachets of tartar sauce. There's a man at the next table reading *FHM,* one of those glossy magazines for men who don't have the guts to buy porn. A bikini-clad actress beams out from the cover, all cleavage and flat tummy. There'll be a suggestive interview inside about what she looks for in a guy, next to a Q&A health page answering readers' queries on penis size and bad breath.

Cohen has had a sandwich at his desk, washed down with a carton of low-sugar Ribena. "I had some e-mailing to catch up on," he tells me as I come back into the office, "a query from a law firm in Ashgabat." I sit at Piers's desk and flick through a copy of *The Wall Street Journal.*

"Where's Murray?"

"He's had to go home. Family crisis. Jemma's fallen off a swing."

"Who's Jemma?"

"His youngest daughter."

This could make it more difficult to print the price sets from my computer.

"So what are we supposed to do?" I ask him.

"You can go, if you like."

This is exactly Cohen's style: probing, arch, ambiguous. The remark is designed to test me. Will I work through the afternoon, or take the opportunity presented by Murray's sudden departure to clock off early? Cohen won't make a move until he knows what I intend to do. If I stay in the office, he'll stay, too. If I leave, he will remain another half hour and then pack up. He can never be anything other than the last man to go home at night.

My best option is to leave now, have a cup of coffee, and return to the office in two hours. By then, Cohen will almost certainly have gone. He's clinical and industrious, but he likes his weekends as much as the next man. I can then pretend to do an hour's work at my desk— for the benefit of the security cameras—during which I can print out the price sets on the LaserJet. That way I'll still be on time for the seven-thirty handover.

"I might go," I tell him firmly.

"Really?" he says, disappointment in his voice.

"Lots to do. I want to go shopping in the West End, get myself some new clothes."

"Fine."

He isn't interested in any excuses.

"So I'll see you on Monday."

"Monday."

Three blocks away, I order a macchiato and a chocolate wafer in a decent Italian café where there's a pretty waitress and a fuzzy TV bolted to the wall. The BBC is replaying highlights from the Euro '96 soccer tournament—a Czech player saluting the crowd after chipping the goalkeeper, Alan Shearer reeling away from the goal with his right hand raised in triumph. Simpler pleasures. My neck starts to hurt from craning up at the screen, so I turn to the copy of *The Times* that I brought with me to pass the time until four o'clock. I read it almost cover to cover: op-eds, news, arts, sports, even the columns I usually hate in which overpaid hacks tell you about their children going off to nursery school, or what brand of olive oil they're using this week. I drink two more coffees, lattés this time, and then make my way back to the office.

George is still on security duty as I come in through the revolving doors.

"Forget something, did we?"

George has just come back from holiday. He looks sunburned and overfed.

"You won't believe this," I tell him, all casual and relaxed. "I got all the way home, made myself a nice cup of tea, and was just settling down to watch *Grandstand* when I remembered I had some letters to finish by Monday morning. I'd forgotten all about them, and my notes are here in the office. So I had to get on the tube and come all the way back."

"That's too bad," says George, rearranging a bunch of keys on his desk. "And on a weekend an' all."

I walk past him toward the lifts, clutching my security pass in the sweat of my palm. I have to wait for some time for a lift to arrive, pacing up and down on the cold marble floor. George ignores me. He is reading today's *Mirror* next to the flickering monochrome of five closed-circuit televisions. The crackle of his newspaper provides the only noise in the reception area. Then a lift chimes open, and I ride it to the fifth floor.

The coffees have started to kick in. I am fidgety without being any more alert. If I can see that Cohen is still working at his desk, through the glass that separates our section from the lift area, I will leave the building for another hour. If Cohen has gone home, as I expect he has, I can proceed. Panpipe music issues from a speaker above my head.

I emerge slowly from the lift as the doors glide open and immediately look through the window partition in the direction of Cohen's desk. My view is partially obscured by a rubber plant. I carry on to the door of the office, still looking around for any sign of him.

Keep moving. The cameras are watching. Don't loiter.

The team area appears to be clear. No sign of Cohen. His briefcase has gone, and his desk has been tidied the way he leaves it night after night: neat piles, immaculate in-trays, a squared-up keyboard with the mouse flush along one side. It's all about control with Cohen, never letting anything slip. Even his Post-it notes are stuck down in exacting straight lines.

I sit at my desk and disturb the screen saver with a single touch on the space bar. Why is this suddenly so hard? I had not expected it to be as difficult as this. There is no risk, no chance of trouble, and yet I feel somehow incapable, lost in an immense space surveyed by invisible eyes. Even the simple process of keying in my password feels unlawful. I should have done this yesterday, not now, should have let the printout get lost in the constant traffic and buzz of office life. To do this alone on a Saturday afternoon looks all wrong.

So I wait. As a smokescreen I type e-mails that I don't need to send and fetch reference books that I flick through ostentatiously at my desk. I go to the gents', fetch coffee from the machine, drink water at the fountain, overdoing every aspect of normal everyday behavior for the benefit of anyone who might be watching. I do this for the better part of an hour. It is unthinkable that George is watching with any great attentiveness, yet I go through with the absurd routine. I am held back not by cowardice, or by a change of heart, but by the simple panic of being caught.

Finally, at around five o'clock, I resolve to do what I came here to do. I sit at the computer and load the file. Three clicks of the mouse and the document opens up on the screen.

There are four pages constituting about thirty seconds of normal printing time. The Print dialogue box prompts me—Best, Normal or Draft? Grayscale or Black & White? Number of copies? I go for the default setting and press Return.

The file spools over to the printer, but it takes longer than usual to emerge from the LaserJet. I busy myself with other tasks, trying not to look distracted by the yawning gap of time. I pour myself a plastic cup of water at the fountain, but my nervousness is all-consuming. When the fax machine on the facing wall beeps with an incoming message, the shock of it causes me to spill a small amount of the water as I am bringing it up to my mouth.

Why was I not more prepared for this? They've trained you. It's nothing. Be logical.

I look down at the printer, willing it to work, and, finally, the first page discharges, smooth and easy. Then the second. I look closely at the two sheets of paper and the printing quality is good. No smudges or runovers. The third page follows. I try to read some of the words as it comes out upside down, my neck twisted around, but I am too disoriented to make any sense of it. Then I stand over the printer, waiting for the fourth and final sheet.

It isn't coming out.

I wait, but there's no sign of it. The printer must have run out of paper.

The drawer is stuck, and I have to give it a sharp tug before it opens, but there is still a half inch of A4 paper lying inside the machine. I slam it shut, but this has no effect. It is as if every piece of hardware in the building has suddenly shut down.

There must be a bad connection somewhere, or a fault with the main server.

And I am on the point of crouching down, ready to trace leads and check power cables, when I hear his voice.

"What's this?"

Cohen is absolutely beside me, shoulder-to-shoulder. Not looking at me, but down at the printer. I breathe in hard and cannot disguise the sound of it, a startled gasp of air as my face flushes red. His breath smells of menthol.

Cohen has picked up the three sheets from the printer tray and started reading them.

"What do you want these for?"

If you ever get caught, they told me, don't answer the question. Deflect and deny until you know that you can get clear.

Think. Think.

"You gave me a shock," I tell him, mustering a half laugh, in the hope that this will explain my blushing. "I thought you'd gone home."

"I was on the sixth floor," Cohen says coolly. "Library."

I didn't hear the lift. He must have used the staircase. I look down at his shoes, silent suede loafers.

"What do you want this for?"

"The commercial price sets?"

"Yes," he says. "The price sets." He holds up the first page and flaps it in my face.

"I needed a copy at home."

"Why?"

"Why not? So I can get on top of my work. So I can see the long-term picture."

Don't go on too long. The bad liar always embellishes.

Cohen nods and mutters, "Oh."

I look back at the printer, trying to avoid his eyes.

"So what happened to shopping in the West End? Got to get myself some new clothes, you said."

"I had some letters to finish by Monday. Forgot."

"And this, of course," he says archly, passing me the sheets of paper.

Cohen knows that something is not right here.

The fourth and final page has emerged into the printer tray without my realizing it. I bend over to scoop it out and tap the pages into a neat pile, stapling them in the top left corner. Cohen walks back to his desk and takes a pen out of a drawer.

"I'm going now," he says.

"Me too. I'm all done."

"Better switch off your computer, then," he says, housing the pen in his jacket pocket.

"Yes."

I move around to my desk and sleep the system. It folds into a slow screen saver, colored shapes in space disappearing into a vast black hole.

He is already halfway to the exit when he says, "Couldn't you have written your letters at home?"

"What?"

Pretending not to have heard him buys me the time to think of a reason.

"I said couldn't you have done the letters at home?"

"No. I had all my notes here."

"I see. Bye then."

"See you, Harry."

He turns the corner and disappears, taking the stairs all the way to the ground floor. I continue to sit at my desk, wanting to clutch my head in my hands and sink to the floor. After all the planning and preparation, it seems extraordinary to me that something should have gone wrong so quickly.

I put the documents into my briefcase, place the letters beside the postage meter, shut off the lights in the office, and take the lift to the foyer. The blur of aftermath makes it impossible to think at all clearly. I leave the Abnex building without speaking to George and disappear out onto Broadgate. It's five thirty.

Some things become clear as I walk around.

I may have overreacted. What did Cohen really see? He saw Milius, the new boy, doing some printing. No more, no less. He saw letters on my desk, cold cups of coffee, the outward signs of an afternoon's work. Nothing untoward about that. Nothing to make him suspect sharp practice.

What do I know about Cohen? That he is guileful and malevolent. That he is the sort of person to sneak up on a colleague in a deserted office on a weekend afternoon and get a kick out of giving him a fright. Cohen feels simultaneously threatened by what I am capable of and contemptuous of what I represent. He's just another Nik, snuffing out his insecurity by making others feel uneasy.

But he will be watching me that much more closely from now on. It was my first mistake, the only thing to have gone wrong so far.

Why didn't I see him coming?

23

THE CASE

Just after six, still feeling restless and shaken, I take a slow, half-empty tube to West Kensington. I have rationalized what happened, and yet it continues to play on my nerves. There should have been a clean through-line of action in the last six hours, right up to the handover this evening, but it has been disrupted by Cohen and by my own stupidity.

Emerging from the underground station into a humid September evening, I walk slowly, clutching the briefcase tightly in my right hand. Sweat has warmed the handle, making it clammy to the touch. The contents feel almost radioactive, as if they will somehow burn through the leather case. This thought in itself strikes me as absurd, yet I cannot shake it off. I want to stop and open the briefcase to check that the documents are still inside. Dog walkers and lone queers pass me as I walk through Hammersmith Cemetery, and each one appears to steal a glance at the case, as if aware of its contents. Their faces seem full of bored, suspicious loathing, and this only deepens my sense of isolation. I was warned that the first drop would be like this, but the chaos of it has completely bewildered me.

Approaching the door of Saul's apartment building at seven fifteen, I turn around in the street to check for evidence of a tail. There is an old lady loitering near a fenced-off expanse of grass, but otherwise the road is deserted. I look closely at the cars parked up and down the length of Queen's Club Gardens, but all of them appear to be unoccupied. Now there is not solely the probability of American and British surveillance, which I had anticipated, but the added problem of Cohen. It is as if I am expecting him to appear around the next corner at any moment.

Saul buzzes me in without saying hello and I climb the four flights of stairs to his flat. This is a slow business. My mind has been scrambled by the afternoon's events and my body feels tired and cumbersome. Yet the optimism contained in his smile as he opens the front door momentarily lifts me. I had forgotten just how much I rely on him for a sense of being *liked*. He plants his arm across my back and gives it a slap.

Katharine and Fortner have come up behind me on the stairs. They are so close that Saul asks if we have come together. How could I not have seen them after staring so long down Queen's Club Gardens? They must have been parked a long way from the building, watched from a distance as I entered, and then followed me up. As soon as I see them, my stomach tightens.

"Hi, sweetie," Katharine says, kissing me on the cheek. Her face looks puffy up close, suddenly middle-aged. "You okay?"

"Fine, thanks," I say. "Fine."

Both of them look unnervingly focused. Fortner's complexion is almost gray against the faded white of his shirt, but there is a look of intense concentration in his fixed, still eyes. In his left hand he is holding a single bottle of wine wrapped in thin crepe paper, and in his right a tanned leather briefcase that I have not seen before. He will be using this to carry my documents away.

Katharine surges forward to plant a kiss on Saul's cheek and compliments him on his clothes. He is wearing a cream shirt and a trim pair of dark moleskins with what look to be a new pair of running shoes. Saul has always had the money to buy decent clothes. He and Fortner shake hands as we shuffle around, putting our jackets and coats in the hall.

With Saul's back turned, I set my briefcase down next to an old umbrella stand and look to Fortner for approval. He nods quickly, letting me know that he has registered where it is. I look back at Saul to check that he has not seen this exchange, but he is speaking to Katharine, unaware. It occurs to me that I have still not properly considered the implications of allowing a handover to take place here. Should Saul ever find out, the consequences would be enough to end our friendship, yet I barely feel a jolt of betrayal. I have to concentrate so hard nowadays on every aspect of my relationship with Andromeda that there's no time to consider anything as mundane as friendship.

"Everything all right?" Fortner says to me, not bothering to lower his voice.

"Absolutely."

"Did you find that stuff we needed?"

Across the hall, Saul is still talking to Katharine, though she must have one ear listening in on what we are saying.

"Yeah. I got it. It's there."

I nod in the direction of the briefcase. Fortner sets his own down beside it.

"Nice goin'."

"Come through and I'll introduce you," Saul is saying, and he guides the three of us into the sitting room.

I just float through the next half hour, oblivious of the others, unable to concentrate on anything beyond the possibility of discovery. We are introduced to Dave, Saul's friend from Spain, and Susannah, his girlfriend. They are the only other guests, which concerns me. Fortner's absence, when it comes, would not be so noticeable in a larger crowd of people.

Dave is a squat thirtysomething, bald before his time, with a generous smile stitched below weak eyes. Susannah is also short, but pale and thin, with vanished tits and charity shop wardrobe. I distrust her immediately and think of him as ineffectual. He has a slightly desperate way of looking at me, a craving to be friendly and affable. Saul pours us all a drink and a conversation develops among the five of them to which I make no contribution. The utter pointlessness of getting to know new people, given my present situation, is palpable. Smells of garlic and wine drift in from the kitchen, where Saul goes from time to time to check on the food.

Toward eight o'clock, as we are standing up to go to the table for dinner, Dave asks me how I know Saul.

"Old school friends," I tell him. "From way back."

"Listen to him," Saul interjects loudly from across the room. "From way back. You never used to say that, Alec." He looks over at Katharine. "You two are turning him into an American. The other day on the phone he told me to have a nice day."

"Oh bullshit," I say, but the way this comes out it sounds angry and petulant. There's a sudden embarrassed silence among us, and Saul grimaces, a joke gone wrong.

"All right, all right," he says, and his face fills with disappointment. He has been growing more impatient with me in the last few months, knowing that something in our friendship has changed, but without any real knowledge as to why. I don't telephone Saul as much as I used to and don't have the time to send him jokes via e-mail. We haven't been out for a drink, just the two of us, since Christmas of last year, and I have entirely lost track of his career, his girlfriends, his worries and concerns. This is how I imagined things would pan out, but now that something has gone wrong, the burden of secrecy feels suddenly overwhelming. With Kate gone, Saul is the one person I might trust to talk to about what happened this afternoon. I want to tell him the truth, I want to tell him exactly what is going on. This constant entanglement with bluff, double-bluff, second-guess, and guile is wearing. Any notion of trust or honor that I ever had has vanished. My life has become a wall of lies shored up against the possibility of capture. I cannot recall what it felt like just to sit around this flat in the old days, watching videos with Saul and pissing away our teens and twenties.

"Telecommunications," Dave is saying, to no one but me. We are sitting beside each other at the dining-room table, Katharine and Fortner at either end, with Saul and Susannah opposite us.

"What about them specifically?"

"You know how they're paying for the Internet and all the fiber optic networks?"

Has he been talking to me about this before now? Have I missed something? Have I just been nodding and mumbling at him, my mind drifted off elsewhere?

"No. How?"

"Answering machines."

"What do you mean, 'answering machines'?"

Dave leans forward, plucks a napkin from his side plate, and places it on his lap.

"Before answer phones came along, you just dialed a number and let it ring out, right? If somebody wasn't in, you hung up and there was no charge for making the call. But all that's changed now that everybody has an answering machine. Whenever you make a call, it kicks in after two or three rings. So a connection's been made, right? And if a connection's been made, then you've added to your phone bill. They have a minimum charge of four pence, so it adds up. How many answering machines do you think there are in the UK?"

"I have no idea."

"Maybe fifteen million, conservative estimate. So every time somebody rings those machines, British Telecom is making sixty million pence, which is . . . which is . . ."

The night is still while Dave makes his calculation. I do it for him.

"Six hundred thousand pounds."

"Exactly," he says. "Thank you."

Susannah is reacting to something Saul has said. She has a laugh like a broken fan belt. There's some kind of mousse appetizer in front of me and I am already halfway through it.

"But of course the really smart thing about answering machines is that you have to call back if someone leaves you a message. So that's another guaranteed call for BT, another four pence minimum. It's no wonder they make the profits they do. What is it? About seven hundred and fifty pounds a minute?"

"Is that how much they make?" Katharine asks. Suddenly the entire table is listening to Dave's monologue.

"Apparently. And it doesn't just stop with answering machines. There's call waiting now, too. That's the most craven one of all. You ring up a friend, and even if he's on the line talking to someone else you're made to wait. Beep. Beep. *Please hold the line while we try to connect you. The other person knows you are waiting.* And it goes on and on. Fucking woman sounds like Margaret Thatcher. So you're there, you're holding the line, but they're not trying to connect you. Like fuck they are. They're just happy to let you run up your bill."

"That's right," says Fortner. "They are."

He looks relaxed and composed, a drink inside him, safe in the knowledge that the Abnex documents are in the next room.

"And let's say they do." Dave is speaking faster and faster, gesturing wildly, cutlery in hand. I look across at Susannah, but she has nothing but pride in her eyes as Dave swallows a mouthful of mousse and continues with his discourse. "Then the first person they were talking to has to run up *their* phone bill waiting for the other person to talk to the person who's waiting. That can go on for hours. And even then, one of them will have to call the other back, which is another guaranteed call for BT. And then—and *then*—there are itemized phone bills. If you're sharing a flat with somebody and he denies making that five-pound call to the number listed on the bill, you then have to ring that number up and embarrass yourself by asking who the fuck they are, just so that you can work out if it's your bill or his. You ever done that, Alec?"

"I live alone."

Again, silence settles around the table in the wake of my speaking. Saul frowns and then turns his head to face Katharine, his lips drawn together in a tight, disappointed line. Dave, looking pale and embarrassed, finishes eating, and for a while the only noise in the room is the tinkling of his fork against his china plate, the quick munch of his jaw as he chews and swallows. Saul is already up and collecting the plates before Dave has finished, stacking them noisily and making for the kitchen.

"Can I give you a hand?" I ask, and, without looking at me, he says, "Sure."

"I'll come too," Katharine offers, but Saul gestures at her to sit down.

"Don't worry," he says. "I only need Alec."

Once we are in the kitchen, he turns on me.

"What's the matter with you these days?"

What surprises me about my reaction to this is that I am grateful to him for asking. For a brief moment I consider not bothering to deny any unhappiness. I want the opportunity to unburden myself, but it's untenable. I have to keep up the masquerade.

"I'm fine. Fine," I tell him, managing a smile, but there can be nothing in either my voice or my attitude to convince him of this.

"You're not fine, Alec," he says, the weight of his body shifting forward, coming at me. "You're hardly here. Most of the time I don't even recognize you anymore."

He is keeping his voice low, tinkering with a pan on the stove that has pasta boiling hard inside it. I am worried that Fortner, who is only across the corridor in the chair nearest the kitchen, will hear us, so I move away from the sink and close the door until it is ajar.

"Come on, Saul. Who has the will to listen to a guy they've never met before doing his party piece about answering machines and phone bills? I have a lot on my mind."

"We all work hard, for fuck's sake," he says, but before I have time to reply he has carried a bowl of salad into the dining room and left me alone in the kitchen. I turn to the sink and begin rinsing the plates in a coughing stream of lukewarm water. One by one, I slot them into the dishwasher.

"Is the pasta ready?" he says, coming back in.

"I don't know. Listen, why don't I stay tonight? We can talk then, have a smoke, watch some TV."

"Okay," he says, forking a strand of tagliatelle out of the water. Then, more quietly: "Whatever."

At half past ten, with the main course out of the way, Fortner makes his move.

Saul, Dave, and Susannah are having a conversation about the latest cinema releases, which to me is always the sign of a bad dinner party. Fortner interjects to ask if anyone has seen *Mission Impossible,* and Susannah says yes she has and tells a boring story that reveals only that she has misunderstood the plot. More summer blockbusters are discussed—*Independence Day, Die Hard with a Vengeance,* one with Schwarzenegger I haven't heard of called *Eraser*—and everybody gets to share his views about whether Arnie is past his prime. Dave plays the art-house card by revealing that he has seen "the new Bertolucci." As far as I can tell, it's just a story about a bunch of seedy British ex-pats sleeping around in Tuscany. In the middle of all this, Katharine says simply, "Honey, have you taken your medication?"

Which is Fortner's cue.

"Dunno why I bother," he says, getting up from the table with the slowness of a geriatric. His voice is a low grunt. "Goddamn pills never do any good."

And with that he lumbers toward the entrance hall. He makes this look so natural that the others would never suspect a thing.

Dave carries on: "I often think, would Bernardo Bertolucci have half the reputation he has if his name were Bernard Bell or . . . or Bob Bower or something?"

From the hall I can hear the slap of my briefcase falling onto the carpet, and the successive snaps of the brass catches flying open.

"I mean don't you think that the success he's enjoyed has something to do with the allure of the name 'Bernardo Bertolucci'? He already sounds like a great movie director before he's even shot a frame of film."

There's a rustle of papers in the hall, clearly audible to all of us and not at all like the sound of a pill bottle or a foil pack of antibiotics. Then the briefcase is closed. Almost immediately another case, clearly Fortner's, is opened. The sound of this is much fainter. Only someone who was deliberately listening would hear it. Fortner must have held the catches with his fingers, drawing them up slowly to smother any sound. I look at Saul and Susannah, but they have been sidetracked by Dave, who has segued into *Last Tango in Paris*. I listen for further noises, but Dave's voice smothers everything. Katharine catches my eye, but the expression on her face does not change.

Then, at a convenient break in the conversation, Saul says, "I'll get pudding. Will Fortner want any, Kathy?"

This could be dangerous. If he heads out into the hall, he may see Fortner. I try to think of a way to delay him, but Katharine reacts more quickly.

"Hey," she says, thinking on her feet. "Before you do that, just tell me about something. It's been bugging me all night. You see that book there?"

"Which one?"

Saul is wavering near the door, looking back at her.

"On the second shelf."

"Here?"

Saul points to a book with an orange spine, coming back into the room.

"No, just a little farther along. To the right."

"The one by James Michener?"

"That's it, yes."

By now we have all swiveled and are looking at the book in question.

"That's right. Now, was he British?"

"Michener?"

"Yes," Katharine says.

"I don't know," Saul admits. "Why?"

"Because I have an ongoing argument with my father that he's from Connecticut."

Saul doesn't know that Katharine's father is dead.

"I've no idea," Dave says. "I'm fairly sure he's British."

Fortner comes back into the dining room.

"No idea about what?" he says confidently, a spring in his step. Everything must have gone smoothly.

"Oh, it doesn't matter," Katharine tells him, settling back into her chair with a faint grin. "D'you want any dessert, honey?"

There is pudding, there is cheese, there is coffee.

My sense of relief at the success of the handover has made adrenaline gradually dissipate from me like a deep, muscle-softening massage. For the first time in hours, I begin to relax. Out of this comes a tiredness that flattens me toward eleven o'clock like jet lag. Katharine notices this and offers me more coffee. I drink it and pick at the pudding, a chocolate goo that goes some way to restoring my energy, but it remains difficult to involve myself in the party.

At midnight, Katharine begins to fade and is soon making excuses to leave, which Fortner is only too keen to pick up on. He came here for the briefcase, after all, not the conversation. Having stood up, he walks over and kisses Susannah twice on the cheek and shakes Dave's hand, telling them what a pleasure it's been to make their acquaintance.

"Good-bye, young man," he says to me, placing his arm on my shoulder. "We'll be seeing you soon, I hope."

"I asked him for supper next week," Katharine says, disengaging from her farewell to Dave.

"Terrific. See you then."

Saul then walks them to the front door—I remain where I am, listening to Dave talk about his job—and he sees them out. When Saul comes back, he smokes a joint with Dave in the sitting room while Susannah makes a vague attempt at clearing up. By one o'clock, the two of them have gone out into the hall arm in arm with warm smiles and promises of meeting again that I do not deserve and do not believe.

Saul now goes for a pee and I sit on the sofa. It's late and he's stoned, and, when he comes back, he doesn't want to talk. I was expecting a long, involved chat into the small hours, but he just wants to sit in front of the television watching a videotape of *Match of the Day*. As the cassette is rewinding he asks me what I thought of Susannah, and I say how nice she seemed, how funny and smart and easy, and that seems to satisfy him.

On the sofa, beer in hand, Saul follows the match between Chelsea and Manchester United with the attentiveness of the lifelong fan. I half watch it, my mind wandering back through the events of the day. Fort-ner will be home by now, going through the contents of the file, prepar-ing the information before handing it over to his case officer in the morning. Will Katharine help him with this or leave him to it? A car horn sounds long and hard in Queen's Club Gardens as a Manchester United player is tracked closely down the wing by a defender stooped low like a piano player.

"Andy fucking Cole," Saul mutters. "I know caged hens who are more creative in the box."

Ten minutes later, as I am getting up to go to bed, Saul mutes the sound of the television and looks up at me.

"Alec?" he says.

"Yeah?"

"Sorry I had a go at you before. About Abnex. I think it's great you're doing so well there, doing something you believe in. A lot of people would give their arse to be in your position."

"Don't bother . . ."

"No, hear me out," he says, raising his hand. He's more drunk than I had realized. "I don't have any right to criticize you for working hard, for spending time with people in the business. And I like Fort and Kathy, they're not the issue. I'm just reacting to how little time all of us have now, away from our careers. It's taken me a while to adjust to the fact that we can't always be fucking about like we used to. I don't really know when the fun stopped, you know? We've all had to get a lot more serious."

I nod.

"Truth is, I admire you," he says. "You were in a bad place after not getting into the Foreign Office, and you sorted yourself out."

Now is when it is most difficult. Now is when none of it seems worthwhile at all.

"Thanks," is all I can say. "That means a lot to me."

He leans back and I decide to call it a night.

"I'm bushed," I tell him. "Going to get some sleep."

"Sure," he replies. "See you in the morning."

And he turns back to the TV.

I sleep in the room where I always stay, a study with a futon in it, the walls lined with paperbacks and hefty academic tomes left over from

Saul's days at LSE. I take down a paperback copy of *Out of Africa* and climb into bed, wearing boxer shorts and an old white T-shirt. From down the hall I can hear the roar of a goal-celebrating crowd and Saul quietly shouting, "Yes!" to himself as someone scores. I lie there for a while, trying to read, but my eyes grow tired after a single page and I put out the bedside light.

Then, of course, I cannot sleep.

Every night now for more than a year the pattern has been the same: an urgent need to rest, ignored by my wandering mind, raking over every imaginable thought and anxiety, solving nothing. To sleep so little, so agitatedly, has become commonplace. Yet, somehow, my body has adjusted to being starved of rest. I still manage to work, think, exercise, and lie, but at some basic level I have forgotten how to *feel*. The jadedness is gradually erasing my better instincts, any capacity I once possessed to evaluate consequence and implication. It is as if every time I am woken up at three in the morning by that awful, caving sense of worry that creeps around my subconscious, some better part of me begins to fail. Even a few straight hours of sleep will always be broken before dawn by mind racings, concerns somehow magnified by the quiet and black of the night.

So, as ever, I turn to sex to try to shut it all out, lying there in the dark with the noise of the TV in the distance and some girl fucking me to sleep. She's never anyone I care about, never Kate. Only the ones I tried to have, but couldn't, even some woman I saw at a bus stop who gave me the eye. Every now and again I relive an actual sexual encounter and try to make it better than it was: screwing someone from years back, or Anna again. Tonight it's her, with her showered skin and tits bouncing uselessly above me, that look of sated lust in her eyes that I failed to recognize as malice. Nothing works, though. I hear Saul shut off the TV at around two o'clock and follow the noise of his footsteps going up and down the passage. He visits the bathroom, washes, then turns out all the lights. The flat is quiet.

I find myself thinking back to when I broke up with Kate. Saul and I would spend long hours in a Brazilian bar in Earls Court trying to dream up ways for me to win her back. These talks were mostly serious and full of regret, as the realization that I had thrown away my one pure chance of a kind of happiness gradually dawned on me. But they were also punctuated with laughter and optimism. This was all thanks to Saul—I was a mess. Quietly and selflessly he had watched and understood Kate to a point where he knew us both intimately. And now that understanding was paying off. He could explain her apparent cruelty, he could see when I was allowing a particular line of thought to become warped or exaggerated. It was uplifting in itself just to talk to somebody who also knew and loved her. And he never once tried to make me get over her. In his heart he knew that we should be together, and he wasn't about to conceal that from me. I respected him for that.

Three months later, with ridiculous symmetry, Saul's long-term girlfriend turned around and told him that she was seeing another man. And so we went back to that same bar, only now it was my turn to be the good friend, to be as wise and understanding as Saul had been to me. We sat with our bottles of beer, late-night traffic sliding by outside, and tried to make sense of what had happened. From his coat pocket Saul took out a letter she had written to him, parts of which he allowed me to read. "How sad that two people who once cared for each other so much can end up like this," it said. "Take care of yourself" and "I will always love you." The awful platitudes of separation.

More than anything else, I think, Saul was astonished by the speed with which it had finished. They had been together, on and off, since school. To my knowledge, she was the first girl he had ever slept with.

What he needed then was for me to keep my mouth shut and just drink a beer with him. But I felt some sort of obligation to cure and began bombarding him with half-baked advice and banalities. I tried to tell him that all his fears and insecurities were not worth worrying over, that he should try to shut out all the mental pictures of her infidelity. I told him that the anguish we feel in the immediate aftermath of heartbreak only dissipates in time into prejudice and misinformation. Best to ignore it. None of this seemed to make any impression on him. He looked at me almost with pity. I wanted, absurdly, a transcript of the advice he had given me to read out to him.

The truth of that situation was that he had already made up his mind what to do. He had stopped loving her the moment she had told him about her affair. Very quickly, she had become reprehensible to him. Saul's numbness gave way to a strange kind of relief in a matter of days, as if he was pleased to be rid of someone who was so devoid of basic decency. This strength astonished me. I had thought it would be years before he got over her, that the breakup would be something from which he would never properly recover. But I was wrong.

This memory is in my head for the better part of an hour, all the sides of it, the implications. Then I review the night's events once again, unable to shut them out, unable just to put it all to one side.

I do not once look at my watch—I learned that long ago—but it must be after four when I finally manage to sleep.

Early the next morning, I call Hawkes at his house in the country from a telephone box in Barons Court.

"Could I speak to Paul Watson, please?"

"You have the wrong number," he says, following procedure. Then he calls back immediately, using a secure line.

"Alec. What is it?"

He sounds remote, detached.

"I needed to ask you something."

"Yes."

"Did you ever get caught up in the drama of it?"

"What do you mean?" he says, as if the question were ridiculous.

"Did you ever do things in the course of your work that you didn't really need to do? Did you make things more difficult for yourself because you were deceived by the glamour of espionage?"

"I'm sorry, I'm not following."

"Let me give you an example. Last night, I made the first drop—"

"Yes," he interrupts nervously. He has always been wary of who may be listening in. His has been a lifetime of paring words back, of bending them into ambiguities and codes.

"I was only following instructions, but the Americans seemed to have made things more complicated, more risky than was necessary. Maybe it was a test. I brought a briefcase to Saul's flat—"

"Alec, we can't talk about this."

"What do you mean?" My voice must sound petulant and spoiled. Like the game is over.

"It is not advisable for us to speak anymore."

"Since when?"

"I'm going to be out of contact for some time. You'll be all right. Just retain anonymity. You've been told what to do in an emergency. Go to Lithiby. Do not contact me again. You're doing fine, Alec. You must learn how to do this thing on your own."

24

FINAL ANALYSIS

The year draws to an end.

There are four more drops, one roughly every month, for each of which I am paid ten thousand pounds sterling, deposited in an escrow account in Philadelphia. I will have access to the money when the Americans have the data from 5F371.

The first handover takes place at a West End theater, a simple exchange almost as soon as the house lights have gone down. The next two occur at my flat in Shepherd's Bush, and the fourth inside Fortner's car on the way to Andromeda's Christmas party. That was last week.

Were they straightforward? Yes and no. The actual transactions are always fairly simple: well planned, isolated, unobserved by third parties. There is the small problem of obtaining suitable information, or of getting freely available documents home, where I can make copies. There are security systems to be circumvented at Abnex, random checks on packages leaving and coming into the building.

So JUSTIFY has become routine, just as it was supposed to, just as we had planned it all along. Yet, something in me will not rest. When asked me to do this, to give over the next two, possibly three years of my life, I agreed to it with the private acknowledgment that things would be difficult at times, occasionally even intolerable. The long-term gain, the promise of a settled and fulfilling future, outweighed any immediate reservations I had about conceding to a constant duplicity. The hard fact of being caught between two sides was presented to me as a relatively simple arrangement. It was just a question of maintaining balance.

That is easier than it sounds. A third party was never foreseen. We reckoned without Cohen; we did not factor him in. I was ready to feel on edge, watchful and suspicious, but I expected that to be attended by feelings of elation and personal fulfillment. Instead, because of his constant, nagging presence at Abnex, I feel isolated and consumed by an apprehensive solitude that I am increasingly unable to control.

To give an example. In mid-October, I began to notice that black rubbish bags were being taken from the outside of my building as often as three or four times a week. No other garbage is removed from the road with the same frequency. The council truck is scheduled to come only on Thursday mornings. I could not mention the problem to anyone, for fear of worrying them about the security of JUSTIFY. It was conceivable that American agents were going through my bins as a way of checking on the validity of their agent. This is common practice.

But that was not all. At around the same time in October, I made a telephone call to British Telecom requesting a second copy of my itemized phone bill. I told the assistant that the first had been mislaid and I was late paying the balance.

"Haven't we already sent you one?" the operator asked. "Didn't you request an itemized bill last week? I've got a note here on my screen."

No, I told her, I did not.

So who requested it? The CIA already has a tap on my phone. Was it Abnex? Cohen himself? Or had the operator simply made a mistake?

Thirdly, the post has started arriving later than it did, as if it is being intercepted en route to my flat, then checked, resealed, and sent on. First-class letters take two days instead of one; second-class, up to a week. Parcels have often been tampered with, seals broken and so on.

I expected taps and tails, but everything else is outside normal U.S. and British procedures. It is possible that, because of Cohen, Abnex has placed me under twenty-four-hour surveillance. There is at all times a feeling of being watched, listened to, sifted, followed, pressures exerted on me from all sides. I live constantly with the prospect of abandonment, constantly with the prospect of arrest. Things have been like this for so long now that I cannot recall what life was like before they started. The sensation is not dissimilar to the experience of being ill. The world outside goes about its business, and you cannot even remember what it felt like to be healthy and well.

Walking to Colville Gardens tonight to make JUSTIFY's sixth drop on a cold December evening, I feel tight and self-contained, certain in the knowledge that I am being tailed—by Cohen, by the Americans, even by our side. "Do They Know It's Christmas?" is playing out of the open window of a house on Pembridge Crescent, but there are no visible signs that it *is* Christmas. The streets have not been decked out with lights, there are no glowing trees in the bay windows of sitting rooms, no carol-singing children scurrying from flat to flat in the cold.

In the inside pocket of my long overcoat, zipped up against thieves and spooks, there is a single high-density IBM 1.44 MB floppy disk inside a small manila envelope containing crude oil assay data from a wellhead sample in Tengiz. My adrenaline, as always, is up, my heart beating rapidly with a rush like caffeine pushing me quickly down the street. I tilt my head down for warmth and watch my breath as it disappears into the folds of the coat.

For perhaps the tenth time today, my mind casts back to a confrontation I had with Cohen last week. I cannot ignore what happened, because it convinced me that he is assured of my guilt. This, at least for once, is not paranoia, not just some by-product of my persistent agitation. There are hard facts to consider.

We were standing beside the printer where, three months earlier, he had discovered me spooling out the commercial price sets on that quiet Saturday afternoon.

"Those Americans you've been spending so much time with," he said, adjusting his tie.

"What about them?" I replied, a void immediately opening up inside me.

"Alan has found out about it."

"What do you mean he's found out about it? You two been keeping tabs on me?"

That was my first mistake. I was too aggressive, too early. There was nothing in what Cohen had said to cause me any alarm, simply a sly tone of voice, an implied rebuke in his manner.

"We like to keep an eye on new people."

"What do you mean, 'new people'? I've been with the company over a year."

"Did you know they work for Andromeda?"

"No kidding, Harry. I thought they were guides at the British Museum. Of course I know they work at Andromeda."

"And do you think it's wise to be spending so much of your time with a competitor?"

"Implying what?"

"Implying nothing."

"Why ask the question, then?"

"You're getting very ruffled, Alec."

"Listen, Detective Inspector. If I'm ruffled, it's because I don't like the undercurrent of what you're saying."

"There's no undercurrent," he said, calm as quicksand. "I merely asked if it was a good idea."

"I know what you asked. And the answer is that it's my private affair. I don't keep tabs on what you do behind closed doors."

"So you do things behind closed doors?"

"Fuck off, Harry. Okay? Just fuck off."

At that, both Piers and Ben looked up from their desks and stared at us. Cohen knew he had me cornered so he kept on probing. Typically, he phrased his next remark as a statement, not a question.

"I was simply going to say that they don't ring as often as they used to."

I responded to this without thinking through my reply.

"No, they don't," I told him. "I wonder why that is."

That was my second mistake. I should have reacted to the strangeness of Cohen's observation.

"Look," he said, sympathy suddenly in his voice. "I'm just telling you this because you might need to be prepared for some questions."

"About what?"

"Anybody who spends an unusual amount of time socializing with employees of a rival firm is bound to come under suspicion. At some point."

I had to presume that this was a lie designed to flush me out. He paused, leaving a silence that I was supposed to fill. My body was wretched with heat, exacerbated by the warmth of the office. I managed to say, "Suspicion of what?"

"We both know what I'm talking about, Alec."

"This conversation is finished."

"That's something of an overreaction, don't you think?"

"Fortner and Katharine are my friends. They are not work associates. Try to make that distinction. Your life may begin and end with Abnex, and that's admirable, Harry, it really is. We all admire you for your dedication. But the rest of us try to have a life away from the office as well. You'll find as you get older that this is perfectly normal."

Smirks from Piers and Ben.

"I'll take that into consideration," he said and walked back to his desk.

I ring the street bell of Katharine and Fortner's building and the door buzzes almost instantaneously. They have been waiting for me.

When I get to their apartment, Fortner opens the door slowly and offers to take my coat. I pass him a bottle of wine, which I bought in Shepherd's Bush, and extract the manila envelope from my inside pocket. He takes it quickly, a magician's sleight of hand. Simultaneously he is talking, asking about the weather, hanging up my coat, pointing out a scratch on the door.

"Never noticed that before," he says, rubbing his thumb against it. "Do you want a drink?"

"Glass of wine?"

"You got it."

Katharine is in the kitchen, washing up after dinner. She has had her hair done. It makes her look older. The clock on the wall says ten to nine.

"Hi, Alec. How you doin', sweetie?"

"Fine. Tired."

"Everybody is," she says. "I think it's the change in temperature. Isn't it cold suddenly?"

She comes over to kiss me, a warm dry lingering on my right cheek. In the next room, Fortner starts up some classical music on the CD player, piping it through to the kitchen with a switch on the stereo. The orchestration is loud, talk-smothering.

"Oh, that's nice, honey," Katharine says as Fortner comes into the kitchen.

"Chopin," he says, with no attempt at an accent. "Let me get you that glass of wine."

We have a signal, one of only four, that I use to inquire whether it is safe to talk. I simply put a straightened index finger to my lips, look at either one of them, and wait for a nod. Katharine glances at Fortner and does so. It is safe.

"I had a conversation with Harry Cohen at the office last week that I think you should know about."

"Cohen?" Fortner says. "The one who's always on your back?"

He knows exactly who he is.

"That's him."

"What did he say?" Katharine asks, touching her neck gently with her hand.

"He's noticed that you've stopped calling me at the office. Brought it up out of nowhere."

"Okay, so we'll call a little more. I don't think you should be unduly concerned. Did he say anything else?"

Fortner takes a sip from one of two glasses of wine he has poured near the stove. He hands me the other.

"No, there was nothing else in particular. I just found it odd that he should have brought it up."

"Listen, Alec," he says quickly. "Far as I can make out, this guy has been all over your job since you started. He feels threatened by you, just like they all do. Askin' you questions about a couple of Americans who happen to be working for Andromeda is just his way of bullying you. You gotta ignore it. You're doin' a great job and nobody suspects a thing."

I want to leave it at that, but Katharine comes a step closer to me. She is biting her lip.

"You all right?" she asks. "You look almost feverish."

I sit on one of the kitchen chairs and light a cigarette. My hand is shaking.

"No. I'm well. I'm just . . . I get nervous. I worry about being followed, you know?"

"Natural reaction," says Fortner, still very matter-of-fact. "Be strange if you didn't."

They have bought a new picture, a Degas print in a wooden frame. The one of the girl at ballet school, bending down to tie her shoes. Now, just briefly, I let things slip. My intense desire to talk to someone momentarily outweighs the wisdom of doing so with Fortner and Katharine.

"It's funny," I tell them, trying hard to sound as solid and as capable as I can. "I'm living with this constant fear that some journalist on *The Sunday Times* is going to call me up out of the blue and start asking questions. 'Mr Milius?' he'll say. 'We're running a story in tomorrow's edition that names you as an industrial spy working for the Andromeda Corporation. Would you care to make a comment?"

"Alec, for Christ's sake," Fortner says, putting his glass on the counter so hard that I fear it might break. I cannot tell if he is angry with me for being afraid or for making a direct reference to JUSTIFY. Even in the security of their apartment it was unwise to mention it. "What are you getting so bothered about all of a sudden? There isn't some Bob Woodward out there trackin' every move you make. Not unless you're being dumb."

There is a brief silence.

"*Are* you being dumb?"

"No."

"Well, there you go. Now just relax. Where is all this coming from?"

He doesn't give me time to answer.

"If you're worried about being tailed, we can have one of our own people follow you. They'll know in thirty seconds if you've got a surveillance problem."

The nerve of this. They're already tracking me.

"Great. So now I won't know if I'm being tailed by the CIA or Scotland Yard or a private security firm hired by Abnex."

Fortner doesn't like this now, not at all.

"Now look, Alec. You'd better start being cool about this or you're gonna slip up. When they caught spies during the Cold War, they were sent to Moscow and made into heroes. If they catch you, you'll be sent to jail and get your butt fucked. And if you get caught, *we* get caught. So let's all just calm down, all right? Let's not get too excited."

He sits on the chair nearest mine, and for a moment I think he is going to try to reach out and touch me. But his hands remain folded on the surface of the table.

"Look," he says, taking a deep breath. "Bottom line. If things get too hot, we have a safe house for you here in London. In fact, we have safe *houses,* plural. We can get you in the Witness Protection Program back home, whatever you want."

I almost let out a laugh here, but luckily some latent good sense in me smothers it.

Katharine says, "The important thing is that we are all deniable to one another." Her voice is a welcome balm. "Now, are we deniable, Alec? What is the nature of our relationship should you get caught?"

"I'm not going to get caught."

"*If* you do," she says, trying to be patient with me.

"Friendship. We had dinners and drinks. That's it. No one has ever seen me hand anything to you. Not even in the theater. That's how you wanted it."

"Good."

"And me?" I ask. "Am I deniable to you?"

"Of course," they say in practiced unison. "Absolutely."

Now we sit quietly for a moment, no one saying anything, just coming down off the tension. Katharine gets up and pours herself a glass of wine. I light a cigarette, searching around for an ashtray. The Chopin has slowed to an aching lament, single notes collapsing into each other.

"I don't mean to get tough on you," Fortner says finally, moving his hand closer to mine on the table.

"Look," Katharine says, joining in. "We're here for you. What you're doing must be messing with your head."

This is standard procedure. Officers must combine a firmness of intent with enough flattery and conciliation to keep an agent onside.

"Is there anything else you need to talk about?" she adds.

"No," I reply. "I'd just like to talk business briefly, if that's all right?" Fortner jerks his head up.

"Sure," he says, looking pleased.

"It's just that I have some interesting news."

"Go on," he says, nodding slowly. He needs to shave.

"You know of course that Abnex has been exploring 5F371 in the North Basin?"

"Sure."

I take a long draw on the cigarette. This is what the Americans have been waiting for.

"The exploration work finished as of last week. My team are expecting a geological report containing sufficient 3-D seismic data to depict the extent and location of the hydrocarbon deposits within the field. That could happen at any time in the next two months. If I can get hold of a copy, it should tell you how much Abnex is prepared to pay to get access rights to the oil."

"Good," Fortner murmurs.

"As far as I know, bids are being tabled in early summer of next year. That should allow Andromeda time to outflank us. I can also get you documentation outlining how we plan to export the oil once our bid has been accepted. There will also be maps and information regarding pipelines, terminals, and shipping routes, all of which should be useful to you in making your bid more attractive. And I can get you access telephone numbers and addresses for all the key personnel at each of the transport nodes. There's also a lot of detail on loopholes and flaws in Kazakh law."

"That would be dynamite," Fortner says, leaning toward me. He glances over at Katharine and beams.

I go on: "Abnex has done all the hard work, spent all the money. All you've got to do is outbid us and the field is yours. But it's going to cost you. I want two hundred thousand dollars for the information or I'm out."

"Two hundred thousand?"

"That's right."

"Haven't we been here before?" he says, but the glow in his face betrays an excitement. The geological data is too important to Andromeda for Fortner to risk alienating me.

"I'm aware of that. But this is the crown jewels, Fort, and it's worth a lot more than ten grand. If Andromeda's bid is successful, I'll have made the shareholders millions of dollars. That's got to be worth something. I think two hundred thousand is cheap."

"All right," he says, buying time. "I'm not authorized to green light that kind of money. Let me talk to our people and we'll get you an answer within seventy-two hours. My instinct says it may be a problem, but I'll try to bring them around."

"You do what you have to," I tell him.

It is nearly midnight by the time Fortner shows me to the door.

There are no services running on the Hammersmith and City line, so fifteen minutes later I board what must be the night's last train at Notting Hill station. Empty hamburger cartons have been discarded on the floor, and men in suits are falling asleep against greasy glass partitions. I am tired and find it difficult to focus on a single object for any length of time: an advertisement above the windows, a passenger's shoes, the color of someone's scarf. I look through into the next car half expecting to see Cohen in there, staring right back. My eyes sting and the skin on my face feels tight and dry.

I find it impossible to shut down. I am always thinking, evaluating, calculating the next move. I actually dread the thought of going home for another night of sleeplessness, just lying there in the dark analyzing the day's events, speculating on how much, or how little, Cohen knows. Then I picture Kate asleep in bed, her slim arm draped across the shoulders of another man. Night crap.

Last night, at three in the morning, I got up, put on a pair of jeans and a sweater, and wandered around the dead streets of Shepherd's Bush for over an hour in an attempt to tire myself out with walking. There seemed to be no alternative beyond taking a handful of sleeping pills or sinking a half bottle of scotch, which I cannot do because of the need to stay sharp and clearheaded for Abnex. When I got back to the flat at around four, sleep came easily. But then there were the customary dreams, packed with sicknesses and capture, isolation and pursuit. It's all so predictable, regular as clockwork, and tonight I will have to go through it all again.

I stare into the concave windows of the Central Line train and they warp my reflection like a hall of mirrors. I am split in half by the steep curvature of the glass, a pair of broad shoulders and a tiny, mutated head melting into an inverted reflection of itself.

Two of me.

PART THREE

1997

And ye shall know the truth
And the truth shall make you free.

—JOHN 8: 32
INSCRIPTION IN THE MAIN LOBBY OF CIA HEADQUARTERS,
LANGLEY, VIRGINIA

25

THE LURE

The New Year brings with it familiar clichés of renewal: private promises to take more exercise, to be a better friend to Saul, to get over Kate and find a new girlfriend. I want to exert greater control over my life, to try to get things into some kind of perspective. By the second week of January, however, all resolutions have been set aside, rendered meaningless by the simultaneous demands of Abnex and JUSTIFY. My life simply doesn't allow any opportunity for change.

Everything now is about 5F371. Whenever I am not involved in normal day-to-day activities at work, all my efforts are concentrated on obtaining the doctored North Basin data from Caccia. Andromeda wants the information as soon as it becomes available. The Americans now make that clear in almost every conversation I have with them.

Even during the Christmas break, while Katharine and Fortner were staying at her family home in Connecticut, they phoned me to check up on developments.

Mum picked up the phone.

"Alec!" she shouted, with that strained, impatient bark that got me out of bed on so many mornings as a teenager.

I was upstairs, reading.

"Yes?" I said, coming to the landing.

"There's an American on the phone for you."

I picked up the receiver in Mum's bedroom, having closed the door for privacy. She hung up in the kitchen as I did so.

"Alec?"

"Katharine, hello."

"Hi! We just wanted to call and wish you a happy Christmas!"

Her voice was pitched high and enthusiastic, overcooking the friendship for the benefit of anyone who might be listening in.

"That's very kind of you. Where are you?"

"Back home with my mother. Fort's here. You want to talk to him?"

"Sure."

"Well, just a minute. Tell me what you've been up to."

I told her.

"Great. And is your mom good?"

"Very well. She hates Christmas, but she's well."

"Super. Look, Fort really wants to talk to you so I'll pass him over."

"Fine. See you when you get back in January."

I was wondering why she had bothered ringing. The conversation felt rushed. She had made the call out of a sense of professional duty but had neglected to think of anything to say.

"Hey, Milius. How ya doin'?"

Fortner sounded humdrum and tired. It was ten in the morning on the East Coast.

"Fine. Fine. You?"

"Same old same old. Been seein' some friends. Eggnog and old movies. Fuckin' smoke police at every party we go to. Tell you this, pal. Nowadays it's easier takin' a gun out of your pocket in America than it is smokin' a cigarette."

"It's nice of you to ring."

"Don't mention it," he replied. "Get any gifts?"

"Some. A shirt. A couple of videos."

This was all starting to feel easier. The pressure, for once, was off.

"What d'you give your mom?"

"Stuff from Crabtree and Evelyn. Bath salts."

"Oh," he said, his voice lifted. "Crabtree and Evelyn." He pronounced Evelyn like Devlin. "We have that over here. Makes Kathy smell like a rose bush."

"Good."

"What about that CD you wanted? You get that?"

And straightaway I was back in the fog of duplicity, no break from it. The CD was code we used for the geological data from 5F371.

"No," I said, stumbling for words. Three days away from London and I had forgotten how to lie. "Mum couldn't find it in the shops. But I've ordered one. It should be out in the New Year."

"Great. So I guess we'll see you when we get back."

That was all they wanted to know. As soon as Fortner had established that the data was not yet available, the festive niceties could be dispensed with. It was not a social call.

"How 'bout you come over for supper sometime in January, once we get back?" he said. "Say Wednesday the twenty-ninth?"

Why was he so specific that it should be that date?

"Sounds great."

"I'll get Kathy to fix it up. She's sayin' good-bye. Give our best to your folks."

Folks, he said, plural. A slipup.

"I will," I said, and I was halfway through saying good-bye when the line went dead.

We speak transatlantic on two occasions in January. Both are calls made to the Abnex offices, which I think of as risky and unnecessary. The first is from Katharine in New York, "just calling to touch base." In a ten-minute conversation that can be clearly overheard by Cohen, she makes no reference to 5F371. The second is from Fortner, now in Washington, just two days before they are due to fly back to London. He asks almost immediately about the CD, and I am able to tell him that I have ordered it, expecting delivery within eight to ten days. This is what Caccia has indicated, and he is usually reliable. Fortner sounds pleased, reiterates the invitation to dinner on the twenty-ninth, and quickly curtails the conversation. This angers me. My work phone is presumably tapped, and if an Abnex official happened to be listening in on the conversation, they would surely find the exchange between us odd.

The night that they get back, Katharine e-mails me to confirm the dinner date for the third time. Clearly they have something specific planned. I enter a lie about it in my desk diary: on Wednesday the twenty-ninth, instead of "Dinner F+K," the entry reads, "Cinema. Saul. Maybe *Some Mother's Son*?" a film about Northern Ireland that has just opened in London.

Then it's just a question of waiting.

26

THE APPROACH

The night of the dinner, Wednesday, January 29, is glacial, as cold as it has been all winter, with a freeze chill in the air that might precede snow. Walking to Colville Gardens, I am characteristically apprehensive, and yet there is also an unfamiliar edge to my mood. Although no handover is taking place tonight, the meeting has been arranged a month in advance, which is more than enough time for the Americans to have planned something unexpected. It is too much to suggest that I am being lured into a trap, and yet something is not quite right. Is it only that I am coming empty-handed, without a disk, a file, even a photograph? To meet them purely on the basis of our friendship is both so unnecessary now and so utterly false that it feels almost sinister.

I take a pair of gloves out of my briefcase and put them on. The people around me are moving quickly, hurrying, just wanting to be indoors and out of the cold. I have started to notice a gradually increasing dampness in my left shoe, as if rainwater has seeped through the leather, wetting the sock, but when I stop to check it there is only pavement dreck and muck on the sole, with no sign of a hole or tear. I light a cigarette and continue walking.

Turning right into Colville Terrace from Kensington Park Road, a pair of car headlights flash twice in quick succession on the opposite corner of the street. Two people are sitting inside a gleaming green Ford Mondeo, one in the driver's seat, one in the back. The headlights flash again, briefly flooding the street with light. I stop and peer at the car more closely.

Fortner and Katharine are sitting inside. I cross the street and move to the passenger door. Fortner reaches across to open it.

"What are you two doing here?" I ask, trying to sound nerveless and calm as I climb inside. "I thought we were going to meet in your apartment."

After a last drag on the cigarette, I toss it into the gutter, twisting around in my seat to give Katharine a smile. She looks gaunt.

"Close the door, Alec," Fortner says with heavy seriousness.

I clunk it shut. The interior smells like a rental car.

"When did you pick this up?" I ask, tapping the dashboard lightly. My heart is racing furiously.

"This morning," Fortner says, activating the central lock before turning the key in the ignition. The engine roars briefly and then settles back to a low hum.

"What happened to the old one?"

"Garage," says Katharine, deadpan.

Fortner pulls out into the street. We are heading back up Kensington Park Road.

"What's going on? Where are we going?"

"We're real concerned about something, Alec," he says, turning to look directly at me. "We believe that our apartment may have been penetrated. It may be under audio surveillance. The vehicle also. That's why we picked up a fresh one. The Mondeo is clean."

Fortner grips his hands firmly around the steering wheel, turning back to look at the road. My reaction here will be crucial. I have to get it exactly right.

"Your apartment is *bugged*?" I say, with what may be too much emphasis. "Why would you think that?"

"We picked something up on a routine sweep," Katharine says. She has positioned herself directly between the two front seats, leaning forward between us.

"A routine sweep? So it's something you do all the time?"

"All the time," she says.

Fortner makes a turn into Ladbroke Square. I cannot think what to say to them. If their apartment has been bugged, it may be because of mistakes I have made at Abnex, and that will not have escaped their notice.

"Don't worry unnecessarily," Katharine says, resting her hand gently on my shoulder. "This may have nothing to do with JUSTIFY. It may be completely unrelated. But we're gonna have to make some changes. When are the geological plans due? Any day now, right?"

Suddenly everything is clear. This is all just a bluff. They are trying to move me along, trying to scare me into thinking that we are running out of time.

"Like I told Fortner, I'm expecting them within a week, but there have been rumors of a delay. I'm so low down the food chain I don't get to find out. . . ."

"Well, let's hope it's soon. Now listen." Katharine coughs. "Due to what's happened, and due to the sensitivity of the 5F371 documentation, we're gonna have to ask you to change the strategy of your handovers."

I say nothing, but this is highly unorthodox.

"It's nothing too serious, nothing that you won't be able to handle." After a brief pause, no more than a deep inhalation, she adds, "We're going to introduce a third party."

I glance out into the road, trying to calculate the implications. A third party is outside our arrangement, an unnecessary complication that I have been advised against.

I turn to look back at Katharine.

"The understanding we have is that I am to deal with you and you only. Introducing a third party would be reckless."

"I know that, Alec," she says. "But we can't risk any foul-ups."

Fortner is staying well out of this, just driving the car, his lined face swept by the shifting lights outside. Katharine's voice is close and loud in my right ear and I cannot twist around to look at her for any length of time without causing pain in the small of my back.

"Who is the third party?" I ask, turning back to face the dashboard. "Is he CIA?"

"His name is Don Atwater," she says. "He's an American corporate lawyer who works out of London."

"That's his cover?"

"He helps us out from time to time. That's all you need to know."

"On the contrary. I need to know everything."

"No, you don't," says Fortner, interjecting. There is a light trace of malice in his mood tonight, as if he is disappointed in me. Perhaps they are telling the truth about the surveillance and blame me for what has happened. That thought is enough to make me back down.

"How would we work it, if I agree to go ahead?"

Katharine breathes in hard once again. She will have prepped herself for this part of the briefing.

"As soon as you have obtained a copy of the 5F371 data, you are to call this number."

She reaches forward and hands me a piece of white paper, no bigger than a credit card. It has a seven-digit number written on it in neat black ink.

"When they answer, you are to give your name and ask if your dry-cleaning is ready."

"My dry-cleaning?" I ask, stifling a surge of incredulous laughter.

"Yes," she replies soberly. "They will say that it is ready and then hang up. That is your signal to us that we are ready to go."

"I just ask if it's ready? Nothing else?"

"Nothing."

A car cuts us off at some lights and Katharine says "shit" through her teeth as she is rocked by the sudden braking. I have lost track of where we are: the West End? Kilburn? Farther north than that?

"That night," she says, "make your way to Atwater's London offices in your car."

"Where does he work?"

"Cheyne Walk. Chelsea. SW3."

"I know where it is. Which end?"

"Close to Battersea Bridge."

"What if I'm working late?"

"You won't be. He's not expecting you before midnight."

Again Fortner comes in: "And you should not arrive there before that time."

"Midnight?"

"Midnight," Katharine confirms. The switch between them is disorienting, like a tussle for power. "Now, the most important thing for you to be doing en route is to watch your tail."

"Tell him about the bike."

"I was going to," Katharine says impatiently. "If you want, we can put a motorcycle outrider with you throughout the journey. He'll keep an eye on things."

At this, I lose some cool.

"Fuck, Kathy. How serious is this? If they're onto me, it's too risky.

If there's a chance of being followed, I shouldn't do it. We should close it all down for a while."

"Not necessary," Fortner says, making a slow right-hand turn. "An outrider is routine with something this important."

"Well, you can forget it. I'll go alone."

"Your choice," he says calmly. "Your choice."

We have stopped at another set of traffic lights. A small group of teenage girls wearing too much makeup passes in front of the Mondeo, laughing in a squawking pack. They are dressed in miniskirts in spite of the cold. When we have pulled away, Katharine continues talking.

"Once you have left your apartment, make sure that you drive directly toward the roundabout at Shepherd's Bush. As if you were heading to our place."

"Why?"

"I'm coming to that," she says, not wanting to be rushed. "Go right around it and come back on yourself down toward Hammersmith."

I know why she has recommended this, but still I have to say, "Go right around the roundabout? Why?"

"Best way of shaking a tail," says Fortner, who can't help himself butting in. His voice is low and dismissive. "Take the Shepherd's Bush Road down to Hammersmith, then make your way to Chelsea Harbour."

"Why there?" I ask. "Why not go directly to Atwater's office?"

"There's something you've gotta do before proceeding to Cheyne Walk."

The information is starting to pile up now, and after a tough day at work I am finding it hard to work through all the ramifications of what they are telling me. If their surveillance concerns are a bluff, both Atwater and the briefing are needless, a waste of time. If there is a genuine threat of penetration by Abnex, I am at great risk.

"This is getting very complicated."

"We'll go over it all again before we get you home." Fortner drops down into first gear in a crawl of traffic.

"What happens at Chelsea Harbour?"

Katharine gathers herself.

"There's only one entrance there and one exit. If you still have a tail, this is where you will lose him. Wait inside the complex. It's a left-hand turn if you're coming off Lots Road. Anyone following you will be forced to pass your vehicle once they are inside. When you're sure it's safe to drive on, proceed to Cheyne Walk. Not before. Go back onto Lots Road and drive east toward the river. Don Atwater's offices are at number 77. Park your car—it shouldn't be difficult at that time of night. Once you're inside, hand the documentation to him. Make sure that it is Atwater and no one else. Not his secretary, not the doorman, Atwater. Are we clear?"

"We would be if I knew what he looked like."

Marble Arch looms up on the right.

"Overweight. Puffed-out cheeks. Glasses. He will make himself known to you."

"And what about the money? What about the two hundred thousand dollars?"

"As soon as Atwater has the 5F371 data in his possession, he will notify us and that will trigger the financial transaction in escrow. It will be the sum that you requested. That's been cleared."

As I had expected it would be.

"Can I smoke?" I ask, taking out my pack of cigarettes.

"Be my guest," Fortner says, with a little more relaxation in his manner. "The sooner this upholstery smells of stale tobacco, the better."

I light the cigarette, offering one to Fortner, who declines. Then I request that we go over the instructions one more time for clarity. So he drives for another twenty minutes while Katharine runs them past me once more.

We are almost home when their car phone rings out loud and shrill. The interior of the Mondeo is miked up and Fortner is able to answer the call without lifting the receiver from its cradle.

"Yup," he says.

"Fort?"

The caller, an American, is trying to shout above the roar of the road. His voice sounds distant and warped, as if lost under a great, vaulted ceiling.

"Hi, Mike."

"Hey, buddy. Can you call Strickland ASAP?"

I instinctively flinch away from Fortner when I hear his name, an uncontrolled movement to disguise my surprise. Strickland. The agent Lithiby used to leak my SIS file to the CIA. Is this just coincidence, or is there another level to this, a conspiracy that I'm not seeing?

"Sure," says Fortner quickly, too casually, as if he wants the conversation to end before Mike says anything else. "Usual number?"

Everything that has happened tonight has been curiously unnatural, almost like the rehearsal of real events. Katharine's insistence that I follow an exact procedure, their lies about surveillance . . .

"Yeah, usual number. See you Saturday."

Fortner presses the red button on the handset and Mike's voice disappears.

What would they want with Strickland? What would *he* want with them?

Katharine asks the very same question, but it may be just a bluff.

"Why's he calling?"

"Not sure," Fortner replies, and is it my imagination or does his gaze slip toward me, a concealed warning to Katharine to stay away from the subject? Certainly he does not call Strickland while I am still in the car. Instead, I am driven back to Uxbridge Road and released a block short of my flat.

27

THE STING

I have waited so long for Caccia's people to prepare the data from 5F371 that when it finally arrives there is a hurried sense of expectation that catches me off guard.

It is a gray March day at work. The morning has adhered to its usual routines: phone calls, reports to be written, a meeting with some clients in Conference Room C on the sixth floor. I have a late lunch—steak sandwich, Sprite—in a café down the street, doing my best to avoid making eye contact with two Abnex employees eating spaghetti on the far side of the room. Then, just before three o'clock, I make my way back to the office.

Cohen, who is working at his desk, looks across at me as I come in, putting down his pen.

"Since when did you start getting packages from the boss?" he asks, an uncharacteristic suggestion of defeat in his voice. "Barbara Foster, the chairman's PA . . ."

"I know who she is."

"Well, she left that package for you while you were out getting lunch."

He is pointing at a white padded envelope in my in-tray. I know immediately what it is and experience a surge of grateful satisfaction that proves critical.

"She did?"

"Yeah. Told me to let you know it was there."

I make no gesture to pick it up.

"So what is it?" he asks.

"Probably his remarks on a report I did for the board three weeks ago. The one about Turkmenistan and Niyazov."

"I didn't know you'd done a report for the chairman," he says, a flicker of envy about him as he looks away. His ego has been wounded by a lie. "Can I look at it?"

"Sure. But I'm taking it home tonight. Want to read over what he's said."

Cohen nods unconvincingly and returns to his work. I open my briefcase, drop Caccia's envelope inside it, and, without even pausing to think, retrieve the small card on which Katharine wrote down the contact number for Don Atwater. The card is frayed at the edges now, worn by the constant movement of pens, coins, and files in my case. So keen am I to alert the Americans that I dial the number right away, with no thought of Cohen's proximity, the receiver clamped between my neck and chin. It starts to ring as soon as I have punched in the last digit.

There is no immediate answer, but I wait. Still no one picks up, even after a dozen rings. I am on the point of replacing the receiver, thinking that I have dialed the number incorrectly, when a voice responds at the other end.

"Hello?"

It's woman, Irish accent. For some reason, I had been expecting an American male.

"Hello. This is Mr. Milius calling. Is my dry-cleaning ready? I brought it in last week." As an afterthought, as if to take the edge off the absurdity of what I am saying, I add, "A jacket."

Cohen is tapping something into his Psion Organiser. There is a brief pause on the phone line backgrounded by a rustling of papers. The woman seems vague and disorganized, and this worries me.

"Yes, Alec Milius. Hello," she says eventually. There is relief in her voice, an enthused lilt. "That's fine. You can come and get it."

"I can?" I say, with enthusiasm. "Great." These simple words feel unnatural and self-conscious. "See you then."

"All right," she says, abruptly hanging up.

As I replace the receiver, my left thigh is shaking involuntarily beneath the desk. I need to walk around, need to splash some cold water on my face to throw me clear of worry. In the gents', I run the cold tap for a few seconds, eventually filling a sink. Then I scoop handfuls of icy water onto my face, letting it wash out my eyes and cool my temples.

Having lifted the lever to release the plug, I stare open-eyed into the mirror. Bloodshot whites, tired and weary, with a spot coming up on my nose. I run through Katharine's instructions one more time.

It's watertight. Relax. Just do what you're being paid to do.

Crossing the room to the hand dryers, I stick my face in a rush of warm air, eyes squeezed tight against the heat. Behind me, a cubicle lock snaps open, making me jump. Duncan from accounts emerges from one of the booths looking disheveled. I glance at him briefly and leave.

Toward six o'clock, Piers invites me to join him for a drink with Ben, but I explain that I already have a dinner engagement and make my excuses. I need time in which to settle myself before the handover tonight, time in which to gather my strength.

At half past, I join the early evening rush hour and for once am glad of the people crowding up the tube, glad that we stop between stations and wait in the darkness for the train to jerk just a few yards down a tunnel. It takes three times as long for the sheer volume of passengers to get on and off at each station, and every passing moment shrinks my waiting time before meeting Atwater. I dread the inevitable slowness that precedes a handover, the dead period in which I can only anticipate capture. Every enforced delay is welcome.

It is quarter to eight by the time I get home. A weak drizzle has begun falling outside, a wetness that clings to the roads and buildings, glistening under the street lights. My hair is damp when I get inside, and I dry it off with a towel while boiling the kettle for tea. Then I sit for more than an hour half watching television, my mind working slowly over the details of the plan for the last time: the circuit of the roundabout, the route to Chelsea Harbour, the tenor of the meeting with Atwater. I stay off the booze and occasionally pick at a microwaved potato, but deep concentration has left me with no appetite.

Just after nine o'clock, I go through the contents of Caccia's package. The envelope is padded with bubble wrap and contains a light blue plastic folder labeled CONFIDENTIAL in bold black ink. Inside it there is a twelve-page document with a handwritten covering note attached by a paper clip: "5F371 as requested. Good luck. DRC." These are Caccia's initials. I burn the note in the sink. On the inside back page of the folder, housed within a clear plastic flap, is a CD-ROM marked with the

Abnex logo. When I open the disk on my laptop, bitmap 3-D seismic imagings of 5F371 form on-screen, with magnetic surveys and information on rock samples available in separate files. It all looks realistic. The printed document contains everything from assay data to sources of capital, with details about loans Abnex has taken out to finance drilling operations in the North Basin. There is more here even than I had promised them. I go into my bedroom and take a new A4 manila envelope from my desk in which to place the contents. Once I have put the disk and the documentation inside, I seal it up with a lick. The gum on the flap tastes like curry powder.

The minutes then drag out until ten o'clock. I stare at the envelope on the kitchen table, smoking dumbly, drinking cups of strong percolated coffee that only make me feel more shaky and tense. Finally, unwilling to sit things out, I place the envelope inside a folded copy of *The Sunday Times* and leave the flat.

My car is halfway down the right side of Godolphin Road, about a thirty-second walk from the front door. There has been an ice cream van parked in the same space next to it for weeks, painted with cartoon characters and pictures of Cadbury's Flakes. When Kate was a small child her mother used to lie to her, would tell her that the jingle of the van, the ripple of bells in the street, meant that the vendor had actually run out of ice cream. Kate told me that story on the first night we met. It was one of the first things she said.

Inside the car, buckling up, I realize there are things I have forgotten to do. I should have filled up with petrol, checked the tires and oil, and turned the engine over at least once in the last few days to free it of winter cold. When I put the key in the ignition, the starter motor turns over asthmatically, sounding disconnected and worn, and I switch it off for fear of flooding the engine. At the second attempt, there appears to be less seizure within the system. The starter moans briefly, flicks over twice, but then catches and the engine fires. I whisper a grateful "shit" to myself, switch on the headlights, and pull away from the curb.

There are still plenty of vehicles on the roads: lorry drivers making up time before stopping for a night's rest, cabs shipping people across the city. I drive down Uxbridge Road, join the one-way system at Shepherd's Bush Green, and glide in the wet under the mocked-up Inter City walkway.

Cars are waiting in queues of five or six, preparing to go on to the round-about; with the sheer volume of traffic, I'm concerned that making a full circuit with surveillance check may prove difficult. I sit in the outside lane with my turn signal on and wait for the lights to go green.

As I go around, I check my mirror every other second for any sign of sudden movement behind me—a last-minute indication, a swerve-out or burst of acceleration. After passing the second exit, a cabdriver blasts his horn at me when I cut across his lane, and another beeps as I pass through the traffic lights leading back toward the Green. All the time I am watching as vehicles build up behind me, trying to gauge where they have come from. As far as I can tell, all appear to have entered the roundabout from either Holland Park Avenue, Holland Road, or the Westway. It looks as if no one followed me completely around.

So I head for Chelsea Harbour. Katharine suggested going via Fulham Palace Road, but I take a different route, with which I am more familiar—via Brook Green, Talgarth Road, and Fulham Broadway. The journey takes no time at all. Only once—my eyes distracted by a girl on the North End Road—do I brake fractionally late and almost rear-end a designer Jeep with a skiing rhino painted on its spare tire. Otherwise, the drive is incident free: no tail, no motorcycle outrider, nothing to report at all.

By half past eleven, I have arrived, a full thirty minutes before the scheduled meeting. I look up at the Wharf Tower, London's puny sky-scraper, and consider my options. There is no need to go into the harbour complex to flush out a tail because I have experienced no surveillance problems en route. And my presence there will serve only to alert the Americans to my whereabouts. There can also be no reason why I cannot meet Atwater before the prearranged time. If he's not there, I will simply wait outside on the street until he arrives. There is no advantage in following Katharine's instructions to the letter. Better to put myself in a position of control, rather than play into their hands and be dictated to by others.

So I do not turn into Lots Road. Instead I continue down King's Road until I come to Edith Grove, driving with the one-way system as far as Cheyne Walk. After a brief block in traffic I cross the Battersea Bridge lights and park in the first available space on the left, just a few feet from the statue of Sir Thomas More. From here, it's a short walk to Atwater's office.

There are three white stone steps rising to number 77. I climb them, the file and *Sunday Times* clutched in my right hand, and press a small plastic buzzer marked DONALD G. ATWATER, CORPORATE ATTORNEY. A wild wind is gusting off the Thames; it whips across my face as I stand in the porch. The lock buzzes softly and I push the door.

The foyer is an enclosed hall with high white walls and a checkered marble floor. There is a mirror to one side with a wooden umbrella stand directly below it. Opposite that, above an empty cream mantel-piece, hangs a large watercolor depicting thin children at the seaside, paddling in the shallows. I stop and wait, hearing heavy footsteps coming down a staircase. There is a deep male cough, what sounds like the rustling of small change in a pocket, and then a man comes into the hall through a door in front of me.

Donald G. Atwater is a large, humorless American, full of expensive lunches. He moves toward me more quickly than his short stumpy legs would otherwise suggest.

"Alec Milius?" he inquires in a slurred Virginia drawl. He is holding a small white envelope in his left hand.

"That's right."

"Privilege to meet you, sir."

Sir sounds absurd coming from a man of such size, a man who must be twice my age, but by now I am well used to empty American flatter-ies. He extends a hand, which I briefly shake. His palm is dry and hard.

"You got the package?" he asks.

Down to business right away. No pleasantries.

"Yes. But first I have to ask who you are."

He seems surprised by this and gives me a strange sideways glance.

"I'm Don Atwater."

"Do you have some sort of identification?"

He fishes around in his pockets for a business card, die-stamped with his name.

"Thank you. I just had to be sure."

Atwater cranes his neck back and looks down his nose into my eyes. There is an unsettling quality about this man, a suggestion of lazy ruth-lessness.

"You wanna come in or are you happy doing this out here?" he says, glancing carelessly around. Somehow we have got off on the wrong foot.

"Why don't we just do it here?"

"Fine," he says, curtly.

I take the envelope out of the folded-up newspaper. Atwater reaches out and takes it with a thin smile, his eyes staying focused on the pale manila. He tucks the file firmly under his left arm and coughs at a higher pitch than before. Neither of us says anything, as if in deference to the moment. Then, as this awkward silence draws out, I ask, "Why was it necessary for me to give this to you?"

"Excuse me?" he says. He has a way of talking that implies I am wasting his time.

"This isn't the way we normally proceed."

"I'm just acting on behalf of my client," he says, downcurling his lip. Interesting that he used the word *client* there, singular. He may be working on behalf of an Agency case officer higher up the food chain. But I might be jumping the gun. Atwater could have no knowledge of the contents of the file and consequently no idea of the real importance of JUSTIFY. He may be just what the Americans said he is: a lawyer, acting as a middleman.

"Then is there any reason why your client was so adamant that we meet this late on a weekday night?"

"Mr. Milius," he says, making no attempt to disguise an impatience with my questions. "As I understand it, the fewer people who know about this, the better. Am I right?"

"Right."

"Hence the midnight exchange."

"I'm sorry I asked."

"Not a problem." Atwater reaches out sideways with his right arm and leans against the wall, propping up his vast bulk with a splayed-out hand.

"I have instructions to authorize the release of funds to you in escrow."

"Yes."

He pauses briefly before saying, "The money is being held at the Chase Manhattan Bank in Philadelphia. Inside this envelope you will find the account details."

He passes me the small white envelope, lick sealed and with no writing on it. I place it in the back pocket of my trousers.

"Thank you."

Atwater lifts himself away from the wall and makes a move toward his jacket pocket.

"I also have something that my client wanted me to give to you. A gift. A gesture of thanks."

I was waiting for this to happen. One day.

"My client said that you would understand their not giving it to you in person." He is finding it difficult to extract the gift from his pocket. It is a rigid blue box, something heavy. He eventually frees it and passes the box to me.

"Go ahead. Open it up."

I flip the catch and lift the lid to reveal a silver Rolex watch draped over a hand-stitched baseball. I do not know what is more absurd: that they should have balked at paying me two hundred thousand dollars for the data and then splurged on a five-figure Swiss watch, or that they thought it was appropriate to throw in a baseball as well.

"Wow," I say. "How generous of them."

"What is it?" Atwater asks.

"It's a Rolex," I say, swiveling the box so that he can take a look. He must have known this already. "And a baseball."

"That's a beauty," he says. "Put it on."

I take out the watch, house the baseball in my coat pocket, and thread the broad silver links of the strap onto my wrist.

"Will you thank them on my behalf? Tell them I won't be declaring it as a corporate gift."

Atwater manages a meager laugh and takes a firmer hold on the file as he slips it under his arm. He says, "Of course," as I rattle the watch, which weighs heavy on my wrist.

"I really wasn't expecting anything so generous," I add, privately wondering if the watch contains a bug, a tracking device, a small plastic explosive. This is the ludicrous state of my movie-fueled mind.

"Yes, it is a fine gift," Atwater replies, suddenly sounding bored. His job is done. I have a feeling that he is keen to get rid of me.

"Is there anything else?" he says, confirming this.

"No. Not really. Just to thank them."

Atwater says nothing. We find ourselves swaying in the wind of another lengthy pause. The baseball knocks lightly against my hip bone as I rock from foot to foot.

"Alec," he says finally. "I have things I need to be getting on with. So if there's nothing else . . ."

I have a bizarre desire to keep him here, to ruin his night with a needless hour of talk. This man does not approve of me. I would like him to suffer for that. But instead I say, "Yes, I should be leaving."

And he quickly replies, "Whatever you like," with a quick leftways jerk of his chin.

"Maybe see you again," I say, turning to go. The watch slips on my wrist with the movement of my arm. I'll need to have it adjusted for size. Take a couple of links out.

"Yes."

Everything feels rushed in these final seconds. I shake Atwater by the hand, but his skin is damper than before, a nervous heat spread out across the palm. Then I turn around and pull the handle on the front door. It does not budge. I look back at Atwater, who says, "Wait just a minute," as he hits a small black button to his left. This buzzes the lock electronically and I open the door, passing outside onto the unlighted porch. I am still holding the copy of *The Sunday Times* in case anyone is watching from the street. The door swings shut behind me. Deep inside the hall I hear Atwater say, "Good-bye now," but I am given no opportunity to reply.

I walk back to the car and unlock it just as a little girl in a *Don't Look Now* raincoat is crossing the road from the river, tightly clutching her mother's hand. She looks wise and canny, old for her age, staring at me for that too-long length of time known only to kids. What's she doing up this late?

When the two of them, mother and daughter, are out of sight, I drive away with an odd sentimental feeling that nothing will ever be the same again with Katharine and Fortner. Why I think this now, so suddenly, I cannot be sure, yet the gift of the Rolex has already acted like a seal on our arrangement. They have what they think of as the main prize, and my usefulness to them may well have ended. Often, the immediate aftermath of a handover is like this. There are a lot of questions in my mind, many doubts and queries, but the predominant sensation is one of anticlimax, as the adrenaline seeps away and all that remains is exhaustion. For some inexplicable reason, I start to miss the thrill of the drop, the risk of capture. Everything that follows is dull by comparison. And this feeling soon bleeds into solitude, into self-doubt.

The streets are drenched with the early evening drizzle that turned to rain at midnight. I like the noise of tires on soaked roads, the quick wet whip of water thrown up by speed. In my tiredness, I listen to this sound above the quiet noise of the engine, driving more or less on instinct, barely paying attention to what is happening on the roads. For once, I feel capable of sleep. I can drive home now and get seven straight hours with no need of booze or pills or useless, lust-filled walks around the streets of Shepherd's Bush. The odd, edgy meeting has left me with a rare feeling of calm. Perhaps I know now that the worst is over.

28

COHEN

I see the black Volkswagen in my rearview mirror three times on the way home: once at the lights coming onto King's Road; again on Holland Road, which is where I start to get suspicious; and finally on Goldhawk, when it sweeps behind me as I make a right turn onto Godolphin Road on my way back to the flat. I can't, of course, be sure that it was the same car every time. My mind has been wandering, and the second sighting was obscured by a night bus heading east along Kensington High Street. It would be wrong to write off the reappearance of the same car—same color, same lines—to mere coincidence. Someone might have been tailing me from Cheyne Walk.

So I don't take any chances. I park about five hundred feet short of my front door, which is on the corner of Uxbridge and Godolphin roads. This is farther away than I need to be—there are several spaces nearer to the flat—but I want a good clear sighting of the street. Now I wait, inside the car, staring out through the windshield, waiting for the Volkswagen to reappear. The rain starts up again and an old man appears at a bedroom window high up to my right, closing curtains in a dirty white vest.

Nothing happens. No cars, no pedestrians, no cyclists. After ten minutes I get out and lock up, convinced that there's nothing more to worry about. It's just the play of my paranoid mind, the cautious proddings of self-preservation. So I begin walking toward the flat, relaxed and ready for bed. An animal—but not a cat or a dog—darts across the road in front of me, sleek and wet. Just as it vanishes behind some broken fencing, a car turns into the north end of the street directly ahead of me. I halt beside a wall. The headlights are so bright that I can make out neither the type of vehicle nor its color: it might be the black VW, it might not. The car stops directly opposite my front door, three hundred feet ahead, engine still running.

The driver remains there for several seconds and then moves off, coming toward me now, creeping malignly down the street. Slowly I move forward, edging away from the wall, walking through the pools of orange light thrown onto the road by streetlamps. I halt again almost immediately, pausing under the shadow of an overhanging bush. The car stops 150 feet away, and I hear the gearbox shift into reverse. The driver is backing up into a parking space.

I can see the make now. It's a Vauxhall, like mine: a bottle-green, four-door B-reg with worn hubcaps and a sprig of heather threaded through the radiator. I move out of the cover provided by the bush.

Driver and passenger get out just as I am walking past. They catch me looking at them in a split, nervous instant, and I recognize their faces. I've seen them buying newspapers in the neighborhood, watched them walking to the tube. They live in the next street—Hetley Road—a young couple with a kid. They look startled, wary with mugging nerves, and we do not greet one another.

I walk on, relieved, reaching into my trousers for keys, now just a few paces short of the front door. There is loose change in my pocket, tiny balls of laundry fluff, and an old pack of gum. I look up, tugging the cold keys in my fingers, pulling them free.

He comes directly at me, moving quickly with a flat, focused walk. He's wearing a heavy brown corduroy jacket, gloves, and a black scarf.

Cohen.

He stops, feet scuffing on the pavement as he comes to a halt.

"Hello, Alec."

Cohen's new company car is a Volkswagen. He was taking delivery of it last week.

"Harry. What are you doing here? Been out to dinner?"

"Where have you been?"

"I've been out."

"Where?"

He is breathing quickly. Vapor clouds out into the narrow space between us.

"Are you pissed?" I ask him.

"No," he says with a quiet authority that cancels out any trace of af-fability. He has been rushed to get here but has quickly regained his composure. "I've just come from Cheyne Walk."

I try to work through the consequences of this. He must know something. He must be onto me. Think.

"Where have you been, Alec?"

"I've been on Cheyne Walk as well. But something tells me you al-ready knew that. What's all this about? What are you doing here?"

"Who were you with tonight?"

"Is that your business?"

"Why don't I *tell* you who you were with?"

"Why not?"

He inches forward on the pavement.

"You were with your contacts from Andromeda. The Lanchesters."

I am briefly relieved. He has made a baseless assumption.

"What is it with you and those two, Harry?" I ask, letting out a little sputtering laugh.

"Are you saying you weren't with them, or not?"

The manner in which he asks this worries me. It is as if he already knows the answer to his question. Perhaps Cohen saw Katharine and Fortner going into Atwater's building before I arrived. There would be no logic in that, but it is possible. They may have been there throughout the meeting. I feel suddenly rushed and get lost in the double negative of Cohen's question. Taking a chance without thinking things through, I tell him, "No."

And immediately I sense from his reaction that he has trapped me.

"No? You're saying *no*?" The tone is one of grim sarcasm. "Then why did I see them enter the building you've just come back from half an hour before you got there?"

Why would the Americans have kept that from me? Momentarily this question outweighs the grave fact of Cohen's accusations. I try to stay on the offensive.

"What the fuck were you doing wasting your time following those two around?"

"I wasn't following them," he says unconvincingly. "I was having dinner on a houseboat and I saw them going into the building as I was leaving."

"And you decided to spy on them?"

"An appropriate word, wouldn't you say?"

I take out a cigarette and light it as a means of shutting out the implication.

"Am I not allowed to see the employees of other oil firms after a nine o'clock curfew? Is that it? Is that a clause in my Abnex contract?"

"That's not the issue."

"Well then, I don't know what is the issue. You're wasting your time. I'm very tired. I want to go inside and get some sleep. Maybe we can have a word about your problem in the morning."

This is weak, a thin attempt at escape. And, of course, it does nothing to deflect him.

"You made a telephone call this afternoon," he says.

"I made a lot of phone calls today. That's part of what we do, Harry."

"Ostensibly to a dry-cleaner."

I try to disguise my reaction to this, but some of the shock must seep through.

"That's correct," I reply, not bothering to deny or deflect. Better to find out how much Cohen knows, to listen to the evidence he has compiled.

"You went to the toilet afterwards."

"Yes."

"After you got up from your desk, I pressed the Redial button on your telephone."

It is as if something collapses inside me.

"Why did you do that?"

I do not expect him to answer. Cohen knows he has the upper hand. He came here with enough evidence to flush me out and is interested only in confession. He has acted with a greater swiftness than I would ever have anticipated.

"A woman answered," he says, moving a few inches closer to me so that his face is suddenly bathed in the grim orange glow of a streetlight. He is almost whispering now, as if out of courtesy for my sleeping neighbors. "Do you want to know what she said?"

"You had no right to do that, Harry," I tell him, but my anger makes no impression on him.

"She said: 'Mr. Milius? Alec, is that you?' Now, does it strike you as odd that she should say that?"

"This is ridiculous."

"You must be very friendly with your dry-cleaner to be on first-name terms with her."

"I've spent a lot of money there. We know each other by name. It's not that uncommon, Harry. Did you come here just to tell me *this*?"

In my stupidity, I think that this remark may be enough to deter his questioning, but it is not. What comes next is the worst of it.

"Does the word *justify* mean anything to you?"

His eyes scour mine and I look away down the street, my body suddenly limp with fear. I inhale deeply on the cigarette and try to think of a response. But any reply will be futile. This is over.

"Excuse me?"

"*Justify?*" says Cohen, as if the effort of repeating it has annoyed him. "Does that word mean anything to you?"

"No. Why?"

"The woman on the phone. She had an Irish accent. She used that word as if it were some sort of code. Is that what it is, Alec? Just tell me and let's get this out of the way."

I do not know if he sees my face in the darkness with its flush of humiliation. Perhaps the fall of a shadow saves me, a simple lack of color in the night. I can say only this: "Go home, Harry. I don't know if you're drunk or paranoid or whatever, but just go home. The word *justify* means nothing to me. Absolutely nothing at all."

"Why don't you just tell me what's going on?"

"I'm very tired. You're getting a big kick out of playing private detective and I'm very tired."

"Just tell me. I'll understand, I promise," he says. Then, after a calculated pause: "How much are you being paid?"

"You want to be careful what you say."

"How much are they paying you, Alec?"

Our eyes lock in a tableau of male bravura, a standoff on a street corner. I have to deny this. I cannot betray the truth to him. I must, from somewhere, summon the energy to counterattack. Yet, I feel—as I have felt for so long now—completely worn down by him. Cohen has always second-guessed me. He has always been there, right from the beginning, hounding my every move. How did he know? What clue did I give him to allow his slight suspicion of me to develop into something altogether more serious? What was my mistake?

Again I say, "Go home, Harry. Get in your car and go home."

But he says, "This is not going to go away."

And now it is all I can do to stretch my panic into self-preservation. At least I can find out who else knows.

"Who the hell else have you been spreading these rumors to?"

To ask this is an innate piece of common sense that I am lucky to have struck on. His answer will prove crucial.

"As of this moment, nobody else knows."

This is my only glimpse of hope, and I use it to turn on him, this time with more force.

"What do you mean, 'nobody else knows'? There's nothing *to* know."

"We both know that's a lie. Tonight has proved that."

"Tonight has proved nothing."

I turn in the direction of my front door.

"I'm on the Baku flight first thing tomorrow morning," he says, barely raising his voice. "By the time I get back, I expect you to have spoken to David, to have given him your side of the story. I'm not a rat, Alec. I will not be the one to turn you in. I have always worked on the principle that I would give you the chance to give yourself up. But if you haven't cleared things by the time I get home, I will see to it that you go down."

He turns to leave, without waiting for a reply, heading back in the direction from which he came.

"This is all shit," I call after him, struggling to conceal my desperation. He is already turning the corner onto Uxbridge Road when I say, "Wait. Harry."

He stops, making to come back.

"I'll talk to you tomorrow," I tell him. "Call me from the airport when you're more clearheaded."

He does not reply.

"There are things you should know."

He takes a step forward, intrigued.

"Meaning?"

I have to do this, have to tell him at least something of the truth.

"I know why it is that you have these suspicions. But believe me, things are not as they appear to be. You think you're onto something, but the only person you're going to end up hurting is yourself. In your mind it all adds up, but you have to try and see the bigger picture."

He looks at me with contempt, and then is gone. I am left staring at a section of empty street with no clue as to how to proceed. I tried to make him privy to the complete truth of this. I was prepared to break the central binding law, but he withdrew from it.

A car goes past with the radio on, a song playing loudly that I do not recognize. I feel cold, hungry, and beaten. How quickly failure settles on me. Cohen has won. In this, as in all things, he has proved the better man.

29

TRUTH TELLING

This is what they told me, a long time ago.

Only make contact in the event of an emergency.

Only telephone if you believe that your position has been fatally compromised.

Under no circumstances are you to approach us unless it is absolutely necessary in order to preserve the security of the operation.

This is the number.

I ring from a telephone box outside the Shepherd's Bush Theatre. With Hawkes out of contact, I have no other choice. The woman who answers says, "Two-seven-eight-five."

"John Lithiby, please."

"One moment."

Lithiby picks up.

"Yes?"

"John. It's Alec."

"Yes?"

"We need to have a meeting."

"I see."

It sounds as if the breath has gone out of him. I never wanted to be a disappointment to them.

"Where are you?" he asks.

"Near my home."

"Can you get to the restaurant for midday?"

"I've taken the morning off."

"Good. I'll send Sinclair to meet you. He will escort you to a place where we can speak freely."

At the restaurant off Notting Hill Gate, downstairs out of sight of the street-facing window, I order a bottle of mineral water and wait for Lithiby's stooge.

The only consolation in all this is that I am doing the right thing. It is better to act now, when I can take preventive measures against Cohen, than to let matters get beyond my control.

I never thought it would come to this. I never thought it would be necessary to tell the truth.

Sinclair is on time. He comes down the stairs at a fast clip wearing brown suede loafers and a corduroy suit. There is, as always, too much gel in his hair. He scans the room, sees me, but makes no discernible greeting. His height—six three—is immediately striking. It marks him out. He walks over to my table and I stand to greet him, to shake his firm hand. He looms four or five inches above me, looking down like a prefect. I hate the unearned psychological advantage of the tall, the pay-off from an accident of birth.

"You're lookin' a bit ropy, Alec."

His accent suggests a desire to shake off London vowels.

"I'm not too bad."

We sit down. The waiter, new to the place, comes back with a bottle of Hildon and two menus in his other hand. He pours each of us a glass of water and begins reciting the specials in halting English.

Sinclair lets him get to the third dish before he says, "That's all right, mate. We're not staying."

The waiter looks confused.

"It's not that we don't like it here. It's just we have to be somewhere else."

"I don't understand," he says, a Russian accent. "You don't want eat?"

"That's right," I tell him. "I'll leave money for the water. Just let me know how much it is."

"What you like," the waiter says with a shrug. He walks away from the table briskly, as if we have hurt his feelings.

"Just leave five pounds," Sinclair tells me firmly. "No need to wait for the bill."

I don't like it when Sinclair tells me what to do. There's only a five-year gap in age between us, but he likes playing the slick old hand, the unruffable pro. To irritate him, to make him look cheap, I take a ten-pound note from my wallet and wedge it between the pink tablecloth and a worn glass ashtray. Sinclair looks at it and then stands to leave. I want to let him know that I have access to money.

We cross the room. A Japanese businessman passes us on the stairs with a young Slavic blonde draped on his arm, probably a hooker. She looks drugged out and shamed. Then we go outside onto the street.

Sinclair and I do not speak in the taxi, not out of concern for what the driver might overhear but because there is so little to be said between us. He gives the address of a hotel at the west end of Kensington High Street and spends the rest of the journey looking for signs of a tail out the back window. Aftershave lifts off his clothes, a brutish smell of lavender. I start to dread Lithiby.

The journey takes less than ten minutes. Sinclair pays, makes a big deal of leaving a generous tip, and taps the roof of the cab as it pulls away. We walk up a ramp at the side of the hotel entrance and move haltingly through stiff revolving doors.

The decor is international marble, light and gleaming. A reception desk widens out ahead of us, manned by a slim, mustachioed man and a brunette with galaxies of dandruff stuck to the shoulders of her corporate blazer. I scan the lobby for surveillance. Two tourists—undoubtedly Americans—are sitting on a sofa behind us. There are four Japanese, all men, loitering near a window, a cleaning woman stooped and dusting, a Royal Mail deliveryman with a clipboard making his way across the marble floor, and two young girls giggling near the entrance to a buffet-style restaurant. We have not been followed inside.

Sinclair and I walk to a bank of lifts. There is one already waiting; its doors slide open, and we ride it, just the two of us, to the tenth floor. There is a large mirror inside the elevator car that makes the narrow space feel less claustrophobic. Sinclair brings a mobile phone out of his hip pocket like a revolver and twists it lovingly in his hand. He turns to me.

"We have people on either side of 1011. It's on the top floor, directly above a conference suite, so there's no listening threat from above or below."

We step out of the lift and make our way to the room along a cream-walled corridor, the floor a marie-rose carpet flecked with ticks of blue. Sinclair walks a pace ahead of me, brisk and purposeful. My mind is simply not prepared for the rigors of a debriefing. As we pass room 1010 I can hear voices, relaxed cockney laughter. There are men inside setting up recording equipment, ready to take down everything I say.

Room 1011 is standard-issue. A hard-mattressed double bed with a smooth cream cover lying taut across it. A dressing table with a strip-lighted mirror, a freestanding lamp next to velvet curtains shut heavy against the daylight. There's a smell of cleaning fluids, a sense of the recently hoovered, as if the memories of all former guests have been quickly and efficiently erased.

John Lithiby is sitting in a narrow, high-backed chair in front of the closed curtains. There is a briefcase at his feet, but he has left no trace of himself elsewhere in the room. Sinclair shows me in, nods deferentially at Lithiby, and leaves. I hear the door to 1010 open and close as he enters the next room.

"Alec."

"Hello, John."

He appears to be in a stark, blunt mood. I stand in the narrow space between bed and wall, getting my bearings. I back up and scope the bathroom. Neat soaps in packets, a shower above the bath partly obscured by a blue plastic curtain. Everything so clean.

"Why don't you come in and sit down?" he says. "We can start whenever you're ready."

Nothing about Lithiby ever changes. His shirt is blue with a stiff white collar, the graying hair barbered in an exacting straight line that stretches from the back of his semibald cranium to the upper perimeters of his forehead. The bespectacled, bony face looks drawn out by intense concentration. It is hard to imagine such a man having a private life. I perch on the bed, at the corner farthest from his chair.

"Now, what is the precise nature of the problem?" he says, interlocking long fingers in his lap. "Why have you come in?"

"Last night I dropped off the North Basin report that David prepared."

"We were there. We saw you go in."

"Did your people spot Harry Cohen?"

"Who?"

I have never mentioned Cohen's name in any of my reports to Lithiby. That fact alone will make the next hour extremely awkward.

"Harry Cohen. He works on my team at Abnex. Michael and David know him. Where *is* Michael, by the way?"

Lithiby moves forward and back within the narrow confines of his chair. He looks to have been suddenly constricted by my question.

"I don't know if they did," he says, referring back to Cohen. "I'd have to check the report."

"He suspects that I may be handing secrets to Andromeda."

"Why would he think that?" There is a rising note of surprise in his measured voice.

"He came to my house last night, close to one o'clock. I was back from Cheyne Walk after dropping off the file. He said he'd seen me going into Atwater's building."

"This man has been following you?"

"No," I say, confidently. The lie just slips out because it has to. "But he may have been following the Americans. They've complained of an increase in surveillance."

"Yes," Lithiby says, dismissively. "I would ignore that if I were you. We looked into it. The Americans let you believe their flat was bugged to hurry you along. They wanted the survey of 5F371, and they wanted it quickly. That also explains why they were at Atwater's office last night. We saw them leave ten minutes after you, presumably having taken possession of the file."

"So you don't think Cohen has been following them?"

"We've certainly never seen him." He coughs, once and hard, his lungs sounding old. "Which begs the question, what was he doing there?"

And that is the question I do not want to answer, because it will reveal that I have kept things from them. I try to work around it.

"Cohen said it was just coincidence. He'd been to a dinner party on a houseboat and just happened to be passing Atwater's building."

Lithiby shuffles, pinching the fabric of his suit trousers to loosen them away from his thigh.

"So he comes out of his dinner party, sees you going into a building occupied by two employees of an American oil firm, and from that deduces that you are an industrial spy?"

I admit, "It's not that simple."

"I didn't think it was. I imagine you have a little bit more to tell me."

Lithiby's attitude has already started to bend into a characteristic sarcasm.

I say, "Maybe it would help if I told you exactly what happened yesterday."

"From that we could certainly put together a more complete overall picture."

I steady myself, begin.

"Caccia's report landed on my desk at about three o'clock yesterday afternoon. I immediately telephoned the Americans to set up the meeting with Atwater."

"As you were instructed to do by Katharine," Lithiby says. The smug self-assurance of his voice has started to unnerve me. "Where did you telephone from?"

"From the office."

"Why didn't you use a secure line?"

Another mistake.

"I didn't think Cohen would recognize the dry-cleaner as code."

Saying "dry-cleaner" like this sounds ridiculous. Lithiby breathes contemptuously through his nose.

"But he did recognize it. He suspected that something was up."

"Apparently. Yes."

"Had he been given any reason in the past to suspect that you were involved in something covert?"

"He's been acting strangely toward me for some time."

I do not like admitting this. I did not mention it in any of my monthly reports. Lithiby, who would be justified in becoming angry, looks away and appears to stare at a bedside lamp. He is weighing things up.

"In what way 'strangely'?" he asks. Often he will latch on to individual words, inspecting them for hidden meanings, for ambiguity.

"Cohen was suspicious of my friendship with Katharine and Fortner."

"Suspicious?"

He is still looking at the lamp, gazing.

"He felt it was professionally inappropriate."

"I see," he says, his voice tightening slightly. "Why didn't you mention this before?"

Lithiby closes off the question by turning back to look at me.

"I didn't think it was important."

"You didn't think it was important."

This drifts, an echo that makes me feel scolded and useless. His eyes are gradually narrowing with irritation.

"And although you knew that Cohen was suspicious of your relationship with the Americans, you told us nothing about it and still made the call in his presence?"

I do not reply. There seems no point in doing so.

"How did he react when you were setting up the Atwater meeting?"

"What do you mean?" I ask, buying time.

Lithiby's reply is quick and impatient, a rapid list of questions he considers obvious to the overall design: "Was he listening? Was he alone? Did he look up? How did he react?"

"He did nothing," I say, equally quickly, to match him. "He was working quietly at his desk."

Something knocks against the wall to Lithiby's left, a hard, heavy falling, but neither of us moves. I add, implausibly, "I can only conclude that it wasn't the code that alerted him. It must have been something else."

Lithiby stares hard. My last remark has triggered something. It occurs to me, only now, that because my work phone is tapped by GCHQ, he may already know about Cohen redialing the Irish woman and hearing the word *justify* said freely on the line. If that is the case, he may think of this conversation solely as a test of my integrity. But I cannot tell Lithiby what motivated Cohen to confront me. That information might be enough to persuade him to shut everything down.

"And you have no idea what that something else could be?" he says.

"None at all," I reply.

"And yet from somewhere this Harry Cohen has got hold of the idea that you are handing information to Andromeda?"

"Yes."

Clearly, he thinks I am keeping something from him. There's an increasingly curt, disapproving tone to Lithiby's questions, an impatience with my failure to provide him with satisfactory answers.

"You said earlier that you were certain Cohen hasn't been following you. How can you be so sure?"

"I just know he hasn't been. You get a feel for these things."

"Yes, you do," Lithiby says, in apparent agreement. "Tell me what happened last night. What time did you leave your flat?"

"Ten thirty. Around then."

"And what did you do? How did you get to Cheyne Walk?"

"I drove down Uxbridge Road, got onto Shepherd's Bush Green, did a complete circuit of the roundabout to shake off anyone who might be following—"

He interrupts me. His expression has taken on the sudden alertness of the interrogator who has discovered a flaw. "Why did you feel it necessary to do that if you weren't worried about Cohen following you?"

He has led me into a trap. He wants me to admit that I have been fearful about Cohen for some time.

"I'm not sure I follow you."

"It's perfectly simple, Alec. You can't have been trying to shake off a CIA tail, because you were going to an American drop. That would have been pointless. You must have been worried about surveillance coming from another source."

"Not at all. I just did it because I'd been told to by Fortner."

"You weren't worried that someone from Abnex, possibly Cohen, might be following you?"

"No."

Lithiby breathes in hard, as though growing tired of my lies. I think back to Dr. Stevenson at Sisby, a shrink catching me out over Kate. You get so far into a deceit that it's just too late to get out.

"Let me tell you what I think has been going on here. I think your friend Harry has had his doubts about you for some time. He has followed you around now and again, noted how often you see our American friends, perhaps even sneaked a look in your diary or staked out your flat of an evening. Last night, he followed the Lanchesters to an address in Cheyne Walk. He sees them go inside and then, lo and behold, who should turn up twenty minutes later but Alec Milius. You come out after fifteen minutes, he follows you home, confronts you on your doorstep, and tries to extract a confession."

"That's your theory," I say. "I can see why you might think that."

He was always the smartest of them. It was stupid of me ever to think that I could deceive him. I pick out the hum of air-conditioning in the room, the lunchtime traffic far below, horns and the din of people.

"Why didn't you go to David with this?" he asks, the obvious question to which I have no sensible answer.

"I thought about it, but what could he have done? I didn't want to panic him into shutting things down."

Lithiby appears to accept this, but he asks, "Didn't you ever worry that Cohen might have gone to security at Abnex, that he might have asked them to keep an eye on you?"

I have to give him something. Lithiby won't let this go until I tell him at least some of what he wants to hear.

"I did, yes. I admit it. But I didn't put that in any of my reports because I thought you'd write it off as paranoia. I'm under constant CIA surveillance. You would have said it was just American interference."

"That was a considerable supposition, Alec. We could have looked into things for you. A simple phone call to David."

I try to defend myself, try to erase the slim look of betrayal that has appeared on his face.

"It was too risky. It wasn't worth it. And they only took my rubbish away a few times. It could have been the CIA doing that. In fact, looking back over what Cohen said last night, it probably was."

This does not console him. It appears only to make things worse.

"They took your *rubbish* away? When?"

"Three or four times. It would just vanish."

"And you thought it might have been Abnex doing this and you said nothing?"

"Because I wasn't sure. It didn't seem important enough."

"Does it seem important enough now?"

I am tired suddenly of his persistent scolding, the claustrophobia of Lithiby's disappointment.

"John, I don't want to sit here and be reprimanded by you. I have been out there twenty-four hours a day for the last eighteen months trying to do a job, not knowing where surveillance is coming from, not knowing who I can trust, not knowing what I can or cannot say. Sometimes little things get away from me. I make judgments, good and bad. In this instance, yes, I fucked up. And because of that, Harry Cohen has threatened to turn me in."

"Threatened?" Lithiby says, seizing gratefully on semantics. "You mean he has done nothing so far?"

"I don't know." I can hear myself in the room, the exasperation in my voice. It is beyond me now to try to be calm. I resent Lithiby for extracting so much of the truth from me. "I don't know what he's done. But I'm worried. Cohen's fiancée works at *The Times.* If he leaks the story to her, I'll end up on the front cover of every fucking newspaper in the western . . ."

"Oh, let's not be drawn into melodrama."

My visible sense of panic has seen him slide once more into condescension. This irritates me.

"It's not melodrama, John. This is a very real situation. I am not keen to become my generation's Kim Philby."

At the mention of his name, Lithiby's face folds up. I am overreacting and he knows it.

"It won't come to that. You'll be protected," he says. His voice has slowed to a stall. It is almost as if he is ridiculing me. I stand up from the bed, my back stiff from inactivity. The hotel room feels dark and musty and I walk to the door to flick on an overhead light. Lithiby squints.

"Is that necessary?"

I do not answer, but switch the light off.

"This is the situation, John." I start to move around the room, pacing the narrow corridor that leads from the door to the bedroom, gesticulating, sweating. "Harry flew to Baku this morning on a three-week working trip. When he comes home he expects me to have discussed things with somebody, to have cleared my name."

"So you think no one else at Abnex knows what he knows?"

Lithiby has latched on to this as though it were a sign of hope, and I have no intention of deflating that.

"I'm convinced of it. I wasn't until last night, but I am now. Cohen was very specific about it."

"And you believed him?"

"What reason would he have to lie?"

Lithiby looks at me and smiles with appropriate disdain.

"What reason would he have to tell the truth?"

"He's basically a decent guy, John. He snoops around because he's a company man. He does it out of loyalty to the firm. I trust him to stick to his word. We made an agreement. Now I have three weeks in which to come up with a way of convincing him that I am not an industrial spy, and I need your help in that."

"And what do you suggest we do?"

Lithiby asks this in a tone that suggests he is prepared to do very little. All solidarity between us appears to have vanished.

"Can you talk to Harry?"

"Out of the question. The only people within Abnex who know the truth about you are David Caccia and Michael Hawkes, and that's how things are going to stay. We cannot jeopardize the operation because of one man. The North Basin data is being examined by the Americans as we speak. In a matter of days, they will start to act on the information contained within it. To get to that point has always been the purpose of this operation."

"And it doesn't bother you that Cohen may go to the press and mess everything up before that happens?"

"Of course it bothers me. Do you know what a scandal it would cause if we were found to be selling fake secrets to the Americans?"

"No more of a scandal than that the Americans were buying them in the first place."

Lithiby likes that I've said this. It's the argument that legitimizes his operation. He pushes out his lips to smother a grin that steals up on him. Then he crosses his legs and says with absolute conviction, "Cohen isn't going to go to the press."

"How can you be sure?"

"I speak to David Caccia regularly. He has never mentioned anything about a security alert at the company. Cohen must have kept his mouth shut. And there's no way an employee of the firm would go to *The Times*—girlfriend or no girlfriend—without making certain of his story beforehand. He would need to instigate a thorough internal investigation of your activities before he went to the press. If he was wrong, he would lose his job."

This reading of Cohen's behavior makes perfect sense. With the slow absorption of his logic, I experience a first buzz of relief.

"That is not to say he isn't a fly in the ointment," Lithiby adds. "But Cohen is easily dealt with."

"How?"

He pauses for a moment, as if weighing up a raft of options. Then he leans back in his chair and puts his hands behind his head.

"What would you say were his weaknesses?"

There's relish in the asking. Lithiby has allowed his grin to burn through, not bothering anymore to hide it. This is the part of the job that he most enjoys, slicing imperceptibly through an opponent's Achilles' heel.

"Don't you think it's gone beyond that? Beyond playing psychological games?"

"That's what we're about, Alec. Now what would you say are his weaknesses?"

"He's competitive. Ambitious."

"You see those as flaws?"

"If you can exploit his vanity, yes."

"What else?" He is unsatisfied by this avenue of thought. "What about his fiancée? What's her name, this journalist?"

"Sarah Holt."

"How long have they been together?"

I don't feel like having this conversation, and I am curt, almost rude.

"Long enough to get engaged."

"Is Cohen faithful to her?"

"John, I don't know," I reply, thinking immediately of Anna and Kate. "I assume so. He's that sort of person."

"What hotel is he staying at in Baku?"

"If it's the one we normally use, the Hyatt Regency."

"Fine," he says. "We'll take care of him." Then his face seems to shut down. His appearance takes on the calm detachment of one who has access to terrible power.

"What do you mean, you'll take care of him?"

"I mean just that. We will see to it that Harry Cohen no longer poses a threat to the operation."

"What are you going to do?"

"That will require consultation."

"With whom?"

I am suddenly fearful for Cohen's safety, the first time that I have ever experienced any measure of sympathy for him.

"It's not your problem, Alec. You can relax. Don't let your imagination run away with you."

"I'm not."

"Good," he says, in a tone close to reprimand. "We're on your side. Don't lose sight of that."

"You don't need to worry about me," I tell him, summoning a sort of strength.

Lithiby smiles unconvincingly and takes off his glasses, polishing them on a lint cloth that he has produced from the breast pocket of his shirt. Here sits a man who exists outside the usual parameters of right and wrong. I will one day be like him if they decide to keep me on. He replaces the cloth and molds the thin, wire-rimmed glasses back onto his face.

"There are positive elements to be drawn from this," he says, standing up. He wants to stretch himself out with a little theorizing.

"And what are those?" I ask.

"The Americans know nothing about this. Everything in that respect is going very well and that's in large part down to your efforts. I'm very pleased, on the whole, with the way things have gone."

On the whole.

"Good," I say. "I'm glad."

We are facing each other now, both on our feet, the conversation coming to its natural end. I have a deep need to be away from this place.

"I should be getting back to work."

"Of course," he says, clapping his hands against thin hips. "No point in upsetting the firm."

I turn toward the door, and, as I do so, Lithiby puts his arm around my waist to guide me out. The physical contact is sickening. A card hooked on the door handle reads: PLEASE DO NOT DISTURB. Just as I am reaching for it, he says, "Haven't you forgotten something, Alec?"

We are a pace away from being outside, yet it feels as if I will never leave. There must be something that Lithiby knows, something that I have omitted to tell him. But I cannot think what that might be.

"I'm not following you," I say.

He withdraws his hand from my waist and rests it on the bone of my left wrist. It becomes clear.

"Oh, you mean the watch? The Rolex?" I hold it up and give it a slow shake. "How did you know about that?"

"Katharine was seen buying a Rolex in Bond Street by one of our people. I noticed today that you are wearing a Rolex. I merely put two and two together."

"They gave it to me as a gesture of goodwill. Of thanks. For the North Basin data."

"Did they?" he says, opening the door with a dry smile. "Well done, Alec. That's a good sign. Well done."

Sinclair, I see, is already waiting outside in the corridor. He nods complacently at me as we come out. He's heard everything.

"I'll be in touch," I tell Lithiby.

"Yes," he says, already turning to go back inside. It is as if the vivid glare of indoor light in the passage has startled him.

"Chris," he says, just as an acknowledgment of Sinclair, nothing more.

The single syllable trails off as the door closes, and there is silence now, not a sound from anywhere. Just Sinclair and I standing alone together in the corridor.

Eventually he says, "All set?"

30

LIMBO

And what now?

It appears that I am expected to go about my business as normal, to conduct my everyday life with the same blank regard for routine that I have shown for the past eighteen months. I receive no instruction from Lithiby, no hint or tip about Cohen. I can measure his disappointment in the silence that follows our meeting.

Six days go by. I wait by the phone, sleep only with the help of pills, drink from twilight till 2:00 A.M. Self-discipline erodes. At work I am somnambulant, incapable of clear and sustained thought. Tanya inquires if I am ill—*You look tired,* she says, *you look sick, Alec*—and I leave every afternoon at four, eager for the simple shelter of home.

What has happened is that I have grown bored of secrecy. I have developed a compelling urge to confess. I want now to be rid of all half-truths and deceptions, of all the necessary lies of my life. I have been doing this for so long now that I cannot recall when the deceiving began, when it became necessary, in the name of a higher cause, to be something other than the person I once was.

Did I let this happen willingly, or was I lured into a trap set by Hawkes? I have never been able properly to answer that question. Late 1995 and '96 is a blur of heartbreak and bruised ego. SIS rejected me—but in the next instant, just a day later, I was presented by Hawkes with a plan. At the time it seemed a lifeline thrown by kinder fates, a glimpse at last of something promising. And I grasped at it with no thought to consequence, no concept of its dependence on total secrecy, and with nothing but a young man's blind greed for acclaim.

That, of course, is how the intelligence services operate. They appeal to your innocence, to your secret and grandiose dreams. Any large corporation is the same: get them when they're young, prelapsarian, before they've had a chance to get too disappointed with what life throws at them. Get them when the prospect of being faced with a choice does not constrain but rather liberate; when the thought of the clandestine life is thrilling, not abhorrent.

I no longer recognize the person who made those choices, and yet he was surely a better person than I am now. The one whom Kate knew. If I could only get back to that.

On the weekend of April 4 I set myself to do some clear thinking, but it's vague and contradictory. For a while I convince myself that there was a part of me that was waiting for Cohen, a desire actually to get caught. Something about his persistence was comforting. It offered me a way out. Just below the constant fright of imminent capture, I am experiencing a curious sense of relief, an intimation of rebirth, a feeling of beginning again in the past. To be free of Lithiby, of Caccia and Hawkes, to start afresh, seems possible now.

But to believe this is fatuous. If Cohen bleats, SIS and Five will deny all knowledge of me and I will be left to fend for myself, as a traitor against the state. If the truth comes out—that the Americans have been victims of an elaborate hoax—it will be denied at official levels in the interests of the special relationship. What was Hawkes's line? *We've been hanging on to the shirttails of every U.S. administration since Roosevelt.* That isn't about to change just so that Alec Milius can sleep soundly in his bed at night. I will then be a marked man, the target of an expansive American grudge. Either way, my options are hopelessly limited.

Why did I not see all this coming? Why did I not recognize immediately the grim paradox of the trade? That we are all of us foolishly reliant on the goodwill of corrupt men for our safety and peace of mind. Their loyalty can—and will—vanish in an instant, because everyone must be ultimately deniable. That's what breaks the chain. You came here lonely, and you will leave alone.

Saturday night. There's nothing on TV but talking heads and *Noel's House Party* in "A New York Special." Edmonds has taken the show to a television studio in Manhattan where William Shatner and David Hasselhoff have been invited as his special guests. Next to these tanned, protein-rich megastars, Noel looks like a very small man awed by America. I switch the program off, and the room lapses into silence, the thin electric whine of the TV fading, just on the edge of sound.

There is a buzz on the doorbell, a sharp sudden punch, which kicks me out of the reliable calm of home. What if it's a journalist, a scoop-hungry hack with a TV camera bolted to his shoulder? I have lived this last week in persistent dread of the journalist on the phone, of the item on the six o'clock news. More wild hallucinations. Who is at the door?

It's just a pizza delivery boy, clear skinned and accentless, called to the wrong address. I show him where he wants to go—111B, next door—and he thanks me with a grunt. Going back upstairs, passing all the flyers and pamphlets littering the hall, I allow myself a little knowing smile. Perhaps, at the end of the day, all this is merely appealing to my sense of dramatic effect. Perhaps everything will be fine. Perhaps the Americans will use the data, oblivious of its defects, Cohen will be taken to one side and told to act in the best interests of Queen and Country, and JUSTIFY will prosper. And maybe I should stick to the plan that has existed all along: to leave Abnex in three or four years and accept Lithiby's offer of employment with Five. In the final analysis—Cohen's intrusions apart—I am good at my job. I have a talent for it.

I had thought about a confession to Saul. It came from a deep-seated desire to be unburdened of the facts, a simple need, in the wake of Lithiby, to explain to someone exactly what has been going on. No evasions, no half-truths. The total picture. I would sit him down, apologize for being such a lousy friend, and explain that I used his flat for a dead drop. But what could I expect in return? Forgiveness and understanding? Why burden him with something so beyond his experience? There is nothing Saul could usefully do for me but bob his head sympathetically and pour me another drink.

31

BAKU

At work on Tuesday afternoon, three days before Cohen is due back from Baku, I get a call from Katharine. I am unprepared for the conversation and struggle to summon up the necessary zip. My mind is so slack that I speak only briefly in abrupt phrases that trail off, going nowhere. Katharine, who is evidently cheery and content, picks up on this and after a couple of minutes asks, "You okay?"

"Yes. Why?"

"I dunno. You sound kinda odd. Sad."

I almost believe she cares.

"I'm fine."

"Sure?"

"Absolutely."

We talk about the election. Katharine says that if she had British citizenship she would vote for Blair, because he has the requisite "dynamism" that's lacking in John Major. Fortner, on the other hand, feels sympathetic to the prime minister, seeing him as an essentially decent man laid low by the vanities of his grudge-filled colleagues.

"By the way," she says, changing the subject. "That gift you gave us, the CD. It's great. Terrific. Just exactly what we were hoping for."

I absorb this, the first piece of good news in days.

"I'm glad," I say, but nothing else.

"It took a long time for you to find it, but it was worth the wait."

There's the sound of a tap running in the room where she is talking. She must be using the phone in the kitchen. Fridge magnets, a wooden rack of wines. My concentration wanders. I can think of nothing to say.

"So maybe we'll see you before too long, huh?"

"That would be nice."

I cannot lift myself out of this sapped funk. The intensity I need for JUSTIFY has somehow vanished. I cannot even lie with my voice on a phone.

"You sure you're okay, Alec?"

"Just a bit tired, that's all."

"Maybe you should take a vacation. They work you too hard."

This is when I see Tanya coming out of Murray's office, her eyes flooded with tears. I think at first that she has been fired, but this is sadness for another person; it isn't the grief of self-pity. Her cheeks, the stretch of her face, have flushed to raw pink, like someone with a bad cold. She has a handkerchief balled tightly in her right hand, which she is pressing weakly against her nose. I am the only other person in the office.

"Alec?"

"Sorry, Kathy. Look, can I ring you back?"

"Sure. Get some rest, will ya?"

I replace the receiver slowly, without saying good-bye. Tanya is slumped now at her desk and I start walking over to console her. Murray appears in the doorway, arms propped on both sides at head height.

"Can I have a word?"

He does not wait for me to answer, turning back in the direction of his office on the opposite side of the corridor.

"You all right?" I say to Tanya.

"You'd better go in," she says.

"Shut the door, will you?"

Murray is standing in the bright spring light of his window, which overlooks a merchant bank and a small block of flats. He has his back to me, staring out over the City. He is very still. A man who has found a calm within himself so that he may deliver bad news.

I close the door. Someone walks past outside and I hear a woman's voice, in concerned tones, asking Tanya a question.

"What's going on?" I ask.

"It's about Harry."

Murray turns, and I find that my head lolls down, shamed into staring at the carpet.

"He's been badly injured in a fight in Baku. A robbery. Three, they think, maybe four local boys attacked him. Knives. He's in bad shape."

We'll take care of him.

"He's alive?"

"Intensive care."

We will see to it that Harry Cohen no longer poses a threat to the operation.

"Where?"

"He's in a hospital in Geneva."

"What's the extent of his injuries?"

"Three broken ribs. Internal bleeding. Broken arm, hairline fracture to the skull. They don't think there's been damage to the brain, but it's too early to say. He's not been conscious."

"Does his girlfriend know?"

"Already in Switzerland. Mum and dad as well."

"I'm so sorry."

At this, Murray appears to shiver.

"What are you sorry for?" he says, like a clue to something he has doubted about me. "What does it have to do with you?"

"It's just a figure of speech."

He turns back to the window.

"He's not going to die." The way I say this makes it sound like a statement of fact, not a question.

"No. Chances are."

"That's good, at least. I'd better see if Tanya's okay."

"Yeah. Take her out for a coffee or something."

"Sure."

I leave Murray's office, closing the door behind me. Tanya, still seated at her desk, is being comforted by one of the girls from personnel, who is sitting on her haunches, her arm half around Tanya's back. They both look up, as if expecting me to speak, and I say, "It's unbelievable," but the words may come out too softly to be heard. Neither of them replies. I cross the room, take my coat off the rack, pick up my briefcase, and walk to the door.

"I need some air," I tell them. "I'm going for a walk."

Tanya gives a desperate short nod of assent, her face still blotched with tears, and I make my way to the lift.

———

I can see them close in, the dull glint of a muddied blade, the suddenness of it. They are upon him so quickly. A kick burying into his kidneys, bleeding. The complete lack of any sound. Just the thud of a boot, a punch landing awkwardly across his shoulders, another following instantly, smashing bone. He feels warm suddenly with the blood in his clothes, but the pain in his ribs is wrenching. He can no longer see. There is a taste of vomit growing in his throat.

The stark truth of cause and effect appears now with a clarity that I have never before allowed myself to acknowledge. There is no longer anything theoretical about what I have been doing. My actions have had a direct and appalling consequence. The guilt is overpowering. I have a lurching need to talk to somebody, to confess and to explain. And there is only Saul.

In a telephone box a block away from the office, I dial his number, but it just rings and rings. No one home. I try the mobile, but he has left it on message. He could be out of town on a shoot, or screening his calls. I do not know where Saul is.

"It's Alec. Please, if you get this, can you ring me? At home. I'm going home. It's urgent. I need . . . I really need someone to talk to about something."

A woman has appeared outside the booth, waiting to use the phone. I hang up, and a coin falls with a clatter behind the small metal flap. I retrieve the ten-pence piece from the slot. The woman comes around to my left, but she does not look directly through the glass. She just wants to let me know that she's there. Where is Saul?

Then, like a temptation, I feed the coin back into the telephone and dial her number from memory.

She answers after just a half ring. There's even a little performance in the cadence of her "hello." A need to be liked.

It takes me a beat to respond.

"Kate. It's Alec."

32

END OF THE AFFAIR

I travel to her house in a kind of trance, blank of thought and purpose. The taxi ride becomes a stark fact: within twenty minutes I will be in a room with Kate for the first time in over two years. She didn't sound surprised to hear from me. There was no gulp or awkward silence on the phone, no apparent sense of shock. Just a note of happy surprise, almost as if she had been expecting me to call.

Yes, it's a good time. Come straight round. I understand. Anything.

I pay the driver and walk the short distance to the front door of her house. It's still deep blue, the glass mottled, the base flecked with the scratches of a dog's paw. I glance up at the sitting-room window, looking for a twitch of curtain, some sign of her, but there isn't even a light on inside. So many times I walked up these steps and just the sight of her face would lift me, an inexplicable joy. Will that still happen? Can I still feel things in that way?

So I ring the bell. I don't hesitate. I just press it right away.

Odd not to have keys. Odd to have to wait.

A light comes on in the hall and then the tall outline of her, blurred by the glass. Now comes the first true nervousness, a swallowing void in my stomach. This was a sudden decision. I have not thought it through. Her hand is on the latch of the door.

New haircut. Bobbed. It suits her. In the first instant that I see her I know that it will be possible to tell her everything and to depend on her silence. Kate says my name very softly with a nice ironic smile that does something to diffuse the forced theater of reunion. Then we hug—it seems the right thing to do—but that goes wrong. I lean too far in, across the threshold, and our shoulders collide. We do not kiss.

"I like your hair."

"Thanks," she says, dismissively. "Had it done a while ago."

Her mood is cool, patient but without much warmth. Perhaps that will change. To begin with, she will want to show me that she has moved on. Perhaps for this reason there has been no attempt to look pretty for me. Her face is without makeup and she is wearing her old Nicole Farhi sweater, stretched and holed at the elbow, with a pair of torn blue Levi's. No perfume, either.

She turns and walks back into the hall and I see that she has put on weight, perhaps as much as fifteen pounds. Her hips have widened out. All of us getting older.

"Let's go to the kitchen," she says. "I made tea."

That's her mug on the table, the one with the teaspoon in it. She always liked her coffee that way. She'd lie in bed in the morning with her index finger wrapped around the handle of the spoon, supping with sleepy eyes.

Not much has changed in here. Everything still smells and looks the same. The Hermitage poster from the time Kate went to St. Petersburg is still hanging on the wall, and there's a pile of yellowed newspapers on a wicker chair by the door. Just like the old days. We never got around to recycling. A dishwasher, though, over by the sink. That's new.

"You got a dishwasher."

"Yes."

"They're great. Wish I had one. Saves so much time."

She smooths down her hair, edgy and flushed now. This isn't easy for her. Memories coming back all the time.

"You sounded awful on the phone," she says.

"It's just been a terrible few weeks. I had some bad news."

"No one's hurt, are they?"

"No. Nothing like that. No one that you know, anyway."

She looks perplexed.

"I'm sorry to ring you out of the blue. You were probably busy."

"I wasn't."

Think of something to say. Fill the silence.

"Are we alone?" I ask.

Kate hesitates, gives a look that I interpret as guilt, then says, "Yes," as she touches her chin.

"Good. Just had to be sure."

I sit at the seat nearest the window, weak sunlight on my back. There's a small yellow jug on the table with daffodils in it. Kate goes toward the sink and offers me tea, tapping a steaming pot on the counter. I say no. If I could only tell what she is thinking. Is she still angry with me, or is this slight detachment only nerves? She walks back to her chair, an apple in hand, and sits.

"So what is it?" she asks. She has a genuine look of concern about her, the patience of a true friend, but this may be entirely artificial. She is capable of that, of putting on a show. It's quite possible that she feels nothing but hatred for me.

"I'm involved in something," I tell her, starting out sooner than I had anticipated. "I just needed to talk to someone. Saul wasn't around."

She doesn't react to the mention of Saul's name. He is just someone from her past now.

"So I rang you. That's why I rang you. Because of that. I'm sorry to bother you like this. It just seemed to make sense."

"It's really all right."

She must think it's weak of me to have come here: how could she not? I should have a new life by now, a new girlfriend, somebody else to lean on. To rely on the past like this is pitiful. I've known too many couples who meet up after an absence of a couple of years, and one of them always wonders why they wasted so much time on the other.

"You look tired," she says.

"I haven't been sleeping all that well."

"You sure you won't have tea?"

"Sure."

"Nothing else? Sprite or Coke? Something to eat?"

"Nothing, thanks. You're kind to offer."

"So how come you haven't been sleeping?" she asks.

I take out a cigarette and light it, not bothering to ask if that's okay. I couldn't bear too much politeness between us. My eyes fix on an unpaid bill lying on the kitchen table, £124 to BT. At least they have Cohen in a Geneva hospital with Swiss doctors who'll give him the best treatment they can.

"Alec?"

I had wandered off.

"Sorry. Why am I not sleeping? Stress, I suppose. Just worry."

"About what?"

"All kinds of stuff . . ."

"What kind of things? Why have you come here?"

"I think I may have been responsible for something terrible. For someone getting hurt."

She doesn't visibly react to this. She will just want me to go on talking.

"He's someone at work. I'm in the oil business now. He's on my team." I am starting to speak more quickly now, feeling the rush of the impending confession. "What I'm going to say to you, Kate, you have to swear to tell no one. You can't speak to your dad about this, or to Hesther, or anyone. . . ."

"Alec, I won't. I promise."

"Because no one knows. There's just me and three other men, that's all."

She doesn't bother to reassure me again of her intent to keep her word. She has promised it once, and that, in her view, is enough.

"About two years ago I was approached by someone to be recruited for MI6."

"What's that, like MI5?"

"MI5 is domestic. Six is foreign intelligence. Its proper name is SIS. The Secret Intelligence Service."

Kate nods.

"I did a lot of interviews and exams. The whole process took about three months. The man who approached me was called Michael Hawkes. He knew my father when they were students."

"Did I ever meet him?" she asks, a question that strikes me as odd.

"No. At least I don't think so. Why?"

"Go on," she says.

"He was taking up a seat on the board of directors at a British oil company called Abnex."

"Never heard of it."

"No. It's small."

Kate sips her tea.

"He told me that Abnex was having a problem with industrial espionage, people trying to extract information from employees of the firm to benefit rival organizations. In particular there were two known CIA agents working out of an American oil company called Andromeda, using marketing consultancy as a cover. Since we share so much intelligence with the Americans, and they know our personnel, MI5 couldn't use any of their own people. So Michael asked me if I would pose as a target for them, if I would present myself as somebody who would be willing to hand over sensitive documents in exchange for money."

"Jesus."

"I know." I attempt a smile. "Who would have thought it?"

"And you did it?" she asks, deadpan. "You went ahead with this?"

"I was flattered. I was at a loose end. Yes, I went ahead with it."

She pushes out her lower lip and I feel a need to say, "What young man of twenty-five *wouldn't* go ahead with it?"

Kate responds to this with a twitch of her mouth, which suggests that she can think of several who wouldn't. Steady, able fellows with a puritan streak.

"So that's how I got the job in the oil business. It was put together by Michael Hawkes."

"I see," she says.

"And by David Caccia, the chairman of Abnex, who's ex-Foreign Office, working alongside another man, someone they both know at MI5."

Some dying trace of professional responsibility prevents me from mentioning Lithiby by name.

"Amazing," she says under her breath.

"What is?" I ask.

"I heard that you'd got that job on merit. Because of your languages."

"Who told you that?"

She hesitates.

"I saw Saul at a party a year ago. That's what he said."

Saul never told me anything about seeing Kate at a party.

"That's what people are supposed to think. That's what Saul thinks. He doesn't know about any of this. Neither does Mum. I haven't been able to tell anybody. That's why I made you promise not to discuss it with anyone. I know it's a lot to ask, but . . ."

She says my name softly, to herself, a whispered consternation.

"I've had to maintain complete secrecy. It's driven me crazy. Can you imagine not being able to tell your friends or your family—"

"Absolutely," she says, interrupting me. "I can understand that."

We look at each other briefly, the first vaguely intimate moment to pass between us. Her skin is so close now, the vivid green of her eyes, but the instant passes very quickly. Kate seems to check it. She will not smile at me or show any real warmth, beyond a certain businesslike efficiency.

"But how did they set all this up?" she asks, pushing hair out of her face. "I don't get it. Michael Hawkes and these other people you work for. How did they set you up with the Americans?"

"They leaked my SIS recruitment report to the CIA, having taken out any reference to Michael Hawkes and doctored the psychological profile to make it look like I'd be more susceptible to treason."

"How?"

"Gave me low self-esteem, delusions of grandeur, no money. The classic traitor profile. It was all shit."

"So you're a spy? You work for MI5?"

There's no concealed pride in the way she asks this, only worry in her voice, perhaps even contempt.

"At the moment, I'm what they call a support agent, someone who's not an official employee but who assists the intelligence services in some other capacity. They may grant access to a private bank account for money laundering, or provide safe houses in London, that kind of thing. MI5 have offered me a full-time job if I want it."

I had expected her to be impressed by this, but nothing registers. She says, "Do they pay you?"

"Yes."

But she does not ask how much. "And what? These two Americans think that you're loyal to them and you're not?"

"Yes. Some of the information I've given them is legitimate, but most of it has been doctored. That was the purpose of the initiative."

"And the CIA pay you as well?"

I nod.

She sucks all this in, biting down on the apple for the first time.

"I can't believe this stuff goes on. And I can't believe you're involved in it, Alec."

"It's happening all the time," I tell her, again feeling some need to justify myself. "Everyone's doing it. European countries spy on other

European countries. The Yanks spy on us, we spy on them. There are SIS officers operating under diplomatic cover in almost every one of our embassies overseas."

"So it's a widespread thing?"

The experience of seeing her come to terms with this is bewildering. I had just blandly assumed that everybody knew about it.

"Of course. Let me give you an example. Just the other day, we found out that French intelligence had people listening in on secret negotiations between Siemens, a German technology company, and the South Korean government over a contract to build high-speed trains. Using that information, a French company was in a position to offer the Koreans a better deal and they won the contract."

"It makes you sick."

"I know. Those guys even bug business-class seats on Air France flights out of Paris. We're all supposed to be in this fucking European community to make trading easier between member states, but this is how the real business gets done."

"But with America?" she says. "They're our allies. Why did you have to get involved with them? Why didn't Abnex just prosecute the two people from the CIA?"

"Because it would be politically explosive. And because intelligence people love the thrill of the chase, the satisfaction of knowing that they're getting one over on the other guy. It's all tit for tat."

"Childish, if you ask me," she says, glancing out the window. "What are these Americans called? What are their names?"

"Katharine Lanchester and Fortner Grice. A married couple. He's much older."

Kate clearly has a growing interest in this now, a look of privileged access, though as yet no discernible admiration of my role in it.

"And how did you know that they'd come to you? How did you . . . ? I don't understand how it all works."

I put out the cigarette. It tasted suddenly sour.

"We were going to set up a meeting with the two of them at Abnex to discuss a possible joint venture with Andromeda. There's a lot of that going on in the Caspian Basin, a lot of cooperation. Companies get together and share the cost of exploration, drilling, whatever. That's how I wanted it to go, but Hawkes and my controller at Five thought that that approach would be too obvious."

The sensation of finally being able to break my silence has momentarily suppressed any immediate concern for Cohen. Two years of backed-up secrets, all pouring out in a scrambled rush. I feel loose and relieved to be free of them.

"So we came up with another plan. MI5 put someone inside Andromeda, a guy called Matthew Frears, who was on my recruitment program. He fed us background on their movements, leaked documents, and so on. I then invited Saul to an oil-industry party, and Matthew manufactured an introduction to the Americans, using Saul as cover. Saul didn't know anything about it. Everything that happened after that was carefully planned. It took a lot of organization, a lot of hard work. I saw them regularly, made out that I didn't have very much money. I even had speeches prepared, tracts of dialogue committed to memory."

"How do you mean?" Kate asks. "Give me an example."

It is not difficult to recall the bones of one of the monologues. I lean forward in the chair, and it is like being back in their apartment, weaving a tale for the CIA.

"I was predicted straight-A grades, but I got ill and took a string of Bs and Cs, so I didn't get my chance to go to Oxbridge. That would have changed everything. I meet Oxbridge graduates, and none of them has qualities I don't possess. And yet somehow they've found themselves in positions of influence. What do they have that I haven't? Am I lazy? I didn't waste my time at university. I'm not the sort of person who gets depressed. If I start feeling low, I tell myself it's just irrational, and I pull myself out of it. I feel as if I have had such bad luck."

Kate has a peculiar grin on her face as I continue. I am talking quickly now, giving the words no inflection.

"I want to be recognized as someone who stands apart. But even at school I was always following on the heels of one or two students who were more able than I was. Smarter, quicker witted, faster on the football pitch. They had an effortlessness about them that I never had. I always coveted that. I feel as though I have lived my life suspended between brilliance and mediocrity. Not ordinary, not exceptional. Do you ever feel like that?"

Kate interrupts me: "That's not a prepared speech. That *is* you."

I stare back at her, smarted.

"No, it's not."

She gives a sputtering, patronizing laugh, which effectively kills off any chance of arguing this out.

"Whatever," I say, unconvincingly. "It doesn't matter. Think what you like. The basic idea was that I showed them how unsettled I was, how depressed I had become after breaking up with you. . . ."

At this Kate balks.

"You brought *me* into this?"

I stall. I had not intended to mention her role at all. Her voice quickens into anger.

"Fuck, Alec . . ."

"Relax. It was just cover. In all this time, I must have mentioned your name once to them. Nobody at SIS or Five knows anything about you. You didn't even come up in the interviews."

She appears to believe this, looking visibly calmer almost immediately. I keep on talking, to take her mind off the possibility that she was more acutely involved.

"It was just a way of getting the Americans to sympathize with me."

"Okay."

"That's how I was taught to approach things. Show them something you've lost. That's the first rule. A girlfriend, a job, a close relative. It doesn't matter. Then you confide in them, you show them your weaknesses. Ultimately I gave Katharine and Fortner the impression that they understood me. The relationship between us became almost familial."

"And all the time it was just a pretense. . . ."

Kate has that look she gets when learning lines for a play, an intense concentration, close to bewilderment, furrowing her brow. It makes her look older.

"They were not the innocent party, Kate. They knew Abnex had a small team that was exploring a sector of the North Basin that nobody else had access to. They wanted to get their hands on data from that project. They cultivated the friendship with me to that end. That's how it works. It's grim, and it's cynical, but it's the way of things."

She does not answer. Her half-eaten apple has turned brown.

"So, to cut a long story short, they offered me the chance to spy for them. They made me feel that it would be in everyone's interest in the long run."

"I just don't know how you could do this."

"Do what?"

"Pretend to be something that you're not to people you care about."

"Who said I cared about them?"

"Of course you do. You're not capable of being that cold."

She wants to believe that about me. She has always wanted to believe that people are essentially decent, that they adhere to certain standards of behavior.

"Kate, you're an actress. When you go on stage or in front of a camera, what are you doing but pretending to be somebody else? It's the same thing."

"Oh, please," she says, lifting her face up suddenly. "Don't even attempt to make that comparison. I'm not fucking with people's heads. I'm not living a twenty-four-hour lie. When I come home at night I'm Kate Allardyce, not Lady Macbeth."

"I dunno, there were some nights we were together . . ."

"Alec, please. No jokes."

I try a smile. Nothing from her. I had not expected a reaction like this. I had not prepared myself in any way for being criticized by her.

"I'm simply making the point that it's an act. I had to become someone that I was not. I was paid to put up a pretense. Every time I go to their apartment, I have a particular strategy in mind, something I have to say or do to facilitate the operation."

"Every time you go? Present tense? You're still doing this? But I thought . . ."

The telephone rings on the counter nearest the sink. Both Kate and I start in our seats, eyes briefly meeting, but she is up quickly, answering it.

"Hello?"

When the person on the other end of the line speaks, she turns away from me so that I cannot see her face. It is a man. I can hear the low bass of his voice coming through the receiver.

"Hi. Listen, can I call you back?" she says, suddenly nervous and unsettled. "I'm just in the middle of something. No, I'm fine. I'll ring you in an hour or so. Where will you be?"

He tells her. I look at Kate, standing there lithe and cool, and it's hard to believe that we fucked each other what must have been a thousand times.

"Fine. Lots of love," she tells him.

That's what she used to say to me.

She hangs up.

"You should have taken the call."

"Forget it," she says, scratching the back of her neck.

Why didn't she tell him I was here?

"Who was that?"

She hesitates, ignores the question.

"I'm still trying to get my head around all this. You said when you got here that someone's been hurt. Who? One of the Americans? Is that it? Who is this person you work with who's in trouble? You say he's on your team. Which team?"

"Somebody at Abnex. He cottoned onto what I was doing." After a brief pause, I add, "At least, I thought he did."

I light another cigarette, though the stale tar funk of the last one, lying crumpled in the ashtray, still hangs over the table, a rank odor that Kate detests.

"What's his name?"

"Harry Cohen. He's been at Abnex three years longer than I have."

"How old is he?"

"Twenty-eight."

"And how did he find out?"

"He was jealous of me for some reason. Or wary, one or the other. We didn't ever see eye-to-eye. And he seemed to track me. He always seemed to be on my back."

"Maybe you rubbed him up the wrong way," she says, as if looking to start an argument.

"Maybe," I reply, unwilling to pursue this.

"Maybe," she says again, archly.

It is almost as if she is mocking me. I stop and look at her with a half scowl that has the effect of making her turn away.

"Sorry," she says, flatly. "I didn't mean to . . ."

"It's all right."

"Go on," she says.

So I keep going, trying to explain Cohen as much to myself as to Kate.

"A couple of weeks ago, he followed me home from a drop. I'd left some information for Fortner and Katharine with a lawyer on Cheyne Walk. Harry says he was having dinner on a houseboat down there and just happened to see what was going on. He just knitted things together, like he was looking for a way to bring me down. And when I got back that night, he confronted me. Threatened that if I didn't explain to senior people at Abnex what was going on, he'd do it for me."

Kate again moves hair out of her face, tucking it quickly behind her ear.

"I had no choice but to report all this to my controller. I told him what Harry had done and he said he would take care of it." I pause, looking over at Kate, whose face has hardened further into censure. She knows what I'm about to tell her. There's a grim logic to it.

"After we talked, Cohen flew out to Azerbaijan, one of the old Soviet Repub—"

"I know what it is."

This is short and abrasive, spat out of a hardening in her attitude. There is no sympathy in Kate's eyes, no understanding of motive. Everything I am telling her has merely confirmed what she always suspected about me: that I am deceitful, weak, and cold. When I tell her what has happened to Cohen, she will blame me. And yet I cannot stop now; it has to come out. I have maintained a sense throughout this last half hour of hearing these things for the first time. At last they have been made plain to me, simply by the act of hearing the secrets spoken aloud in a room. There is no ignoring the plain fact of all the lies. If Kate is still the person she once was, the girl I fell in love with, she will despise me for what I have done.

"I've just learned that Harry was in a fight in Baku. Near his hotel. He's been very badly hurt. He might even have brain damage. They've flown him to a hospital in Switzerland."

Kate brings her elbows up onto the table, making a church with her fingers. She still wears that Russian wedding ring her mother gave her. I used to feel for it when we held hands, rolling the cold metal loops up to the knuckle and down. She would take it off when she had a bath.

"And it was your people that did this?" she says. "Because he found out what was going on? Because he knew the truth?"

"Almost certainly. It's too much of a coincidence."

She is silent for a long time. The sense of my shame is sickening.

"God, how you hurt people, Alec." She is shaking her head. "Is he going to be all right? Will he be okay?"

"They think so. Yes."

She looks up at me, and that's when I see pity. Such disappointment that it starts to anger me. I need understanding now, not contempt.

"Kate, if I'd known, do you think . . . ?"

She stands up and walks to the far side of the room, getting herself away from me.

"He's going to be all right." My voice is slightly raised. "They haven't killed the guy. It was just too dangerous to allow him . . ."

She puts out her hand to silence me, a weak floating limb that she retracts almost immediately.

"Let's just not talk about it for a bit. Is that okay? I'm sorry. I know you came here today because you needed someone to talk to, because all this has obviously had a bad effect on you. I can see that, and I'm sorry, I really am. But I'm just so amazed, you know? I haven't seen you in two years, my life has moved on in so many ways, and then this—that you could get involved in something like this. All the things you could have done, and you end up . . ."

Her words trail off. I am too tired to argue, to try to make her see sense. I cannot force Kate to act against her will, to console me with words she does not believe. It was inevitable that she would react in the way that she has. I had allowed myself to forget her true nature. She always speaks her mind, judgmental to the point of being conceited. She sets such high standards for herself and for others that it is almost impossible to move within the narrow confines of her expectations. Kate is incapable of compromise, of seeing another point of view. She demands so much of people that she will only ever be disappointed by them.

Needing to be away from her as much as she needs to be away from me, I stand and edge my way along the table back out into the room. I stand facing her, Kate staring beyond me at an opposite wall.

"I need to splash some water on my face."

No reply.

So I turn and leave the kitchen, walk upstairs to the bathroom, and lock the door.

I see things that are not hers immediately. A can of shaving foam at the edge of the bath. Contact-lens cleaners and a small plastic case beside the sink. Two toothbrushes in the mug beside them. After everything that has happened, now this.

I sit on the edge of the bath, head bowed. On the floor, a pair of white boxer shorts. Why didn't she hide them?

There is a window open and a cold wind buffets the glass, knocking the wooden frame against a brick wall outside. I tell myself that Kate is a pretty girl and that pretty girls have boyfriends and that this is all inevitable. But somehow it doesn't help. Why didn't she hide his things?

I drive myself crazy with images. Don't. It's too late for that. This is payback for Anna, for all of them. One man, two years later, his saline and his toothbrush laid out in the bathroom. You have to get used to that.

It was him on the phone.

I run cold water over my face at the sink but cannot stop the questions, the doubts. That he is good in bed, funny, capable of bringing out qualities in Kate that I suppressed. I cannot stop thinking that he makes her happier than I did.

Does Saul know about this? Did he meet him at that party?

Don't. Don't wonder what he looks like, what he does for a living, how much money he has or what stories he tells.

She will have met his friends.

They would have been to Paris, to movies, cooked for each other and fucked all night. Don't. Don't picture them in bed together, because that has nothing to do with your feelings for Kate and everything to do with your vanity. I just don't want him to be better than I was.

Just let it go. Think about Cohen and let it go.

God, the speed with which she has recovered.

When I come back downstairs Kate has moved into the sitting room, bunched up on the sofa with a fresh cup of tea and a face like stone. She looks different now, now that I know she has a boyfriend, a man living here under the same roof. The one I feared all those nights.

"Not much has changed up there," I say.

She cannot even look at me. My temper snaps.

"Kate, if you want me to go, I'll go. But please, don't sit there with this air of disappointment, this condescension, because I didn't come here for that. I genuinely believe that I would never have done this if we were still together."

"Don't you dare. Don't you dare blame this on me."

"You're right. I shouldn't blame you. It's not your fault. I would have done it anyway. Just like I slept with someone behind your back. It's in my genes, you say. And for the last time, I'm sorry that I took you for granted. I'm sorry I wasn't the person you thought you deserved. You had dreams for me that I couldn't fulfill, and I fucked up. And now I've got involved in a murky business that you find reprehensible. I don't blame you."

She looks up at me, twitching with moral authority. Nothing that I say will ever satisfy her. Let's have this out.

"If I thought this would happen, do you think I would have done it? Do you? Do you think that if I knew it would come to something like this that I wouldn't have put a stop to it? It was straightforward in the planning, that's all I can tell you. I was doing a job that I thought was useful and loyal and significant."

"Straightforward in the *planning*?" Her laugh here is contemptuous, the slender jaw gaped with sarcasm. "Jesus. Straightforward in the *planning*?"

"Let's not do that thing where we pick each other's sentences apart, okay? It's demeaning."

"You never think, Alec. That's just it with you. That's just exactly the problem. It's what happened with us, it's what's happening now. You take things on with no thought to the consequences, with nothing in your mind but how it can make you feel better about yourself. It doesn't matter if it's an affair with a girl at your fucking office or some needless industrial espionage that leads to an innocent guy getting the shit kicked out of him. It's always the same thing. You can't live life without turning it into a lie."

"That isn't the case. It's not that bad."

"Not that bad?" she says. "You never stopped lying to me. For the last six months we were together, we barely slept together. . . ."

Here we go. Actress time.

"Get over it, Kate. It's history."

"And when we did, those few times, I had to shut my eyes, I had to hold off the scream in my head. I did it for you. I let you fuck me because somewhere I still felt love for you, all the time knowing that that love had been corrupted, bit by bit, until all I felt was pity. Toward the end I could barely look at you. I couldn't touch you. And I'm not sure you even noticed that. I would lie beside you in bed and actually dread your weight, your smell. And do you know why? Because you were soaked in lies. Deceit was all over you. I should have been the first person, the only person, that you might have been open with. But instead, I was the one person that you lied to more or less the whole time."

I have heard all this before. The words have changed, but the well-worn message remains exactly the same. It is her standard tactic, a withering assault on my masculinity, disowning our sex life to wound me. My regrets about JUSTIFY, my fears for Cohen, are of no consequence to her. She does not see herself as my friend. There is still too much that she feels enraged by. Nothing has changed, nothing at all. It is still impossible to talk to Kate without her twisting a subject until it becomes a conversation about her. This is the selfishness in her that I had forgotten.

She is still not finished. She puts her tea on the small table beside the sofa and shakes her head with disappointment.

"In the beginning, when we first met, I saw you like someone might see a jigsaw. Just starting off. You were seventeen and I didn't know how you would work out, the shape of you. And then, as I got to know you, as the jigsaw came together, I saw that you were just made up of lies. Not big lies, not all the infidelities or womanizing or cheating or anything really dangerous, but weak, cowardly, fearful lies. And you lied because you were afraid of me. You were afraid of everybody. To console me you would open your mouth and something sweet and caring would come out, but I couldn't know if it was deeply felt. I couldn't know if you really meant it or if you just liked the sound of those words in the room, the way the sentences altered my face. I felt that you were never with me. You couldn't let me near you, you couldn't let anyone near you. Your whole life is just a process of holding people off in case they have an effect on you."

I do not deserve this. She has never found it in herself to forgive me. The damage to her self-esteem was just too great. I came here today on an impulse, to tell her things as a friend that I had never told anyone else. And yet she wants to use my confession as an excuse to criticize me for things that happened between us more than two years ago. The only thing that is of any interest to Kate is Kate. I had forgotten that.

"I'm going to go," I tell her very firmly, with no doubt in my mind that this is the right thing to do. "I don't have time to be talking about this. I need to find out about Harry and then get home. I'm sorry you weren't able to see the bigger picture, I really am. But I'm trusting you not to speak to anybody about what I've told you. You've given me your word, and I trust you. Because if you do, it would certainly mean the end of my career. I could even be killed."

She smirks at this. She does not want to believe any of it.

"I'm serious," I tell her. "So that's it. You've got it?"

"Yes," she says, exasperated.

"Good. Because I'm trusting you."

I travel home numbed by all the bad decisions I have made, each falling on the heels of the other. Young and blind to consequence, I have done and said things that have led me to the point at which I now find myself. This afternoon was just another example, a pointless tracking back into the past.

When Kate and I were together, there was such arrogance in me, an inability to see things for what they were. I just threw everything we had away on a whim and never properly fought to get her back. And then with Hawkes, what was it? Vanity? Is that all it was, a craving for recognition? What do Saul and Kate know that I do not, that they can make the right decisions, that they can appear to live life in the way that it is meant to be lived?

More waiting now. Nothing to be done. Always the ball in someone else's court. So I open a bottle of wine and read for five hours straight about Philby.

I cannot conceive of the scale of his deceit. The entire span of a life lived as a vast deception—to friends, to family, perhaps even to wives. I have done it for less than two years, and the relentless demands of total secrecy have been overwhelming. What must have been going through his mind as he contemplated all of that coming to an end?

Earlier in his career, British intelligence had been convinced that Philby was the Third Man, even to the point of asking for his resignation. Yet they held off, because the consequences of publicly revealing an enemy within outweighed the practical necessity of unmasking him. The shame would have been too much for the establishment to endure. Philby, Burgess, and Maclean all survived undetected for so long precisely for this reason, precisely because of their gentlemanly polish, their wit and erudition. In short, no one believed it possible that such men would betray their country. They induced a sort of class blindness in the intelligence community.

In spite of their suspicions, SIS allowed Philby to operate in Lebanon for some time, using journalism as cover. While still on the SIS payroll he filed for *The Observer,* in between feeding cocktail party gossip to low-level KGB agents in Beirut. Throughout all this, SIS acted as if Philby was a problem that would eventually disappear. Which in the end, of course, is exactly what he did.

When they were sure, when they knew that they had their man, they sent Philby's best friend—his Saul—to Beirut to flush him out. Nicholas Elliott, also SIS, was under instruction to offer him immunity from prosecution in return for a full confession. He was given twenty-four hours to reveal the full extent of his activities, but over that period was left to his own devices. What is astonishing to me is that on the night of Elliott's visit, Philby attended a dinner party at the residence of the first secretary to the British embassy, and then drank himself into a coma on cheap Lebanese whiskey. When he woke up, he made the decision to defect. He contacted his KGB controller, was given false papers as a Russian sailor and spirited back to Moscow on a freight ship before anyone had time to notice.

33

CACCIA

The days after seeing Kate continue to feel awkward and unsettled, like the guilt that follows an infidelity. The morning after I first slept with Anna there was a sense that I had succumbed to a needless temptation with no net gain that threatened to destroy everything. The pursuit was all. To wake up beside her, to adjust to her routines and smells, was the least enjoyable part of it. And yet I went back to her, time and again, for no better reason than that she provided me with a sense of excitement, a pitiful rush of adrenaline.

Telling Kate about JUSTIFY, having not seen her for more than two years, feels oddly similar, for she is a stranger to me now, someone whom I no longer know. The confession was pointless. None of my anxiety has subsided, and, if anything, telling her has actually compounded the problem. I feel no less guilty about Cohen—whose condition in Switzerland is deteriorating—and I have broken my explicit pledge to Lithiby, Caccia, and Hawkes to maintain absolute secrecy.

Perhaps the most damaging consequence of contacting Kate is that there is now someone out there who knows the truth about me. This endangers both her and the security of the operation. Although I can trust Kate to keep her mouth shut in the short term, it may not be too long before she feels the need to open up to someone. There is a sell-by date on secrets.

It is astonishing how quickly things begin to slip out of control.

On the afternoon of Thursday, May 1, election day, I get a call at my desk directly from Caccia. Normally he would never phone me in person. Barbara would do it, or he would send an encrypted message to Uxbridge Road.

When I pick up, he says, "Alec. It's David. We need to have a talk. Right away. Can you come up?"

"Of course."

Instinctively, I look up to check for Cohen's whereabouts, to ensure that he has not overheard the conversation, and it is only after a couple of seconds that I realize my mistake. Tanya is eating a yogurt at her desk and I smile at her as I leave the office, riding the lift to the executive floor.

Caccia is waiting for me on the other side of the elevator doors, alone and trim in a gray suit. It is not his style to look worried, though there is an undertow of concern as we shake hands. He would not have contacted me unless it was absolutely necessary to do so.

"Come into my office," he says, telling Barbara that we are not to be disturbed. She looks up at me warmly, as if I am somebody whom she has been instructed to impress. I smile back as Caccia ushers me inside, closing the door behind him.

"Drink?"

"Not for me, thanks."

"Mind if I have one?"

He turns to a bookcase in the corner of his office, pouring a large whiskey from a duty-free bottle of J&B concealed inside a cupboard. I have been in Caccia's office on only three occasions, twice with Hawkes in the very earliest days, by way of preparation for JUSTIFY, and then several months later with Murray, J.T., and Cohen to discuss a project in Kazakhstan.

"Terrible about Harry," he says.

I do not reply.

"I said, it's terrible about Harry."

Caccia is facing me, a tumbler in his right hand, waiting to see how I respond.

"Yes," I say, slowly. "A terrible shock. Who would have thought a thing like that could happen?"

He murmurs something, and his head drops as if suddenly weighed down by thought. If Caccia is privy to what has gone on behind the scenes, if he has knowledge that the assault on Cohen was authorized by

Lithiby, he does not reveal it. Nothing in his demeanor suggests a willingness to conceal the facts from me. He appears to be legitimately upset. And, of course, it is entirely possible that Lithiby has left him out of the loop. Caccia may have no idea just how close Cohen had come to the truth. On the other hand, Lithiby may have told him everything. At all times, I have to remember that these guys are in a different league when it comes to deception. Whatever they say, they say nothing.

"They haven't caught the bastards who did it," he says. I always forget how well spoken he is, the certainty of his place in the world revealed through polished vowels.

"No. Not yet."

Caccia clears his throat.

"One of our best people, too," he says, a remark that irritates me. He sits down in the high-backed, black leather chair behind his desk. "Normally I would ask how things are proceeding. My impression was that things had been going rather well. Do have a seat."

I sit in a nearby armchair, troubled by his use of the past tense.

"It would appear that we have a problem."

"Really? What kind of problem?"

"We've been keeping an eye on Andromeda, seeing how things proceed with the data you passed to the Americans. At first, they acted exactly as we supposed they would. Two of their employees flew down to Baku to begin negotiating the well workovers for 5F371. They set up meetings with government officials, crossed a few palms, usual sort of thing. The validity of rights was meaningless with the recent change of government personnel, and that was their cue to act. Again, exactly as we thought it would be."

"Yes?"

"Then nothing. This is the point. In the last forty-eight hours everything appears to have ground to a halt. We were expecting them to move quickly, to start looking into the possibility of drilling an exploration well before the end of this year. Now we hear that the Andromeda people are back in London. Cut short their visit. Never completed negotiations for the workover agreements and missed a series of crucial meetings." He takes a sip of his whiskey. "I don't need to tell you that this is strictly *entre nous*."

"Of course."

It always is. Why did he bother saying that?

"You think they smell a rat?" I ask.

"I rather hoped you would be able to tell me."

"Surely it's too early to say. Just because they came home doesn't mean Andromeda have realized there's nothing in 5F371."

"True. True." Caccia is nodding. "But we have another unanswered question. Again, something unusual, against the normal run of things."

I move forward in my seat.

"Fortner was seen in Colville Gardens last night packing up his car. Chris Sinclair tailed him to Heathrow. He was alone. We saw him check on to an American Airlines flight to Dallas, connecting on to Norfolk. The long route to Virginia, in other words. He usually flies United to Richmond via Washington. So it was unscheduled. According to Frears, Fortner hadn't planned to be going away at such short notice. Chris says he had four large suitcases with him, as well as a holdall for the cabin. Paid over two hundred pounds in excess baggage. You know anything about that?"

"Nothing. He and I haven't spoken in over a week."

"And Katharine?"

"Ditto."

"Sounds like a hasty exit to me."

And to me, too, but I reply, "Not necessarily. He may just have had to make an unscheduled visit to Langley."

"Let's hope so."

Caccia takes another long sip of his drink, setting it down on a copy of *The Spectator*.

"We think it would be a good idea for you to telephone Katharine as soon as possible. Try to find out what's going on."

"I can't mention 5F371. That would be too obvious."

"Of course."

"But I can ask her about Fortner. See what he's up to."

"Good."

This appears to satisfy him. Caccia nods, clears his throat, and stares at a painting on the wall. There appears to be nothing left to say. In the silence I feel suddenly awkward and oddly embarrassed, as if I should somehow elaborate on my plan. Then, out of nowhere, Caccia asks if I have voted in the election.

The question takes me by surprise.

"Er, I don't intend to," I tell him. "I take Billy Connolly's advice."

"Oh? And what's that?"

"Don't vote. It just encourages them."

Caccia grunts out a laugh.

"Think Blair's got it sewn up, anyway," he says, standing. I take this as my cue to leave. "Find out what you can, eh?"

"I'm sure it's nothing, David. Just a coincidence."

"Well, let's hope so," he says. "Let's hope so."

34

THINK

Of course, not a day has gone by when I didn't fear that all this would come to an end. And contained in Caccia's warning is an intimation that the game is up, that somehow the Americans have discovered my true intentions and pulled the plug on JUSTIFY. Every instinct tells me that this is the case, yet some grudging stubbornness in me will not accept the situation. It could still be a wild coincidence that Andromeda's people pulled out of Baku just hours before Fortner left for the States with his London life packed into four large suitcases and a cabin bag. There is still that tiny possibility.

There is a message on my answering machine when I get home:

"Hi, man, it's Saul. Listen, hope you're okay. I just got your message from last week. I was in Scotland. Ring me if you still need to talk about whatever it was. . . . Ring me anyway, will you? Do you fancy going down to Cornwall this weekend? I need to talk to you about that. I want to bring someone, try and maybe leave tomorrow night. So . . . give me a ring."

I call him back on his mobile.

"Alec. How you doing? Everything all right?"

He sounds concerned.

"Everything's fine."

"I was worried. You sounded in bad shape. What happened?"

"It was just a scare. Nothing."

"What kind of scare?"

Let's try this.

"Just Mum. We thought she might have a skin cancer, but it turned out to be benign."

"Shit. I'm glad. Send her my best."

"What's this about Cornwall?"

He stalls momentarily.

"I've met someone."

"And?"

"And I wanted to invite her down to Padstow this weekend."

"Why are you asking me? You want my permission?"

He does not laugh.

"No. It's not that. I wanted you to come with us."

"Sounds very cozy."

"It won't be. She has friends down there already. We're going to hook up."

In all probability, events at Abnex will prevent me from going.

"Can I let you know at the last minute?"

"Sure," he says. "No problem. Look, I've got another call coming through. We'll speak first thing tomorrow."

I take a lasagne out of the freezer and microwave it for dinner, finishing off a bottle of red wine that I opened last night. I have to prepare now for Katharine; it needs to be just right. There are two crucial things to find out: why did Fortner go to the United States on such short notice, and what happened in Baku? It should be easy getting an answer to the first question. Katharine will most probably volunteer all the information we need. Whether she reveals that Fortner has gone to America will be a first signal. If she lies about that, we may have a problem. Finding out about Baku will be more difficult. She would never bring up 5F371 on an open landline, though it may be possible to ask a more general question about Andromeda, which could lead to her revealing something about the present situation.

I also need to recapture something of my customary mood. The Alec they knew before the attack on Cohen was chirpy and biddable, untroubled by matters of conscience. It will be essential not to sound nervous or distant. Nothing can seem out of the ordinary. This has to be just another phone call, just the two of us touching base after a break of six or seven days. There's no hidden agenda. We'll just be two old friends talking on the phone.

I wash up my plate, put it on the rack, light a cigarette, and go out into the hall to make the call.

Their number rings out, long enough for me to suspect that Katharine is not in. She usually picks up promptly, and sure enough the answering machine kicks in after several seconds. This is frustrating. My mood was exactly right to handle the conversation. Not too tired, not too tense. Oddly calm, in fact.

The beep sounds.

"Katharine, hi, it's Alec. Just calling to—"

There is a loud scraping crash on the line, as if the phone has been dropped on a hard wooden floor. Then a thud and a tap as Katharine picks up the receiver, her voice coming through.

"Yes?"

"You're there."

"I'm here."

"Screening your calls?"

"No. I just got in."

"From work?"

"From work."

She sounds immediately detached. I feel a rushing heat across my forehead and extinguish the cigarette.

"Everything okay?" I am trying to sound as easygoing as possible.

"Oh, everything's just fine," she says, a little archly.

She waits for me to respond and, when I do not, says, "So, what are you calling about?"

In any normal conversation between us, there would be friendly inquiries after my mood, about Saul or Mum, my work at Abnex. Perhaps even a joke or a story. But nothing tonight, merely this odd reticence.

"Just to see how you were. How things are going."

I wish I could see her face.

"I'm fine, thank you."

"And Fort?"

A fractional pause.

"Oh, he's fine, too."

This is said with no feeling.

"Katharine, are you okay?"

"Sure," she says, lifting herself. "Why?"

"You sound odd. Are you tired?"

"That must be it."

I should end the conversation here. She knows something, she must do. But is that simply paranoia? How could the Americans have any idea of the truth?

"You should get an early night," I tell her.

"I have to go out."

"For dinner?"

With a low hum she confirms this.

"Who with?"

"Just some friends."

Where is the detail, the shading-in? She is being stubbornly, deliberately obtuse.

"Anyone I know?" I ask.

"No."

A longer pause now, so much so that I think she may be about to end the conversation. Finally she asks a question.

"So what've you been up to these last few days?"

"Not much," I reply.

Then I recall lying to Saul about Mum before dinner, a conversation that the Americans may have tapped and alerted her to.

"There was one slight scare, but otherwise everything's been fine."

"What kind of scare?"

For the first time she sounds interested by something I have said.

"Mum thought she might have a skin cancer, but it turned out to be benign."

"That's a relief. And how's Kate?"

Nothing prepares me for the shock of this, a carefully weighted jab exactly timed for maximum impact.

I manage to say, "What are you talking about?" although my voice cracks like an adolescent on the word *talking*.

"I asked after Kate."

They have got to her. Kate has been burned.

"But you know I don't see her anymore. I haven't seen her in over two years."

"That's not what I heard. Fort says you two still sleep together, for old times' sake."

"Why would he have said that?"

"You mentioned it to him one night when the two of you were out drinking. Or don't you remember?"

That was months ago, a slight lie in a pub just to fill the silence. Instinct tells me to deny all this.

"I don't remember ever mentioning that to him."

"Were you bragging, Alec?"

What does she want to hear? I do not know what Kate has told them. Then—a chink of light—it occurs to me that someone from their side simply saw me going into Kate's house last week. They know no more than that.

"Was it male bravado?" Katharine is asking. "Was that what made you say it?"

"Not necessarily."

"So you two still hook up from time to time? How come you never said anything to me?"

Her voice becomes significantly warmer with this question, more friendly and engaging. Is it possible that she is simply jealous?

"It was private. Kate wanted me to keep it a secret. She has a boyfriend. I'm sorry I told Fort and not you."

"That's okay," she says calmly.

"You can understand why I didn't say anything. Not even Saul knows that I still see her."

"Of course," she says, creating a brief lapse in which an instinct to get away from any talk of Kate fatally overrides my common sense. I ask, "How come Fortner is in the States?"

And there is silence. And nothing I can do to retract the question.

"Why do you ask that, Alec?"

I can say only, "What?"

"Why would you think Fortner is in the States?"

"Isn't he? I just assumed he wasn't home."

"Why didn't you ask if he was here?"

"I'm sorry. I'm not following you."

"It's very simple, Alec. How did you know my husband had gone to America?"

I am trapped now, with no way out of this but ineffectual bluffs.

"I just assumed. It sounded like he wasn't around. Usually I would have talked to him by now."

She'll never buy that.

"You just assumed."

I go on the offensive. It may be the only way to distract her.

"Kathy, what are you getting at? You're being really odd tonight."

Then it is as if every sound around me has suddenly ended, a tunnel of silence into which Katharine whispers, "My God, it is true. I could not believe it until I heard it from you directly. I would not believe them."

"Believe who?"

Very slowly, she says, "You're so dumb, Alec. How did you know Fortner was in the States? Isn't that revealing a little too much of what you know?"

"I don't understand what you're getting at."

"You want me to *tell* you why he's there?"

"Maybe we should talk another time, Kathy. I don't know what's got into you, but . . ."

"He's there because of your fucking girlfriend."

I have a sensation now of cold fear, like falling through space in a dream and the black ground rushing up to meet me.

"Kate's apartment is bugged. It has been ever since you told Fortner you were still seeing her. Just like your home is bugged, your car, your telephones, Saul, your mother's place. Everyone is being listened to."

My body goes stiff with panic. It was nobody's fault but my own. They heard everything I said to Kate.

"And you know what the irony is. We almost shut it down. You never visited Kate, and we figured you weren't about to in the future. It was a sleeper, but Fort insisted we keep it on. He had some hunch you might go there someday, said he knew how you felt about her. I gotta hand it to your people: 5F371 was a smart plan. You guys worked us over. Nice little Alec hands over 3-D seismic imaging showing the strong possibility of oil in a field where none exists. Caccia has known all along that the crude was beaten out of it by the Soviets in the sixties and seventies, but Andromeda buys out Abnex's validity of rights, drills an exploration well, spends—what?—about three hundred million dollars, and find nothing when we get there. Meantime, the Azerbaijani government loses confidence in Andromeda and, next time around, is more open to the idea of joint ventures with Abnex. Only you messed up, Alec. You couldn't keep your fucking mouth shut. You went soft on them."

To hear her anger spat back, the triumph of it, sickens me almost to the point of retaliation.

"You gonna say something, Alec? You got anything you want to say to me?"

Only Hawkes's voice in my head, like an invocation, prevents me from tripping into confession. When caught, he said, deny everything, if only for the sake of legal process. Never admit charges, never verify their accusations, however much information they may appear to have against you. The other side will always know less than you think they do. Resort to lies.

"I have nothing to say to you, Kathy. And frankly I'm disgusted that you think this about me."

"Oh, get off it, Alec." She is shouting now, making no attempt to control the flow of her rage. "Have you no self-respect? Is your vanity so great that you crave this kind of recognition, from men like David Caccia, from men like Michael Hawkes? It's pitiful, truly it is. I'm flying to Washington tonight. Do you understand that? My career is most probably over. How does that make you feel?"

"It has nothing to do with me."

"Oh? And how do you spin that one?"

"I'm not spinning anything."

"Why don't you just have the guts to come out and admit what's going on here? It's over, Alec. You're beaten."

I know that she is right. The situation is out of control. Whatever happens now, this is over.

"I am not beaten, Kathy. No one is beaten. This is all . . ."

"Why are you bothering to deny this? Is that what they taught you, huh? Is that it?"

And suddenly I snap. I just let it go.

"Listen. This is the game we're in. It's that simple."

There is a momentary silence as she acknowledges that I have broken cover for the first time. But her anger soon returns.

"The game? Doing undercover work for a snake like John Lithiby? You have any idea of that guy's record, Alec?"

"And what about you? You work for an operation that helped to arrest Mandela, that relocated Nazi war criminals. . . ."

She emits a dry and contemptuous laugh.

"That's ancient history. We both know that. It's a freshman conspiracy theory."

"You want something recent? Okay. I'll give you something recent. We've just caught American intelligence agents hacking in to the computers of the European Parliament. CIA people trying to steal economic and political secrets, just like you, just like Fort. Just doing their job, in other words. That computer linked up to five thousand MEPs, researchers, and EU officials with their confidential medical and financial records, all of which the CIA would have had no hesitation in using if it gave them some leverage. So don't lecture me about ethics."

"So that's all this is? Tit for tat?"

"If you want to see it that way, sure."

"What are you saying, Alec? That SIS isn't doing exactly the same thing with its own European allies? Are you so blind that you think the good old Brits aren't up to that? You really suppose your government is too clean to spy on its EU partners?"

"Not at all. But that's how all of this works. You spy on me, I spy on you. And every government in the civilized world spends millions of dollars going round and round in circles."

"There are too many people who know about this, Alec."

"Meaning?"

"You work it out."

"Are you referring to Kate?"

She says nothing.

"I said, are you talking about Kate, because if you—"

"All I'm saying is that there are people who are going to want payback for this."

"You leave me alone. You leave her alone."

But Katharine's voice suddenly slows into intimidation.

"You haven't heard the last of it."

And the line goes dead.

35

FAST RELEASE

GCHQ picks it all up and within ninety minutes Sinclair has been dispatched to bring me in. He rings the buzzer downstairs impatiently in hard electric bursts lasting four or five seconds. It is just past ten o'clock.

"You'd better come with me," he says, when I open the front door. "No need to pack."

His expression is one of worn distaste. Most probably Lithiby summoned him from home just as he was preparing to go to bed. He betrays no sign of pleasure at my failure; there is just a weary contempt on his neat, tanned face. He never liked me. He never thought I was up to the job. They should have given it to him and then none of this would have happened.

I go back upstairs and put on my jacket like a condemned man. I have a few cigarettes in the inside pocket, also my wallet and an old pack of chewing gum to see me through the night. Then I lock up and go outside to the car.

We say very little to each other on the journey. Sinclair will not reveal where we are going, though I suspect that it will be a safe house and not Vauxhall Cross or Five. I cannot tell how much or how little he knows about the conversation with Katharine. Lithiby would have given him only a sketchy outline on the phone, just enough to make him realize that JUSTIFY is blown.

Sorting through the debris of what Katharine has said occupies my mind for the whole journey. There is no order to this. I experience an acute sense of self-hatred and embarrassment, but also an immense anger. I thought that I had experienced the last of failure, seen it off for good, but to have messed up like this is catastrophic. It is a personal defeat of a different order from anything that has happened to me in the past. There is also concern for Mum's safety, for Saul's, and for Kate's. She knows everything about JUSTIFY, but I cannot think that Katharine's words were anything more than scaremongering. Kate poses no threat to them. Why should they harm her? And I feel a curious sense of annoyance with her, too. Though none of this is Kate's fault, she was the source of my failure. Were it not for the hold that she exerted over me, I would never have gone to see her, far less lied to Fortner about the two of us still being lovers.

On just one occasion, about five minutes into the journey, I attempt to make conversation with Sinclair. A cool night wind is drumming into the car through an open window, and I think I detect the sour vapor of alcohol on his breath.

"It's funny, you know," I say, turning toward him as he comes off the Westway, heading north toward Willesden. "After everything that's happened in the last few—"

But he stops me short. "Listen, Alec. I've been instructed to keep my mouth shut. So unless you wanna talk about New Labour or somethin', we'd better just wait till we get there."

The street is narrow, poorly lit, suburban. Of the dozen or so houses lining both sides of the road, only two or three have lights on downstairs. It's late, and most people have gone to bed. Sinclair pulls the car over to the right side of the road, scraping the hubcaps against the curb as he attempts to park. "Shit," he mutters under his breath, and I unbuckle my seat belt.

A man is walking a dog on the opposite side of the street. Sinclair tells me to stay where I am until he is out of sight. Then we both get out of the car and make our way up a short driveway to the front door of a detached house with curtains drawn in all the front windows. He taps once on the foggy glass of the door, and I am surprised to see that it is Barbara who opens it from the other side. She greets Sinclair with a tired smile but shoots me a sour look that breaks from her face like a snake. No more pleasantries. That is not required of her now.

The hall is covered in a dirty brown carpet that continues upstairs to the first floor. There are two umbrellas and a walking stick in a stand beside the door, and a bright oil painting of a mountain hanging to our right as we come in. Magnolia paint covers all the walls and ceilings. It is as if we are encased in the mundane. The safe house smells stale with lack of use, yet it hides interrogations, solitudes, enforced captures. People have not been happy in this place.

Barbara ushers us slowly into the kitchen, which is where I see the three men for the first time. I was expecting Hawkes to be here, but he is not among them. Standing left to right in front of a bank of bottle-green kitchen cabinets are John Lithiby, David Caccia, and an older, bespectacled man in his late sixties. I have never seen him before, this portly, stooped Englishman with a lonely, cuckolded look in his eyes. He has an air of long experience, and the others appear quietly deferential toward him.

All three are probably wearing the clothes in which they went to work this morning: Lithiby in his customary blue shirt with its white collar, Caccia still in his gray flannel suit, the third man in cords and a tweed jacket. Dressed in jeans and a sweatshirt, I feel untidy and slack beside them, yet their formal clothes are incongruous in this kitchen with its cheap fixtures and fittings, its linoleum floor patterned with worn beige checks. They are visitors here, too.

There are three mugs of tea resting on a Formica-topped table in the center of the room, brown milky fluid gradually souring in dregs at the base of each.

I try to gather myself into courage by speaking first, looking at each of them in turn.

"Good evening, David. John." I look directly into the glasses of the older man. "Sir."

"Good evening to you," he says. He has no accent, but there is a gravelly resonance in his voice like that of a well-trained actor. I notice that his shoes are brown suede, one of them stained.

"Have a seat, Alec," says Lithiby, failing to introduce me to the older man. I would have preferred to remain standing—and he knows that about me—but this is typical of the way Lithiby operates. He is a student of control, of bending others to his will.

I sit with my back to the door. Barbara makes herself scarce, most probably to the sitting room nearby, where she will record and minute the conversation that follows. Sinclair loiters near the sink and Lithiby tells him to make four cups of instant coffee, an order he obeys like a butler.

"You take milk, don't you, Alec?" Sinclair asks.

Never accept tea or coffee at an interview. They'll see your hand shaking when you drink it.

"Black, please," I reply. "Two sugars."

Caccia now sits on my left. I take out a cigarette.

"This is okay, isn't it?" I ask him, holding it up. I want to hear Caccia speak.

"Of course, of course," he says breathlessly. "This isn't going to be anything sinister, Alec. We just want to have a little chat."

I light the cigarette. Sinclair puts a small white plate in front of me to use as an ashtray. They've got him well trained.

"Aren't you going to introduce me, David?" I say, nodding toward the old man. I wouldn't have had the nerve to say that to Lithiby.

"Of course," Caccia says quickly. "Forgetting my manners. Alec, this is Peter Elworthy."

A cover name.

"How do you do?" I say, trying to stand up to shake the old man's hand. My legs get trapped under the table as I say, "Alec."

His look here is revealing: Elworthy knows exactly who I am—of course he does—and gives a passing glance of annoyance. He lacks entirely Caccia's easily peddled charm and, unlike Lithiby, is too old for me to make any sort of a connection with him.

"How do you do?"

His suit is a very dark tweed with a waistcoat underneath. Men of his age often don't seem to mind being too warm in the summer months. And although it is late now, he looks sharp and alert, more so than Caccia, who looks significantly more tired than he did this afternoon.

"Do you know what the Russians are up to these days?" Elworthy appears to have directed the question to Lithiby, who is standing beside him.

"No," he replies, as if he has learned his lines.

"Rather than track down all their traitors, the KGB—or whatever those fellows are calling themselves these days—are trying to turn them into double agents, to play them back against our side. They even have a number that the Russian agents can telephone if they're having second thoughts and want to turn themselves in. The Yeltsin government then offer them money to feed us disinformation."

"Is that right?" says Lithiby blandly.

Elworthy continues, "The Americans are finding it difficult to re-cruit new officers as well. You need fluency in two or three languages coupled with a high level of computer literacy. And if one has those as a graduate, why opt for a CIA starting salary of thirty thousand dollars when Microsoft will pay three times that amount?"

"Mossad has the same problem," Lithiby replies. "We all have."

Caccia looks down at the table as Elworthy moves farther toward me. "My feeling is—"

I interrupt him.

"Can we cut the shit? Is that possible? We all know why I'm here, so let's talk this thing out. Stop fucking around."

Elworthy looks taken aback: I would almost say that he is impressed. I do not know where this courage has come from, but I am grateful for it. Nothing is said for a few moments. Sinclair takes the opportunity to place two mugs of coffee on the table. He passes one to Lithiby, but El-worthy raises his hand.

"Listen to me, young man." He leans on the table, palms down, fin-gers spread out like a web. "I will do this in my own time."

His voice is a dark hiss. It has shifted from nonchalance to malice in a matter of seconds. Only now do I realize the extent of their anger. All of them.

"I apologize. I'm just a little edgy. You bring me out here in the middle of the night . . ."

Elworthy stands again, leaving sweat prints on the red plastic surface of the table as he rises to his feet.

"We understand," Caccia says, interjecting gently. He has obviously been designated to soften me up. "This must be as difficult for you as it is for us."

"What does that mean?" I say, turning to him. I had not intended to lose my temper so quickly. "How can this in any way be as difficult for you as it is for me? Is *your* life in danger? Is it? Are your friends and fam-ily safe? Have you just fucked something up on this scale?"

"Let's calm it, Alec, shall we?" Lithiby says, walking across the room toward the door. He is soon directly behind me, and his presence is enough to make me want to move. I pick up my cigarette, push back the chair, and stand up. Sinclair looks briefly startled. The cigarette has left a tiny nicotine smear on the plate.

"Where are you going?" Lithiby asks.

"Just let me walk around, will you? I think more clearly that way."

At some point I have accepted that this will be my last encounter with any of them. They are preparing to cut me loose. It is pointless to hold out any hope of a reprieve. After this, there is no chance that MI5 will keep to their promise of a permanent job. That was conditional solely on the success of the operation.

"Why don't you tell us what happened tonight," Elworthy announces, his voice back to its characteristic level of flat understatement.

I inhale very deeply on the cigarette and almost choke on the smoke.

"You know what happened," I tell him. "You heard it all. There's nothing for me to add."

Behind me, Lithiby says, "It would be helpful, nonetheless, if we could get a handle on things from your point of view."

"What, so that Barbara can get it all down for the record?"

"You're being very aggressive, Alec," he says. "There's really no need."

Perhaps I am, and this checks my rising anger. Perhaps I have read the situation incorrectly and have not been summoned here simply to be mocked and fired. There may be a chance that they are prepared to notch this up to experience.

"I don't mean to be that way," I reply. "You can understand that it's been a bad day."

Caccia smiles. He is still sitting at the table, fingers playing idly with the handle of his mug. He has always looked too well preserved, too decent and respectable, to be involved in something like this. A diplomat out of his depth, a dull foil for Hawkes. Caccia was never SIS, merely window dressing.

"Of course," says Lithiby, empathetically. "Why don't you sit down and tell us what happened?"

His trickery has the effect of putting me once again on my guard.

"I've told you, John, I prefer to stand. All that happened was this. I had a meeting with David at Abnex this afternoon. He told me that our people had seen Fortner skip the country, and that Andromeda had pulled out of Baku. That was it. I feared the worst, though David didn't seem too upset. Looking back on it now, that was disingenuous." I glance down at Caccia. "You must have known that I was blown, but you wanted me to be the one who found out why. You wanted me to be the fall guy."

"There's no truth in that whatsoever," Caccia says, maintaining his cool. "There is only one person responsible for this cock-up, and that is you."

"But you weren't to know that, were you? At that stage you had no idea why these things were happening."

"What happened when you got home?"

Lithiby has interrupted, trying to prevent things from escalating into a full-scale argument. I am still surprised by how quickly I have allowed the civility of the meeting to break apart.

"I made the phone call. You heard it all for yourselves. Surely I don't need to go over all that?"

Elworthy coughs, an old man's way of saying that he wants to be heard.

"That won't be necessary," he says. "But we need to know about this girl. Kate Allardyce. We've had a problem with her before, haven't we?"

Elworthy looks across at Lithiby and I instinctively follow his lead. He nods just once.

"A problem with Kate?" I reply. "What do you mean? Who *are* you, anyway? Nobody has even told me how you fit into things."

Elworthy ignores this.

"In your first meeting with the friends," he says flatly, "you led the interviewer to believe that you were still involved with her."

"What does that have to do with anything?"

"There's a pattern of deceit, Alec, don't you see?" Elworthy is now to my left, no more than a foot away, with Lithiby closing in on the right. It is like a pincer movement as Lithiby says, "You've tried to pull the wool over our eyes about her before. We'd like to know what role she has in this. How does Kate Allardyce fit in?"

What is this assumption they have made about Kate? Where is it coming from? Have they got to her, too? I cannot think how to reply.

"Alec?" Caccia says, trying to prompt me into saying something.

"She doesn't have any role in this," I tell them. "This is a blind alley. That was the first time I'd seen her in over two years."

"When?" Elworthy asks very quickly. He is convinced that there is more to this.

"Last week. When I went to her house. When I told her about what happened to Harry in Baku. About JUSTIFY. About all of this."

"And she knew nothing of it before?"

"No. Of course not."

They appear to have had doubts about her for some time. Trained to see trickery in even the most blameless situations.

"So how is it that the Americans discovered what was going on?"

This comes from Caccia, and I hand him a look of derision.

"Are you not getting this, David? Can you guys stop asking all these fucking obvious questions? You know how the Americans found out. They had her fucking house tapped."

"But why?" says Elworthy, and the malice returns now to his voice. He doesn't like the fact that I have been disrespectful to Caccia.

"Because I lied to Fortner about her. Told him we were still seeing each other. This is all on your tape. You heard the fucking conversation with Katharine. They put a bug in Kate's house."

"Just because of that?"

They think I'm lying.

"What other reason would they need?" I ask, exasperated.

"The fact that you were still sleeping together hardly justifies a wiretap."

"On the contrary," I reply. "If tonight has proved anything, it's that Fortner was entirely justified in making that decision. After all, that's what caught us out."

"That's what caught *you* out," Elworthy replies.

I look at him, itching to retaliate, knowing that what he has said is entirely justified. Now he begins to pick over his words, choosing them with great care, like a politician wary of being caught out by semantics.

"You asked who I am," he says. "I will tell you. There are people in this room who are answerable to me. That is all that I am prepared to say. What I have come here tonight to tell you is this. In view of what has happened today, we are terminating our arrangement with you. I imagine that you might have expected as much."

I nod.

"You will be only too aware that we are under no obligation to keep you on as a support agent. Your contract is with Abnex Oil. Whether or not David decides to renew it is a matter to be settled entirely between the two of you, with the possible input of Alan Murray. The position of the Security Service is straightforward. We are letting you go."

Only Sinclair has the guts to look at me. Both Lithiby and Caccia stare down at the floor, briefly ashamed by what Elworthy has said. The room is suddenly very silent, as if even the walls are absorbing the news. Then Caccia speaks.

"Abnex is in a similar bind, I'm afraid. After what has happened in the last few days, we feel it would be ill-advised for you to continue as an employee. There may be risks involved. I'm thinking, for example, about Harry coming back to work in due course. How will he feel if you're still on the team?"

I am enraged by this.

"I am not the one responsible for what happened to Harry. . . ."

"That's not the point I'm making," says Caccia. "As far as he is concerned, you are a liability, an industrial spy, for God's sake. The last thing we need is for him to start digging all of this up once it's been put to bed."

"Whether I'm there or not won't stop him doing that."

"Oh, I think it will," says Lithiby, and I see that they have agreed to present a united front against me. Tonight is not about argument or debate. Tonight is about eradicating Milius.

"So I've outlived my usefulness. Is that it? You just wash your hands of me, after everything I've done?"

"You will receive a generous payoff from Abnex Oil," says Caccia, blinking rapidly.

Lithiby again interrupts.

"We suggest that you get out of London for the time being. Take a holiday or something. Let the dust settle."

I actually laugh at this, at the effrontery of it.

"Take a holiday? That's it? That's your advice?" Even Elworthy, for the first time, looks uneasy. "And where do you think I should go? Where's nice this time of year? Do I check the brakes on my car? Spend the next thirty years looking over my shoulder?"

"That is an overreaction," he says, though, with the knowledge of what happened to Cohen, it is the least authoritative thing Lithiby has said all night.

"I'll tell you what I want," I say to them, and for a moment it is as if I have a measure of control. Having expected to be sacked, and having no great wish to remain at Abnex, the single thing I care about now is my safety. I look Lithiby directly in the eye. "Before I leave here tonight, I need concrete assurance that you will negotiate with the Americans on my behalf to guarantee that I go unharmed."

It is some time before any of them responds.

"We'll see what we can do," says Elworthy.

"That isn't good enough," I tell him, pacing toward the door.

"Well, it's unfortunate that you should think that," he replies. "I would remind you that there are more important things at stake here than misguided concerns about your safety."

"Such as?"

"We must protect the institution of secrecy, first and foremost. We told you that you had to be completely deniable. You failed in that respect."

"The institution of secrecy?" I am almost shouting. "That is meaningless. What the fuck is that above a man's life? I could be killed when I leave here. Had that thought even occurred to you? Or is it simply that you don't care?"

"You are being relieved of your responsibilities. That is our position. By speaking to Miss Allardyce you broke the very code on which this organization depends for its security and well-being."

I look away from Elworthy, to Lithiby, a flash glance of anger.

"And did John think about Harry Cohen's security and well-being when he ordered a gang of Azerbaijani thugs to beat the crap out of him?"

"Excuse me?"

Lithiby has taken a step forward.

"You know what I'm talking about."

"I suggest that you withdraw that remark, young man," Elworthy warns.

I do not do so.

"John had nothing whatsoever to do with what happened to Harry. That was simply an unfortunate accident."

"Is that right? And how would you know?"

Lithiby's face has darkened to a scowl.

"You're out of your depth, Alec. I suggest that you do not make enemies of us."

"I'm not interested in your suggestions," I reply, and before I have properly thought it through, I issue them a clear-cut blackmail: "You have given me an ultimatum. Now let me give you one. If I do not receive clear indication that you have negotiated with the Americans to ensure my safety, I will send full details of JUSTIFY to a national news-paper."

This threat, which I had only briefly contemplated on the journey from Shepherd's Bush, does not appear to worry them. They would have expected it.

"You'd be wasting your time," says Elworthy. "We will simply D Notice the material."

"Then I'll publish overseas. In France. In Australia. Fancy another *Spycatcher*? Don't you think *Pravda* or *The New York Times* would be in-terested in a story like that? It's news that's fit to print, wouldn't you say? And I'll put everything about JUSTIFY on the Internet. Everything. You have no jurisdiction there."

"Two things will happen if you do that," he says, very calmly. "First, no one will believe you. Second, you will be prosecuted under the terms of the Official Secrets Act."

"Then it's simple," I tell him. "You keep your end of the bargain and nothing will happen."

"Why?" asks Caccia, whose voice seems to hide a measure of con-cern. "Why should we keep our end of the bargain when you have failed so completely to keep yours?"

"That's just the way it's got to be. And if either myself or Kate or anybody is so much as winked at by you or the CIA, I will make arrangements to have every detail of this operation made public."

"We will have to talk to her," Lithiby suggests.

"No. You will not. She has nothing to do with this. And if I hear that Kate has been approached by any of you, that will be enough to set things off."

There is a knock at the door. It can only be Barbara.

"Come in," Caccia says.

"Telephone call for you, sir," she says to Elworthy. I didn't hear a phone ring.

"Thank you." He turns to Lithiby. "Will you excuse me?"

Lithiby nods and Elworthy shuffles next door. Barbara, looking at four washed-out faces, says, "It looks like a Labour landslide."

"Really," Lithiby murmurs. None of it makes any difference to him.

"Yes," she says. "Lost every seat in Scotland, by the looks of things."

"Every seat?" Sinclair exclaims, his first input since we arrived. "Christ."

A car sounds its horn in the street outside.

"There was one other thing."

Lithiby is talking to me.

"Yes?"

Very calmly he says, "They weren't married."

"Who?"

"Our American friends. Not even a couple. Thought you'd like to know."

"What do you mean they weren't married? How long have you known this?"

Of course. Separate bedrooms. The age difference. The lie Katharine told me about her miscarriage. All just cover.

"Not long. Two, three weeks. I was surprised you didn't have any suspicions."

"I did."

"They weren't in your reports."

To have been lied to for so long about a thing so obvious. I am momentarily blunted, consternation draining away any control I may have had over the meeting. That was Lithiby's deliberate intention, to throw me off guard.

"Alec?"

"Yes?"

"I said it wasn't in any of your reports."

From somewhere I summon the energy to challenge him.

"What does that matter now?"

Lithiby does not reply. He glances across at Sinclair, and I could swear that he was smiling.

"How did you find out about this?" I ask.

"Deep background," Lithiby says, as if that explains everything.

"Why would they bother to pretend?"

He is interrupted by Elworthy's coming back into the kitchen.

"Labour landslide," Caccia says to him. "The Tories are out."

"Is that right?" he says, his reaction muted. "Well, here's to the tedious and predictable triumph of moderate politics."

Caccia grins smugly.

"I have had a chance to think," Elworthy says, turning his attention to me. "I suspect that we are all rather tired of threats and innuendo. It's late, and I suggest we call it a day. Alec, you will hear from us in due course about the matters discussed here this evening. It only remains for me to remind you that you are still bound by the terms of the Official Secrets Act."

"And it only remains for me to remind you that you have an obligation to protect me. Set up a meeting with the Americans, or I will make good my promise to go public with the story."

Elworthy merely nods, knowing that his hands are tied.

"Chris will drive you back," says Lithiby.

"Fine." I look down at Caccia, still seated at the kitchen table, and say good-bye. He does not answer. Lithiby manages a contemptuous nod, but both Barbara and Elworthy remain silent.

Nothing else is said.

We pull up outside the flat at around 3:00 A.M. Sinclair surprises me by switching off the engine.

"Where will you go?" he asks.

It is some time before I answer, dazed, "To Scotland, I think." The lie is pointless. They will find me wherever I go, but I do it out of spite. "A friend of mine has a place in Perthshire. He invited me up this weekend. I'll probably stay there for a while."

Sinclair looks ahead at the street and appears to be summoning up the courage to say something.

"I admire what you did tonight," he says, very softly. "The way you handled yourself."

"Thank you."

"Didn't let them push you around."

"I appreciate you saying that. I really do."

"It's funny," he says, laughing gently, though it appears that he has been overtaken by reflection. "I never liked you much before. Jealousy or something. And now that's it, you're out of it, just when things were starting to look okay. Most probably you and I will never see each other again."

"Most probably."

"You're all right, Alec," he says, and he takes his arm off the steering wheel to shake my hand. "You're gonna be all right."

Inside the flat, I switch on the television to catch the tail end of the election coverage. Just as Barbara said, the Tories have been obliterated. Perhaps it is just my solemn mood of regret, but it is hard not to detect in the government's downfall a spitefulness on behalf of the electorate. Good and able men are being made to suffer for the failures of a very few. I even feel sorry for Portillo, who is beaten out by an ineffectual Blairite clone with a weak mouth and puppy eyes.

But what I will not allow to happen is a slide into self-pity. There is no time for that. The utter disappointment of the last several hours actually motivates me to move against them, to make good the threat against MI5. If I do not act now, they will regain the upper hand.

So, in front of the TV, with the sound muted, I compose letters.

To Lithiby, I restate my intention to release a complete account of JUSTIFY on the Internet and to sell the story to foreign publications unless he receives a valid guarantee of my safety from the Americans. I write, "There will be an anonymous third party in a position to release all information when and if he is instructed to do so."

That person will be Saul.

To Caccia, I write a brief letter of resignation from Abnex. This is pointless, given that tonight he effectively fired me, but a vague and petty stubbornness in me will not allow him the pleasure of formally handing me my notice.

And to the Chase Manhattan Bank at 1603 E. Wadsworth Avenue, Philadelphia, I fax instructions to transfer funds from escrow to a dormant account in Paris set up by my father more than fifteen years ago and left to me in his will.

Only my mother knows about that. A family secret.

I stay awake until dawn as the BBC reruns pictures of Blair standing outside his constituency office, acknowledging the extent of Labour's victory. In his moment of triumph, after a carefully stage-managed campaign in which he has been presented as a mature and thoughtful politician undaunted by the prospect of high office, the new prime minister appears suddenly adolescent, almost on the verge of tears. Suddenly the prize for which he has worked so tirelessly, the culmination of his consuming ambition, stands before him. And as he comes to terms with the weight of the responsibility that has been placed on his shoulders by millions of people, right there in front of the cameras it is possible to see Blair experience a dawning realization: there is a price to be paid for success. He actually looks panicked by what he has achieved.

This is something that I have come to realize far too late. That we allow ambition, the hunger for recognition, to blind us to wider consequences. We are encouraged to pursue goals, to make the best of ourselves, to search for meaning. But what does a person do when those dreams come true? What is the next step?

36

WEST

Eight twenty P.M. Ten minutes until we are scheduled to leave. On the far side of the neat gravel path a man is standing, back straight, head level, eyes closed. He wears purple shorts and a plain white T-shirt bearing the inscription MOON in narrow black letters. A canvas bag lies at his shoeless feet. Slowly, he moves his legs apart. Then the man lifts his arms in a wide arc above his shoulders, palms up toward the sky, until his body forms a composed, tranquil cross.

Fifteen feet to his left, two women, both in jeans, stand up from their bench and drop two empty Diet Coke cans into a wire-mesh bin. They move away.

The man's mouth opens, emitting a just-audible noise, a sustained meditative *yawp* out into the trees. For a moment, the stillness of it erases all the white noise of London. Then a creak of the metal gate at the entrance to Queen's Club Gardens, and Saul appears, shouldering an overnight bag.

The first thing he says is, "She can't come. Says she's going to drive down first thing in the morning. You all right? You look knackered."

I ignore this.

"Can we just head off?"

I am anxious to leave, keen to be out of London. Whatever self-confidence I had is gradually draining away to a constant fear that what happened to Cohen will happen to me.

"In a minute. I told her to come over so I can give her instructions about how to get there."

I look back at the man. From the canvas bag he extracts a sandwich and begins eating it in a pool of fading sunlight. Behind him, an elderly couple are playing tennis on a hard court, the slow thock of balls like a clock.

There is no one else in the gardens. No one who could be watching me.

"Seen much of Fort and Katharine?" Saul asks, and the question catches me off guard.

"A little. Their contract at Andromeda hasn't been renewed. They're thinking of moving back to the States. In fact, I think it's definite. They may be gone by the end of the month."

I am so tired of lying to him.

"That's a pity," he says, gazing at the sky. "It'd be good to see them before they go." There's a check-shaped cloud above his head like the Nike logo.

"I'll try to fix something up."

Saul bends over now to tie his shoelaces, and I say what I have to say while I don't have to look into his eyes.

"I may have to go away, too."

"Really?" he says into the ground.

"Yeah. Abnex has a posting overseas. Something came up. In Turkmenistan. It would just be for a year or so. I think it would be a great opportunity."

He stands up.

"When did this happen?"

"Just last week."

"You're not going straightaway?"

First thing this morning I booked a cross-Channel ticket to Cherbourg, leaving late on Monday afternoon.

"No. Most probably not."

"Good," he says, relaxing immediately. Then he looks across at the gate.

"Here she comes now."

Saul's new girlfriend is tall and slim and attractive—they always are—with dark hair cut short to the nape of the neck. A little like Kate's new bob.

"Hi," he shouts out enthusiastically, though she is still some distance

away. The girl gives a stiff wristy wave and then looks beyond us, apparently at the tennis court. When she arrives, she says nothing at first, just
glances at me, and then wraps Saul in a hug and a kiss. I am briefly envious. She has a slim, supple waist and a lightness about her.

"And you must be Alec," she says, breaking away from him to shake
my hand. "I'm Mia. Pleased to meet you."

She is American.

"You're from the States?" I ask.

She looks irritated.

"Canada. From Vancouver."

Just seeing them together casts my mind back to when Kate and I
met for the first time. We were seventeen, what now seems an absurdly
young age to be about to embark upon the relationship we had. Barely
old enough to express ourselves. It was at a party in the school holidays.
I remember a lot of weak beer and girls in miniskirts. Kate came right
up to me, just seemed to know it was the right thing to do. We were
standing over a bale of straw, surrounded by people dancing to Dexy's
Midnight Runners, and within minutes were hidden in some dark quarter of a vast garden, kissing. Everything was new back then; all we did
was react to things.

For some reason, we started climbing a tree, Kate first, me right behind her, just the rustle and scrape of the two of us against the branches
and among the leaves. She lost her footing. Flecks of sooty bark puffed
into my eyes. I lifted my hand to catch her in case she was about to fall.

"You okay?" I asked, calling up at her.

Even then, within moments of our meeting, I wanted Kate to feel
safe. It happened immediately.

"Yes," she said, and there was a certain stubbornness in her voice
that I noticed, and liked, right away. "I'm okay."

And she kept on climbing.

Saul is talking Mia through the route to Cornwall. When they're done,
I shake her hand, she wishes me well, and he walks her back to the street.

"See you at the weekend," she calls back to me.

"Yeah. Looking forward to it."

And five minutes later, we are on our way.

Saul is driving his wideboy Capri, a dark blue V-reg with seventy thousand miles on the clock and a bonnet the size of a Ping-Pong table. Gradually we shunt our way through the preweekend traffic, which has clogged up the M3 from Sunbury right out to Basingstoke. The Capri feels low and heavy against the road. When I lean back in the passenger seat, the darkening sky entirely fills the windshield.

After an hour, the traffic starts to free up and we move at a steady seventy-five. I put on a tape—Radiohead's *The Bends*—and watch the flat suburban heartlands flick by.

"You want to get something to eat?" Saul asks, overtaking a caravan. "I was going to stop at the next place we see."

"Sure."

It is the first time I have felt like eating in twenty-four hours.

"There's a McDonald's at Fleet services," he says, winding down his window and letting a half-smoked cigarette firework on to the road. "You feel like McDonald's?"

"Whatever."

Two miles later, I spot a glowing yellow M hanging low over an off-ramp encased in black trees. Saul comes off the motorway. The passenger-side mirror is not aligned, so I turn around sharply in my seat and look out through the back windshield.

Three vehicles follow us up the exit.

In the car park, Saul swings into a space alongside a gray BMW. The Capri gives a growling cough as he shuts off the engine. Two of the vehicles behind us went straight on to get petrol. The third, a hatchback Volkswagen, has parked seventy feet away, disgorging young children who run gleefully into the building. An Indian woman wearing a sari is stretching nearby, rolling her neck in a slow clockwise loop.

The restaurant is as bright and sterile as the Abnex offices. There are no shadows. People drift about in the white light, fetching straws and napkins. They queue up four deep at the tills, munch Big Macs at clean-wiped tables. Kids are greedy for plastic figurines and pots of ice cream threaded with furls of chocolate sauce. There's a constant noise of demand.

A middle-aged man standing near me is looking around the place with a flinching bewilderment, as if he has been deposited here by accident from another era. The queue moves quickly. We are flanked by young couples and boys in shell suits, overweight salesmen, and girls in bright pink, too young to be wearing makeup.

At the counter, an acne-soaked teenager in a purple hat takes our order for food. I pass Saul a five-pound note, but he wants to pick up the tab.

"I'll get it," he says, pushing my hand away.

Twenty minutes later we are back inside the car, my mood flatly resigned to a long, dark journey with no end until well after midnight. Saul has a polystyrene cup of Coke wedged between his thighs and a postburger cigarette hanging from his mouth. It's my turn to drive. The Capri feels heavy as I reverse out, as if it, too, has eaten too much, too quickly. Saul clicks in *The Bends* again and sits back in the passenger seat with a deep sigh. Within ten minutes he is asleep and I just listen to the songs.

> *And if I could be who you wanted,*
> *If I could be who you wanted*
> *All the time.*

The rain starts coming down at around eleven fifteen and doesn't stop all night. I worry that the heavy car will skid on the road surface and it's a job to keep my concentration. The motor driving the windshield wipers is sluggish, and as a consequence my vision is constantly blurred by the glare of oncoming headlights refracting through the water-covered glass. Saul naps through all this with heavy catarrh snores and an occasional groan.

The traffic gradually evaporates the closer we come to Bodmin. Now and then a vast, speeding lorry will roar past in the wet, throwing up spray and mud, but otherwise I have the road to myself. There's just a feeling now of wanting to get there, of the quest for sleep. For fifteen minutes on the Dorchester road, I was tailed by a black Rover, the same make of car that Sinclair was driving when I first met Lithiby. But I am past caring. Let them waste their time. They know where I'm going. They know where to find me.

I wake Saul when we enter Little Petherick, the last village before the turnoff to Padstow. He makes a show of being disturbed, rubbing his eyes with his knuckles like a sleepy child.

"Where are we?"

"London."

"Seriously."

"Nearly there. I need you to show me the way."

"Fucking rain," he says.

I have pulled the Capri over to the side of the road, the wipers flapping irregularly, left to right, right to left. The tired old engine turns over. Across the street there is a man loitering alone in a bus stop, trapped by the weather. He stares at us from under the peak of his baseball cap, colorless eyes in the wet gloom.

"Take the second left after this village. Sign saying Trevose."

"Then what?"

He starts imitating Katharine's voice.

"Road forks, so go real slow," he says. "Flirt with me awhile, turn right at the traffic lights, and then I'll leave my husband and elope with you."

I wheeze a fake laugh.

"It's easy from here," he says. "Just head down to the sea. I'll show you."

Saul makes coffee when we arrive and I smoke a cigarette in the kitchen as he busies himself finding blankets and towels. The house feels damp. In the distance I can hear steel halyards pinging in the wind against masts. Otherwise, it is utterly quiet.

I like it down here. London makes you forget the simpler pleasures of being away from a city. The loose give of the warming sand after weeks of walking on pavements and hard floors. In the summer that brilliant clean light, and the feeling of salt drying against the skin. Then evening sunsets blink off the surface of the water, like flashbulbs in a floodlit stadium.

Saul comes back into the kitchen.

"I'm not actually all that tired," he says.

"Me neither."

"You want a drink? I think there's a bottle of wine here somewhere."

He finds it and sits down with two tumblers, a radio on in the background playing country music. I pour the wine and we toast the weekend, glasses clinking over the table. A car drives past outside, close to the house at a crawl, and I think that it might be about to stop on the drive when it suddenly moves away.

We talk for perhaps an hour, and it surprises me how easily I disguise my apprehension from him. I am thinking always of the consequences of telling Saul about JUSTIFY, of asking him to release details to the press and on the Internet should anything happen to me. But I can stay focused on what he is saying. Any thoughts I might have about the timing of a confession exist only as an undercurrent to the conversation.

Saul is preoccupied by his work, thinking of chucking his job and going into finance. He says, "After university, we all went into television for the glamour. I thought TV would provide some outlet for self-expression, but a lot of the time it's just tedious and vain, full of guys with goatee beards wearing Armani suits. I need to make some *money.*"

I don't try to sway him one way or the other. I simply hear him out. It is the longest and most fulfilling conversation we have had in over eighteen months, just the two of us talking into the night. All the time I am conscious of a thawing in Saul's attitude toward me, the gradual reconciliation of a ten-year friendship that had been allowed to fester and grow stale. The old-established ties were always there: they simply needed to be rekindled.

When both of us are slightly drunk and, although not tired, starting to think about going to bed, Saul's mobile phone goes off. It is still packed inside his overnight bag on the kitchen floor, the ring muffled by clothes.

"Who the fuck's that?" I ask, looking at the clock on the wall. It is half past three in the morning.

"Probably Mia," he says, getting up out of his chair and struggling to retrieve the phone. "She always calls late. Doesn't sleep."

But it is not Mia.

The signal is bad, and Saul has to go outside to take the call. When he comes back into the kitchen, he tells me that Kate and her boyfriend have been killed in a car accident. He tells me quickly and without inflection, the news of her death first, then the place where the crash took place, and the name of the boyfriend. William.

He says that he is so sorry.

I cannot stay in the room with him. I do not even ask a question. I am outside, through the open door, and stumbling on gravel, his voice behind me just a single word: "Alec."

There is no feeling in me but rage. No sadness or pain, just a sense of powerless anger, like punching air. I turn and am conscious of Saul, standing in the doorway, his head absolutely dropped, not knowing what to do or say. She was his friend, too.

And the boyfriend. He got caught up in it, and they took him as well. His life meant nothing to them.

"Who was driving?" I ask, and, at first, Saul does not hear me. I have to repeat the question, my voice louder.

"Who was driving?"

"I don't know," he replies, and he uses this as an opportunity to come toward me, out onto the drive. "It was Hesther who telephoned. She had to tell her parents. That's where she was calling from. Said they were at a party or something. Coming back. That's all she said."

"No other cars? No drunk driver or . . ."

"Alec, I don't know. She didn't say. Do you want to go back to London? What do you want to do?"

When you are with somebody, when you love them, you think about their loss, what it would mean to suffer their dying. I thought of this always with Kate: illness, accident—even a car crash. Her going off on a journey and simply never coming home. I was aware that these fears contained an element of expectation, perhaps even of hope that something *might* happen to her. Why? Because that would make people sympathetic toward me; it would give my life a certain drama. To lose your first love. It had the character of tragedy.

There is nothing of that now. Only the hideous noise of impact, an inhuman sound. And Kate's eyes at this moment. I see Kate's eyes.

How did they do it? Brakes? Tires? Were they forced off the road? What person has it in him to order the deaths of two young people?

"What happened?" I ask Saul. "How did it happen?"

"I really don't know. We should go back," he says. "Maybe sleep and then go back to London."

I agree with him, without thinking it through, looking directly at him for the first time. We just stand there, saying nothing, and Kate is dead and Saul does not know why.

And now the first doubts come, the first ugly glimpses of self-interest. I realize that I am not safe—that Saul is not safe—not here or in London, not anywhere now that this has happened. They will find us and, without hesitation, move again.

He is offering me a cigarette, already lit, and I take it.

"Let's get in," he says.

"Yes."

In the house, things move slowly. Saul is quiet and still, sitting at the kitchen table, knowing that there is nothing he can say. I move about the room, boiling a kettle, making tea. I find that it helps me not to stay in one place. Occasionally he will speak—a question, some expression of his concern—but I barely respond. I can say nothing of what I am really feeling, for the simple reason that it is inexpressible without resorting to the truth.

With the clock at five thirty I suggest to Saul that he go upstairs and get some sleep. He agrees and turns at the door and asks me twice if I will be all right. I nod, manage a smile, even, and say that I will wake him in a few hours.

"I probably won't sleep," he says.

As soon as he has gone upstairs, I go out onto the gravel drive and walk along the main road, heading downhill in the direction of the sea. The color of night has shifted to a deep blue, which makes it easier to spot the telephone box on the first corner leading into Padstow.

The door to the booth opens heavily. I struggle with it, weakened by the hopeless knowledge that this is all that I have left. Three phone calls.

I put a pound coin in the slot and dial Katharine's number.

It connects immediately, but there is only a rising three-note message where her voice used to be.

The number you have dialed has not been recognized. Please check and try again.

I press Redial, forcibly with the point of my thumb.

The number you have dialed has not been recognized. Please check and try again.

She has gone, on a plane to join Fortner in the States. The man who is not even her husband. Their work is done.

I try Hawkes.

Nothing. A busy signal both at his house in the country and at the flat in London. Both lines busy at a quarter to six on a Saturday morning. If he is here, he knows about Kate. He knows that I want to talk to him. They are all of them cowards.

I have one final chance.

The number rings and I hold on, for twenty or thirty seconds, waiting. Then, finally, a woman's voice, tired and suspicious, says, "Two-seven-eight-five."

"I want to speak to John Lithiby. This is Alec Milius."

She buys time.

"Who?"

"This is Alec Milius. Put me through to John Lithiby."

"I'm afraid that won't be possible, sir. Mr. Lithiby will not be available until Monday morning."

"Then give me his home number."

"You can understand that—"

"I don't give a fuck about what I can understand or what kind of policy you've been told to follow. Just tell him that Kate is dead. Tell him that Kate Allardyce is dead. They killed her, and they will kill me unless—"

"Dead?" she says, as if she has heard of Kate, as if she knows who Kate is.

"That's right. In a car crash. Tell him this. Get him to ring me. Tell him that if he doesn't contact me, I will put everything on the Net. Do you understand? Everything. There is someone else who knows. Tell him to speak to the Americans, let them know that. Someone else. Get Elworthy if you have to. . . ."

There is a brief silence, and then I can hardly believe what happens.

The woman says, "I will be sure to give Mr. Lithiby that message on Monday morning."

And she replaces the handset.

I stand in the phone booth holding the receiver and there is nothing left to do. I press Redial, but the line is now busy. I try Hawkes again at both numbers, but it is pointless. He is still engaged, town and country. Caccia will be the same, Sinclair also. I do not know how to reach Elworthy. I push open the door of the phone booth and go outside.

They had no intention of striking a deal with the Americans. They do not even know that I have threatened to expose them. The Americans have no idea what is at stake.

This is what they have decided on. To ignore Milius, to exclude him until he is taken out of the equation. They are counting on the Americans. Counting on a shared understanding. A special relationship.

Saul must be told what has happened. They have to realize that there is someone else who knows. That is the only way. And yet to tell him is to place him in danger. To tell him is to make him into another Kate.

Walking back up the hill, I can see a light on in his house. Saul's bedroom. He may still be awake.

When I get upstairs he is slumped in an armchair, still fully dressed, but asleep.

I close the door and walk back downstairs to the kitchen. My laptop computer is in a plastic bag on the backseat of the car. I find Saul's keys, go outside, and take it out.

Then, at the kitchen table, I begin to write everything down.

At nine Saul comes downstairs, saying that he has managed a few hours of sleep. I am standing by the sink.

"How about you?" he asks, glancing at the computer and frowning. He is wearing a different shirt.

"I've just been thinking about things. I can't seem to remember anything about Kate. I'm trying to summon up memories, but they're just not there."

He nods, still unsure of how to look at me.

"Maybe it's too early," he says.

"I can't seem to picture or recall anything we did together. All I keep thinking about is her mum and dad, and William's parents. Did you ever meet him?"

"A couple of times."

"It just seems so long ago now. Two years since we split. She had a whole life that I knew nothing about. It's as if I was a different person back then."

He does not answer.

I had boiled the kettle shortly before he woke up, and he makes himself a coffee, going out onto the drive with the mug.

This is probably the best time. When he's outside. Still early in the day.

Always where Saul is concerned there has been this conflict in me between doing what is necessary and expedient, and what I feel is right. Always I have been trying to suppress my more calculating instincts in order to behave as would a good and loyal friend.

But it is hopeless. I am so inured to moral consequence that I do not even consider whether he will forgive me. I simply walk outside into the gathering light and open the driver's door on the car. Reaching inside, I switch on the radio, tuning it to the nearest station.

"What are you doing?" he asks gently.

"It's necessary," I reply, and Saul looks bewildered. A song is playing and I turn up the volume, leaving the door of the car open.

"What do you mean, 'It's necessary'?"

I have to keep him out of the house, in case they have had it wired.

"Don't go back inside for a bit, okay? And don't get too close to the car."

"Alec, turn it down, what are you . . . ?"

"I know what happened to Kate. I know why they were killed last night."

"But we both . . ."

He starts to reply but then stops, putting the mug of coffee down. Saul looks up at me, his face suddenly altered by fear.

I move a step closer to him. I want to lay a hand on his shoulder, to assure my friend that everything is going to be all right. And then I say, "There are things that I have to tell you."

ACKNOWLEDGMENTS

I am enormously grateful to the following people for their assistance and encouragement: Lucy Almond, Otto Bathurst, Lucinda Bredin, Camilla Kingsland, Alex and Jonathan Capel, Henry Carpenter, Jolyon Connell, Jeremy O'Grady and all the staff at *The Week,* Marcus Cooper and Grahame Cook at BP, Ian Cumming, Leslie Daniels, Caroline Dawnay and Jago Irwin at PFD, Sarah Day, Janine di Giovanni, Angus Graham-Campbell, Melissa Hanbury, Annabel Byng, Rupert Harris, Ed Heathcoat-Amory, James Holland, Trevor Horwood, the late Mary Huffam, JJ Keith, Nicki Kennedy and Jessica Buckman at ILA, Jeremy Lewis, Nick Lockley, Tif Loehnis, Kirsty Gordon, Luke Janklow and Claire Dippel at Janklow & Nesbit, James Maby, Josephine Mackay, Jamie Maitland Hume, Rupert Morris, Kerin O'Connor, Charlie Oliver, Simon and Caroline Pilkington, Andrew Ramsay, Charles Spicer, Yaniv Soha, Frances Sayers, Diane Reverand, Regina Scarpa, and everyone at St. Martin's Press, Katharine Road, William and Mary Seymour, Simon Shaw, Christian Spurrier, Hilary Tagg, Martin Vander Weyer, Ralph Ward-Jackson, Joanna Haddon, Rowland White and Tom Weldon at Michael Joseph, and Angus Wolfe Murray.

For additional information about the secret history of British intelligence after 1945, I relied on Tom Bower's excellent biography of Sir Dick White, *The Perfect English Spy.* Pete Earley's account of the Aldrich Ames affair, *Confessions of a Spy,* was just as helpful.